THE HOUSE AT THE
Bottom of the Hill

Also by Jennie Jones

The House on Burra Burra Lane
12 Days at Silver Bells House

THE HOUSE AT THE *Bottom of the Hill*

JENNIE JONES

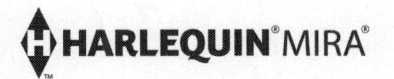

HARLEQUIN® MIRA®

First Published 2015
First Australian Paperback Edition 2015
ISBN 978 174356987 0

THE HOUSE AT THE BOTTOM OF THE HILL
© 2015 by Jennie Jones
Australian Copyright 2015
New Zealand Copyright 2015

Except for use in any review, the reproduction or utilisation of this work in whole or in part in any form by any electronic, mechanical or other means, now known or hereafter invented, including xerography, photocopying and recording, or in any information storage or retrieval system, is forbidden without the permission of the publisher.

This book is sold subject to the condition that it shall not, by way of trade or otherwise, be lent, resold, hired out or otherwise circulated without the prior consent of the publisher in any form of binding or cover other than that in which it is published and without a similar condition including this condition being imposed on the subsequent purchaser.

All rights reserved including the right of reproduction in whole or in part in any form.

This is a work of fiction. Names, characters, places, and incidents are either the product of the author's imagination or are used fictitiously, and any resemblance to actual persons, living or dead, business establishments, events, or locales is entirely coincidental.

Published by
Harlequin Mira
An imprint of Harlequin Enterprises (Australia) Pty Ltd.
Level 4, 132 Arthur Street
NORTH SYDNEY NSW 2060
AUSTRALIA

® and TM are trademarks of Harlequin Enterprises Limited or its corporate affiliates. Trademarks indicated with ® are registered in Australia, New Zealand and in other countries.

Printed and bound in Australia by Griffin Press

About the author

Born and brought up in Wales, Jennie Jones loved anything with a romantic element from an early age. At eighteen, she went to drama school in London, then spent a number of years performing in British theatres, becoming someone else for two hours, eight performances a week.

Jennie wrote her first romance story at the age of twenty-five while 'resting' (a theatrical term for 'out of work'). She wrote a western, but nobody wanted it. Before she had time to get discouraged, a musical theatre job came up and Jennie put writing to one side.

Jennie now lives in Perth, Western Australia, a five-minute walk from the beach that she loves to look at but hardly ever goes to—too much sand. She returned to writing four years ago and says it keeps her artistic nature dancing and her imagination bubbling. Like acting, she can't envisage a day when writing will ever get boring.

The House at the Bottom of the Hill is the third book in Jennie's Swallow's Fall series, following *The House on Burra Burra Lane* and *12 Days at Silver Bells House*.

For Elisabeth

One

Daniel Bradford leaned his shoulder against the doorframe of Kookaburra's Bar & Grill and settled in to watch the ruckus at the northern end of Main Street. Observing the redhead deal with the townspeople had become a daily ritual, as long as he wasn't too close to the kerfuffle.

She'd only been in town two weeks and already she had the committee on her back. The war council, Dan called them, and Swallow's Fall Community Spirit committee members weren't easy to appease once a person put their noses out of joint.

The redhead stood in front of her pink B&B facing the small group, shoulders set, arms at her side, chin raised. She had pluck, he had to give her that.

He crossed his arms over his chest and ran his gaze down the length of the one-street town, thanking his lucky stars he'd been born even-tempered, fair-minded and patient.

Another glorious day in the Snowy Mountains. The November sun high in the sky. The soft breeze from Mount Kosciuszko blowing the dust off the multi-coloured rooftops and swaying the boughs of the claret ash trees lining the street. Swallow's Fall:

population ninety-nine and rising but it wasn't the population surge on Dan's mind.

'Morning, Daniel.'

'Mornin', Mrs Tam.' Dan lifted a hand to the owner of the petrol station as she waddled by on the other side of the street, her black hair knotted in its customary bun and her apron tied tight around what remained of her waist. Nice old girl. Not interested in interfering, but happy to keep an eye on those who were. He indicated the B&B with a nod. 'You going on down?'

'Wouldn't miss it. There's talk of a meeting.'

'Yeah,' Dan said under his breath, 'I bet there is.'

Six years he'd waited to get Kookaburra's Bar & Grill ready for change. An iconic, colonial-style double-storey building standing proudly in the centre of Main Street with cast-iron balustrades and columns at its main doors. Open early, closing late: that was Dan's vision for the future, once he'd got the seven bedrooms renovated upstairs. The town committee didn't know he'd rekindled his long-term plans for the hotel and he wasn't about to tell them. Timing was everything in Swallow's Fall. Or it had been, before the redhead arrived.

Not so many visitors for Swallow's Fall now summer was almost upon them, just those wanting farm stays and walking holidays but they'd seen more tourists the last couple of winters—the best season for the Snowy Mountains. People winding their way from the beaches in the east to the ski slopes in the west, with Swallow's Fall sitting patiently in the middle, waiting for trade. With Dan's hotel, it wouldn't only be the bar that prospered. The town would be given a rejuvenating kick too. If he got the war council on his side.

What he didn't understand was why pretty little Miss English Chick had chosen this remote township. She was as misplaced around here as a snowflake in the outback. Twenty-seven months the B&B had been up for sale without a nibble, then suddenly,

Red was lugging expensive tools from her brand-new 4WD into the seen-better-days house. And now she was paying the price for not adhering to small-town rules. Something Dan understood. It had taken him two years to gain acceptance himself.

'I got that ice cream made for your restaurant, Daniel. Chocolate bubble gum flavour.' Mrs Tam shook her finger at him, batting her eyelashes in her gentle manner. 'Wasn't easy.'

Dan uncrossed his arms and thumped a hand against his chest. 'You're the best woman in town but don't tell the other ladies I said it. It'll be on the menu tonight.'

She tilted her head coyly. 'Anything to help a handsome man, Daniel. Anything at all.'

Dan smiled, and shoved his hands into his trouser pockets. Damned if he knew how it worked, but people seemed to shine when he smiled at them, and mostly, Dan liked smiling.

He waved Mrs Tam on her way, and followed her progress.

A grand little house, the B&B, even if it was a pink-puke colour. Weatherboard, with a grey metal roof that gleamed with the lustre of a tarnished silver sixpence when the sun rose high in the sky. Three bedrooms, two on the top floor for guests and one on ground level. A veranda ran along the front, shading two picture-perfect windows either side of a bright red door. And if a person were to park their backside on one of the locally made rocking chairs the redhead had bought from the Granger's Art and Craft Centre, they'd have a panoramic view of not only Main Street, but also the boulder-studded hillside behind the town, protecting Swallow's Fall from inclement easterlies.

'What's going on?'

Dan looked over his shoulder as Ethan Granger, the town's vet, came up the steps from the street and onto the wooden walkway that served the shopping side of Main Street.

'Same as yesterday and the day before,' Dan said, indicating the B&B with a jut of his chin

Ethan stopped beside Dan and let his two-year-old son, Lachlan, slide down his leg.

Dan glanced at the bar's noticeboard on the walkway to Ethan's left and the one-hundred-dollar note pinned to it. The noticeboard had been framed in a lockable glass case. That had been before Dan arrived, but story was, Ethan had placed a bet on how long it would take him to get Sammy Walker, as she was then, to marry him. They'd had their wedding seven weeks later with the whole town in attendance. That one-hundred-dollar-note was a talisman to the townspeople. The kind of local tale that warmed people's hearts. 'She's hardly set foot in town,' Dan continued, 'and already she wants to make changes. Damn silly, if you ask me.'

'Well, she's not asking you and you can't blame her for starting on the renovations straight away. The place needs a helluva pick-up.'

True, but what sort of a pick-up would she give it? She didn't fit the country ambience. Too polished looking. He hadn't had call to shake up many cocktails since he'd bought the bar, but he could spot what drink a punter would ask for as soon as they stepped through the swinging doors, and the redhead was *all* martini. Lovely looking lady though. Even from a distance his curiosity was piqued. But she wasn't his type: Dan liked women who were happy to share a sizzling couple of dates, and content to wave goodbye when the time came. And as Red didn't look the type to want to date a guy like Dan—why was he even contemplating the issue?

'She should have known better than to rip in straight off with her ideas,' he said. Maybe he shouldn't have left it so long before introducing himself. All he'd done was nod and wave. He really ought to have initiated a casual meeting and given her a few tips on how to tread slowly with the committee but he hadn't wanted to get caught up in the argument because that would mean he'd have to take a side. Too late now, and anyway, he'd wanted a bit of time to study her and suss her out since her plans would affect his.

'Considering the competition?' Ethan asked, with a smile.

Dan pulled his hands out of his pockets. He hadn't, and, yeah, it irked him somewhat. He'd been forced to acknowledge his lack of foresight in not buying the B&B for himself. Six years ago he'd have fallen over his big feet to buy the house. But he'd been too engrossed in his plans for Kookaburra's to realise he'd let a good investment go begging. It could have been a decent hideaway a stone's throw from the bar; somewhere he could have holed up after closing time, instead of in the make-do back room where he'd been living. He'd intended renting the B&B for a few months so his work guys had somewhere to stay but hadn't got around to contacting the real estate agent. He supposed he could still put the guys up at the B&B, provided the English chick lasted long enough to begin hosting guests.

'Sammy wants you over for dinner again,' Ethan said. 'She said soon would be good, since you've got Josh behind the bar in the evenings. How's that working out?'

Josh Rutherford. Twenty-three years old. A decade younger than Dan and filled with the adventurous streak only the young felt they had a right to. Dan nodded. 'He's a hard worker. Learns fast.'

Ethan peered out at the street. 'It's good of you to give him the job. Running the craft centre for us doesn't bring in enough money and he's not getting much carpentry work these days either. He wants to leave town.'

'He's wanted to leave town for the last six years.'

'Last eight.' Ethan hauled in a breath. 'Anyway, glad it's working. I like to watch out for him.'

Dan looked down at Lachlan, still holding tight to Ethan's jeans. Lochie looked up and gazed at Dan with sky-blue eyes.

Dan winked. The little boy's features crumpled and he thrust his face against Ethan's leg.

'Here,' Ethan said to his son, digging into his jacket pocket. Lochie's face brightened and he reached up with chubby hands. 'Careful, now. Go easy on him,' Ethan said as he handed his son a small bundle of fur.

'What's that?' Dan asked.

'Guinea pig.'

Lochie sat on Ethan's boot, held the animal against his chest and bent his sandy head to kiss it.

'Do you have to carry it around with you all day?' Dan asked.

'Only when I've got Lochie with me.'

'Wouldn't want to forget it was in your pocket and sit on it.'

Ethan laughed, a great rumble from deep in his chest.

Dan grinned at his friend. It wasn't often a person made Ethan laugh but it was a dynamic sound when it happened. The man was full of energy and warmth, held carefully within most of the time, unless he was looking at his wife.

'How is Sammy?' Dan asked.

Ethan's smile broadened. 'As big as the new artists' wing on the house, to hear her tell it—but happy.' He looked at Dan, perhaps expecting a response that showed Dan understood the intricacies involved in dealing with expectant wives.

Dan nodded. 'Good. When is she … due?' Pregnant women might be delicate looking but Dan knew they were more resilient than a five-a-side rugby team. He'd happily load their shopping into their cars, or take their arm when they needed to get from the wooden walkway down the steps to the road but when they started talking to him about how good it was to be settled, Dan's status as practically the only single man in town put him on the defensive against their resolve to see that changed. Not the kind of urging a determinedly single guy would ever be completely comfortable with.

'She's due in six weeks,' Ethan said. 'Little Edie is going to be our summer baby girl.'

'And how's how our old summer boy doing?'

Ethan chuckled. 'Grandy's doing well. Junior said he's complaining. They're not likely to let him out of hospital for another couple of weeks though.'

'Gave us a scare.'

'Well, Grandy doesn't do anything by halves.'

'It'll be good to have him back in town.' Dan didn't know what had startled the townspeople more—the thought of losing their patriarch or the sight of the air ambulance chopper landing on the field behind the stock feeders'. Dan missed the old man's dry humour. Main Street wasn't the same without Edmond Morelly sitting outside his hardware store, taking the sun and keeping an eye on the township. Although after the bout of pneumonia he'd come down with, it was unlikely the townspeople would allow Grandy the freedom he was used to. More than likely, one of the women would force him out of his farmhouse and into some hastily built retirement bunker. Dan had his money on Grandy. Ninety-five or not, the man was a force to be reckoned with.

Ethan lifted his chin and gazed down the street. 'You spoken with her yet?'

'The redhead?' Dan looked back up the northern end of Main Street. 'Nah, not really. Given her a wave and whatnot.'

'Whatnot?'

'You know. A smile, a welcome.' But no advice. Another stab of remorse about his lack of gentlemanly qualities hit Dan in the stomach. 'She hasn't been in the pub, and I don't expect she will any time soon.' And it would be best if she stayed away. He'd spent the last fortnight leaning on the bar listening to what people were saying about her. Like she'd been sacked from her job in England and was skulking in the Australian countryside using the B&B as a hideout. Or worse, she'd run off from an angry boyfriend she'd been two-timing. Mostly, Dan gave a nod and a grin, but he drew the line at discussing what she'd be like in bed when some of the farmhands and graziers from out of town started on that subject. He knocked those conversations on the head and turned them to his favourite subject: rugby union. He wasn't interested in the redhead's love life—if she had one.

'Thought you might have taken a closer look,' Ethan said.

Those vibes of interest flared. 'Not in the way you're thinking, mate. Not my type.'

'Okay then.' Ethan scooped up Lochie and the guinea pig and turned. 'So why are we standing here watching her when we've got hotel plans to look at?'

Charlotte Simmons pulled her shoulders back and eyed the mob standing in front of her. Only six people but two of them held high seats on the town committee and had enough community rope to hang her.

She'd thought she was bringing herself to a quintessential Aussie country town, but it seemed she'd travelled in a time warp. They turned quirky into an art form. Surely there was nowhere else in Australia like Swallow's Fall?

Sweat trickled beneath the collar of her white linen shirt but she ignored the need to waft the collar and get some cooler air blowing down her spine. She smoothed the palms of her hands over her beige cotton skirt and raised her chin instead. At least Daniel Bradford had disappeared inside Kookaburra's instead of standing there watching her. Not much of a conversationalist, Daniel—well, not with her; usually showed her his back after one of his off-hand waves. That's all she'd seen of him: his broad back and relaxed shoulders. Couldn't say what he looked like up close.

He had a great bum though. A *fabulous* bum. A twelve out of ten rating masculine butt. He had the respect of the town too, something she definitely didn't possess, but he'd been in town for years, was practically home-grown. She'd been here two weeks and so far it felt like a life sentence.

Charlotte looked down at Lucy, her dog, and the only friend she had. She tickled Lucy's ears; a young Australian Shepherd she'd found along the highway on her way down here. She'd emailed and posted lost dog notices at every vet surgery from here to Canberra but no-one had come forward to claim her.

'Right then,' Mrs Johnson said, opening the debate.

Charlotte straightened and gave the committee a smile. Two months, three, maximum, and she'd be gone from this unexpectedly perplexing town. *Please don't let it take any longer.*

'Good morning,' she said. 'How nice to see you all … again. Can I offer anyone a cup of tea?' She indicated the door behind her. 'Kettle's on.'

Mrs Johnson—or Mrs J, as she was mostly called—folded her arms over her lightweight summer jacket, her sharp gaze raking Charlotte's face as though trying to place her. 'Jug,' she said in a considered tone. 'We're a little old-fashioned in Swallow's Fall. We call it a jug.'

Charlotte took her focus off Mrs J's penetrating gaze and shook away the concern that the woman knew about her. How could she? Charlotte had spent only the first six years of her childhood in Australia before the nightmare event that had forced her relocation from an outer suburb of Sydney to the village of Lower Starfoot-in-the-Forest in Yorkshire, England. Mrs J might know about the event from twenty-three years ago, but not about Charlotte's involvement. 'The jug's on then,' she chirped. Her smile had surely petrified into a gaping grin and she'd never again be able to lick her lips, which were dry, like the roof of her mouth. 'And I have a fresh batch of lemon tartlets, if anyone's hungry.' Most days they partook of her home-baked fare as they stood around on her front lawn, attempting persuasion.

'No time for picnics,' Mrs J said. 'Let's get this sorted.'

The temperature of the situation must have risen this morning.

Charlotte eyed the group. Mrs Johnson. Sweet-natured Mrs Tam. Mr and Mrs Tillman, who ran the stock feeders'. Their oddball twenty-year-old twin daughters, who didn't quite fit in with their 1950s floral dresses and studious natures. One had a purple streak in her hair and the other a tattoo of a scallop shell on her shoulder. Charlotte wondered why the twins hadn't left home and made their way to the city.

'It's our understanding,' Mrs Johnson said, 'that you're planning on repainting the weatherboard on the B&B.'

Charlotte nodded. 'Sunflower yellow.'

'And we're not saying it's a bad thing,' Mrs J continued as though Charlotte hadn't spoken. 'The house needs a new coat of paint and it's decent of you for wanting to pep it up.'

'Thank you.'

'That bad storm we had a few years back did a lot of damage, and our good friends, the Cappers, didn't have the money to renovate, with hardly any customers and their income dwindling as it did.'

'I understand,' Charlotte said. One of the first things she'd done was repair the sorry state of the veranda railings and put down new turf in the front garden. 'It's good of you to take an interest, with me being new. How kind of you all.'

'That's why they moved west to their son,' Mrs J said, steamrollering Charlotte's sarcasm. 'Forced to retire because the B&B wasn't producing an income. So what we really want to know is how you think you could do any better because this is a difficult town to live in.'

Wasn't it just? 'Well ...' Charlotte hadn't given any consideration to answering this question. She hadn't expected such opposition. Or was it interference? 'I'll advertise. Although it might take a couple of months before the house has guests.' Not that Charlotte would be around to see them. The only advertising she intended was putting the B&B up for resale—and she couldn't do that without first giving it a cosmetic makeover. It was in a worse state inside than she'd realised.

Mrs Johnson stared at her, face puckered as though she'd taken a sip of strong coffee, expecting it to be weak tea. 'It's been pink for as long as any of us can remember.'

'So yellow would be a refreshing change.'

'Pink,' Grace Tillman said, nudging her husband, Ted, in his tank of a chest.

'Pink,' he responded on cue, frowning like a disgruntled Buddha. 'Can't go changing it now. We had photos taken of the town four years back—we haven't got money in the kitty to have more done. We have our own website, you know, and those pictures are up on it. That's the first impression people get when they go wandering the interweb.'

Charlotte withheld her smile at the idea of the world looking for the dot on the map called Swallow's Fall.

Ted puffed up like one of the local corroboree frogs, although there was nothing endangered about him. 'This B&B is part of our legacy and we're proud of our history. Why, it's practically heritage ranking, is our B&B. It has to remain flamingo pink.'

'My B&B,' Charlotte said. Parts of the inside were certainly worthy of a museum, but she'd better not mention that. No wonder it had been on the market forever. If it took too long to settle the repainting issue, let alone what she needed to do inside, she'd never resell the place; she'd be here through summer, autumn *and* winter.

'It's our further understanding,' Mrs Johnson said, 'that you're planning on putting kiddie beds in the rooms for young children.'

Charlotte drew her bottom lip between her teeth. 'Yes. So families can stay.' Small families—two parents, one child. The rooms weren't big enough for more.

The group shuffled and sighed, signalling an overall impression of wrongdoing.

'The Cappers only had couples,' Grace Tillman said. 'They advertised their place—'

'My place now.'

'—as a retreat for adults.'

The bedrooms upstairs were sweet, in a bijou, chintzy way, but you could fit a trundle bed or a cot if needed, so what was the problem with catering for children? The house was small and currently a bit dated but had enough love in its rafters to make families want to stay for the night—cheaply—and have a hearty, home-cooked breakfast the next morning before moving on. Which is why Charlotte felt it would sell once she'd done some cosmetic renovation.

'This is a main thoroughfare off the Monaro Highway,' Grace continued, her plump cheeks reddening with every word. 'We have a responsibility to our visitors. We can't go about our business constantly watching for kids running out of the B&B.'

Six cars an hour was a main thoroughfare? Charlotte put her politest smile back in place. 'I recognise it's a busy little town and that it's growing. I have thought about the Main Street issue. I'm going to build a fence around the front garden.'

Silence.

Charlotte stilled. What had she done now?

'A f–f–fence?' Ted Tillman spluttered. 'We've never had a fence around the B&B. What colour are you going to paint *that*?'

Charlotte held her breath a moment. 'I was thinking ordinary white.'

'A yellow house and now a fence, for crying out loud. What next?' Ted took hold of his wife's arm. 'Come on, Grace. We need an official town meeting about this.'

Charlotte breathed deeply. 'No need for a meeting, surely?'

'A fence around the B&B front garden, young woman,' Ted said, his tone reminiscent of a brewing summer storm, 'would run up against the bus depot and possibly interfere with the shire's transportation arrangements. You'll need *permission*. And let me tell you, it might take months. The shire is busy, you know. They've got pot holes on the highway to consider before they jump to your wants and needs.'

Charlotte glanced at the shire's distinguished depot: a green barricade railing and an open-sided shelter.

'Nothing to worry about,' Mrs Johnson said as Ted stormed off, pulling his wife behind him. 'Town meetings are a normal practice when something major is happening. You'll find that out.' She turned to the old 4WD she drove. The thing screeched like a pandemonium of parrots whenever she fired it up. Why hadn't the committee done anything about that?

Charlotte glanced over her shoulder at her own brand-new 4WD she'd thought would give a better impression of fitting in than the swanky sports car she'd driven in England. Stuff the fitting-in—she'd never fit in here. Good job she didn't want to.

The Tillman twins looked at each other and back to Charlotte. 'There's plenty for you to find out,' the one with the purple streak in her hair said. The one with the tattoo of a scallop shell nodded in agreement.

Charlotte sighed.

'Don't go worrying too hard,' Mrs Tam said once everyone had gone. 'Ted's in charge of the gavel. Likes to bang it whenever he gets the chance.'

Charlotte already felt the weight of it. Right on top of her head.

'And I do like to give Ted the chance to let his emotions out,' Mrs Tam continued. 'He's been under the weather recently. Too much study of space travel and the like. And there's the trouble with—' Mrs Tam pursed her mouth, suggesting she'd like to say more but felt she shouldn't.

'I'll keep all that in mind,' Charlotte said.

Mrs Tam looked at Charlotte, head tilted, dark eyes searching Charlotte's face. 'Are you sure you haven't been in town before?' She smiled. 'Maybe it's that beautiful hair of yours making me think I've seen you somewhere.' Charlotte swiped at her shoulder-length hair, pushing it from her face and rolling her shoulders in an attempt to release the self-consciousness settling on them. She'd never been here before. Didn't want to be here now but had forced herself to come, and buying the B&B had been her only option.

She glanced down the street to Kookaburra's where Daniel and Ethan Granger had been standing. Charlotte had seen Ethan around but hadn't met him yet. He was quieter-looking than anticipated. Big though; six-foot-five, easy.

She'd be less tense if she kept an open mind about the best way to approach him, but the questions she had for him might anger any man, especially if the townspeople already had wind of something amiss about Charlotte's sudden arrival. They were so unexpectedly closed off and protective of each other. She'd have to think about backing down a little, not rushing things. Taking her time would be hard, though. She had so many questions and she needed the answers in order to move on. She had a new life to build, away from this place and free of fear.

Ethan didn't look like his father, or even have the same surname, but was he built the same way, emotionally? Perhaps he was different to Thomas O'Donnell.

Charlotte didn't know, but she was here to find out.

Two

Charlotte locked the front door, slid the bolts into place top and bottom and hooked the chain into its lopsided brass slot. The red paint had chipped where her old screwdriver had slipped. She wasn't an expert handywoman but she knew how to put chains and bolts on doors—when she had the right tools. A new screwdriver was on her shopping list.

It was silent outside. Dark.

She turned to the hallway, fighting fatigue and the dreaded sense of claustrophobia the darkness gave her. She switched the hall light off and the upstairs light on. The large peonies on the flocked wallpaper looked like splashes of raspberry cordial in the evening shadows.

'Goodnight, Lucy.' The dog lay in her basket in the laundry area off the kitchen.

Charlotte held her breath, counted to five and released it, putting more than usual mental effort into ignoring the shadows around her as she made her way to her ground-floor bedroom.

It had been years since the panic overwhelmed her to the point where she wanted to hide beneath her bedcovers, but tension after the death of her gran nine months ago and the loss of the world she'd loved had nudged the fear again. Two weeks in Swallow's Fall and the angsts were back with a regularity more worrying than the bodily incapacities that came with them: clouded vision and nausea that played a skipping game in her stomach; that terrible closed-in sensation. And the dream.

She closed her bedroom door, holding on to the tarnished brass knob as she turned the old-fashioned key in the lock. She moved to the window, slipped her hand between the closed drapes and checked that the window lock was hooked properly. She shuffled the heavy brocade fabric, folding one width over the other; locking out the night.

She got into bed and switched off her table lamp. A light was on in the house; she didn't need one in her bedroom. She'd taught herself to sleep without it. *There's no monster now*, she reminded herself. *He's gone.*

She turned her mind to the jobs on her list. The hall carpet had seen better days and her kitchen could do with an overhaul worthy of two rubbish skips—and she had a pink house to be repainted yellow. Not that she wanted to go overboard with renovations, but the quicker she got the B&B ready for resale, the faster she'd be out of this town. It was nothing like the village in England she'd grown to love. She treasured wide open spaces but there was too much landmass in Australia. Too much country to become too damned lonely in.

She'd go for a run tomorrow. That would help relieve the sense of the townspeople not liking her, not wanting her, disturbing her normally happy-to-be-alone attitude. Mrs Tam was helpful but Mr and Mrs Tillman were troublesome. Mrs Johnson was probably more bluff than bite ... and Sammy Granger. She was on the committee and had been welcoming the few times Charlotte had met her but it would be a colossal mistake to befriend the woman who was married to the man she'd come to town to meet.

She scrunched her eyes closed and ran a hand over her face. Why should she care what anyone thought about her? She wouldn't be here long enough for any of it to matter.

She saw an image of Daniel Bradford resting against the doorframe of his Bar & Grill, arms folded, one leg bent, his weight on his hip. She surprised herself by smiling as she shrugged her shoulders beneath the eiderdown and shuffled her head into the pillow. At least she'd removed the fear of the dream, although she hadn't expected to fall asleep with a picture of Daniel Bradford's firm backside in her mind. Still ... if that's what it took. She yawned, snuggled further. The man had a fabulous bum.

Neither had she expected to get a first-rate view of it so soon, but here it was in daytime, right in front of her in superb display. Clothed, of course—encased in washed denim so soft looking she could imagine the smoothness of it on the palm of her hand.

The farming aromas of cracked feed and chicken pellets stifled her breath as they did every time she came into the stock feeders' establishment. The smell of hay and sheep wafted through the open barn doors at the back along with the sound of the twins' laughter, but she couldn't take her focus off Daniel Bradford's tight, two-hundred-squats-a-day backside. He must work out. A lot.

Ted Tillman had his head bent over a brochure and Daniel was leaning on the counter, nodding at whatever he was being shown. He had his left foot on an upended crate so the denim of his jeans creased where the top of his leg met his hip. The length of his back and legs said six-foot-two, and the firmness of his thighs said runner, or football player. The jeans were what might be called a comfortable fit on an exceptionally taut body. The white shirt he wore, tucked into the waistband of his jeans, showed off a torso that tapered from wide shoulders to trim waist. His brown belt looked old; a scratched leather favourite, or perhaps the only one he owned.

Her consideration slid downwards again and her focus got snagged on a small rip in his jeans below the left back pocket. About three centimetres long, it was only slightly frayed, suggesting it hadn't been torn for long. He might not even know it was there.

'Good morning.'

She shot her gaze up to his face and didn't know what feature to look at first. His short brown hair should be ordinary by anyone's description, but it was thick and glossy. His eyes were the colour of sable and his tanned skin suggested he liked being outdoors.

Charlotte gathered herself. *Stay calm. He's just a guy.* So why did she feel like panting the way Lucy did on warm afternoons?

'Something wrong?' he asked with a quizzical half-smile.

'There's a queue,' Ted said, both hands flat on the counter as he leaned forward, his frown meant to scare.

'It's okay,' Daniel said to Ted, taking his foot off the crate and turning to face Charlotte. He hooked his fingers into the back pockets of his jeans, and thrust his left leg forwards.

Alright, so he wasn't just any male specimen. *Hot farmhand on hay stack*, the caption said, as a vision of Daniel Bradford standing on the baler of his John Deere tractor erupted in her head. Wearing only his jeans, with fifty-five hay bales he'd hefted at his booted feet, he ran a long-fingered hand down his bare chest where rivulets of dirty sweat trailed down to his … Charlotte looked down at his—For God's sake. This was not the dream she should be having. Not in daylight.

'Looking for something particular?' Daniel asked, amusement in his tone.

The flame of embarrassment singed her cheeks. He'd caught her looking.

'I wanted some screws,' she said in a breathy little voice. Where had *that* come from?

'You're in the wrong place. You need Morelly's hardware across the street.'

Did the man have any idea what havoc that shirt wrought with a woman's imagination? Strong neck, toughened shoulders, an expanse of iron-hard chest and a firmed abdomen—all barely concealed by his thin cotton shirt. Given her reaction to him so far, all this masculinity spelled trouble.

'Screwdriver,' she managed. 'I need a Phillips head for the screw-in type of screws.'

He grinned the sort of grin obviously meant to please anyone who wanted to catch it. Charlotte did her best not to be knocked sideways by the sexual vibrancy of it.

'Screwing?' he said, his voice lowered to a soft, deep vibrato. 'I think I know just what you need.'

Oh, trouble alright. Hotshot-charm-boy trouble. 'Screw *in*,' she said firmly.

Ted Tillman coughed. 'So, shall I order the charcoal briquettes for you, Dan?'

'Yeah, please, Ted. One ton.'

'One t–ton?' Ted stuttered. 'What are you going to do with a t–ton of charcoal?'

Daniel spoke softly. 'Thinking of throwing a barbecue at Kookaburra's on Friday nights throughout summer. Something different for the punters.'

Ted closed the brochure and puckered his mouth and brow.

Daniel turned a confident-looking smile on the stock feeders' proprietor. 'First night I do it, you and Grace get a free feed. Put the charcoal on my tab, would you, Ted?'

Ted's brow relaxed. 'That's very generous—a free feed, eh?' He slapped the brochure. 'Not sure how this will go down, but I'll order the briquettes for you. Can always send them back if we decide we don't like Friday night barbecues.' Ted looked around Daniel's shoulder at Charlotte. 'You wanted something?'

'Dog biscuits.' Charlotte turned, picked up a fifteen-kilo plastic sack and nearly dropped it—it was heavier than anticipated. She'd intended to buy the five-kilo bag but couldn't bring herself to look weak and fainthearted in front of these men. She had an unflinching public image to maintain. She hoisted the bag under her arm and turned to the counter.

'Cash for smaller purchases,' Ted said. 'EFTPOS for others but I don't accept American Express.'

'I know, you've told me before.' No tab for Charlotte. She deposited the sack onto the counter and dug into the pocket of her A-line skirt for her purse.

'Where's your dog?' Daniel asked.

'Outside.' She inhaled the aroma of coffee coming off him in waves. Freshly ground beans. Strong and sweet.

'*Ted!*'

Mr Tillman moved towards the sound of his wife's voice, his footsteps shuffling on the grainy floorboards. 'Coming, honey. Guess what's happening at Kookaburra's on a Friday from now on—and we're getting it free!'

'I've left the correct money on the counter,' Charlotte called. Didn't want him creating a fuss in the street, saying she'd left without paying. That would only give him another reason to bang his gavel. Whatever the emotional problems Mrs Tam had been referring to, Ted didn't appear to be having any trouble with them today.

Hotshot held his hand out. 'Dan Bradford. Good to meet you at last.'

She grabbed the sack and dragged it to the end of the counter. 'At last? I've been in town a fortnight.'

'Been meaning to call. Thought I'd let you settle in first. Didn't want to crowd you.'

'Very kind of you. Especially as I have a gathering over at my place most days.'

He grinned. 'I did wave.' He thrust his hand further forwards.

Churlish not to take it, but she kept her hand on the sack of dog biscuits. 'Charlotte Simmons,' she said, much preferring the prim tone to the breathy voice.

He leaned closer. 'We have a custom in Swallow's Fall, Charlotte.' His expression looked more amused than perturbed by her discourteous manner. Those coffee beans must be expensive because the unexpectedly rich aroma teased her nostrils and made her mouth water. 'We shake hands and we help each other out whenever we can.'

Charlotte bit back the retort on the tip of her tongue. Not wise to bring up her thoughts about how *helpful* the townspeople were while Ted was still in earshot. She slid her hand into Daniel's, where it was immediately engulfed. 'Nice to meet you. At last.'

He cocked an eyebrow. 'You been waiting for an introduction?'

Charlotte tilted her head. 'Is there a queue?'

His smile broke. Clusters of lights danced in the depths of his eyes. She drew a steadying breath. Could he do that on purpose?

'Seriously,' he said, breaking the spell and releasing her hand as he stepped back. 'I'm happy to meet you. I was going to pop into the B&B and introduce myself later this morning.'

'Glad to have saved you a chore.'

'Now I've seen you close up, I guarantee it wouldn't have been a chore, and I apologise for not having introduced myself before now. Will you forgive me?'

Fabulous looking, great physique—good job she wouldn't be in town long enough to consider how she'd react if he threw his bounty of masculine charms her way. There hadn't been time for relationships or love affairs these last two years and she certainly wouldn't be looking for any in the antiquated, backward town of Swallow's Fall.

She grabbed the sack of dog biscuits, settled its bulk on her hip and tugged at her skirt, which had ridden too far above her knees. She thrust her purse into her pocket, and headed for the door.

'Can I give you a hand with that?' he asked, following her out.

'I'm fine, thanks.' The plastic was slippery and the biscuits inside shifted with each step. She stopped by Lucy and resettled the sack.

'Here, give it to me.'

She angled away. 'I'm *fine*.'

He let his arm drop and produced another smile. 'Stubborn, huh?'

'Capable.'

'It's that red hair,' he said with a grin.

'Titian.'

'Highball red. Not quite ginger.'

Highball? Was he referring to her as a cocktail? And it was hard to ignore the 'ginger' remark, but Charlotte found the willpower.

Daniel glanced at Lucy as the dog unfurled, yawned and shuffled closer to Charlotte's feet. 'Will she bite?'

Charlotte shrugged. 'Don't know.' *Hopefully.*

He hunched down, elbows resting on his knees and checked the name tag on the dog's collar. 'Hi, Lucy. How's your day?'

Lucy gave him a dog smile, mouth open, tongue lolling, eyes bright with curiosity.

Flirt. Charlotte would have to give her dog some lessons on dealing with certain types of men. 'Come on, Lucy.' She checked for traffic. Nothing coming. She stepped off the pavement with Lucy at her heels and headed for the wooden walkway on the other side of Main Street. She needed milk and coffee from the grocer's. They didn't stock expensive coffee beans and she'd pay a hundred dollars for a real coffee right now, but granules would have to do.

Lucy padded after Charlotte, Hotshot Bradford right behind the dog.

Charlotte halted outside the beauty parlour, next door to the toy shop. Both were closed. Cuddly Bear Toy Shop was only open a few hours each day but the beauty parlour hadn't had its doors open once since she'd arrived. Why the town had a place like this, she had no idea. She'd wanted to stop and peer inside any number of times but never spent time dawdling on Main Street in case someone cornered her and asked more questions about colour schemes, but the sack of biscuits was heavy so she took the opportunity while she had it.

She slid the sack down her leg, plopped it on the ground and looked up at the creamy facade, the bronzed trim, and the curly signage on the window. *'La Crème Parfaite. Cherishing the woman within,'* she read aloud, wondering how much cherishing the women of Swallow's Fall demanded. Obviously not much, since the place was locked up. She stepped closer to see what was written beneath. The font, a small italic, read, *For women passing through and those stuck here.*

She spluttered a laugh. Someone with spirit had written this. It lifted her mood, a heartfelt, fun moment she hadn't expected.

'Who owns this place?' she asked.

Daniel was studying her, his smile tinged with surprise.

Charlotte scowled and picked up the sack. Across the road, a blonde got out of a little sports car. Elegant wasn't the right word for her … perhaps sleek suited. She looked about Charlotte's age but a lot trendier.

'There she is now,' Daniel said. 'The beauty parlour owner.'

'Who is she?'

'Julia Morelly.'

The woman moved to the back of the car. She reminded Charlotte of a gazelle—long neck, slim legs, thin arms and wrists and there was a casualness in the way she moved, as though she were out shopping for silk scarves on Bond Street, not running a beauty parlour in a miniscule alpine town in the

Snowy Mountains. She opened the boot of her car and took out a stroller. Slamming the boot closed, she unfolded the stroller, locked it into place, pulled the sunhood down and turned. She pushed the empty stroller along the road, upended its front wheels with seeming care as she wheeled it up the pavement and headed for the stock feeders'.

'What's she doing?' Charlotte asked.

'Practising.'

'For what?'

'Having a baby.'

'She's pregnant?'

'No, she's practising.'

Charlotte checked his face to see if he was joking.

'Julia's got a sperm donor in Canberra. She wants a baby and he said he'll give her one.'

Charlotte raised an eyebrow. 'That sounds a little calculated.'

'Nah. You'll understand when you get to know her. She's had a lot of boyfriends. Got fed up with men and came home a year ago. Opened up this place, although she doesn't get many customers wanting her fancy treatments, so she decided it was the right time to become a mother.'

'Is this man going to help with the child? Or is it a business arrangement?'

Daniel shrugged. 'All I know is they don't do it.'

'Don't do what?'

'*It*. They have it … you know …' He grinned. 'Medically done.'

Ah. *It*. 'IVF,' she said in a serious tone.

'Yeah.' His grin and narrowed eyes spoke a dozen silent but explicit words. 'Boring, huh?' He stood there, all lean beef and brawn, the dazzling smile and laidback demeanour pronouncing *sex, sex, sex*. Could he do that on purpose too? Make a woman think about sex?

Okay, so it wasn't just coffee she was missing.

Charlotte moved off smartish in case the heat on her face showed up as a blush. Titian red and pink wasn't the best colour match. 'This is one strange town,' she muttered.

'It's taken you two whole weeks to discover that?' There was a laugh in his tone as he followed her.

Charlotte walked past the grocer's—she'd pop out later and get the coffee and milk; couldn't carry everything now anyway. She walked straight past Morelly's hardware store too, even though the doors were open and the copious, dusty-smelling shelves would house any number of Phillips head screwdrivers. Young Mr Morelly chatted effusively to a customer. *Young* was obviously a euphemism for *pensioner who wouldn't retire*. He had to be close to seventy.

'Didn't you want a Phillips head for all that screwing you're going to be doing?' Daniel asked.

Charlotte ignored him. Not worthy of a sensible woman's answer.

The door to Kookaburra's was propped open too—and there was that tantalising smell. Dark cocoa-flavoured roasted coffee beans. She slowed and sniffed the air, drawing the fragrance inside in the hope it would stay all day.

'Fancy a coffee?' Daniel asked as he brushed past her, the coffee-bean smell overlaid with a lighter, summery fragrance of aftershave; a hint of sliced melon and sandalwood shavings. He pushed the door to the bar open and looked over his shoulder. 'You must have noticed we're the only two sane people in town. Let's get together and talk about that.'

Unfair. Just unfair. She'd get down on her knees for a real coffee. 'No thanks.' It had been fifteen days since she'd had a flat white.

'Come on in and tell me your plans for the B&B.'

She definitely wouldn't be doing that. 'I hope you're not trying to chat me up.' It came out snappy but he had no right being so tantalisingly masculine either.

'I'm not making a pass,' he said in a surprised tone. 'You don't interest me that way.'

'You don't interest me that way either.' All she had to do now was inform her libido of this decision.

'You think I hadn't noticed? You're not exactly Miss Forthcoming.'

He said it with a smile but he made her sound like a fractious beauty pageant contestant, arguing with the judge because she hadn't got the crown. She was already on the wrong side with the community, and now here she was getting offside with Hotshot. She knew he'd be trouble—just knew it from the start. How dare he make assumptions after such a brief acquaintance?

'I don't intend to argue with you, but you did ignore me for two weeks.'

'Come on, Charlotte. I waved. And I apologised.'

'And I don't fall easily for smarm.'

'Smarm?' He stepped back. 'Look, I asked if you'd like a coffee, not to marry me.'

'What's going on?'

Charlotte started, turned to the man who had spoken and dropped the sack.

'Careful.' Ethan Granger stepped forwards and bent to catch it. 'You okay?'

The breath drained from her lungs. Ethan was a giant of a man. 'Yes, I'm fine. Thank—thank you.' Although she was desperate to look up at him again, she kept her gaze on his chest. She was so close she saw the way it rose and fell with each steady breath he took. *Look up at him. Look at his face. Who does he look like?*

She looked up, her breathing shallow with worry. Sandy-coloured hair, a bit tousled. Piercing blue eyes that held a reflection of the smile on his firm mouth. A handsome giant. O'Donnell hadn't been this tall, had he? Hard to tell, she'd only been six years old and most men were tall to a child. She pushed anxiety down and concentrated, with an almost greedy need, on every feature of this man's face so she could evaluate it later—when she wasn't so close to him.

'Take it easy there, Charlotte,' Daniel drawled.

Charlotte jumped back—she'd forgotten he was there. She snapped her head his way, and met his frowning contemplation.

Dan lowered his head and studied her. One minute she was behaving like a debutante fighting to be the first to shake the hand of the queen, and the next she was a bundle of nerves, as though she'd tripped on her dress in front of the crowd, her face drawn with tension, lips parted in surprise—or worry.

When she'd laughed about the signage on the beauty place her face had bloomed with joy, her eyes sparkling with frank and open amusement. Lake-green eyes, the colour of still water at dawn, more vibrant because of her pale skin and hair colouring. A hell of a good-looking woman, and he'd caught her happiness for a second too. Hadn't lasted long.

'Nice to meet you at last,' Ethan was saying. 'You've met my wife, Sammy, but I've been a bit busy of late. I apologise for not having visited you sooner.'

'Please don't worry. Sammy was—Sammy was very kind.'

Dan's frown deepened. Charlotte was looking up at Ethan from beneath her lashes, studying him intensely, as though *he* were the newcomer in town.

Ethan didn't appear to notice. 'Well, if there's anything we can help you with, just call.'

She was blinking too fast, as though the sun had blinded her. 'Thank you.'

Jesus. She was batting her eyelashes at Ethan the way Mrs Tam did at Dan.

Dan stepped forwards, took the sack of dog biscuits from Ethan and held it out to her. She hadn't batted her auburn lashes at him but that didn't mean he wouldn't hold true to his offer of assistance. 'Hold it in both hands if you won't let me carry it for you.'

She seemed to sink into herself, the skin on her face paler than a vanilla milkshake. Her eyes narrowed with a muddled look, as though she'd got herself tangled in something bigger than she could cope with. A bolt of tenderness hit him in the chest. The same kind of sensation he got when he looked at Sammy walking along with her baby bump. Or when little Lochie looked up at him with his soulful gaze.

'You're going to need a hat, Charlotte,' he said softly, keeping her perplexed gaze locked in his. 'You'll burn in the sun.' And what could be worse than seeing that beautiful skin marred?

She reached for the sack.

'Why don't you let me carry it for you?'

She all but grabbed it from his hands. 'No, thanks. I'm fine.'

Stubborn, alright. 'Okay, well hold it flat or you're going to wrench your arms out of their sockets.'

'I will. Lucy.' She looked behind her. '*Lucy.*'

'She's right there,' Dan said, pointing at the walkway where the dog sat at Charlotte's feet.

'Oh, yes.' It looked like she could hardly catch her breath. 'Okay, well. Bye.' She nodded at Ethan, flicking another look at him as she moved off. She didn't look at Dan.

'Watch your step at the end of the walkway,' Dan said.

'I will.'

'So we'll make a coffee date for another time?' he called.

She glanced over her shoulder. 'Yes. Lovely.'

Lovely? Where'd that come from? She wasn't thinking straight. She'd called him smarmy, refused his friendly offer of coffee and started bickering with him. And all that had stopped the moment Ethan turned up.

'What were you pestering her for?' Ethan asked.

'I wasn't pestering. I asked if she wanted a coffee but she wasn't in the mood.'

'Yeah, right.' Ethan laughed. '*Let me carry your bag,*' he mimicked. '*Buy a hat, little Charlotte. Watch your step, sweetheart. Don't strain your precious arms.*'

Dan frowned. 'Give me a break. She doesn't need anyone watching her back, she's got a two-foot-long copper pipe soldered to her spine.' Or so Dan had thought. Now he'd met her he got the impression there was a lot more going on inside her head and that perhaps her straightened spine was armour against … something.

Ethan cocked an eyebrow.

Dan sighed. 'I was just trying to behave a little friendly like, and it didn't work.'

'Looked to me like you were planning on becoming her *special friend.*'

'No chance.' Whatever Charlotte's bemusement was about, Dan didn't want anyone thinking he had some obsession with her just because she'd fluttered her eyelashes at Ethan and not him.

He peered at Charlotte's retreating back, her hair afloat around her rigid shoulders, billowing like the fringe on a silk shawl.

'Look at your mother,' his father used to say when he watched Dan's mother walk around the house, or the garden. 'Whips my breath away.' Dan's breath had been whipped from him too. He'd had nine years of love from his parents and not a second more. They'd died and he'd lost the chance to grow up sheltered by that love, living in a male-dominated world with his grandfather after that. Life hadn't allowed for a lot of emotional to-ing and fro-ing, unless his team lost on home turf or the muffler fell off the ute while doing a hundred and twenty down the freeway.

He'd been almost captivated by the sound of Charlotte's laughter, and when her smile reached her eyes, a pang of pure pleasure had ricocheted in his chest. All eyes, cheekbones and pointy little chin, impish—light and wonder, as though the child she'd been still danced inside her, yet somehow was only allowed out for special occasions.

Too reminiscent of everything in his own childhood. All the love stuff he'd missed out on. He turned to the door. 'I told you, she's not my type.'

Three

Dan turned a slow circle on the upper level of Kookaburra's, taking in the crumbling plaster and hundred-year-old cladding that hung in tatters from the now mostly fallen partitions of the seven original bedrooms. No need for bedrooms in a hotel that didn't get any customers after the First World War. The rafters above him groaned and the wind whistled through the frames of the seven neat windows looking out onto a balcony running the entire top level of the hotel.

Dan was a qualified draughtsman and knew enough about buying, renovating and selling-on properties to produce his own reality television show. Turning properties around was how he'd made his money, although granted, this renovation would be the biggest of his life. He'd applied for and received an extension to the original development approval licence. One of the reasons he'd bought the place was because the development proposal had already gone through the shire and had been accepted. What he hadn't counted on was the townspeople's reservations about the actual build. He'd learned, quickly, that they'd only agreed to the changes because they hadn't thought for a moment that the previous owner would get the hotel up and running, but he'd been a home-grown and well-liked man, so the committee had humoured him.

Then he'd moved overseas and Dan had turned up. Sparks had flown as everyone fretted about what the new guy was going to do. They didn't want change. They were scared of it so Dan had decided he didn't need to do anything fast and had been content to mosey around for a few years, settling in and finding his feet. And anyway, there weren't as many tourists passing through back then and Dan had learned the virtue of patience in Swallow's Fall as he waited for the right moment to announce his plans.

As owner-builder he had to abide by certain rules, given the size of the development. Which meant he'd have to hire professionals to undertake the plumbing and wiring and most of the re-build. Which meant he needed somewhere for them to stay.

He wandered to one of the windows and rubbed at the grime. Swallow's Fall had enough historic attractions to show off. The pioneer cemetery with white bunting along the fence line. The Town Hall, and its noticeboard with renovation updates and a thermometer chart tracking the dollar donations—the jackpot still a decade off by Dan's reckoning. The stock feeders' with its oversized neighing plastic horse out the front. Morelly's hardware store got a look in too, usually by the men, the women trotting their kids inside Cuddly Bear Toy Shop two doors down—when it was open. The craft centre just out of town made some profit, showcasing the skills and wares of the locals.

He looked over at the B&B. Red was out early this morning, the dog at her heels in the front garden. She was dressed for exercise, Lycra running shorts and a big grey sweatshirt. No hat. She did a few waist twists and took off at a jog, heading for the hill on the eastern side of town. Lucy bounded ahead of her.

Dan stepped back from the window. She was good-looking, yeah, and there was sweetness within her, but there could only be one explanation for how she'd reacted to Ethan: she had to be attracted to his friend. His *married* friend.

Dan turned, jogged down the stairs and crossed the bar, his deck shoes squeaking on the polished floorboards. 'Josh, I'm going for a run.' He headed behind the counter to his room at the back of the bar.

Josh paused at the dishwasher, a glass cloth in his hand. 'Didn't you go first thing this morning?'

Dan rolled a shoulder. 'Yeah.' He went running every morning, unless there was a metre of snow. 'Only did ten kilometres though. Feel like finishing it off.'

'I'll come with you.'

'Sorry, mate, I need you to restock from last night. The backup mixers are low. Next time, huh?' He often ran with Josh and enjoyed the competition. Josh was taller than Dan but Dan was faster. They pushed each other in companionable sportsmanship. Today he needed to get Charlotte alone.

Dan slammed his bedroom door behind him with his foot. He kicked off his shoes, undid the buttons on his shirt and dragged it off his shoulders. He pulled off his jeans, hopping to the chest of drawers. He yanked out a pair of cotton rugby shorts and a crumpled but clean white T-shirt.

Where the hell had he left his runners? He turned, scanning the room. The king-size bed sat in the middle, sheets and blankets in a mess, pillows propped against the wooden headboard; one on the floor. The room was spacious enough to be his away from it all bolt-hole. He had a small study area set up by the window. His home gym equipment took up nearly half of the room. A dumbbell rack served as a bedside table—enough space to balance his alarm clock on top—not that he needed a wake-up call; he rose before sunrise. The only piece of equipment that didn't see any action, except in deepest, darkest winter, was his cross-trainer.

He grinned. His king-sized bed hadn't seen much action lately either, but he took his thoughts off that.

His runners were where he'd thrown them that morning after his usual six a.m. fifteen-kilometre run: in the doorway to the bathroom, half hidden under the towel he'd discarded after his weight session.

He dressed, and headed out the back door and down the alleyway. She was halfway up the hillside. She wasn't running, but she had a reasonable pace going considering the hill was steep. It wouldn't take much to catch up with her, but Dan ran the other way—he'd bump into her when she got to the top of the hill.

He headed north out of town, picked up the pace and took the bush track leading off Main Street. His breathing pattern settled quickly, his lungs like healthy bellows by the time he got to the other side of the hill. He'd seen her, almost at the top, as he ran between the granite boulders that were scattered on the hill as though randomly dropped like marbles from the hand of a giant.

At the top of the hill, he paused and looked out over the pastures. A bit parched but not bad yet. Not damaged by drought. The sunlight cast a golden colour over the tops of the many hill crests. Deep in the valleys the land was still dark green, dotted with snow gums, which were the strongest trees he'd come across. In winter, the boughs cradled the snow, dipped and bent, patiently waiting for spring.

Lucy trotted over the crest, yapped, and went into a gallop, heading for him.

Dan turned his back to the ridge and jogged on the spot.

Lucy barked, circling him.

'Hey, girl. How's it going?'

Two barks.

'Is she nearly here?'

One bark.

Dan grinned and bent to scruff the dog behind her charcoal, black and white ears. She rolled onto her back. 'You're nothing but a flirt.' He tickled her stomach. The white hair on her belly, peppered with the odd copper spot, felt soft and warm on his fingers.

He lifted his hand and clicked his fingers and Lucy twisted her body to sit, as fast and agile as a Jack Russell after a rat. She watched him, waiting for another command. Yeah, she was a good example of the breed, quick-minded and trainable. Dan shook the paw she held up for him. She wouldn't see much ranch action around here, but she might be a useful search and rescue dog.

'Lucy!' Charlotte called out behind him.

'Help me out here, would you, Luce?' Dan said. 'I need to talk to her, so if you could make it look like you need a rest, I'd be grateful.'

Lucy got to her feet, circled Dan and plopped her rump on his shoe just as the redhead came over the ridge.

'Lucy!'

'She's right here,' Dan said, waving.

'Oh.' Charlotte stopped, her chest and shoulders heaving beneath her baggy sweatshirt.

'You okay?'

She flipped the lid of a plastic water bottle and drank. 'Fine. A bit hot.'

'Nearly summer. You're going to need a hat sooner than later.' He was repeating himself and he doubted she'd listen, but he didn't want her to burn. She was used to the English climate, not the Aussie one and even in the Snowies the sun could be unkind.

She wiped her mouth with the back of her hand and slapped the bottle's mouthpiece down. 'You're not wearing one.' She ran a hand through her hair. It was darkened, like treacle, and a little frazzled looking. Exhaustion came off her in waves.

'You okay?' he asked again.

'I'm just getting back into exercise. It's been a while.' She sat on a rock and peered at Lucy, still sitting on Dan's foot. 'Lucy,' she said. 'Come here, girl. Want some water?' She squeezed water from her drink bottle into a cupped hand. 'Come on.'

Dan nudged the dog by lifting his foot slightly. She took the hint, walked across to her mistress, lapped at the water and trotted back to sit on Dan's foot.

Dan shoved her off gently, and walked over to Charlotte. He sat on the boulder next to her and leaned forwards, elbows on knees. He took a deep, easy breath, and caught the scent of her. Since when had exhaustion come bottled in a fruity orange perfume? 'So,' he said casually, 'what type of running do you do? Just jogging?'

She straightened. 'I told you, I'm only jogging because I haven't exercised for a few months.'

'So what are you into when you're in shape? Marathons?'

She cast a sideways glance. 'Are you suggesting I'm not in shape?'

Dan splayed his hands. 'Hey, I'm just making conversation.'

She pulled her knees together. 'Sorry. That was a bit defensive of me.'

An apology? Man; that mellowed the tone of the conversation. Which was just as well because he intended to delve deeper into her interest in Ethan and what her plans for the B&B were.

'It's lovely up here,' she said.

He scanned the horizon, the pull of contentment in his chest as familiar and necessary to him as breathing. 'You'll see the summer wildflowers soon. I don't run this field from December to January, too many flowers to squash underfoot.'

'Are they pretty?'

He looked at her. Her eyes were silky green and her skin smooth although flushed. He nodded. 'Cover the whole hillside.' He raised an arm and swept it across the vista in front of them. The hillside rolling down to the town, the crops of boulders, the narrow bush tracks, the creeks and the main road in the distance. 'When they're in full bloom this hill looks like some watercolour painting of the olden days.'

'Who owns that house over there?' She pointed to their left.

Dan smiled. 'Kate and Jamie Knight.' The high, slanted rooftop of the town's stonemason and his fashion designer wife steepled from the grey-green of the treetops to poke at the wispy cirrus clouds above.

'Kate is best friends with Sammy Granger,' Dan told her. 'They know each other from way back. Used to work together. Both fashion artists, although Sammy is more landscape than fancy clothes these days and Kate has an online dress shop, or whatever you call it.'

'A fashion business online? Good idea.' She paused, frowned a little. 'I haven't met either Kate or …'

'Jamie Knight. Local stonemason. He built Ethan's new veterinary surgery on Burra Burra Lane.' Dan paused after mentioning Ethan's name. 'Kate and Jamie are away at the moment. In Sydney.'

'Working?'

'No. They're adopting a child. They're finalising whatever it is they have to finalise.'

'Wow. Do they have children of their own too?'

Dan shook his head. 'Can't, or so I believe.' He and Jamie were good buddies. The guys of a certain age in town stuck together when the opportunity arose. Exercise, the odd boys' night out at Kookaburra's. Same as the women did, when they got a chance.

'So they're bringing a baby home?' she asked.

'No. A young teenager. A boy.'

'Good for them,' she said softly.

Dan happened to agree. He'd guessed a fair amount over the last few years, and had seen—as had everyone in town—the pain of disappointment in his friends' eyes as each year went by with no child appearing for them, but Dan had never pushed either to tell him their business. Neither was he going to gossip about them.

'I saw a little animal that looked like a mouse the other day,' Charlotte said suddenly.

He turned to her. 'A pygmy possum? You actually saw one?'

'If that's what it was. I thought it was injured at first, it just sat there and didn't move when I walked up to it.'

'Do you carry your mobile phone when you're out running?' He scanned her torso but couldn't make out anything beneath the oversized sweatshirt.

'Do you?'

Dan looked up. 'I asked you first.'

'No,' she said. 'I don't.'

'Well, you might want to.' He could see her now, lost and sunburnt with one small drink bottle. Someone was going to have to look after her; give her a few pointers on surviving an Aussie summer.

'Why do you keep telling me what to do?' she asked.

'Don't get prickly, Charlotte. I was only making an observation.'

'It was the way you made it.'

Dan laughed and put a hand on his thigh. 'Why is it we can't have a normal conversation without bickering?'

'No idea, but you start it. Every time.' She cricked her neck and rolled her shoulders.

Dan wasn't convinced the squabbling was entirely his fault, and if she looked at him he was pretty sure he'd see the vulnerable look in her eyes. The one she tried to cover up. Maybe she was trying to be tougher than she was.

'If you find an injured animal and you want to save it you'd need a phone to call someone, wouldn't you?'

'Like who?'

Dan studied her to make sure he wouldn't miss her reaction. 'Like Ethan.'

The blush already on her cheeks from the exercise spread to her throat.

So Ethan *was* on her mind. 'Or if you don't want to call Ethan for some reason—' like because she had the hots for a married man and didn't want his *wife* picking up the telephone '—you could call someone in the wildlife rescue group.'

'I don't think the mouse animal was injured, it was just quiet.'

'It was a pygmy possum. They hibernate beneath the snow through winter. But they're nocturnal. I'm surprised you saw one.'

'So it was probably sleepy,' she said, tilting her head.

'Or simply mesmerised by you,' he said quietly, thinking that any creature would be dazzled by Charlotte Simmons.

She stared at him, blinked a few times as she sussed him out—he could tell, her emotions sat on her face, readable for anyone who was interested. She wasn't about to give him a flippant response though, not if he read the sudden spark of laughter lighting her eyes correctly. She bit her cheek and looked away.

Dan grinned. 'You almost smiled there, Charlotte. Careful. Next thing you know, you'll be falling for all the small-town charisma and magic.'

She huffed a derogatory laugh. 'Don't hang around waiting for that to happen.'

Dan stood. If she wanted to get a decent footing in town before she started her business, she'd have to fall for the town because if she didn't, she'd never fit in.

He jogged on the spot, mindful of keeping his body warm. 'Might want to do the same thing, Red. Keep warm.'

'I'm boiling hot. And don't call me Red.'

'Stay focussed. Keep your concentration on the task at hand—exercise.'

She swept a hand along the crest of the hill. 'Feel free to jog off.'

'Doing the manly thing first. Making sure you're okay to putter on down the hill without help.'

She stood and turned her back to him. 'There isn't much that'll take my concentration off whatever I'm doing.' She crossed her arms over her front and grabbed her sweatshirt at the hemline. She peeled the sweatshirt up, revealing a white singlet top fitted tightly on her torso. She pulled the sweatshirt over her shoulders, then over her head—where it got caught. Blindfolded by the clothing, she struggled to get her arms out.

Dan ran his gaze over her, giving a fair amount of consideration to how much and why she wasn't his type. He'd only seen her wear clothes that skimmed her body without touching it—apart from the voluminous sweatshirt. Her blouses weren't baggy but neither did they cling. Skirts above her knees with no swing to them. Although her legs were shapely: smooth calves, knees that bordered on knobbly but a person would only notice if he looked hard.

She turned in a circle as she yanked at the top, her red hair flying through the neck. She didn't have the full, ripe figure he usually went for, but she had eye-catching womanly curves. Who knew she'd been keeping a figure like that hidden beneath her demure clothing?

Not your type, mate. Remember?

'So how's the B&B shaping up?'

'What?' she asked, voice muffled in the cloth of her sweatshirt. She gasped as it came off her head, hair flying around her face. 'What did you say?' Still puffing, she knotted the arms of the shirt around her waist and ran both hands over her head, taming her titian hair.

Dan sucked in air. *Red*. He meant red hair.

She parted her lips and licked them with the tip of her tongue. Her mouth was full and pouty. Too big for her face. He groaned inwardly. Who was he kidding? Her mouth was sexy as hell. Any second now he'd be dribbling. He took up his jog again, willing everything stirring below his waist to lie low.

'I said, how's the B&B coming along? Got many renovations to do?'

'I have a few plans, as I'm sure you're aware.'

He questioned her with a cocked eyebrow.

'I'm going to paint it yellow.' She stared at him, a defiant look, hands on her hips. The Lycra shorts clung to the top of pale-skinned thighs. Good muscle tone in her legs.

He took his focus up to her face. 'Yellow?'

She pulled the legs of her shorts down. One sprang right up again. 'Sunflower yellow.' She hauled it down once more.

'Need some help?'

She paused, drawing her titian-coloured eyebrows together. Red! He meant red.

'Not your shorts,' he said. 'The B&B.' He couldn't prevent his grin at her look of indignation. 'Just thought you might like someone on your side with the war council.'

'What's that?'

'Swallow's Fall Community Spirit committee.'

'And what do you think about me wanting to change the colour of the B&B?'

'I don't care what colour you paint it. Paint it purple if you like. It won't interfere with my business. Kookaburra's is halfway down Main Street and is obviously a hotel.'

'You've got rooms? I thought it was just a pub.'

He stopped jogging, tilted his head, put his hands to his hips and spread his feet, echoing her stance. 'In Australia we often call a pub a hotel. No, I haven't got rooms.' *Yet.* 'And it's not "just a pub".'

'Have you got a thing going on with Mrs Johnson?' she asked. 'You sound just like her.'

'Don't go all spitty about the people here. They're all right. You have to learn to get on with them.' She didn't seem prepared to even try. 'Mrs J is okay ... well.' Dan gave in; he knew his townspeople. 'Some people are a little odd, but they've got their reasons. Has Ted told you about his obsession with space and aliens?'

She shook her head.

'Has Mrs J introduced you to her pig, Ruby? She walks her on a lead.'

'No, she hasn't. I'm not liked, as if you didn't know. But I don't care about that.'

'You have to care if you want to become part of the community.'

'Perhaps I don't want that.'

'What do you mean?'

'Nothing.'

Great. Now she'd turned sullen. He tried again. 'Well, you've got some friends. There's Lucy. There's me.' He smiled. 'And there's Sammy—and Ethan.'

She looked up and blinked rapidly, putting her hand up to cover her eyes from the sunshine streaming over her, giving her a warm, charismatic glamour. The lady was a cocktail of fascination. No, wait—he wasn't sure she was a lady yet.

'Sammy and Ethan Granger,' he said. 'Happiest married couple I've ever known.'

She skimmed her gaze along the grassy bank then tilted her face to Dan. 'Do you know Ethan well?'

'Yes.'

'He seems friendly—like a big, handsome giant.'

Jesus, she was really after Ethan! He could hardly believe it of her. 'Like your men big and brawny, do you?'

'I like men I can respect.'

'He's married. He's in love with Sammy. He won't be looking your way.'

'Are you suggesting …?' She yanked at the sleeves of her sweatshirt, tightening the knot at her waist. 'How dare you!'

Dan jogged on the spot.

'You know nothing about me,' she continued. 'And how about you? Do you have a little fancy piece around town you're hiding away?'

'So you're denying it?'

'I'm getting a little sick and tired of the people in this town.'

Dan stopped jogging. Twice she'd made a disparaging remark about not caring about the town or what its people thought of her. If the B&B meant so little to her, why was she here, doing it up?

'So quit,' he said. 'Sell up. Leave.'

She lifted her gaze to his. Her body had gone so still he wasn't sure if she was even breathing. His throat thickened. He hadn't meant to pounce on her like that. What was wrong with him?

He turned from her to glare at the scenery and to give the compassion he felt for her time to settle inside him. Red stirred up feelings of protection he'd never thought he'd have reason to call on, and getting offside with her wasn't going to help anyone. It certainly wouldn't get his seven ensuite bedrooms built easily.

He turned back and found her looking at him, eyes veiled in something looking too much like worry, the corners of her full mouth turned down. Damn it. Her all-too-perfect sweetheart-shaped face and the deep vulnerability he read in her eyes were going to be the death of him.

'I apologise,' he said quietly. 'I had no right to make assumptions about you.' But she'd gone into some kind of shock when she met Ethan yesterday. What else was a guy supposed to think other than that sparky little Red had been knocked off balance by Ethan's good looks—or whatever a woman went for in a guy?

And what was it with all the off-hand quips about not caring what anybody thought about her? It was as though she had no intention of joining the town's fold.

He stepped towards her. 'Can we please start again? Shake?' He thrust his hand out and gave her his boyish grin, although for the first time ever, it was hard to produce, because he now had the impression her arrival in Swallow's Fall had a lot to do with Ethan and little to do with wanting to run a B&B.

She lifted her arm, paused, then slid her hand into his.

The slightness of her fingers and the softness of her skin surprised him. He pressed her hand gently. 'Friends?' he asked.

She gripped his hand, squeezed hard.

A pull of amusement bit through the tension in his chest. She was going to be a tough adversary. A pretty one though, and he kind of liked that a lot.

'Acquaintances,' she said, and pulled her hand free.

Four

Ted Tillman banged the gavel so hard on its indented wooden plinth four hands shot forwards to settle the cups and saucers on the trestle table.

'Order, please. Take your seats.' His voice boomed with command and a ring of self-importance.

Charlotte put a finger under the collar of her blouse, tugged at the sudden tightness of it and ran her gaze around the Town Hall. The preservation notice outside stated the building was safe for use but the inside needed a fair amount of refurbishing. A kitchen alcove was obviously in the midst of renovation, the cupboards sanded back to the original wood and a large white sink sitting on the stone floor, unplumbed but spotless and shiny. Multi-coloured bunting strung on all four walls bobbed and flapped as the townspeople moved around the room, chatting, whispering, some laughing, as though they were about to see a blockbuster movie—or witness a hanging. They gathered metal-legged chairs from stacks at the back of the hall and organised them into rows in front of the committee table where Charlotte sat.

She settled her breathing as people took their seats. The fluorescent strip lighting on the vaulted ceiling created little sparkles on the large glitter-ball hanging incongruously from the centre truss. They must use the Town Hall for dances and parties too, not just newcomer slaughterings.

She'd been seated at the far end of the committee table and nobody had sat next to her. Look at the criminal. Spotlight the new woman who dared to make a revolutionary suggestion.

The door flew open, sending a rush of warm evening air into the room and ruffling the minutes from the last committee meeting. Ted slapped his hand on the papers.

'Sorry I'm late.' Sammy Granger walked to the top table and swung into the seat beside Charlotte. 'Hi, how are you?' she asked, moving the chair back to accommodate her baby bump.

'I'm fine,' Charlotte said, and added a small smile.

'Thought you might need some company. It's a lonely spot in the dock.' Sammy grinned, her face flushed, russet hair flying around her shoulders; a blast of vitality in an overcrowded room. 'How many times has he banged the gavel?' she asked, a smirk on her face.

Charlotte munched on her bottom lip. 'Eight.'

'Oh good, I haven't missed much.' Sammy pulled a pot of tea towards her and poured a cup. 'Ethan said to say sorry he couldn't make it. He's on Lochie duty.' She patted her stomach. 'I've got Edie.'

Memories of what Daniel had accused her of swept over her in mortifying waves. She'd have to watch how she behaved next time she met Ethan. Her eagerness at wanting to judge him had tripped her up, resulting in Hotshot thinking she *liked* Ethan. Well, she did like him, but not in the way Daniel meant. Ethan appeared calm and tolerant when she'd half expected a monstrous chip off the old hideous block: O'Donnell. She settled in her chair. There wasn't time to contemplate O'Donnell now and she didn't want to have a conversation with Sammy about Ethan, in case Sammy got the same—wrong—impression Daniel had: that she was after Sammy's husband.

'Cuddly Bear Toy Shop is yellow,' Ted began, the authority in his voice drowning the chatter and halting Charlotte's thoughts. 'We can't have two buildings the same colour. It wouldn't work.'

'Here we go,' Sammy said. 'He thinks he's an ace batsman but he usually lobs off course, so if he throws the gavel at you—duck to the right.'

Charlotte laughed suddenly and put her hand over her mouth when committee members stared at her.

She glanced at the back of the room and got caught in the amused gaze of the town's charmer. *Oh no.* Why was Daniel here and why did his presence make her feel more exposed than she already was? She cleared her throat—loudly. Everyone turned to her.

She squared her shoulders and put her most cooperative smile on her face. No way was this town going to disregard or overthrow her plans. 'I'd like to say something, please.'

Nobody spoke.

Charlotte took it as acceptance and stood.

'Cuddly Bear's yellow is lemon with royal-blue trim and signage,' she began. 'It's the darker blue on the toy shop that stands out, not the yellow, and it's practically the other end of town. My sunflower yellow weatherboard might balance things out a bit.'

'There's nothing needs balancing,' Ted said. 'You've got to paint it pink again.'

'I've decided on yellow.'

'Pink.' Ted gripped the gavel and swung it in a circle.

Mrs Johnson coughed and shuffled in her seat next to Ted.

He jumped and looked down at his ankles as though something had bitten him. He seemed to get his official demeanour back quickly. 'Please sit down,' he said to Charlotte, with strained politeness. 'You'll get your chance to speak later.'

Charlotte doubted it but at least she'd got a please out of him. She snuck a look at the back of the room. Sure enough, Daniel had a grin on his face, although he covered it quickly with his hand.

She sat, a sense of defeat gnawing at the pit of her stomach. Sammy patted her hand under the table.

'We're worried what sort of clientele we'll get if it's bright yellow,' someone in the audience said.

'Exactly.' Ted lifted the gavel and shook it at his comrade sitting somewhere on the right of the room.

'We don't want hippies down this way,' a woman said in a pinched tone.

Hippies? Charlotte bit into her cheek. What era were these people from?

'It does need some work though, it's a bit of a mess.'

'It's lovely on the inside. Is she going to change that?'

'Rose Capper kept it immaculate,' some old man said in a glum tone. 'What's going to happen to it now?'

Charlotte gasped at the offensive implication. Enough. She stood. 'I beg your pardon. I ran a bed and breakfast with my grandmother for the last ten years in England. I assure you I not only know how to run a small business efficiently and profitably, I also know how to *clean*.'

Her heartbeat knocked in her chest so fast she thought it would be heard in the back row. These people were harder to deal with than the executives in Yorkshire who had coerced her into selling her home and business. But she hadn't gone down without a fight.

Silence. Uncomfortable silence at her outburst. Something they obviously weren't used to, and although she still held fast to her right to speak up, her outburst had been of the tempestuous variety—no help to her case whatsoever—and was now irretrievable. She glanced at Ted, who was still glaring at her. She sat.

'Right.' Ted swung the gavel and looked back to his audience. 'There's another business item for the evening that might help us out of this dilemma. We've had a townsperson enquire as to whether or not he can join the committee.'

Sammy leaned towards Charlotte. 'That's funny, I hadn't heard anything about a new committee member. They're precious about who gets to view the gavel out of session.'

Ted Tillman flipped the gavel in his hand and used it to point to the back of the room. 'Daniel Bradford, please stand up.'

Everyone turned in their seats. A few laughed, good-heartedly. One whistled and others applauded.

Charlotte almost choked.

Daniel rose from his seat, stuffing his hands into his pockets, a quiet smile on his face. Unruffled, relaxed, he looked like a clean-cut, well-respected member of the community. Which, unfortunately, he bloody well was. Daniel nodded. 'Thank you, friends and neighbours. I appreciate your warm response.'

Huh. Charlotte folded her arms.

'I've asked to join the committee as I feel I can help with this delicate situation we find ourselves in. You're all busy people, and I'm happy to step in and mediate.'

Charlotte glowered. He was talking about her as if she wasn't here.

'I think we all agree Miss Simmons has the best interests of the B&B at heart. It's just that she might need some guidance in town matters. I've met her and I can honestly say I believe we can find a satisfactory solution to this problem.'

She was the problem, but how was he going to *satisfactorily* handle her?

'I'd be delighted to help out in whatever way I can.' He grinned, looking boyish and ... charming, damn it. 'Firstly,' he continued,

'I suggest we have one town member act as a go-between. Someone who can shadow the process. Someone who has knowledge of building works and the requirements therein.' He put a hand over his heart. 'Me, if you'll accept me on the committee.'

Smarmy.

'Those for, raise your hands,' Ted said, gavel lifted to shoulder height.

About forty hands went up in the air, with a few murmurs of appreciation.

'That's obviously a vote of confidence but we must do things properly.' Ted cleared his throat with a bumptious cough. 'All those against, show your hands.'

Charlotte shot her arm in the air, dead straight, fingers stretched.

'You don't count,' Ted said, and banged the gavel.

Charlotte stacked three chairs from a row at the back of the hall and shunted them into a corner with the other piles, intent on her task and on not feeling isolated.

The judges at her trial were evading her as though her very presence in their Town Hall might cause the infrastructure of the historic building to crumble at any second. As though she were some newly discovered stone-decaying fungus. Best not go into the kitchen to help with the washing up—being ignored from a distance was the better option.

'I'm hoping you're not going to give me too much trouble during this process.'

Charlotte slotted the last chair onto a pile of others and turned to Daniel. 'You've done this on purpose,' she said. 'Because I don't respond to your little-boy-gorgeous manner.'

'I wouldn't say I was gorgeous.'

Well, he was—to look at, not so much to hold a conversation with. 'Don't pull your fast charm on me. I know what you're up to, and you're wrong.'

'What am I wrong about?'

'About …' *Ethan.* 'You know.' It wasn't only his opinionated observations about her fancying Ethan she'd have to watch out for. His very presence appeared to be unravelling the unflinching image she'd been portraying.

'No, I don't know,' he said, head tilted in a jocular manner.

He knew. And if he was going to be close to her during this mediation process, with all his mighty charm and expensive-coffee-bean aroma, she might succumb and lose her steadfast image altogether. What would she be left with then? A shell. A lonely woman on a quest that was beginning to torment her and twist her priorities. 'Why are you so keen on scrutinising my every move in town?'

'You mean the committee thing?' He shrugged. 'Just being friendly.'

'No, you're not. You're up to something.' Not that she could think of one single thing he might be up to, but it certainly wasn't because he wanted to be close to her. Like—really close.

'You're the one who's up to something, Red.'

'I bet you ten dollars I'm not.' Lie. Big fat lie. One she'd have to hide from him. Especially if he got close. 'And stop calling me Red.'

'No deal. I bet you a five-K run you *are* up to something. And note I said a *five*-K run, since I doubt you're up for distance.'

Charlotte knew he was teasing but why couldn't he just leave her alone? What was his problem? 'Distance?' she said, pulling her shoulders back. 'You have no idea how far I can go but you're going to find out.'

'Hi, what's going on?' Sammy asked, poking her head between them and glancing from one to the other with the look of a tolerant mother about to break up a kindergarten quarrel.

Daniel hitched a thumb Charlotte's way. 'Red and I are just getting acquainted.'

Sammy slanted a look at him. 'What's got you suddenly interested in joining the town committee?'

He gave her an indulgent smile. 'Not what you think.'

She smirked right back. 'Did I say anything?'

'You don't have to, you've got the nesting look on your face.'

Sammy poked him in his chest with her finger. 'I'll get to the bottom of it, you know I will.'

He patted the top of her head. 'There's nothing going on. Keep your nose out of it.'

Charlotte stepped back from their banter.

'Not so fast.' Sammy grabbed the sleeve of Charlotte's blouse. 'Let's get out of here now. It takes them ages to wash up while they chat about what's gone on and my feet won't put up with standing that long.'

Charlotte indicated the committee members who were gathered around the gavel, collecting papers and collapsing the trestle table. 'I should help.' Her tone didn't suggest complete happiness about the idea, but at least she'd made the effort.

'Dan will do that for you.' Sammy nudged him hard in the ribs. 'Won't you?'

He grunted in mock pain. 'Will I?'

'Hey, everyone,' Sammy called out. 'Charlotte wants to help clear up, but if you don't mind, I'd like her to walk me to my car. Is that okay?'

A few murmurs, some nods and very few smiles.

'I'll walk you both down the street,' Daniel said.

Sammy flounced past him, tucking her arm through Charlotte's as she went. 'But then we wouldn't be able to talk about you.'

He grimaced. 'Go easy on me, will you?'

'Don't worry,' Sammy said to Charlotte as they walked down the darkened street. 'The townspeople will come around.'

Charlotte breathed in the quietness of the town. What were the chances? She stared at her little B&B at the end of Main Street, the flamingo pink colour subdued by the dark and the glow of the street lamps. It looked like a flushed rose beneath the night sky. It looked a little special. Maybe this was the way the townspeople saw it.

'Dan's coming over for dinner one night next week,' Sammy said as they walked past the pioneer cemetery with the ever-present white bunting on its picket fence. 'Will you come too?'

Uh oh. 'I don't mean to be rude, Sammy, but is it just him or will you have other guests?'

Sammy glanced over her shoulder and raised her russet-coloured eyebrows. 'You don't like Daniel?'

Charlotte didn't underestimate the coyness in Sammy's tone. 'Let's just say we don't appear to be able to speak nicely to each other, as I think you noticed.'

'Something already happened between you?'

'We had a bit of a to-do the other day at the stock feeders'.' And another on the hillside. And another tonight.

'An argument?'

'Not exactly, but he was rude.' So had Charlotte been. He was so provokingly charismatic she forgot her manners when around him. 'Well, he was sort of rude,' she conceded.

Sammy didn't respond.

Charlotte swallowed a sigh. She'd belittled a friend of Sammy's and was behaving in a standoffish manner to what was obviously a genuine hand of friendship. 'Although he's nice to Lucy,' she admitted, 'and she seems to like him.' Worst luck.

'Everybody likes him,' Sammy said. 'Dogs, old ladies, drunks.'

'He's a hotshot charm-boy.'

'I know. That's what makes him so attractive.'

How lucky was Ethan to have captured a wife like Sammy? A bright, vivacious woman who oozed family joy and was obviously deeply in love with her husband. 'You can say that safely,' Charlotte said. 'You're married.'

'Safely?' Sammy stopped, eyes wide. 'Has Dan made a pass at you?'

'Certainly not. He doesn't like me.'

'Has he flirted?'

'No—he doesn't like me.' *He thinks I'm after your husband.*

'Come on, give. What's happened between you?'

'Well, when we first met at the stock feeders', he seemed to be …'

'Flirting?'

'No. He twisted my words—'

'Into some sort of flirty banter?'

'More suggestive than that.'

'Flirty suggestive?'

Charlotte gave Sammy a can-we-stop-now look.

Sammy grinned. 'What were you talking about?'

'Screwdrivers.'

Sammy wiggled her eyebrows. 'Sexy stuff.' She moved off down the street. 'Do you remember what he was wearing?'

Charlotte followed. 'A white shirt, a scratched leather belt and faded jeans.'

'What shoes was he wearing?'

'I didn't look.'

Sammy glanced over her shoulder. 'Didn't get past those jeans, huh?'

Charlotte couldn't still the deepening warmth Sammy's offered friendship built in her chest. She wasn't staying in town long, but so far it had been a lonelier road than anticipated. She decided to try out this offer of friendship. 'He's got a nice butt, I will say that for him.'

Sammy spluttered a laugh. 'There's nothing better than staring at a good-looking man in a pair of jeans.'

Charlotte gave in. 'It's a *very* nice backside.'

Sammy slowed her pace. 'I'm trying to figure out if he's keen on the committee, or keen on you.'

'That's a no regarding me.'

'I'm not so sure.' Sammy turned. 'Did he give you his sparkly look? The one where lights flicker in his eyes?'

The dancing flecks of charm. 'Do you see them too?'

'Charlotte, there isn't a woman in this town—or likely anywhere Dan's been—who hasn't been mesmerised by those lights.'

'Except me.'

'Yeah, right.' Sammy leaned closer and lowered her voice. 'Picture it. You're with him, close to him. It's dusk. It's so quiet you can hear the mice scuttling behind the skirting boards in the empty bar. The air is warm. He leans towards you, tips his head and …'

Charlotte's breath hitched.

Sammy offered a grin. 'I'll let you imagine the next part for yourself.' She moved off towards a big blue ute.

'Believe me,' Charlotte argued, following. 'The spark between us is a follow through to instant dislike of each other.'

'Yeah,' Sammy said as she beeped her remote at the ute. 'And I'm *so* not pregnant.'

'You getting friendly with the new woman?' Mrs J asked Dan.

Dan kept his sigh to himself, took his focus off Sammy and Charlotte standing by Ethan's ute, and turned to Mrs Johnson. 'Nope. I'm helping everyone out here, that's all.'

'You've got a grin on your face every time you talk to her.'

'She likes arguing. I'm happy to oblige.'

'Bit of a surprise, seeing you stick your hand up for the committee.'

Dan gave her a quick grin. 'Surprised myself but sometimes I feel the need to help people.'

'Something familiar about her but I can't put my finger on what.'

Here we go. Dan crossed his arms and settled in for the duration of the post-mortem. Whenever there was an inquisition regarding some poor sucker in town who'd done something questionable, somebody always piped up and said they'd heard this or that tittle-tattle. Dan had learned fast that it was best to let people talk themselves into and out of it again.

'Don't want you falling for her until I know what she's up to,' Mrs J continued.

Falling for her? Where had Mrs J got that idea?

'I've got a nose for the suspect, Daniel, and she's prime.'

'What do you mean?' Dan wondered if the old girl had heard the one about the two-timing redhead hiding from her furious boyfriends.

'Not sure yet, but I recognise her from somewhere. It's her hair, something about her colouring.'

Or the one about Red tying up an intruder in her home and using him as her sexual slave for three days before turning him over to the cops.

Dan shook that tale from his mind. He didn't like the sound of it now any more than when he'd first heard it over the bar. And anyway, he wasn't falling for her.

'Ted said the same thing,' Mrs J said. 'He recognises her too. And while I'm on the subject of Ted, please be aware Grace said he's having a few of his space-and-alien turns.'

'Right. But he hasn't disappeared yet.' Dan hooked a thumb up at the heavens.

'Not yet—but you of all people will remember how hard it was for him and Grace the last time he … disappeared … seeing as you found him.'

Poor old Ted and his obsessions. He had too many problems on his plate. 'I'll keep an eye on him. Well.' Dan uncrossed his arms and looked over Mrs J's shoulder. 'I'll give them a hand with the trestle table and then it looks like we're done for the night.' He glanced down. 'Nice of you to keep me informed of things, Mrs J.'

'Don't mention it. You've proved yourself a worthy and valuable addition to the town.'

Yeah. Dan nodded and shifted his stance. The old girl hadn't spoken to him for the first six months—thought he'd be bringing showgirls to the bar or something equally outrageous. What the townspeople forgot—or didn't care to consider—was that Dan was country born and bred, like they were. Different town though. Might as well have been a different planet, now he thought about his first few years in Swallow's Fall.

'And we look after our own,' Mrs J continued.

Her words brought a sudden but pleasant warmth to his chest. 'Thank you, Mrs J.' One of their own, huh? Not bad for six years of effort ... and patience.

Mrs J looked around Dan's shoulder, out the open door and down the street. 'Do you fancy her?'

Jesus. Why was everyone so interested in what he thought of Charlotte? He glanced out of the door as Sammy drove away, Red giving a wave and walking slowly, a little ponderously maybe, towards her B&B. Couldn't a man hold a conversation with an attractive woman without it going to council?

He turned to Mrs Johnson and opened his mouth. *Did* he fancy her?

'No,' he said.

Mrs J stared at him. Damn it. He'd paused too long and the old girl's internal gossip receiver sparked the air as it charged.

Five

Charlotte squinted as the morning sunlight caressed her face. She leaned against the doorframe of her B&B, new screwdriver in one hand, the telephone in the other.

Early Monday morning in Swallow's Fall and the town getting ready for its day.

It would be late Sunday night in Starfoot; maybe a few young people showing off with rowdiness as they made their way home from the local pub, giving the Yorkshire residents something to complain about the next morning as they queued for bread at the bakery and discussed the building of the new two-storey hotel on seventeen acres of good old English soil, a quarter of an acre of which had once been Charlotte's.

'So,' Sammy said down the phone. 'Dinner. Saturday night, six o'clock. I've got a roast planned and I'm going the whole hog since Ethan wouldn't let me go to the barbecue last Friday due to my swollen ankles.'

A twinge that felt suspiciously like misery because she hadn't been invited to Kookaburra's first Friday night barbecue gripped Charlotte's chest. Then again, nobody had needed invites, the notice had been plastered on the pub's front window. *Family barbecue, family fare, Friday night fun.* She could have gone. Except who would she have spoken to or sat next to?

'Did you hear me?' Sammy said. 'Saturday, dinner, our place, and I've told Ethan to make sure no animals get sick after five p.m. otherwise they'll be answering to me.'

Charlotte smiled. 'Does he always do what you say?'

'I wear the pants around Burra Burra Lane. He knows it and the animals know it.'

'I hope you don't mind my asking again, Sammy—but is it just me and Daniel, or will you have other guests?'

'Just you two.'

Charlotte lifted her eyes to the street as the man in question took the steps from the walkway outside Kookaburra's two at a time and walked across the road towards the stock feeders'. Lucy trotted at his side. Traitorous four-legged friend.

Charlotte stepped back and behind the door.

'You still there?' Sammy asked. 'You keep going quiet.'

Charlotte nodded.

'Look, Charlotte,' Sammy said, admonishment in her tone, 'I know it's hard but the only way you'll get yourself accepted is to accept people first. Believe me, I know how this is done.'

'If you say so.' She hadn't wanted to make friends but neither had she expected to be disliked. Having to befriend the townspeople was a setback but without doing so there'd be no progress.

'Six o'clock. Don't be late or I'll get Dan to drive back and pick you up—in fact, that's a brilliant—'

'No, thank you,' Charlotte said quickly. 'I don't need a lift from Hotshot. I'll drive myself.'

Silence.

Charlotte nipped at her bottom lip with her teeth. 'Sammy, are you planning on trying to push Daniel and me together?'

'Yep.'

'Oh.' She paused. 'The air bristles between us every time we meet,' she argued. 'You noticed that the other night.'

'Yep.'

'You're not going to believe me when I say, again, that we don't get on. We don't like each other.'

'Nope.'

Charlotte sighed. 'You're incorrigible.'

Sammy laughed—a merry chirrup. 'Yep. See you Saturday if not before.'

Charlotte put the telephone and the screwdriver on the hall table. It seemed ungracious not to accept the blossoming of a friendship with Ethan's wife, and Charlotte had a hankering for a friend, but she hadn't intended to latch onto the hand Sammy was offering. Get in, crack on and get out had been her plan, although she'd known what she was getting into by buying the B&B and how much effort it might take to resell it. Not that she needed the money from the sale; she had enough money to see her through two lifetimes, courtesy of those hotel executives, and would return every penny to have her old life back—but that wasn't possible.

Finding the B&B for sale had been fortuitous—she had no idea how she'd have stayed in town during her investigations otherwise, or what excuse she could have given for popping back every day if she'd booked into one of the neighbouring towns' guest houses or hotels. But then she hadn't thought her plans through properly. She'd simply waltzed into the real estate office in Canberra waving her cheque book and smiling at the amazement on the saleswoman's face as she made a cash settlement, just below the already reduced asking price, for a property that had been on the market for over two years. Given the list of renovations she planned, including some that weren't necessary but would certainly give the house a genuine sparkle, perhaps she'd also bought it for the challenge of bringing it back to life.

Disappointment at her lack of judgement thrust a wedge into her resolve to be unflinching and stubborn. She turned from the door, walked halfway down the hall and stopped. She leaned her forehead against a flocked peony on the wallpaper and braced herself against the wall. 'You came here to get answers,' she whispered. She'd never intended to charge in and ask Ethan the questions straight out—she'd hoped to discover more about him and how he was involved first. Now she knew the people in Swallow's Fall, she understood her cautious approach had been the right approach. But she should be getting on with finding those answers—before she got too deeply enmeshed in the lives of the townspeople.

An image of Olivia Simmons's caring face shone through Charlotte's unease and she had a sense of her gran hovering around her in a cloud of comfort. She'd clung to the safety of Gran's hand every day for the first three months after being whisked from Australia to that foreign place. Gran walked her around the village, introducing her to the pond where they fed the ducks and named each one, playing a guessing game the next time they visited to see if they could pick out Griselda from Giuseppe or Mozart from Miranda. And eventually, after months of counselling—walking with Gran to the red-brick Victorian junior school. Being handed over to the principal and left there for six hours, during which time Charlotte had learned with startling alarm how dissimilar she was from other children.

Face the fear, the counsellors and psychologists told her as she'd grown to teenage years. Remember the event without reliving it. They taught her to delve into her psyche and evaluate, almost as an outsider, the events that had harmed her and left her motherless, but nothing would erase the vision of the pictures she'd drawn as a six-year-old: stick figures in pools of blood; dark hands curling around wardrobe doors, ready to grab her …

'No dream,' she whispered. 'Not in daytime.' All the psychologists in the world could go to hell. She wouldn't be over the nightmare until she knew the truth about Thomas O'Donnell.

She didn't have her answers from Ethan yet, shouldn't make any judgements, but when you faced the man whose father had killed your mother, the man who was probably your half-brother—there were undoubtedly going to be a few shaky moments and any number of dilemmas.

'Hi.'

Charlotte jumped.

'Knock knock.' Daniel rapped his knuckles on the open door. 'What are you doing? Taking a closer look at that fancy wallpaper, huh?' He ran his gaze over it. 'Please tell me you plan to steam it off.'

Charlotte moved from the wall. She planned a lot of things and none of them were his business. 'What do you want?' she asked, crossing her arms beneath her breasts.

He gave her a lazy salute. 'Mediation duties. Thought I'd start right in.'

'How generous.'

'Don't mention it. Great to see you so enthused.' He put one foot on the step to the house and a hand high on the doorframe. His height and the self-assured grin on his handsome face blocked the daylight.

Handsome? Had she decided on that? Sporty, lean, charm-mongering, six-foot-two Hotshot with incredible dancing lights in his eyes. She sighed inwardly. Yes. That's what handsome was and it was standing in her doorway framed by sunlight.

'I nearly brought you a coffee,' he said, 'then figured you might like to see inside Kookaburra's instead.'

He must have his coffee machine up and running already, or perhaps he'd been handling the beans, because the aroma of Ethiopian mountain coffee emanated from him.

'Arabica?' she asked.

'Sweetest coffee berries there are.' He took his hand off the doorframe and stepped inside. 'Smell like blueberry jam and cocoa.'

She inhaled, clamping her lips together and sucking in her cheeks but the taste of a dark, strong, milk-topped flat white swirled in her mouth.

He pulled the door to behind him and did a double take at the bolt on the top, the brass chain in the middle and the bolt on the bottom. 'Did the Cappers do this?' He touched the new brass chain plate she'd just re-fixed to the door and wiped some of the flaked red paint off. 'You did this?' He turned, smiling. 'You hiding the crown jewels in here? Is that why you left Britain?'

Charlotte put one foot behind her to ensure an even distribution of weight and to stop herself from stepping away from the waft of coffee and aftershave that was becoming too recognisable as heady. Sex and coffee. The combination and lack of both could make a girl giddy. 'What sort of coffee machine do you have?'

'Deluxe,' he said with a caress in his tone. 'Eighty-three kilos of metallic black, chrome-panelled action.'

Boasting now, was he?

'Two steam wands.'

Show-off.

'Five-thousand-watt power rating.'

Coffee. Real coffee. 'So how does this mediation thing work?'

'Atta girl.' He stepped from the door.

Charlotte unfolded her arms, tipped her head and took a breath. *Get this done*. That was the way forwards. 'Alright,' she said. 'I'll give you some notes on what I'm going to do, you take them to the committee and get back to me tomorrow. How does that sound?'

'Tomorrow? It could be a whole year before they give you the thumbs-up.'

He had to be joking. 'I don't have to listen to what anybody says,' she told him. 'I own Bottom of the Hill Bed and Breakfast. I can do what I like as long as it's within building regulations.'

'Bottom of the what?'

'Hill.'

'You're giving the place a name?'

Well, of course she was, although she hadn't meant to tell him. It had slipped out, but as anyone in business should know—as coffee Hotshot himself should know—the key factor when selling involved credibility. And a seemingly innocuous little something extra would tip the scale for a prospective buyer. 'I was considering it.' Giving the B&B a name suggested it was a lucrative, ongoing business and a good exit strategy always gave the best return. She'd learned that in Starfoot.

Except that regarding Swallow's Fall, it was a lie. There was no good faith and no steady stream of customers, but that didn't mean there couldn't be.

'Why bottom of the hill?' he asked. 'You're set on the entrance to town facing Main Street and we're on the flat.'

'And there's a hill on the eastern side of town. The one I run on, the one you don't like squashing wildflowers on, and my B&B sits at the bottom of that hill.'

'The hill you *jog* on—you're not up to running yet, you're still getting in shape.' He paused, but not long enough for Charlotte to respond to yet another of his teases. 'Let's keep the new name quiet for the moment, shall we? We've got enough on our plates.'

'We?'

He slid his fingers into the pockets of his jeans. 'We don't want to rub the committee the wrong way with too many ideas. I don't know how things work in England, but out here, life is slow.' He pulled a hand out of his pocket and skimmed it across the air, palm down. 'We glide, we take things easy, we *relax*.'

'I'm happy to relax but I'm not waiting a year before I ...' She faltered. *Sell*—she'd been about to tell him she planned on selling up. 'Before I paint the weatherboard.' The second slip-up in front of him.

'You've got to back down, Charlotte, in order to go forwards.'

'What do you mean?'

'I mean you've got to chill. Get them on your side first. Do something for them. Show them a gesture they'll appreciate.'

'Like what?' What did they want—a bunch of flowers? She'd been here three weeks and hadn't got further than fixing the veranda and laying new turf.

He shrugged. 'That's up to you. But you can't run them over with your stubborn streak. That'll get their backs up even more.'

'They started it.' She'd been nothing but friendly from the moment she arrived; had baked pastries and cakes every time they turned up on her doorstep. They'd eaten her fare but hadn't returned the bonhomie. If they now thought her terse and non-communicative, that was their problem—and their fault.

'Look. I'll give you an example. When I first got here, the wall behind the bar was putrid green. I waited three months before I repainted it a darker green. That didn't get noticed, so the month after I painted it a shade of green with dark blue tones. That got noticed, but people liked it because it was still greenish.' He took a breath. 'The next month I took the green out and painted it a deeper blue. People liked that because they'd got used to the blue. They forgot about the green. Two months later I painted it navy. Everybody patted me on the back for a job well done.'

He *had* to be joking. 'It took you seven months to change the colour from green to blue? That's nutty.'

'That's Swallow's Fall.'

Green and blue were almost the same colour, in certain lights. Changing pink to yellow was ... nothing like the same.

She breathed deeply and took her gaze away from his scrutinising expression.

Why was she so keen on yellow anyway? What did it matter when she'd be leaving as soon as she'd found the courage she hadn't realised she lacked to talk to Ethan privately? She could agree to paint it a softer rose colour and let it be. Pink wasn't too bad, as long as it wasn't flamingo pink.

She straightened and looked Daniel in the eye. It was the principle, not the colour. Yellow. She would paint her little house sunflower yellow if it killed her. If it meant she had to stay here right through summer into autumn. Which meant she'd have to pretend to be getting along famously with her mediator.

'What do you need to know?' she asked.

He smiled, took a step towards her. 'First off, don't worry about the committee. I'll handle them. My role in this is to help them, and you.'

'I thought I'd make a start on the inside first,' she said, looking around the wide but shabby hallway. 'Then get around to the weatherboard colour later, when I get a better footing in town.'

'Now you're talking. I knew you'd see sense.'

She fired him a look. 'You know nothing about me.'

'I know you'd like a coffee. You've got that "hanging out for caffeine" look in your eyes.' He put a hand on the banister. 'So where shall we start? Upstairs?' He took a few steps up the stairs. 'You'll need to get the bedrooms sorted first, if you want guests soon.' He paused, smiled down at her. 'I know a couple of guys who might be your first customers.'

She wouldn't be having customers.

He gripped the banister in one of his big hands and shook it. 'Bit wobbly.' He bent to inspect something and pulled the carpet back from the stairs. 'Dry rot creeping in.' He straightened. 'They'll probably last a year, but you ought to tend to them sooner rather than later.'

She'd be long gone in a year; she'd be gone in two months if they'd just let her paint the damn weatherboard. 'I'll deal with the banister but the stairs can wait.'

'If you've got the capital, you ought to deal with it now.'

'I'll wait.' No need to tell him that the hefty capital she had would be sending her straight back to Britain on a first-class ticket and to a new life. Free from fear ... and free from interference, and free from the not inconsequential charms of a honed six-foot-two guy with a great butt.

He swivelled on the fourth step and sat on it, elbows on knees. By the look on his face, he was pondering more than the creaky staircase. He nodded at the door. 'One question—no joking, no bullshit—what is it with the locks and bolts? You think you're going to be invaded or something?'

Charlotte didn't answer.

'You're getting all defensive again, Red.'

'You're throwing your smooth, sexy charm around. It grates on me.'

He grinned. 'So now I'm gorgeous *and* sexy? What's not to like?'

Another slip-up. Time to knock his inferences and suggestiveness on the head and get her own brain functioning around something other than coffee and sex. She moved to the banister and rested a hand on the wooden knob. 'Let me tell you the definition of charmer.' She cleared her throat. 'Quote: An entertainer exhibiting a professed ability or power to charm a venomous snake. Unquote.'

He studied her for a long time. Three beats, four, five ...

'Looks like it's not working on you,' he said softly. He stood, head tilted, brow drawn. 'Let me give you the lowdown on uptight. Bad-tempered, snooty, repressed—'

'*Repressed?*'

'Inhibited—and I don't mean shy—and frightened to death of making the wrong decision. I reckon you'd rather shave that red hair off than admit you were wrong about anything. You've got a marker for yourself and you've put it real high on the board.'

Charlotte blinked and closed her mouth to stop from answering. Quite a speech. She must have pissed him off big-time. Had she meant to do that?

He jumped the three stairs down to the hallway and strode to the door.

'You'll never attain the mark, Charlotte.' He yanked the flyscreen open and turned to her. 'Not until you liberate yourself from the rigid corset you put on every morning. Shake up your skirts and dance a little, why don't you?' He stormed down her path, the flyscreen slamming shut behind him.

Shocked, Charlotte wavered in a haze of angst about apologising— and even worse, possibly telling him why she was here.

Ethan.

Dan glanced up when someone knocked on the door.

'Man,' he murmured, but didn't move from behind the bar.

The redhead stared at him through the glass panel.

'It's open,' he called.

She stepped half inside, holding onto the door with her hand and resting it against her shoulder. 'I came to apologise. And for that coffee, if it's still on offer.'

Dan didn't answer.

'Pissing you off wasn't my intent,' she said. 'I got carried away.' She paused, looking as though she was gauging her next words with caution. 'I also think it would be good idea to accept your offer of mediation.'

'Alright then.' Dan threw the cloth in his hand over the rim of the stainless steel sink. He strode across the wooden floorboards and pulled the half-opened door she was leaning against out of her hands. She stumbled into Kookaburra's, steadied herself and swung around to him.

'During which process,' she said, with a business-like expression, 'I promise to be the politest I possibly can be while around you.'

'Do you always change your mind so fast?'

'Depends what's on offer. Right now, I could do with a real coffee.'

He smiled and let the door swing closed. 'I might need something stronger.' This bar was his home and he didn't want bad feelings in his environment; it took more than a mop and a bucket of water to wash them away. And maybe this time they'd talk without bickering. Dan rolled the sleeves of his shirt up and moved behind the bar. Shame Mrs J wasn't here to witness his tetchiness with the redhead first-hand. It would sure stop the gossip.

'You didn't come to the barbecue last week,' he said. 'Why not?'

'I didn't think I was invited.'

'Nobody was invited. There was a small dollar charge per head and me and my cook threw some sausages and steaks on the hot plate. Everyone had fun. You should have come.'

'Who would I have spoken to?'

'Me.'

'We'd have ended up arguing.'

The woman had layers of vulnerability beneath that bristly veneer. 'You're right. Glad you didn't come. Might have made me look too macho when everyone knows I'm just an easy-going, friendly country boy.'

Her smile appeared quickly, but she angled it away from him. One layer stripped. How many more to go? Dan let his own smile form. Felt like he couldn't keep it contained when she was around. 'Where are you from?' he asked as he pulled the portafilter from the coffee machine.

'From just outside Harrogate in England,' she answered, slipping onto a stool.

'Big town, huh?'

She tugged at the thin cardigan she wore. 'No. A village called Lower-Starfoot-in-the-Forest.'

'Sounds like a fairy tale,' he said as he packed the portafilter with ground beans and tapped it down.

'It was, once.'

Dan glanced at her. 'Fancy place, is it?'

'If you like village ponds, Maypoles and ye-olde-type buildings.'

'Flat white or latte?'

'Flat white. So who's your cook?' she asked, picking up a laminated bar menu and running an eye down the list.

'Me and Lily Johnson.'

'Mrs J's daughter?'

'Yep. Mrs J looks after Lily's kids while she works. Lily's divorced, and Mrs J lost her husband a few years back so the ladies and the kids live together. Seems to work well for them all.'

She glanced back at the menu. 'Not bad.'

'We keep it small. People don't like change.' Dan was sure she almost laughed at that.

'Does Lily do all the cooking while you swagger around the bar being a hearty country boy with your customers?'

'Mostly,' he said, deciding the gentle barb was merely one more layer stripped from her prickly nature. 'I'm a dab hand in the kitchen though.' He nodded at the menu. 'Chilli is my speciality. Chilli chicken, chilli mussels, chilli con carne. Give me a chilli pepper and I'll create mouth-watering magic for you.'

'Really?' She turned the menu over. 'Who does your desserts?'

'I get most of them delivered.'

'Mmm, shame.' She put the menu back into its metal holder. 'You could expand your business if you offered home-made desserts. I doubt even the steadfast citizens of Swallow's Fall would refuse a good selection of cakes and tarts.'

'Is that what you offered in your quaint English B&B?'

'Yes. I trained as a pastry chef.'

'Can you make all the fancy doings? The éclair things and the sweet puff pastry stuff?'

She gave him a perplexed look. 'Of course. I'm a *pastry chef*. I had a small side business running alongside my bed and breakfast. I catered for parties and weddings.'

Dan pursed his mouth. Pretty much all he offered at Kookaburra's was shop-bought tiramisu cake and lemon meringue pie alongside Mrs Tam's home-made ice creams. 'Impressive,' he said.

'Thank you.'

'Why did you leave?'

She paused a fraction too long. 'Adventure.'

No way did he believe that. 'And you thought you'd get it in Swallow's Fall?' He smiled at her. 'Come on, give. Why are you here?'

She leaned an elbow on the bar. 'I thought we'd formed a truce.'

He poured milk into a stainless steel jug and lifted it to the steam wand. 'We have. We don't trust each other, so all questions we ask are fair and equal. Any answers decided on are up to the individual but open to suspicion from the other.'

She rested her chin in her hand and arched one delicate eyebrow. 'For a moment there, I almost fell for your country-boy charm.'

Cute expression on a cute face, especially with the light of cheekiness glowing in her eyes. But she was the one with charms. Beneath her expensive, slightly conservative clothing, Charlotte had a body with any number of fascinations a guy might be tempted by. Not that he'd admit to anyone that he'd noticed.

He looked back to the jug as the milk heated, circulated and gradually began to rise up the sides. 'I'm your negotiator. I need to know more about you so I can get everyone on your side.' He withdrew the jug, set it down and wiped the steam valve with a damp cloth. He took a cup and saucer off the stack sitting neatly on top of the coffee machine.

'How?' She leaned forwards, watching him work.

'You're new in town. I can help you get settled.' He made sure the portafilter was tightly secured and turned the hot water knob on full. After a few seconds, her nose twitched as the scent of coffee pouring into the china cup reached her.

'Don't know if I'll ever actually … settle.'

'I'd like to know why you need so many bolts on your doors,' he said quietly.

She sat upright on the stool and turned her attention away from the coffee. 'General security.'

'Kinda touchy on the subject, aren't you?' She didn't answer and the light had gone from her eyes. 'I'm pretty good at sussing people out,' he said. 'And I think you're scared of something.'

'And I'm pretty good at not letting anything slip—should there be anything to let slip.'

'So are you hiding from something? Or someone?'

She smiled, looking sweet and saucy suddenly. 'Do you want to hear about how I was fired from my job as a waitress and why I'm sulking here in the country? Or would you prefer the tale about my angry boyfriend … the one I was three timing?'

'Three, huh? That must have tired you out. Personally I prefer the one about you tying up an intruder in your house and using him as your sex slave for three days before turning the poor wasted bugger over to the police.'

The cheekiness left her eyes and she shivered slightly. 'I imagine you would.'

Damn. She obviously hadn't heard that story. Bloody idiots from outside town. Good job they were contractors and not around all the time or he might be tempted to visit one or two of them and put them straight with a punch to the jaw. Perhaps he should have done that in the first place. He picked up the milk jug and banged it on the bar to settle the milk then swirled the jug to get rid of any bubbles.

'Make that a takeaway, would you?'

'Those stories came from guys passing through, Charlotte. The ones that had seen you and fancied you. They won't be back, so don't worry about it. But as far as general gossip goes there's nothing you can do. Unless you tell someone why you're here, they're going to make up stories. And they're wondering why you're here.' He bent to the shelf beneath the coffee machine for one of the takeaway cups.

'I'm here because …'

Dan stilled. She swivelled on the bar stool to face the windows and the street. She'd been about to open up to him, he sensed it. Was she starting to trust him? Perhaps he really could help her. Perhaps they'd become friends—eventually. He poured the espresso shot into the takeaway cup.

Why the nerves and the occasional shadows fluttering beneath her eyes? She was flicking at her hair as though there were a bug in it. Was she more hurt by the townspeople's attitude than she was letting on?

'What's upstairs?' she asked, head tilted back as she gazed at the ceiling.

'The old rooms from a hundred years ago. Falling to bits though. Mainly storage space now.' He poured the thickened milk onto the shot of coffee.

'Must be a big space.'

'Three hundred and fifty square metres' worth.'

She got off the stool and walked into the centre of the bar where a wooden balustrade separated the drinking area from the family restaurant, still gazing up at the ceiling. 'You could have a whole apartment up there.'

Dan picked up a skewer and drew a heart-shape through the light froth of milk on her flat white, something he'd normally only do with a latte but he figured what the hell, Red needed something to make her smile.

'Three apartments, probably,' she said.

Or seven redeveloped hotel rooms. 'Yeah, well, I like my back room.' He pressed a lid onto the cup, firmed the rim and walked around the counter. 'No sugar. I figure you're sweet enough without it.' He handed her the coffee.

'Such potent charm.' She took the coffee from him and sipped.

'Careful, it's hot.'

She looked up at him. 'I'm sorry, the charm remark was uncalled for. It slipped out. Your coffee is delicious.'

Backing down again?

'It's hard to keep secrets in this town, isn't it?'

Dan kept his gaze on her and off the ceiling, where it wanted to go. 'What do you mean?'

'Nothing.' She turned from him.

Jesus, for a second he'd almost panicked. If his intentions to open up the hotel slipped out before he was ready to face the council, he'd be burned alive.

'Anyway,' she said. 'Thanks for the coffee. Oh, and by the way, I'll drive myself on Saturday night.'

'What's happening Saturday night?'

'Dinner at Burra Burra Lane.'

'You're going?'

'Yes. Got a problem with that?'

Well, at least he could keep an eye on her. Since his interest in why she was so guarded about being in town had heightened, so his fear of her coming between Sammy and Ethan had lessened. Sure, Ethan was in the picture somehow, but she'd shown such genuine outrage at his inference that he believed her. Man, he was doing a lot of reading of her recently. 'Is anyone else going?' he asked.

'No, just you and me.'

This was Sammy's doing. He wondered if Charlotte knew that. 'They're not trying to … you know—I mean I hope Sammy hasn't got the wrong idea here.'

'Don't worry. Sammy knows I can't stand you.'

'You think that's going to stop her?'

'I know two things: I like your coffee but I don't like you. Three things actually: you don't like me either.'

'Yeah.' One minute she was easing up, the next she froze faster than a drainpipe in winter. She charged him down every time he attempted to kick the ball of bad-temper away from them, giving him no chance of a drop goal. What had happened to make her plug such a solid stopper into the valves of her heart?

He stepped away, raised a hand in farewell. Why should anything to do with her heart interest him? 'Okay. See you Saturday then. Glad you don't expect a lift.'

Six

'Oh, shit.'

Dan sprinted from the edge of the hill at the northern end of town and charged into the alley behind Kookaburra's. He'd been up half the night poring over plans for the hotel, mapping out a time frame for when and how the work could start, in order to get over the tension yesterday's encounter with Red had left him with. It looked like he was about to pay the price for a later than usual morning run.

He stopped outside the locked back door of the pub, got his breathing under control and stared at seven crated toilets sitting in a row alongside his garage.

'They're not supposed to be here,' he told the truck driver, who stood with a clipboard in his hands.

'Says there you ordered them,' the guy said, thrusting the paperwork and the stub of a pencil at Dan.

'Yeah—ordered, paid for—and requested they be stored.' Dan grabbed the pencil and signed the invoice beneath his company name.

The guy shrugged. 'Can't take 'em away, not without express consent from head office and given the thirty-minute time difference between us and Adelaide, they're still closed and I've got other deliveries to make.' He took the clipboard, ripped off the top copy of the consignment note and handed it to Dan.

Dan shoved the stub of pencil behind his ear and glanced over the truckie's retreating shoulder to where the back alley curved and led onto Main Street.

'Lucy,' he called as he spotted the dog lingering at the far end of the alley. 'Come here, girl.' He clicked his fingers and beckoned her.

She began to trot to him but sidled to the side of the alley as the truck fired up.

'Hang on, mate,' he called to the truckie. He walked down the alley, took hold of Lucy's collar and persuaded her to follow him with little words of encouragement.

The truck's reversing lights came on as Dan got Lucy to the back door of the pub.

He bent and rubbed his fingers beneath her collar—pink with little diamond-like stones—giving her a scratch. 'Where've you been, breathing so hard?' He grinned at the dog, ripped the bottom off the consignment note in his hand, grabbed the pencil from behind his ear and wrote on the scrap.

He folded it lengthways and tucked it safely around Lucy's collar. His note might even make Red smile. Recently, that happened at the rate chickens grew teeth. Which was partly his doing for getting so stuffy with her yesterday. It wasn't Red's fault if Sammy had decided to push them together.

'Go on home.' He straightened and shoved Lucy off gently in the direction of the B&B, then followed the truck as it backed down the side of Kookaburra's and onto Main Street, alerting the town to its presence as its reversing beeps sliced into the quiet of the morning.

'Have you seen Lucy?'

Dan spun around to Charlotte. 'She was around the back, I just sent her home.'

'Oh. Thanks.' She'd been running, and was wearing the tight-fitting sleeveless vest and the hip-hugging black Lycra shorts, but no baggy sweatshirt.

'Where's your hat?'

'Don't start, charm-boy.' She leaned forwards, hands on her knees and took a number of ragged breaths.

'Training for our five-K run?' he asked.

'I didn't take you up on the bet, remember?' She nodded at the truck. 'What did you have delivered?'

'Seven toilets.'

'Huh?' she asked, face scrunched.

'Backup mixers,' he said offhandedly, taking her arm and leading her to the side of the walkway as the truck moved off. 'We go through them like a soda fountain gone dry now summer's just about here.' He checked the street. All Tillmans were out, the twins standing so close it looked like they'd been glued together. Grace was staring at the truck and Ted had his official look on his face. Dan clamped his teeth together.

'Ouch! You're squishing my arm.'

Dan released the pressure. 'Sorry.' He rubbed the reddened fingerprints he'd made. Such tender skin. Warm from her exercise and smooth to touch.

'Can I have my arm back now?'

He let go, holding the warmth from her skin in the palm of his hand as though he didn't want it to fade. Christ, he wasn't getting starry-eyed about her, was he? He was looking at her only as a possible friend, right?

She was smart, in intelligence and style. Her usual attire spoke of expensive department stores and speciality boutiques. She'd bought the B&B with cash, according to speculation. She'd turned up completely unexpected and caused a stir. Why? What *was* she doing here?

'Want a coffee, Red?'

'No, thanks. I'm too busy. And don't call me Red.'

'Perhaps I'm chatting you up.' Perhaps he was.

'Pfft.'

'Not working, eh?'

She started jogging on the spot. 'Let me know when the committee gives me the okay for my list of renovations, would you?'

'Will do.' He nodded down at her legs. 'What distance did you sprint today?'

'Ten K.'

'Bullshit.'

She backed off, still jogging, an upbeat grin on her face. 'You know, one of these days I might fall for you and your provoking charm.'

Dan's grin grew. And one of these days he might like that a lot.

She turned and ran towards the B&B as Lucy galloped from the alley, yapping and twirling her lithe body in the air next to her mistress. Well, what do you know? He'd made Red smile. Which, given his reaction, could be dangerous.

He turned and eyed the Tillmans. The ladies went back inside but Ted glared. Dan raised a hand and smiled.

Ted didn't wave back.

Dan breathed deeply and headed over to the stock feeders'. 'One ton of charcoal briquettes and seven toilets,' Ted said. 'Is there something you're not telling us, Dan?'

'Eh ...' Dan shoved his fingers into his jeans pockets. 'Actually, Ted—'

'Expecting a big turnout for your barbecues after last Friday night, are you? Planning on extending the bathrooms in the bar, eh? That's gonna stuff up the plumbing. Council won't like it. Extra drains, you know...'

This was a chance to come clean but it was too soon. He hadn't fully evaluated how he was going to let them know what he was up to. If he came out and admitted he was planning a hotel now, the resulting interrogation would create a commotion so big it'd be talked about for the next ten years. He'd be knocked off his feet by the squall.

A vision of Charlotte standing in the bar, looking up at the ceiling and pondering the upstairs space came clearly into his mind. He looked Ted in the eye. 'I'm renovating the upstairs area and turning it into an apartment for myself.'

'With seven bathrooms?'

Got him. The old boy wasn't interested in the renovating—not if it simply meant an apartment. 'Nah, course not.' Dan pulled his fingers from his pockets and folded his arms across his chest as he pulled his shoulders back. 'Got the order wrong, didn't they? Only ordered one toilet, now I'm stuck with seven.'

'Well, don't go getting any ideas now you've got an additional six toilets, will you?'

'Like what?'

'Like opening up in the day. Selling alcohol during the day.'

'Happy to open up for anyone who wants a coffee, morning or afternoon.' He should get the official paperwork from the Office of Liquor, Gaming & Racing any time now, granting him an extension for the all-day opening licence.

'Yes, but not for paying customers. What was the Simmons woman doing inside the bar yesterday? And just now. She got something wrong with her arm? The way you were holding it, I thought for a second you might be getting all gooey about her.'

It wasn't only Mrs J who had a gossip antenna tweaked for perfect reception. And what business was it of Ted's if Dan had been getting smoochy with Red? But Ted appeared to be getting wound up. Perhaps he'd just come from his computer and space research. That always set him off. 'She likes coffee.'

'So she's reacting to you?'

'To my what?'

'The mediation. Is she coming round to our way of thinking?'

'Oh, that. Well, I reckon we have to give her a bit of time to adjust to our ways.'

'You've been mediating for a week. You said you'd charm her.'

Dan had an uncomfortable impression he just had. She'd certainly charmed *him* with her teasing, buoyant smile. 'Give her a chance, would you? How about we give her a gesture?'

'Such as?'

'Is there anything wrong with the picket fence idea?'

'Mmm.' Ted chewed his bottom lip. 'It'll take her a while to get shire approval.'

'So why don't we say she can apply for it? That'll give us all some breathing space.'

'Just don't like it when things are done so fast and behind our backs.'

'Right.' As if that was news.

'There's something not quite right about her, Dan. I feel it. Right here.' Ted tapped his chest. 'I've got a nose for these things. I'm going to Google her.'

'No need for that. She's trying to do the right thing. Give her a few more days, eh?'

'What's she doing here?' Ted asked. 'Why does our little town interest her enough to have boarded a flight from England? Why would the likes of her want to run a business in a town like ours if it wasn't for disreputable motives?'

Dan couldn't rightly answer those questions but if ever there was a moment when he should show Red some support, it was now. He was breaking down her barriers, but he needed a bit more time to suss out how he'd done it, because all he could think of was her soft arm under his hand and the pretty smile she'd produced for him—even if it was a tongue-in-cheek smile—and how all that had left him feeling a bit giddy.

Ted didn't give him a chance to answer. 'There's something familiar about her. It's like I've seen her before. Not recently—a long time ago. And I don't feel it was a pleasant experience. I'm open to all possibilities not of this earth,' he said. 'I've made studies and the like, and as such, I think I'm qualified to recognise what's not quite right.' Ted gathered himself like a peacock settling its ruffled feathers. 'There's nothing on the interweb about the galaxy, habitable planets or aliens I haven't researched.'

'It's called the internet, Ted.'

'Google. Takes you places, Dan.'

Dan nodded.

'We're an exoplanet here in Swallow's Fall.'

Sounded technical enough to be plausible.

'Things have dimmed in town since her arrival. It's a bit like transits. Planets crossing in front of their host star and dimming the light. *She's* dimmed our light.'

'Charlotte,' Dan reminded him, wondering if Charlotte realised she'd hit the final frontier when she moved into town.

Ted looked down the street as though looking into the future. 'My ultimate goal is to be taken and remember it.'

'Steady now, Ted.' This is what Mrs J had warned Dan about. He followed Ted's gaze down the street. Last time this happened, Ted got lost for four hours before being found in the back field, apologising to everyone for being away so long; he thought he might have been gone with the aliens for a month, but he couldn't remember any specifics.

'I'll have to keep my focus sharp if they take me. I believe they're very demanding.'

Dan put an arm over Ted's shoulders. 'Tell you what. I'll do the Googling on Charlotte, in case you need some … time out.'

Ted firmed his mouth. 'It might be best. I don't want to start my search and then find myself somewhere north of the Milky Way without means of contacting my loved ones at home.'

'Don't worry, mate, I'll do a thorough job. If there's something to be found on Charlotte, I'm the one who'll find it.'

'Apparently you're very tired when they return you to earth.'

'I bet.'

Ted took Dan's hand in both of his and gripped hard. 'Thank you, Dan. I appreciate this. You'd look after Grace and the twins for me, wouldn't you?'

'You can count on it.'

Ted moved off and Dan headed over to the beauty parlour where Julia was unlocking the door for Mrs J. Mrs J must be getting her hair done or something.

'You were right, Mrs J,' Dan said. 'Looks like Ted's hoping to be abducted.'

'Oh God.' Mrs J stood stock still. 'Does Grace know?'

Dan shrugged. 'She's his wife, she ought to see the signs first.'

Julia grinned and Dan shot her a warning look while Mrs Johnson stared across the street at the petrol station. Suddenly there was female business to be done.

'Mrs Tam, could you come over here for a minute, please?' she called, giving Mrs Tam the news when she joined them.

'Oh good heavens.' Mrs Tam patted her bun. 'Does Grace know?'

'I'm about to tell her,' Mrs J said. 'She probably hasn't noticed, she's been busy with sewing for the twins for Grandy's birthday party.'

'Does this mean you don't want your facial today, Mrs Johnson?' Julia asked.

'Can't go pampering ourselves while there's trouble brewing.'

Mrs Tam primed herself, heaving her bosom and squaring her shoulders. 'Ever since the twins came home with all that trouble they brought with them, poor Ted hasn't been right. It's like he's developed stress-related hypochondria.'

She looked more perturbed than Dan liked to see. 'It'll be fine,' he told her. 'And the twins haven't been prosecuted and nor are they likely to be—'

'Please don't bring that business up now, Daniel,' Mrs J said, pointing a finger at him. 'There are more important matters to discuss.'

Dan straightened and gave her a salute. 'You're right. What can I do to help?'

'Once I've got the key to the committee safe from Grace, I'd like you to go and grab the gavel. But do it surreptitiously and look after it.'

'Not a problem. I'll come with you to see Grace, then nip over to the Town Hall and collect it.' Last time Ted had gone off into outer space the gavel had gone missing too. He couldn't remember what he'd done with it and the loss of it put him in bed for an extra week.

Mrs J drew in a long breath. 'It's a bad time for Ted to be going into space with his aliens. There are decisions to be made on the committee.'

Julia grabbed the silky scarf around her neck and stuffed it against her mouth.

Dan's smile warmed his soul. This was one crazy town. How could anyone not love it?

Seven

'Oh, bugger.'

Charlotte slowed to a walk as she entered the town from the southern end. She sucked in air, her lungs burning from the sprint she'd forced herself into for the last two kilometres after jogging up the hillside and down—twice. Maybe she should have given herself a day off. Yesterday's run had worn her out but somewhere in her mind was the thought that one day she might actually beat Hotshot.

Lucy galloped on with a full tank of youthful vigour and headed for the mob outside Morelly's hardware store. Were they waging war about her colour schemes again? No. Too many of them. Something else was going on.

Problem was, how to slip past them? If she strode down the middle of Main Street she'd look like she was ignoring them. If she walked up the steps to the walkway she'd look like she was hoping to join them.

Oh great. Lucy was sitting, calm as you please, on Daniel's foot. If she called out to the dog she'd draw attention to herself and—worst-case scenario—Lucy might stay seated at Daniel's feet and ignore Charlotte.

No choice then. Heaving in another breath as her heart rate subsided, she climbed the stairs in front of her and padded cautiously down the walkway. She passed the closed beauty parlour, the empty toy shop and the grocer's store but stopped a few metres short of Morelly's. More people stood there than she'd seen in once place since the committee meeting. Must be something major to see this many townspeople out and about on a weekday afternoon.

'Let's listen to what Josh has to say,' Daniel said, both hands raised, obviously trying to temper the reactions of the people in front of him, who were talking over each other, agitated, as though attempting to get their own opinion aired before someone else butted in.

'What kind of mood is he in, Josh?' Ethan stood between Josh and Daniel, his son in his arms.

Josh hooked his thumbs into the belt loops on his dark blue jeans. He had his shirt tucked neatly into the waistband and he wore a good leather belt. He'd been polite the two times Charlotte had met him and hadn't come to any of the meetings or mentioned anything about colour schemes.

The Tillman twins were next to him, staring, arms folded as though waiting for him to make a mistake. During one of their rare keen-to-chat moments, they'd cornered Charlotte inside the stock feeders' and spoken of Josh and their utter disappointment in him. Apparently he used to be a cool-dude type in his younger days but was growing more urbane and detached than either twin appreciated. Charlotte suspected it was more a case of the tall young man standing next to Ethan not being particularly interested in the retro-style attractions either of the twins offered. She couldn't say the same for the grinning, sporty-looking blonde teenager who stood the other side of him. Gemma Munroe, the toy shop owner's daughter. She opened the shop for a few hours at the weekends.

Josh cleared his throat and stepped away from the twins. He bumped Gemma's shoulder, turned and apologised. She smirked up at him, made a quick remark and nudged him in the chest. Josh paused, then faced the town.

Despite her reticence about doing so, Charlotte stepped forwards in order to hear better.

'He's getting tetchy in the hospital,' Josh said. 'Told me he'd be mighty pleased if some schmuck from town could go get him sometime soon.'

Ethan laughed and Lachlan put his hand on his face and smiled. Ethan covered the boy's hand with his own and planted a kiss on his sandy-coloured head, settling him against his shoulder: a picture-perfect show of unconditional love in the midst of a raucous mob, who also seemed to love them without reservation. A satisfying scene to view, if you were involved and included.

Charlotte was overcome with a memory of her gran loving her, guiding her and giving her strength until she wasn't able to do so any longer. Even now, Charlotte felt their connection, like an aura that descended from above and gently surrounded her.

She caught Daniel's eye.

He nodded down at Lucy, who still had her rump nestled on his foot, and winked at Charlotte, his grin so smug she nearly laughed. She gave him a rueful smile instead, but genuine amusement prodded the surface of it. She'd caught up with Lucy yesterday where Dan said she would, coming out of the back alley behind Kookaburra's. She had a note tucked in to her collar: *I don't serve dogs not on a lead.*

Charlotte couldn't remember what a chuckle was, let alone a guffaw, but his note had made her laugh harder than she had in years. She hadn't even *giggled* for over nine months. Sometimes that charm of his worked, and she admitted to a niggling doubt that he turned it on purposefully.

'Grandy said he doesn't want any fuss for his birthday either,' Josh said to Ethan, bringing Charlotte out of her thoughts.

'Damn.'

'Damn,' Lochie parroted.

Ethan smiled an apology at the group and swung his son to his other arm.

'If we tell him about the party, he might have a *real* heart attack,' Mrs Tam said.

Sounded to Charlotte like the man in question was too bull-headed for that.

'Ted's got the new bunting,' Grace said. 'We've got to have the party, he was stringing it up in the Town Hall all weekend.'

Charlotte ran her gaze over the mob, then checked herself. Referring to them as a mob sounded uncouth and impolite, even in her head.

'Hi.' Julia Morelly edged back from the group and made her way to Charlotte's side, pulling her empty stroller with her.

'Hello,' Charlotte said. 'It's Julia, yes? You own the beauty parlour.'

The sleek blonde nodded and gave Charlotte what she could only describe as a 'once over'.

'Fantastic hair,' Julia said.

'Thank you.'

'Too many muted tones though.' Julia indicated Charlotte's grey sweatshirt, tied around her waist and hanging over her black Lycra running shorts. 'Let's grab one of Kookaburra's coffees and discuss things at the La Crème Parfaite one morning.'

'Love to.' Charlotte wasn't sure about being undressed and re-styled, if that's what Julia wanted to do but the coffee part sounded good, as did a morning chat with Julia. 'Good name, by the way—for your business.'

Julia laughed. 'Named it in a fit of pique. Probably should change it.'

The name suited the business and the person who ran it. Charlotte would be disappointed if it was changed to something dull like Julia's Place or Snip 'n' Shimmer.

'Here.' Julia flipped her contemporary and sophisticated pinstripe suit jacket to one side and dug into the pocket of her matching pencil skirt. The only incompatible thing about her up-to-date ensemble was the pair of bright white slip-on sneakers. 'My business card and a list of treatments.' She nodded behind Charlotte to where her parlour was all locked up. 'Only open when I'm called these days.'

'Told you Julia would want to get her hands on you.'

Charlotte stepped back to allow Daniel to join them. It wasn't Julia's hands he made her think about though, it was his. The palm of his hand had scorched her skin yesterday when he'd rubbed the spot where his grip had hardened. So close to him now, she almost felt the heat flare up again. She pulled at her running vest, then realised she'd exposed too much cleavage. She tweaked the scooped neckline an inch. Then another. 'It's warm,' she said, fanning her face with her hand when she noticed Daniel watching every move her hands made. 'Been running.' That should excuse any additional pink tones on her skin.

Daniel leaned in slightly, cloaking her with his now recognisable fragrance of melon, sandalwood and coffee berries. 'How many K's did you sprint?' he whispered.

'None of your business.'

'I'm guessing two.'

How did he know that? Charlotte put Julia's card in the change pouch of her shorts and looked back at the group outside the hardware store, who were still discussing a party. 'What's happening?'

'Grandy's coming home from the hospital in Cooma,' Julia said.

'And Ted's about to disappear.'

Charlotte stifled a smile. Up in a puff of smoke hopefully. 'Where is Ted?'

'Grace put him to bed and locked the door.'

'He's ill?'

Julia laughed. 'Sort of, bless him. It's bad timing though, because he's in charge of organising Grandy's ninety-fifth birthday party.'

'Grandy dislocated his collar bone trying to trim the wisteria on his house.' Daniel indicated the way Charlotte had run into town. 'He lives just out of town.'

Charlotte had thought the farmhouse on the southern outskirts of town, tucked back from the road but only a five-minute walk away, just one more empty, probably neglected, house. Pretty it was, too. Charlotte had stopped her run to take a surreptitious look from the roadside. The place was quiet, with an empty, lost feel, so she'd snuck down the driveway a dozen or so metres and taken a look. It wasn't fancy or grand but the single-storey house, the gardens and driveway were exceptionally well kept. The wisteria was thick and rambunctious, still blooming with its pink flowers and practically covering the front of the house, apart from where the windows poked through. The paddocks to the back meandered as far as the eye could see, all the way towards All Seasons Road and the craft centre Josh ran for the Grangers, maybe as far as Sammy and Ethan's homestead.

'Trouble was,' Julia said, 'Grandy was halfway up a twenty-foot ladder at the time. His foot slipped off the rung and he tumbled to the ground. He didn't tell anyone for three days—thought he'd pulled a muscle.'

'Is that why he's in hospital?'

'No,' Julia said, 'he caught a chill. Turned into pneumonia the next week, but we didn't know that. Coupled with his bad arm going numb, we thought he was having a heart attack.'

'Why didn't he go to the doctor?'

'Doc only visits once a month,' Daniel said.

Charlotte hadn't considered the things the town lacked. There wasn't a police station either. Even the library was mobile—only calling in once a fortnight. 'I hadn't thought …' she said by way of an apology. 'How difficult.'

'We called the Community First Responders unit,' Daniel continued. 'Because we thought it was his heart, they called for an urgent response, and the helicopter took him to the hospital.' He folded his arms across his chest, which only sent Charlotte's gaze firmly to his upper torso and his fanned pectoral muscles. He wore a white T-shirt today, tucked into his pale blue jeans. 'You'll soon get a heads-up on how things work. We don't have much. Too small. In fact we're pretty much forgotten.' It didn't seem to worry him—or Julia.

'Grandy's peed off,' Julia said. 'Hates being away from his farm—not that he does any farming any more, but he loves his house and his land.'

'Sounds like a strong-minded man.'

Julia laughed. 'I should know: he's my grandfather. Now we're trying to figure out where to put him. We don't want him living on his own and he won't come and live with me and my dad—' she nodded at Junior Morelly, '—because he says it's too far out of town. He's planning on putting a camp bed in the hardware store and living there if we won't let him live in his own house.'

'He's certainly drawn quite a crowd,' Charlotte muttered, and immediately shifted her gaze to Julia, hoping she wouldn't take that as a barbed remark.

Julia smirked. 'Bigger crowd than has ever been over at your place, huh?'

Charlotte gave a half-grimace, half-smile. 'Sorry about that. I'm a little touchy these days where crowds are concerned.' She felt Daniel's attention rest on her.

'Not surprised. Don't worry about it.' Julia shrugged it off.

'Well, this isn't getting anything sorted fast,' Mrs J said.

Julia and Daniel returned their concentration to the group.

'He'll insist on staying in his own home,' Daniel said. 'We know that. What we have to do is find him a housekeeper.'

'He won't have anyone live in with him,' Grace said.

Charlotte took a half-step towards Julia. 'He wouldn't object to someone doing his washing and cooking though, would he?' she asked quietly. 'Maybe popping in now and again to check on him?'

Julia leaned Charlotte's way. 'Yes, he would. Stubborn old coot.'

Stubborn maybe, but obviously well regarded—and loved.

'So we put in some amenities,' Daniel said. 'Safety rails and the like. Get him one of those lift-up armchairs, so he feels he's still got his independence. Then we sneak up on him and do what we need to do anyway.'

'Like what?' Josh asked.

'Like hiding his twenty-foot ladder for a start.'

'Like his washing,' Grace said. 'I'll do that.'

'My Lily could cook for him,' Mrs J said. 'Nothing wrong with a few frozen meals so long as they're home cooked.'

'He's good with the microwave,' Junior said. 'But he does like a fried egg sandwich.'

'I'd be ever so worried about him forgetting to switch the gas stove off,' Mrs Tam said. 'Or the heater. I have trouble remembering those things myself and I'm thirty years younger than him.'

'Whoa!' Daniel stepped away from Charlotte and Julia, inserting himself into the group with ease. He had both hands raised but he was smiling. 'Give him a chance. He's got his eyesight, his hearing and his common sense.'

And he had the town, Charlotte thought. The old man had obviously run the town most of his life, given the concern about his imminent return. They were at his back, looking out for him and willing to give up their own time to care for him—albeit behind his back.

Understanding hit her where it mattered—her heart. She'd looked after her gran for two years before she'd died, but she hadn't been alone. All Olivia's friends—aged from fourteen to eighty—had helped. They'd cared for Gran while Charlotte worked the B&B, keeping her entertained by reading aloud, or pushing her in her wheelchair around the park and letting her watch the lawn bowls. Gran had had many people at her back too.

'I'll re-do the bathroom for him,' Josh said.

Ethan nodded. 'I hoped you'd say that. I'll help you with it where I can.'

'Me too,' Daniel said. 'I'll draw up the plans. Between us we can get whatever's needed at wholesale price.'

Ethan shifted Lochie in his arms. 'All we have to do now is figure out where he can stay until all this is done.'

'He can stay at my B&B.'

Silence struck—Charlotte had never experienced such excruciating quiet.

'That's very kind of you,' Ethan said at last.

He didn't say any more and nobody else spoke.

Charlotte held her breath. Whatever the reason for her outburst of generosity, she'd made herself responsible for an old man who lived in a pretty farmhouse a five-minute walk from town. She looked at Daniel for some sort of support as her unease increased.

He cleared his throat and walked back to her side. 'What a generous offer, Charlotte, thank you.' He held his hand out.

Charlotte slid her fingers into his and shook his hand. He squeezed her hand slightly, a promise things would be okay, but the puzzled look in his mink-brown eyes told her he was questioning her. Why? How could she do any harm to him or the town by looking after an old man?

'Not sure if Grandy will accept that,' Mrs J said but didn't offer any further negativity.

Charlotte looked at Julia, who was looking at Charlotte's and Daniel's hands—still bound. She slipped her hand free and instantly missed the reassurance of its strength.

'He'll like sitting on the veranda,' Junior Morelly said contemplatively.

'What about all the renovating you're doing at the Cappers' place?' Grace asked. 'He'd be in the way.'

'My place—and he wouldn't be in the way.'

'He won't be able to manage the stairs,' Grace said.

'He can have the ground-floor room. I'll move upstairs.'

'Are those rooms ready for use?' Daniel asked; again, that interrogative look narrowing his gaze.

'Yes. They're lovely rooms. They only need cosmetic attention but that can wait.' Wait? Had she just said that?

'He'll enjoy the dog's company,' Junior said.

Ethan laughed. 'He'll likely enjoy Charlotte's company too.'

Charlotte smiled at Ethan. Gran hadn't been alone, not for a minute during the last years of her illness. Grandy shouldn't be alone either. Not when he was so well loved. Not when Charlotte appeared to be the only person with the means to house him in the centre of town, which was where he wanted to be. She'd enjoy the company in the house herself. Might not feel so outcast and lonely if there was someone to look after and care for.

'I'd pay you for his board and such,' Junior Morelly offered.

'How much would you charge?' Grace asked.

'Um ...' Charlotte clasped her hands in front of her. 'I wouldn't charge him anything.'

'That wouldn't be right,' Ethan said.

'I wouldn't charge,' she said again, enforcing her point politely. 'I'd be happy for his company.'

'Sounds right funny to me,' Grace said. 'Not charging. Thought you were planning on running a business.'

'I'm not open for business yet.' Neither would she ever be. 'But I'd like to show some goodwill.'

'Like a gesture?' Mrs J asked.

Charlotte jumped on that. 'Yes.' That's what Daniel had suggested she do—offer them a gesture. She turned to the group. 'I'd be delighted to have Grandy stay at the B&B.' Maybe delighted was the wrong word but if it meant her offer hastened the approval of her renovation ideas, she was all for taking it on.

The ensuing silence sparked a new anxiety. If they refused her offer, she'd be left feeling less welcome than she had since her arrival. Which was infuriating, given that she wasn't supposed to care.

Eight

Small business owner beats multinational hoteliers Forsters at their own game

Dan rolled his chair closer to the desk and his laptop and skimmed the British newspaper article, surprised he'd found something about Charlotte so soon.

The buyout turned into a battle as 29-year-old Australian-born Charlotte Simmons …

Australian born? He shifted the lid of the laptop until the early morning light from his bedroom window didn't reflect on the screen so much and went back to the start of the column.

Charlotte Simmons could not have saved her childhood home and thriving B&B business from the big guns, but she gave as good as she got and gridlocked construction of a seventy-room hotel and golfing resort, costing Forsters hundreds of thousands of pounds. Miss Simmons' tenacity must have surprised the

Forsters executives and their lawyers during their bid to purchase her quarter-acre property in Lower Starfoot-in-the-Forest, near Harrogate, Yorkshire, to add to the land already in their possession.

Dan grinned as a vision of Red staring down Forsters executives came quickly to mind. He wouldn't want to be too close to the heat of that bonfire.

Miss Simmons met with Forsters at the British multinational's company headquarters in Surrey this week and walked away with three times what her property and its future livelihood was worth.

'Good for her.' He couldn't halt the swell of satisfaction, but he'd bet his left arm she hadn't expected the dogmatic will of small-town inhabitants to bring her plans in Swallow's Fall to a standstill. He smiled. He might feel a tug of pride for her but Red had no patience. Nothing new there.

But what had brought her back to her native country? Charlotte's battle had happened nine months ago. She'd been in Australia a couple of months now.

The answer probably lay in the reason why she'd left in the first place. The article said she'd lost her home, not just her business, and stated she'd been in England since childhood. Yet she hadn't let anyone think she was anything other than British. Why would she hide the fact that she was born in the same country as those who were against her? It was as though she didn't want them on her side. Or had no reason to seek their acceptance.

He shut his laptop down, pushed from the desk and moved from the contemplative atmosphere of his room into the all-consuming silence of the empty bar. He grabbed a cold bottle of beer from the fridge, gripped the top in the palm of his hand, unscrewed the cap and flicked it into the metal bin beneath the counter. He took a long drink of the beer and wiped his mouth with the back of his hand.

Charlotte would be worth a bob or ten now but she hadn't bragged about her success. If Firecracker Red had moved to Swallow's Fall because she wanted out of the rat race and into the slow-placed groove of country life—*remote* country life—there'd be only two reasons why: either she was running from or searching for something. Whichever reason, she hadn't been egged along by some life-changing wish to come here, she'd made a deliberate move. She'd chosen this town.

He took a slower pull of his beer. Hadn't he done the same?

Six years ago he'd been in north Queensland, flushed with more than the heat. He'd worked hard, had his fun and played the field with a choice of attractive, decent women, not to mention the occasional adventurous one. He'd made his money—a considerable amount—but apart from his success as a draughtsman and his ability to put in dedicated hours of hard graft as he renovated a dozen properties for resale, not one calculated and disciplined task he'd set for himself had fulfilled his expectations. He'd forced himself to sit back and think about where he was and where he wanted to be.

Funny he should see now how clear that choice had been, as he looked out of the window onto Main Street and the town he had such a blistering fondness for. It hadn't been a desire to change gear that had been *his* motivation for moving back to the country either. It was the culmination of a cycle. He hadn't bought the hotel and moved to Swallow's Fall to transform himself, he'd bought it to come home.

Charlotte stared Daniel in the eye, hand on the flyscreen door. 'If you're here to chat about the bet you think I accepted, please don't bother.'

He held out a takeaway coffee. 'I just love that happy face of yours. What's got your back up this time?'

Charlotte took the coffee from him. 'My wallpaper steamer.'

He looked over her shoulder, down the hallway. 'Not going to ask me in?'

She stepped back. 'Watch your step.'

'Man, what are you doing with all this stuff?' He pointed to the under-stairs cupboard where the tools Charlotte had bought in Canberra were normally kept neatly.

'Getting on with my renovations.' Before purchasing the property, she'd been shown enough photos to know about the peony-flocked wallpaper, the peeling kitchen and laundry bench tops and the 1960s farmyard-scene paper lining the back of cupboards and wardrobes.

'And what's wrong with your steamer?'

'It won't steam.'

He walked towards the jumble of boxes and tools in the hallway. 'Want me to take a look? What a mess,' he added, stepping over extension leads, a sander and a large plastic tool box.

Charlotte clamped her lips together, trying to hold back the sulky frame of mind she hadn't been able to shake all morning. On the one hand, it was great the townspeople had agreed to her suggestion to have Grandy stay, but on the other hand—what the hell had she been thinking? The older Mr Morelly might be sitting on her veranda through winter—this year and the next. She could see the newspaper advertisement now:

For Sale. Delightful B&B tucked in quaint country town. Goodwill included in the form of a 95-year-old man with a stubborn temperament who stays free of charge.

On Monday she'd said yes to dinner at Sammy's place. By Wednesday she'd offered her house to Grandy. She'd also taken up some fanciful challenge from Daniel and put her concentration into running and getting fit when she should have been renovating. At this rate, she'd never get Ethan alone. Never get out of this town. Never get her new life.

'How come you're suddenly working so hard?' Daniel asked.

'I need to do as much as possible before Grandy moves in.' And she could move out.

'You've only got four days.' He unplugged the steamer from the socket, checked the tank she'd filled with water, then pulled and tugged the hose that ran from the tank to the rectangular steam pad. He unscrewed it from the base, shook it and screwed it back in.

'I've got to start somewhere,' Charlotte said, her voice filled with the frustration building inside her.

'Okay, stop getting touchy.' Daniel hooked the hotplate pad onto the steamer stand and bent to turn the machine on at the wall socket. The water tank gurgled. He twisted her way and grinned.

'That was lucky,' she told him.

He switched the steamer off. 'How come you softened up and offered to let Grandy stay here?'

'I've been told by practically everyone it's not certain he'll *want* to stay.'

'He will. So wallpaper first, then what?'

'The upstairs rooms.' They only needed decorating but the back bedroom—her room, the one she'd offered to the old man—was in need of the most renovation and would now have to wait.

'What's the sander for?'

'After I've taken up the lino in the kitchen, I'm going to sand the floorboards. But I can't do that until Grandy leaves.'

'Grandy won't mind the noise, he'll probably help you.'

'Yes, good idea. Until the dust from the sander gets on his chest and sends him right back to hospital.' Imagine the furore.

They'd kick her out of town for sure. Or bury her alive in the pioneer cemetery. Who'd feed Lucy then?

Lucy. Charlotte's shoulders sank. Who would take the dog when she left? Taking Lucy back to Britain meant getting her through all the regulations. She'd need a pet passport, which might take months to obtain, and vaccinations, and perhaps a stay in quarantine. Miss her though she would, Charlotte couldn't put the young animal through the loneliness of all that.

'When are you starting work on Grandy's house?'

'Got to draw up some plans first, then order gear from Canberra. What's wrong, Red? You're looking real sulky.'

'Thanks for the observation. How much do I owe you for the coffee?'

'Fine.' He raised his hands in surrender. 'I get it. You're having a bad day.'

Her 'day' had started at three a.m. when she'd woken for the fourth time. But it wasn't because of the dream—her mother had been on her mind in the shadowy hours of the night. She wrapped her hands around the coffee and sipped. At least the caffeine kick would keep her going for a few hours. 'Put it on my tab. If I'm allowed a tab?'

'Well, now, if you want a tab I'm going to have to ask a few questions about your credit rating.'

'Fine. I'll pay cash.'

'What's wrong, Charlotte?'

Charlotte chewed on her tongue but the question she needed to ask danced on the tip of it. 'Why did I offer to let Grandy stay?'

'You don't want him now?'

'Of course he can stay, it's just that …' She was getting caught in a mesh of charm called Swallow's Fall.

'Could be you're coming round to us.'

'Huh.' Her sulkiness was a defence mechanism aimed at hiding her nerves and one sleepless night too many meant she couldn't keep the tone of it out of her voice.

Pulled from her bed by an intense force—a will she wasn't sure was hers alone—she'd settled in the warmth of the kitchen, with Lucy at her feet, and made a list of exactly what it was she was here to do: see Ethan and pound him with questions until all the fearsome ones were answered and she was free to leave. But there was something else hovering—and unattainable. A quest for happiness … a chance at happiness? Charlotte didn't understand it, and pushed it to the back of her mind.

'Any news on my weatherboard colour?'

'I'm going to see Ted now, see what I can do for you.' He paused. 'What was your B&B in England like?'

'Home.' A single word, but an all-encompassing, dreamy depiction for her Starfoot habitat.

'So why'd you leave it?'

'I sold up. After my gran died.'

'Couldn't bear the memories, eh?'

All her memories had been bulldozed and now sat beneath the eighteenth hole.

'I did the same thing when my grandfather died. Just sold up, and moved on.'

'Where are you from?' she asked, sipping her coffee.

'Small town in south Victoria.' He bent and picked up the extension cord. 'Went to Queensland after that and made some money. I was a draughtsman, then I got into renovating properties.' He glanced at her. 'You must have made a reasonable living in your B&B. I hope you get the same here in Swallow's Fall or you might have wasted your investment.' He put the extension cord on top of the tool chest and put both into the under-stairs cupboard. 'Hope you haven't got a large mortgage.'

'Worried about my tab?'

He hauled the sander into the cupboard, followed by all the other bits and pieces Charlotte had pulled out to get to the steamer. 'Coffee's on the house.'

'Any time I want one?'

'Any time.'

She'd found friends here in Swallow's Fall and all she was doing was knocking them back; Sammy, Julia—Daniel. His handshake yesterday—a simple touch but a gesture of strength she'd responded to, along with his likeable, easy grin and the energetic, peppy fragrance of him ... All of it had become as familiar and as tasty as the whisky-orange marmalade she scraped on her toast each morning. But she wasn't supposed to be getting acquainted with any of these people. This wasn't her home. She didn't have a home.

'Okay.' Daniel moved to the front door. 'Enjoy your coffee, Red. I'll check in with Ted about the weatherboard.'

The lump in her throat threatened an emotional storm. Charlotte swallowed it.

'Hey. You fancy a run today?'

'No, thanks.' Even her voice sounded thickened. 'Wouldn't like to think of you trailing behind me for so long.'

'Stamina, Red. How much have you got?'

Was he talking about the renovations or the run?

'Might take more endurance than you think you've got to get yourself sorted here.'

The renovations then. But she sensed there was more; something to do with her. 'You watch out for your own back, Hotshot.'

'I'll do that. You watch out for yours. I'm right behind you. Catch you later.' He left, closing the flyscreen door behind him.

Charlotte held her breath and counted to five. Tears stung her eyes. Thank God they hadn't fallen in front of him. She put the takeaway coffee on the hall table and scrubbed at her face.

Slivers of memories, once gold, now a little tattered from overuse, like the broken spine of a beloved book, crowded her thoughts. The back of her legs itched on the coarse fabric of the train seat. Her knee-high socks kept slipping to her ankles. *We're going on an adventure,* her mother said. *We're starting again.* Or had she said, *It's just you and me, it always has been and always will be?* The shudder that ran through Charlotte ripped at her skin. Her memories were twisted with so many theories about what had happened before the vicious, horrible night her mother was killed by O'Donnell that it was no longer clear if that train ride was real, a dream, or just a wish to make the possible circumstances of her parentage better than they actually were. The mere thought of having the monster as her father made her want to retch.

Ethan was the person she needed to sort it all out. He'd have the answers about O'Donnell.

The train journey, if she and her mother had taken it, had been exciting and probably felt longer because she'd only been four or five years old. Her mother moved them from the city of Sydney to the suburb of Campbelltown, where Charlotte had started school. *That* little girl's world had been a playground with laughter and a Raggedy-Ann doll called Lucy. Lucy had been with her in the wardrobe. Lucy had clung tight. Lucy had been frightened too.

'Cooee.'

'Mrs Tam—just a second.' Charlotte walked to the front door and opened the flyscreen. 'Come in.'

'Thank you, Charlotte, but I can't stop. Just wanted to give you this.' Mrs Tam handed over a bottle filled with dark syrup. 'Blackberry wine. Here—' She produced a small glass from her pocket. 'Have a taste.'

'It's just gone lunchtime. I'm not going to make the right impression if people see me slugging your wine at this time of the day.'

'Oh, go on with you.' Mrs Tam thrust the little glass forwards. 'Just a tot. It'll do you good—you look a bit peaky.' She peered around Charlotte's shoulder. 'Out with the old, in with the new, is it?' Mrs Tam stepped inside. 'This house was built in 1860, you know.'

'Really? I thought it was later.'

'It's the oldest house in town. It would have been a slab and bark hut to begin with. Built by the grazier whose son later built the Grangers' place on Burra Burra Lane. Then someone rebuilt it in stone and corrugated iron. There wouldn't have been anything fancy like the veranda and all those intricate mouldings on the posts and railing. Those were added later, as was the weatherboard.'

Charlotte hadn't been given any history of the property. Might be worthwhile looking into its provenance—for resale value, not because she was overly interested. Mention of the weatherboard made her think of Ted and the committee, and the ten-litre pots filled with sunflower yellow paint she'd been planning on buying. They hadn't been meeting up on her front lawn recently, due to Ted being in bed.

Mrs Tam took the bottle off Charlotte and poured a shot into the glass. 'Word association, Charlotte.'

'For what?' Charlotte sipped the blackberry wine. 'Mmm, this is good.'

'Make it every summer. Have a tot more.' She poured another measure into the glass before Charlotte had a chance to stop her. 'Sunflower yellow. Nobody grows sunflowers around here.'

'Are you saying I should consider keeping the weatherboard pink?'

'You're a smart woman, Charlotte. I'm sure if you think about it you'll come up with an idea for changing the name.'

'But not the colour?'

Mrs Tam took the empty glass out of Charlotte's hands and handed the bottle back. 'The sunflower is a lovely plant—but rather large and in your face, don't you think?'

A bit like me, thought Charlotte; swaggering around, too big for my boots. She screwed the cap onto the bottle of blackberry wine. She'd danced into town with her ideas of sunflower-coloured paint jobs. The people in this quaint, slightly weird little town would recognise the sunflower but wouldn't identify with it.

Grapefruit yellow? Lemon, citrus? Too insipid. That would be like Julia calling her place Snip 'n' Shimmer. She needed something countrified. 'Honeyeater yellow.'

Her neighbour's interest sparked. 'Now there's a colour I wouldn't mind seeing on the weatherboard of this house.'

A tingle brushed Charlotte's spine. The regent honeyeater birds—what was left of them—lived on the eastern side of New South Wales, in the wooded forests. She knew that because she'd bought flora and fauna books from the art and craft centre, but it didn't matter where the honeyeater birds' habitat was, it was their history that would tie in with the townspeople. The bright yellow on their chests would be the perfect colour for the weatherboard too. 'With wagtail-white trim.'

Mrs Tam's eyes twinkled. 'Why, I can practically see it. Sitting proudly at the entrance to town.'

So could Charlotte—she saw her house blending in. Swallow's Fall was a little piece of country not yet taken over by the economies of commercialism. They'd been forgotten in the industrialisation spurt of the last fifty years and had been hindered by that but they didn't care. They liked what they had because it was precious to them. Something Charlotte understood only too well. They preferred the old ways. They were private landowners too, each and every one of them. How many towns, in today's world, could boast of that? Nobody rented in Swallow's Fall. They lived in

Swallow's Fall and put their hard-earned money not only into their own coffers but those of the town. No wonder they were stand-offish. It was pride.

Mrs Tam patted the bun on top of her head, a sagacious gleam in her eye. She nodded at the bottle of blackberry wine in Charlotte's hand. 'Have another, then put it in the refrigerator, it's best when cooled.'

As Mrs Tam walked down the path and onto Main Street, a tentative burst of sunshine entered Charlotte's world. She walked along her veranda and looked east towards the hillside hiding the roots of the wildflowers she hadn't seen. Nor was she likely to now she'd finally got an understanding of how to move forwards. Maybe when she left town they'd appreciate that she'd created something for them to hold on to. Maybe that would atone for the friendships she was shaking off and guarding against.

'Honeyeater yellow,' she said quietly.

'He's in bed but he's up for visitors and looks respectable,' Grace said as Dan followed her down the hallway of the home above the stock feeders'. 'I've got him where I want him.'

Dan kept his smile neutral as he listened to Grace list the benefits of having Ted in bed. His own ideas of keeping someone indefinitely in his bed were a lot more colourful.

'How are your apartment plans coming along?' Grace asked as she stopped outside the bedroom door.

'What apartment?'

'Your apartment. Top floor. The one with seven toilets.'

Dan lengthened his spine. 'Oh, that apartment. Fine. Good.' He nodded.

'Here he is,' Grace said, ushering Dan into the room before her. 'Now don't go taking up much of his time. I want him rested, not riled.'

Dan turned to the man in the bed as Grace left, closing the door behind her.

'Quite a picture, eh?' Ted asked.

Hard as it was to stop his grin from forming, Dan managed to keep his smile polite. 'How are you, Ted?'

Ted heaved himself upright in the bed, a pile of plump pillows behind him. Dressed in pale blue pyjamas buttoned to his Adam's apple, ironed and undoubtedly starched by the stiff look of the collar, he resembled a stuffed teddy bear. A grouchy one that hadn't got to the picnic.

'How do you think I am?' he asked. 'Been stuck in here thirty-six hours now.' He indicated the bedroom door. 'She's a maniac for rules. Sergeant Major Grace, that's what we should call her.'

Dan thought it wise not to answer.

Ted pinned him with a narrowed look, his eyes like glass marbles in a pie-crust face. 'The Simmons woman. We've been thinking.'

'Charlotte. What have the committee been thinking?'

'She's saved us a mighty amount of worry by having Grandy stay at the B&B.'

'I'm hoping to persuade you into allowing Charlotte to apply to the shire for the fence.'

'"Yes" is our decision.'

'So soon?'

'She advised us of her intentions—'

Something Dan hadn't done.

'—and while she did rush in, she's done nothing wrong—*yet*.' Ted's tone was grave. 'So we're going to grant her wish for the picket fence.' He sniffed. 'As long as it's white and not yellow.'

'I'll let her know.'

Ted leaned forwards. 'I wonder if we ought to reconsider the weatherboard colour.'

Dan's humour fled. Seven months he'd waited to paint one frog-green wall to smooth navy blue. Two and a half years to renovate the dining area so it didn't look like it came out of the fifties—which it had—and six years to get to the stage of planning the upgrade of seven hotel rooms. 'So you're going to let her paint it yellow?'

Ted shook his head and leaned against his pillows. 'Absolutely not. I'm going to advise her to paint it white—if she won't keep it pink.'

'How are you going to do that?' Beneath the immediate problem of how to handle both Ted and Charlotte, Dan had a sneaky wish to watch the pyrotechnics. He'd give a thousand dollars to have been in the solicitor's office in England when Firecracker Red held her ground. Ted didn't stand a chance.

'I've been chatting to people and I've decided it'll be nice to see the B&B operational again.' Ted folded his arms, his gaze on the ceiling as though he'd discovered something satisfactory about himself. 'So long as there aren't *too* many tourists in town, of course. It's not as if she's planning a full-blown hotel, is it?' He snuffled a breath. 'Talking of plans, how's the top-floor apartment coming along? I don't know what you'll do up there with all that space. Going to use the back room for storage are you?'

Dan pulled in air. Jesus, give him strength. 'My apartment plans are in motion, nothing definite about what I'm going to do with that space yet—just at the starting point really.' He cleared the discomfort from his throat. 'Tourists aren't such a bad thing you know.' No—best get off that subject until he'd straightened out everything else. 'Do you want me to tell Charlotte about the weatherboard?'

'No need. I'm going to write her an official letter.'

Something else they were going to throw at her. Dan wondered how she'd cope with it. Those petal-shaped spots of skin beneath Charlotte's eyes concerned him; tender damage from worry or sleeplessness. She was hiding so much and it looked like it was all getting to her.

If only she'd open up to someone. Maybe Sammy or Julia could prise the reason out of her, but Dan had a hankering to do it himself.

He pushed from the chair and wandered to the window while Ted picked up paperwork from his bedside table and shuffled through the documents. Dan pulled the edge of the net curtain to one side and stared at the house at the bottom of the hill. The front lawn stretched like a carpet of unblemished green since Charlotte had put down the new lawn, apart from the fallen gumnuts scattered on it. The shingle path led straight from the roadside to the steps of the white-painted veranda. The corrugated metal roof ought to be replaced, although he'd miss the tarnished silver sixpence look of it when the sun sank in the west each evening.

He ran his gaze over the stone chimney stack and down to the eastern end of the garden, where a six-metre-tall snow gum sat to one side of the veranda, shading and protecting the house. It would have been no more than fifty centimetres high when William Swallow, the town's namesake, had parked his horse and cart next to it in 1843 and settled in to recover from his broken leg.

He looked across the road to Kookaburra's. His confidence must be taking a bit of a dive. What he planned was a much bigger change than getting a couple of rooms at the B&B ready for occasional guests—his plans involved continuity, growth for the town. If he'd started the conversation slowly he might have turned the townspeople around within a year. Red appeared to have done that within a month.

He leaned against the windowsill and folded his arms across his chest. 'Got to word this letter carefully, Ted. She's doing us a big favour having Grandy.'

Ted nodded. 'Piped up with her offer fast, didn't she? She's one of *those* types.'

'What types?'

'Bossy.' Ted lowered his tier of chins and whispered, 'I have a similar problem with Grace, so I know what I'm talking about.'

Dan nodded in the expected male-companionship manner, but Grace wasn't bossy. Not really. She'd been worried sick about her husband and the twins. And while Ted was here, weaving plans to get Charlotte to do his bidding, his capable wife was running the store.

'Did you find anything about her on Google?' Ted asked.

'Not a thing.'

Ted grunted. 'Must be something somewhere. Might take a look myself. Got nothing else to do.'

Dan left his position against the window and walked back to the chair he'd vacated. 'Leave the Googling to me.' He picked up the chair, swung it around, placed it closer to Ted's bed and sat. 'We've got an important letter to write so let's get it done.'

He needed to stay close to everyone in order to traffic-manage the unexpected events hampering his own plans. Best get Ted off the internet search before he discovered what had happened to Charlotte's English B&B. The story didn't stop there, and Dan wondered if it even stopped here, in Swallow's Fall.

Charlotte hiccupped. Late afternoon and dozens of raspberry cordial-coloured peonies began to meld one with the other. One slug of blackberry wine too many?

Drinking. At four o'clock on a Thursday afternoon. She stilled in the hallway, the water in the bucket she held sloshing over the rim, and stared at the wallpaper steamer, then sighed. Was it even worth starting now?

A snuffling noise. 'Lucy?' She turned to the kitchen but Lucy didn't come bounding out of her laundry bed. Loose again.

Probably over at the pub with her country boyfriend, Daniel, no doubt getting watered and fed scraps from the kitchen.

Another snuffle sound, then a snort.

Charlotte put the bucket down and walked to the open front door. A bulbous white animal barrelled its way to the closed flyscreen door on squat but strong-looking legs. Legs with trotters.

Charlotte stepped back from the pig on her doorstep and pondered the notion of homemade wine creating hallucinations. The tip of the pig's big round snout pressed against the flyscreen, its dark little eyes staring. It was the size of a fridge. It couldn't be wild because it was wearing a harness.

She shooed it with her hand. 'Go away.' What was the number of the local wildlife rescue group?

'That there's Ruby and she don't take kindly to shooing.'

Charlotte looked up as Mrs Johnson moved from the veranda post she was leaning against and walked forwards. So this was the pig Daniel had mentioned, the one Mrs J took for a walk on a lead. 'Good afternoon,' Charlotte said. She eyed the pig as it waddled backwards to let its owner come closer to the door. A pig with manners. Well, this was Swallow's Fall. Anything could happen.

'Steaming off the wallpaper then?' Mrs J asked, nodding at the hallway behind Charlotte.

Charlotte was mindful of Daniel's feature wall in the bar. Seven months to change the colour. 'I'm afraid I have no choice—it's a bit threadbare in places. But I'm sure it was lovely when it was first hung.'

'It's not definite Grandy's staying yet,' Mrs J said. 'He might not want to.' No friendly banter being swapped here. Mrs J didn't waste time getting to the point.

'That will be up to him,' Charlotte said, 'but the offer's there.'

'He likes sitting on the veranda and watching the town.'

'With a fried egg sandwich.'

'Smart, aren't you?' Mrs J waved a hand at Charlotte's raised eyebrows. 'I'm not being rude, I'm being pleasant.'

Charlotte forgave herself for making an honest mistake.

'Some say I'm the negative type,' Mrs J said, bending to click the lead onto the pig's body harness. 'But it isn't true. Personally, I think I'm getting soft.'

Charlotte grinned, then wiped it off her face as Mrs J straightened and looked her in the eye.

'Things have been tough since I lost my husband.'

That's right—Daniel had mentioned her loss. 'I'm so sorry.'

'I wasn't saying it for pity, I was just saying. My daughter, Lily, she lost her husband in a divorce. Got Lily and her kids, Andy and Jane Louise, living with me now. Helps a bit. We pool resources.'

'Daniel said Lily is a great cook.'

'You're not such a bad cook yourself. Those tarts and cakes you make are professional looking—and tasting. Mind if I come in?'

Was there a choice? 'Please do.' Charlotte held the door open.

Mrs J hooked Ruby's lead over the arm of the rocking chair on the veranda.

'Will that be enough to keep her tethered?' Charlotte asked, eyeing the pig.

'Probably not if she takes a mind to wander.' Mrs J walked into the hallway.

'Should I get her some water—or something to eat?'

'She's partial to the odd banana, if you've got any to hand.'

Charlotte bowed her head with true hostess grace. 'It's Ruby's lucky afternoon, I bought a bunch from the grocer's yesterday.'

Mrs J pulled a hipflask out of her pocket. 'Understand you've been tasting some homebrews.'

Charlotte eyed the hipflask with suspicion.

'Thought you'd like to try some of mine,' Mrs J said. 'Potato wine.'

'I'd be delighted, Mrs Johnson.' Anything to get her out of the house—taking the pig with her.

'I won't beat around, I'm here to suss you out.' Mrs J moved the hipflask to her left hand and held out her right, fingers stretched, arm straight. 'So if you don't mind, I'll call you Charlotte and you can call me Clarissa.'

Mrs Johnson had a girly name? Charlotte hadn't considered what her Christian name might be but if she had, she'd have put a bet down on it being a staunch, strong female from the Bible: Ruth, Deborah, Rachel. Or maybe something from the movies. Cruella.

And how much sussing out was Charlotte about to endure?

Nine

A minor bump to a guy's confidence didn't mean the guy had buckled. Dan's composure had been pranged yesterday and the result was a small dent. Nothing that couldn't be panel-beaten and resprayed. But like all unexpected events, his slight—*slight*—downbeat reaction about how he'd got things wrong and Charlotte had got them right needed closer inspection and thought.

He made a smooth, even draw on the beer tap, waited a few seconds for the head to rise and fall, and drew again until the ale came to the top of the glass with minimal head.

Basically, he was going to have to lie some more in order to smooth his way around the many issues. The committee, Ted, Charlotte—and the women in town. Handling guys was one thing; give 'em a beer and start talking sport. Handling women and their talent for discovering truths, Dan hadn't had much practice at. He needed inside info from someone who had a long-time association, as in a marriage. His opportunity had walked into the bar five minutes ago.

He put the pint on the counter. 'So you've been let off Sammy duty tonight?' he asked Ethan.

'Pushed off, more like.' Ethan took a sip. 'Said I was getting underfoot and kicked me out of the house.'

'How long before she goes into ... you know, gives birth?'

'Just over three weeks. We'll head into Cooma and stay there a few days before the baby's due so we're near the hospital. It's all getting a bit close for comfort. Got an agency vet assistant arriving in a couple of days.'

'Experienced?'

'I hope so. Isla Maxwell. Agency said she was driving down from Queensland. I just hope she'll cope. And stay.' Ethan nodded at the bottle of beer beside Dan's hand. 'What about you? You don't usually drink on duty.'

Dan took a slug of his cold one. 'Had a tough day.'

'How tough?'

'People are asking questions about my apartment.'

'What apartment?'

'Exactly.' Dan scanned the bar. It was gone nine o'clock, only a few stragglers left, all men. The kitchen had closed a half-hour ago. Dan liked to let Lily leave early on a Friday night. Josh was at the far end of the bar, serving the few guys Dan knew he'd be kicking out in under an hour's time.

He leaned on the counter and spoke quietly. 'I sort of got myself tangled up in a lie.' He raised his hand as Ethan lifted an enquiring eyebrow. 'A partial lie.'

'A little white one, eh?'

'Maybe the size of Mount Kosciuszko.'

'I take it this is to do with your hotel plans.'

Dan nodded. 'Seven toilets arrived unexpectedly early and I made up a story about renovating the upstairs area for an apartment.'

'That'd make a damned big apartment for one single guy.'

'They haven't figured that out yet.'

'The war council guys?' Ethan put his glass down. 'Maybe not, but wait until the ladies hear about it. They'll suss you out faster than a tumbleweed gathers dust.'

'That's what I'm worried about.' Grace already knew about it, which meant most of the women in town knew about it.

'How'd you get the idea in the first place?'

'Charlotte asked what was upstairs and mentioned it looked a big enough space to have three or four apartments up there.'

'Or seven ensuite hotel rooms.' Ethan grinned. 'How's it going with Charlotte?'

'I think she might be warming to us.'

'Just as well, because Sammy is out to marry you off to her.' Ethan lifted his ale and took a drink, all the while staring at Dan over the rim of the glass. 'Just warning you.'

'What is it with women?'

'Better get used to them—or get a handle on how to read them. There are more women arriving in town every time we look around. Kate married Jamie. Julia's back for good. Charlotte arrived out of the blue and now Isla Maxwell.'

'At this rate we'll be overrun with them by next spring.'

'Let's get back to your marriage plans.'

'Sammy's marriage plans,' Dan said, straightening. 'Charlotte isn't my type.'

Ethan smiled. 'Sammy's got her heart set on a winter wedding.'

Dan grimaced and looked away, but the pull of amusement sat inside him. Him and Red, bickering their way down the aisle. 'I don't think she'd take me.'

'You're quite a catch. Apparently.'

'Give over, would you? Red wouldn't think twice about running me over in her shiny 4WD.'

'Given her a friendly little nickname, have you?'

'Yeah—Firecracker.' Okay, maybe sometimes he thought of her as Sexy Red.

'Can't promise anything but I'll try to put Sammy off.'

'Just make sure you do that before the lovebird dinner tomorrow night.'

They glanced to the far end of the counter as one of the guys from the small group still in the bar let out a disgruntled cry and thumped the counter with his fist.

Josh stood behind the bar, unflinching, both hands flat on the counter. 'You've had enough,' he said. 'I have the right to refuse to serve you.'

'I'm asking for one last beer before closing, that's all. And I don't like being refused.'

'You just have been,' Josh said.

The guy turned to his buddies at a table behind him, and grinned. 'Look at me, I just got refused a drink.'

His group of mates laughed. 'You gonna play games?' one called. 'Or do something?'

Ethan picked up his glass and sipped his ale. 'You wading in?'

Dan shook his head. 'Nah. Watch this.'

The loudmouth turned to the bar with a show of bravado and smirked at Josh.

Josh's mouth moved to something like a smile but everything else about him was stilled.

The guy lifted his arm fast, fist clenched, and swung but Josh was faster. He grabbed the man's wrist and stopped the punch. 'My apologies,' Josh said, teeth gritted as he held the guy's arm mid-air. 'Didn't realise you wanted to play games.'

The guy grunted, his face split in pain from the pressure but his resolve strengthened as he stared Josh in the eye.

'Arm wrestling you wanted, was it?' Josh asked. 'Why didn't you say?' He slammed the guy's arm onto the bar, the crunch of a possible broken thumb making the guy squeal, the thud rattling the glasses in their wire trays on top of the counter.

Ethan hissed in a breath. 'Ouch.'

'You lost,' Josh said steadily, unfazed. He released his hold of the man's arm. 'Twenty minutes till closing, gentlemen,' he called to guy's mates. 'And I'm no longer in the mood for games.' He picked up the glass cloth on the bar and pulled the wire tray closer to him.

Dan picked us his bottle of beer, took a swig and grinned at Ethan. 'Thank God we still have a set of guys in this town who won't take shit from donkeys.'

Ethan nodded at Josh. 'It's good to see him handle himself that way.'

'He'd take them all on, if he had to.'

'I know that. Just saying I like it when a man doesn't feel he has to until he has to.'

'Yeah.' Dan didn't condone roughness in his bar, but it sent a spark of pure joy up his spine on the occasions it happened. Nothing like a good tackle or a brush against imminent danger to make a man feel like he still had robust health and the balls to take on a troublesome situation.

'Okay,' Ethan said. 'So let's get back to this lie you sort of got yourself tangled up in.'

'If anyone's likely to figure out what I'm up to, it's Charlotte. That's what worries me.'

'You'd best go see her then. Make some appeasement and sort it out now, before it trips you up.'

'Yeah.' There wasn't time to dawdle either, things were moving too fast. He took a last swig of his beer. He could leave Josh here with the loudmouths. Ethan wouldn't go anywhere while they were around.

'Charlotte's smart, Ethan. She'll think I'm taking business out of her hands.' Which he would be, and the raw feeling of being accountable for that scoured his conscience.

'Knock knock.'

Charlotte turned. Oh, great. Hotshot. The denouement of the day.

'What do you want?' she asked tersely. She'd downed three gallons of water, felt sick after eating a bread and butter sandwich for supper, could do with a strong flat white and still hadn't managed to make a start on the peony wallpaper due to Mrs J's potato wine-fuelled interrogation.

'Got some news.'

'I'm more in need of coffee.'

'You okay?'

She checked him out. Nothing in his hands—no bottle of home-brewed cyanide. 'Come in. Everyone else has.'

Mrs J's visit had left her slightly tipsy, starving, and overly concerned about how much information Clarissa would eventually extricate about why Charlotte was in town. Her questioning hadn't been specific, more of a fact-finding mission and possibly just genuine nosiness.

'The committee have accepted my decision about the picket fence,' Daniel told her as he stepped inside. 'You can apply for shire approval.'

'*Your* decision?' She moved towards him but was pulled to a halt when the steam pad hose stretched to maximum length. She shook the pad in his direction. 'It's my fence. My decision. They can't dictate to me—'

'Whoa there, Red. Careful with the hot stuff, eh?' He nodded at the steamer. 'Why don't we switch it off for a minute? What the hell are you doing with it on at this time of night anyway?'

'Trying to get it done!'

He took the hot pad from her hand, hooked it on the rack and bent to turn the steamer off. He straightened and sniffed. 'You been drinking?'

Charlotte stifled a groan. Surely this amount of attention qualified for a public holiday? Even the twins had waved in unison as they stopped to pet Clarissa's pig. 'Does the fence have to be pink?' she asked.

'White. Just as you wanted. Aren't you going to thank me?'

'Thank you,' she said, brow furrowed, gaze to one side. 'Although I'm not sure what to think about this yet.'

'What do you mean?'

She had her word-association paint colours mentally listed, which should appease the most colour-blind of citizens, and she was on good terms with the pig who'd eaten her afternoon tea. She had a faithful dog, she'd shared blackberry and potato wines with the important women in town, and even though Clarissa hadn't exactly put out a hand of friendship, some sort of boundary had been jumped with the handshake. Not leaped, but jumped. 'For sticking your nose in my business,' she said, folding her arms and deciding on a fried egg sandwich for supper.

'Come on, Charlotte. I'm doing the best I can here. If you keep fronting up with your prickly attitude—'

'Prickly?'

'—you're going to get a big fat *no* slapped on your wishes.'

'Well as it happens, I'm forging ahead. And I'm doing it without your assistance. Your mediation skills are no longer required, so go away.'

'I'm trying to do what's right for you. And for me.'

'What do you mean, for you?'

'There are things you don't … I mean, there are a couple of things I haven't …'

'Haven't what?'

He hung his head and sighed in exasperation but Charlotte didn't know if it was because of her 'prickliness' or because of whatever it was he hadn't been able to voice out loud.

'Nothing,' he ground out. 'Bad timing. I shouldn't have come over.'

'So why did you?'

'Don't worry. I'm going.' He pinned her with a look of indignation. 'I'm just trying to do the best thing for the town and everyone in it.' He pointed at her. 'Including you!'

He stormed out of the door and thundered down the path into the night, the epitome of pissed-off male: jaw squared and chest forwards, the set of shoulders stiff and his backside looking absolutely taut and terrific.

'How'd it go?'

'You're still here?' Dan asked. 'Haven't been called home by the wife?'

Ethan's mouth moved to a slow-forming smile. 'That bad, huh?'

Dan pulled a cold beer out of the fridge behind the bar, unscrewed the lid and drank. He wiped his mouth with the back of his hand. 'Sorry, mate. Didn't mean to spark up like that.'

Ethan laughed. 'You didn't tell her about the hotel plans.'

'Didn't get a chance.'

'But you made the effort?'

'Sort of.' He winced. 'No.' God, the woman confused him with her cascading emotions. 'I can't do that until I know she won't go telling people about it—and she practically threw me out of her house so I didn't get a chance to say anything, but if news gets out about the hotel—it ought to come from me.'

'So tell them.'

'I'm figuring out how to do that.'

'You've got a hell of a lot to do before the wedding then.'

Dan allowed his smile to form and took another opportunity to ask his friend a question. 'You and Sammy. You don't bicker or anything.' He'd watched them together, loving each other, loving Lochie, but he wanted to know how it worked between them. Really worked. 'How do you do it?'

'I don't do anything. I just love her.'

How had his parents done it? Dan tumbled back to his childhood, looking for moments where the air between his parents had been less than warm. Times when they argued. None came.

'You're getting tangled in something bigger than a white lie,' Ethan said.

Wasn't he just? 'I've no doubt I'll find a way out of it.'

Ethan put his ale down and stood, grabbing his coat from the stool next to him. 'The lie?' he asked. 'Or the wedding?'

Charlotte stepped outside the front door and breathed the cooling night air. Here she was, up too late and standing alone. What a strange and unexpected day. Were the townspeople coming round to her? How had that happened?

The street lamps threw pockets of light down Main Street. A light shone from behind the curtained windows of the Tillmans' place. They must still be awake. On the other side of the street, Kookaburra's blinds were down, indicating it was closed but the lights were still on inside. Daniel must be cleaning up. He was lucky, being patient enough to wait seven months to paint one wall. He must love it here. Had settled for this type of lifestyle because he wanted it.

She walked along her veranda and looked towards the east and the hillside, then turned for the door and paused as her eye caught the outline of foliage. A plant pot sat next to one of the rocking chairs.

She bent to the plant and lifted the label on the stem, twisting it so she could read it. A wisteria. A *pink*-flowering wisteria.

She dropped the label and straightened. One more reminder the townspeople wanted her to keep the house pink. Ted? No, not Ted—he was still confined to bed for some reason.

She stared at the plant in its terracotta pot and for a second was overcome with unwanted tenderness. This little house, sitting in its orderly spot at the beginning of Main Street, could be a true success story as a business and a wonderful home for whoever ended up buying it. Why couldn't the townspeople see what was in front of them?

A glint of white caught her eye. An envelope had been tucked into the pot. She withdrew it, knocked off the potting soil clinging to its edges and opened it.

Dear Miss Simmons,

It is with a spirit of generosity, which we hope will be reciprocated, that we write to advise you of our most civil yet resolute request that you keep the weatherboard on our grand little B&B pink.

Civil?

It is our preference that all remain calm and well-mannered during the necessary but possibly difficult mediation process before us. We are aware of your strength of character and courteously request you use self-control when evaluating the situation. We feel sure that with some astute and well-meant persuasion by our chosen mediator, coupled with an attempt from yourself to put a halter on your obviously resilient nature …

'I don't believe this!'

… that a satisfactory result can be gained for all concerned.
Yours sincerely,
Swallow's Fall Community Spirit committee members, one and all.
PS We thank you kindly for offering our B&B as a suitable, yet short-term, accommodation facility for our much revered and loved patriarch, Mr Edmond Morelly. We feel sure our thanks

will find you amenable to changing your opinion and mindset regarding the colour of our B&B.

Their B&B!

Charlotte screwed the letter up and threw it onto the plant, more steam emanating from her than from the wallpaper steamer she'd been switching on and off all day.

Ted had written this—from his sick bed, no doubt. The air in his bedroom must be suffocated with his animosity. The entire committee had probably been sitting in Ted's stuffy little bedroom watching him write it. Egging him on while Grace served tea, giving him tidbits of advice: 'Tell her this' and 'Don't forget to mention that'.

Pink. Bloody pink.

One moment they appeared to be grudgingly accepting her and the next ... What game were they playing? She had a good mind to paint the weatherboard neon green and snub the pig next time she met it. Cruise up Main Street in her 4WD doing seventy kilometres an hour and hopefully run Ted down.

She cradled her head in her hands. What was this place doing to her? She was here for a purpose. To see Ethan and get herself sorted so she could return to Britain and start her life anew— without the torments and dreams. Who cared what colour the bloody house was? It wouldn't be her looking at it every day. She'd got herself involved without meaning to.

She spun around and gulped the night air. Where was the businesswoman? The one who carried lists, and wore a neat little frown and neutral colours? Not the one who'd dug out a rose-coloured skirt earlier this evening, slipping it on and teaming it with a soft white jersey top, then stood admiring herself in the mirror. *Pink.* She was even wearing pink

'You *are* getting soft.' She was planning on decorating the house and furnishing it with old-time ornaments and paintings as though it were her own. That wasn't business—it verged on being interested. Teetered on the brink of caring.

A drink was in order. A real drink. And given her frame of mind, a damned good bickering wouldn't go amiss either.

There was only one place she was certain she'd find both.

Ten

'I'm closed.'

'I know that. Do you think I'd come in here if you had customers?' Charlotte pushed through the doors and stepped inside Kookaburra's. 'Your doors aren't locked.'

'Just got rid of the last punter.' Daniel cocked his head, making no move to hide a judgemental assessment of her. 'And I had to lift him and throw him out so you can imagine my mood. What can I do for you?'

Charlotte rolled her stiffened shoulders. It was less than a minute's walk down Main Street from the B&B to the Bar & Grill but her annoyance had lessened with each step. Damn that soft moonlight and the gentle beams from the street lamps, making the street look homely and magical and softening her heart. 'I need a drink. A real drink.'

'Why?'

'This is the stubbornest town I've ever come across.'

'Yeah. You fit right in.'

Charlotte thanked God for the bickering. Something she could handle. 'I knew being in your company would return me to myself. Keep going. Tell me something awful about me.'

'Be my pleasure.'

She slid onto a bar stool and leaned her chin in the palm of her hand. 'They're getting at me again.' The misery of this problem made her head heavy in her hand. 'They put it in writing this time. It's official when it's been typed on the town's letterhead.'

'Yeah, I bet it is. So what can I get you?'

'Someone left a plant on my veranda.'

'Nice of someone, giving you flowers.'

'It's a *pink*-flowering wisteria.'

'So it's a commiseration drink you're after?' He tipped his head. 'Or just my company?'

His company? Well, she couldn't deny she'd sought him out. 'I'll have a Cosmopolitan, please.'

'That's a pretty serious drink. Can you handle it?'

'Yes.' If she could handle potato wine, she could handle a martini.

'Don't want to have to scoop you off the floor.'

'No heroics necessary. Can I have a Cosmopolitan or not?'

He didn't respond.

'Fine.' She got off the stool. 'If you don't want me here, I'll leave.'

'Okay, stop. Sit down.'

Charlotte sat, sighing her impatience out.

Daniel pulled a bottle of vodka and a bottle of Cointreau off the shelf behind him. He poured a measure of each of the spirits into a silver cocktail shaker, added cranberry juice, and squirted in the juice of a lime. He screwed the lid on the shaker and shook it. 'I think they're genuinely starting to like you,' he said.

'Or trying to kill me off with kindness.' And alcohol.

'How?' He poured some of the cocktail into a martini glass.

'They're playing good-cop, bad-cop.' She pulled the glass towards her. 'I met the pig.'

'Oh-oh. That's a sure sign. They're coming round.' He tapped his chest. 'And you've got me to thank for that. Your gorgeous, sexy mediator.'

She almost smiled. He was back to being Hotshot. She sort of respected this side of him. It was almost like having a friend. She sipped her sweet red martini. 'You haven't heard anything yet. It gets worse. Mrs J told me to call her Clarissa.'

'Why?'

'Because that's her name!'

'Is it? Man—even I didn't know that.'

'See? It's scary. Why are they doing it? Next thing you know, Ted'll be asking me to stroke his gavel.'

Daniel spurted a laugh. 'That isn't gonna happen. Not while Grace is around, anyway.'

'It's not funny.' She banged her hand on the counter. 'I'm in trouble.'

'Yeah, you are. You're coming around too. You're starting to like us.'

The truth of it nearly choked her. She swallowed the last of her drink without tasting it. 'Is that why I offered to let Grandy stay?'

'Could be.' He took the empty glass off her.

'I'll have another please. It's thirsty work, being misunderstood.'

'Your choice but don't forget I'll kick you out if you cause a scene.'

'I don't get drunk. I've proved that by drinking home-brewed wines all day long.'

'Whose wine?'

'Mrs Tam's and Clarissa's.'

'You didn't get a visit from Ray Smyth? He makes the best home brews.'

'No, who's he?'

'Ray runs the farm the other side of the hill. Top Field. He's a top guy too. Got a little thing going on with Clarissa.' He grinned.

'A little thing as in ...'

'Exactly what you're thinking, Red.'

Wow. Clarissa was doing the naughties with farmer Ray? There was hope for this town yet.

Daniel poured another Cosmopolitan from the shaker into a clean glass. This time he topped it off with a cocktail cherry.

'The sun's yellow, and the sun's always happy,' Charlotte said bringing the conversation around to what she really needed—justification of why she was feeling so upset about the possibility of being liked, and why it mattered so much if she was wrong—and wasn't liked.

'But the sun's not pink,' Daniel said.

'Flamingo pink.'

'Puke pink.'

She looked at him from beneath her eyelashes, humour penetrating the gloom. 'I knew you'd understand.'

He gave her a smug grin. 'That's my job. I'm a bar owner. I know how to make people feel better.'

'When you're not kicking them out.'

He put the drink in front of her. She took a slug and was surprised to find she'd downed most of it. They didn't make martini glasses as big as they used to. 'They're only coming around to me now because I'll be housing Grandy.'

'Not necessarily. You can be charming when you want to be.'

'Name one time I've been charming.' She'd been rude on so many occasions—perhaps she deserved their interference.

'You cook all those fancy tarts and cakes for your executioners. They usually eat them when they're around your place, attempting to persuade you to think the way they think.'

'Some persuasion.'

'I typed the letter.'

Her eyes popped open, along with her mouth. 'You too, Brutus?' She expected deceit but not of this magnitude.

He moistened his lips with his tongue. 'Ted was going to force you to keep it pink or paint it white. So I got involved—to give you a fighting chance.'

'Did you leave me the plant?'

He didn't answer.

'I don't believe it!' He must have dropped it off when he came over earlier.

'Now don't get all huffy. I gave you the plant to soften the blow of the letter. I didn't think about a pink connection. It's just a bush in a pot.'

What was it she was doing that got his back up? Why didn't he like her? She dragged her glass closer.

'Look.' He slid the glass away. 'We're in this together, whether we like it or not. I'm the facilitator between you and the town committee. We're stuck with that because the other option is to let them run things their way.'

'What's in this for you?'

'Ah. Well.' He took a breath and looked her in the eye. 'You were right, I am up to something and I don't want the committee knowing too much too soon.'

Interesting. 'What?'

He shifted his stance. 'I'm going to renovate the upstairs space and turn it into … an apartment for myself.'

'Why would you be concerned about annoying the committee over that? Are you painting it yellow?'

'I'm not concerned, I just know how things work. I told you—you've gotta stay calm, chilled, relaxed, and lead people into your plans. Weave around them a bit.'

'So you're having trouble with them too?'

'Kind of.'

'Welcome to the club.'

He studied her for long seconds, his features contemplative. 'Might be best if we join forces and show each other a little admiration.'

She pulled a face. 'We argue all the time—how are we going to get over that?'

'I'm sure if we put our minds to it we can find something complimentary to say about each other.'

Fat chance.

'I'll start, since you're suddenly shy and retiring.'

'Yeah, right. That's the new me.' She settled her chin in her hand and waited.

He put both hands on the counter and hauled in a breath. 'Charlotte, you have beautiful hair.'

She lifted both eyebrows. 'What colour is it?'

'I think you called it ... titian.'

She shook her head. It was easy to read his thoughts. 'Red' and 'ginger' sprang to his mind faster than he could thumb through the pages of a thesaurus.

'And you've got a pretty smile.'

She thinned her lips and scowled at him. 'How would you know? How many times have you seen my smile?'

'Haven't seen it since Tuesday.' He leaned on the bar, arms crossed, head bent towards her. 'And come to think of it,' he said softly, 'I've missed it. Smile for me, Charlotte.'

Her reaction fluttered inside her, like moths caught in a glass jar, their wings beating uncontrollably. Was this the moment Sammy had spoken of? He was close, and it was late and silent. If she listened hard she'd probably hear the mice scurrying behind the skirting boards. 'I can't smile,' she said, before the story in her mind moved forwards to the next part. 'I've lost my smile.' The part where he kissed her. 'I haven't smiled for months.'

'Yes, you have. You smiled outside Julia's place the day we met. You smiled at me on Tuesday when I pretended to chat you up. Your smile makes you glow.'

The lights danced in his mink-brown eyes and the moths escaped their jar and flew to her chest in a rush of exhilaration. The air stilled between them and for a moment ...

Charlotte cleared her throat. 'You're not getting smarmy on me, are you?'

He straightened. 'Not a chance. I'm just trying to make you feel better. That's my job.'

Thank God. For a moment she'd almost been tempted to kiss *him*. She leaned across the bar, grabbed the cocktail shaker and poured a third glass.

'Now it's your turn.' He turned on his smile. 'What's great about me?'

Easy. She picked up her drink. 'Your bum.'

Dan blinked. Had she said *bum* as in reference to his backside, or had she called him a bum?

'*Very* nice backside,' she said. 'It's tight.'

Man. How many times had she taken a look at his backside, and what went through her mind when she was staring at it? Sex? Did he make her think sexy thoughts? 'Tight, huh?'

She put her glass down, lifted her hands and cupped the air as though she were holding a basketball. 'Tight.' She wriggled her fingers until he all but felt the thrill of her touch.

'Rugby union training,' he told her, trying to appear nonchalant. When her pouty mouth wasn't thinned to a straight line there was enough fascination about her to make him want to kiss her. 'Lots of squats.'

'I do squats too. And I run.'

'I know, I've seen you out jogging, remember?'

'But you didn't think to compliment my bum, did you?'

'Well ...' Careful, now. What did she want? An exposition on how pert it was? 'I did take a look.'

'When?'

'When you were taking your sweatshirt off once. You have a nice bum too.' He hoped he hadn't gone too far by saying so.

'Pathetic attempt at making me feel better.' She swung off her stool and faced the doors, thrusting her bottom at him, looking over her shoulder. 'It's much tighter now I've been running.' She slapped it. It hardly wobbled.

Dan swallowed hard.

'Go on,' she said. 'Tell me what it's like.'

'I'm thinking.'

'What do you see?'

A softly rounded feminine backside, enclosed in a pink skirt, hiked up a little since she was bent forwards. The type of bottom he wouldn't mind taking a firm hold of and hauling against … 'I need a closer look.' He walked around the bar until he stood behind her behind. 'Yeah,' he said, studying it. 'It is firmer now.' It wasn't any firmer at all. It had always been a pert, sweet peach shape.

'Go ahead, slap it.' She slapped it.

He raised his eyes to the ceiling then brought his gaze back to her. Her green eyes were wide, challenging him … and a little dazed looking. A Cosmopolitan daze.

He took hold of her shoulders and returned her to the bar stool. 'I'll get you a coffee.' He went behind the bar, flicking the switch on the coffee machine.

'I can't have coffee, I'll never get to sleep.'

Dan picked up a cup and saucer. With the amount of wine she'd had and the three martinis she'd downed in the last ten minutes, chances were she'd sleep for a week.

She sat on her bar stool, wriggling the pert bottom that hardly wobbled as she settled herself. 'This is fun,' she said, smiling.

Who'd have thought it? He'd made her smile. Would she remember tomorrow, in the hung-over light of day?

'The next stage is to tell each other confidences,' she said, getting herself cosy on the stool. 'That would prove the beginning of a true camaraderie against the war council.'

'Not sure I have anything I want to tell you.' If he didn't count the hotel rooms and the research he'd done on her. Thank God he'd told her about the letter. It was some compensation for the other underhand deeds.

'Come on, come on.' She wiggled her fingers. 'Tell me something personal.'

Like how the embers of temptation in his belly flared when he looked at her mouth? 'Ah ... I'm ticklish.'

Her eyes widened. 'Where?'

'That's two secrets, we shook on one.'

'Did we?' She drew her brow. 'I don't remember shaking hands on anything.'

'Well, there's my secret. Now tell me yours.'

She took a deep breath and sighed it out long and hard. 'Okay.' She hunched her shoulders and leaned across the bar. Dan bent down to her. She turned her face until her mouth was close to his ear, her breath warm on his skin. 'I haven't had sex in ages,' she whispered.

His heartbeat flatlined.

'*Ages*,' she said again, her breath tickling his cheek. She pulled back. 'I wouldn't be surprised if I'd forgotten how to do it.'

'Right.' He cricked his neck and rotated his shoulder, the right one, which had got dislocated more times than he remembered. Best to focus on that. The agony when he'd fallen on it in a particularly vicious tackle and it popped again. The pain when it was snapped back into place. The misery of—

'I haven't had sex for so long I can't remember what noises I make.'

He slapped the bar. 'Too much information, Charlotte. Time to get you home.' He walked around the counter, turning the coffee machine off as he passed.

'So soon? What about my flat white?' She pulled back when he took hold of her arm.

'Come and get one tomorrow. You'll need it.' The hold he had on her arm wasn't tight, just firm enough to ensure she accompanied him.

'I can't go out the front,' she complained. 'I'm tipsy. I'll ruin my reputation.'

She was only just starting to get one, and if she was found stumbling in his arms she'd lose it. *In his arms*. 'We'll slip out the back then.' What noises *would* she make? Little, *do that again* moans? Or deep, *I love the way you do that* sighs?

'Don't even think about it,' he mumbled.

'What?' she asked, slipping her arm around his waist and leaning into him.

He hooked his arm around her shoulder and shunted her forwards.

'Hey, you're squishing me.'

'Too bad.'

Dan leaned his weight on his hip and strummed his fingers on the frame of the laundry door at the back of the B&B while Charlotte fiddled with the keys.

'Here,' he said, taking them off her. 'Let me, or we'll be here till sunrise.' He opened the flyscreen door. 'What is it with you and locks?'

'There are two doors, two locks.'

'I can see that.' She had enough keys on the key ring to dam one of the fast-flowing mountain creeks. 'Why so many, Charlotte?'

'I lock the dream out.'

'What dream?'

'I won't dream the dream tonight because you're not the monster.'

'You're not making any sense, sweetheart.' He got her through both doors, and closed them quietly behind them, still holding on to her arm.

'I'll be dreaming about how you look in jeans and nothing else,' she said, grinning at him.

He stared into her darkened eyes. 'Is that right?' He brushed a thick lock of titian hair from her brow. If she wasn't sleepy drunk he'd plant a smacker on that lush mouth—to shut her up and halt the flow of images in his head of her watching him walk away, of her looking at his backside. Hell—of him putting his hands on *her* backside. 'You going to remember anything about tonight when you wake up?'

'I never forget anything. I have a memory like an elephant.'

'If you say so.' He led her through the kitchen. Lucy perked up on her bed, but didn't move. Dan kept Charlotte moving down the hall ahead of him.

'You can stop right there.' She turned and put the palm of her hand on his chest and pushed with more force than he thought she had. 'This is my bedroom. Go away.'

He raised his gaze over her head and took in the room. It was quaint in its tattiness, with a neat little chest of drawers, an old-fashioned wardrobe and a thick, buff-coloured eiderdown on the bed. The curtains were open.

He removed her hand from his chest and walked around her.

'What are you doing now?' she asked, turning and stumbling over a pair of fluffy slippers on the floor.

'I'll close these curtains for you.' He looked at the window: fastened, latched and locked.

'Thanks for walking me home. You can go now. I'll lock up behind you.'

She had an issue with locks but he was stumped as to why. 'Why don't you just get into bed and go to sleep? I'll lock up behind me.'

She shook her head in firm denial. 'I'll lock up behind you.'

'Okay then.' Best not irritate a tipsy woman.

'That way I can take another look at your bum.' She giggled as she followed him out of the bedroom and down the hall.

He stopped at the kitchen door. Lucy still lay on her bed in the laundry, not perturbed by anything. 'If there's anyone creeping around outside, which there won't be—' He switched the hall light off. 'Lucy will warn you.'

She slapped into his back and pushed him away from the light switch. The light came on and she glowered at him. 'Don't switch my light off. It chases the monster.'

This was getting silly—she wasn't making any sense. Okay, she'd had one too many, but this wasn't banter. She had a real issue with something that scared her.

He took hold of her arms and pulled her close to him. 'Look at me.'

She blinked up at him, her lips parted.

'Don't be frightened, Charlotte. You're safe, okay?'

Her gaze clouded, tears formed in her eyes. 'I hate the monster. I have to get rid of him.'

He nodded. 'Alright then, let's get rid of him together. Come on.' He led her back down the hall. She stumbled beside him, soft and drowsy, so he put his arm around her waist and half carried her into her bedroom.

'Let's take your shoes off, shall we?' He wasn't about to undress her; she'd be okay sleeping in her clothes for one night.

'I'm so tired I could sleep for a week.'

'Yeah, I know. You're tired.' He pushed her gently to sit on her bed and bent to take her shoes off. The skin of her ankle was warm in his fingers. He slid his hand down over her smooth heel, pushing her shoe off, until he held the arch of her foot. He ran his hand up to her calf muscle. Soft skin, the muscle a little knotted. But he wasn't here to give her a sports massage. He pulled her other shoe off, let it fall to the floor and stood.

She lay back on the bed, the tips of her hair bouncing over the buff-coloured eiderdown in a tangle of fiery red. 'Come on.' He took her by the shoulders and moved her across the bed so he could pull the eiderdown up and over her.

She snuggled in, then wriggled, lengthening her body and reaching behind her. 'My skirt's too tight.' She undid the button, unzipped the skirt and wriggled again as she shimmied it over her hips.

Dan looked away. 'Done?' he asked as his gaze burnt a hole in the ceiling.

'Done.'

He looked back and shut his eyes quick-smart, but not before he'd caught sight of her white underwear. Man, what was he doing playing babysitter? He tugged the eiderdown from beneath her legs, pulled it up and over her body and tucked it in at her shoulders.

'Thank you,' she murmured. 'Goodnight.'

'Goodnight.'

Her eyes were scrunched closed and her lips compressed. Something *was* frightening her. He leaned over her, stroked the hair from her brow. It was wispy in his fingers. 'Go to sleep, Red. You're safe.'

'I'm safe. Thank you.'

'Okay, sweetheart.'

He stayed watching her. After few minutes her breathing evened out to the gentle rhythm of sleep. He pulled the bedroom door to but didn't close it and made his way to the kitchen. 'You hear anything, Luce, you bark, okay?' Now *he* was getting silly. What would the dog hear? There was nothing dangerous in town. Nothing that would harm Charlotte. The loudmouths from the bar would be long gone.

He made his way to the front door, bolted it top and bottom, put the brass chain into its slot and went back to the kitchen. 'I'm going out the laundry way,' he told the dog. He didn't want to be caught creeping out of her front door after midnight.

He pulled the snub on the lock so it would catch when he closed it. He couldn't bolt it though, and she had this fetish for bolts and locks. He propped the empty rubbish bin against the laundry door. If anyone tried to get in, Lucy would bark, and if he kept his bedroom window open all night, he'd hear her. He'd be down Main Street in two ticks. If anything went amiss. Which it wouldn't, so why was he getting all concerned and tender about Red?

Eleven

Bounty and beautification. Dan took both into consideration whenever he turned a property around, but that had been for profit. Kookaburra's had good bones and he was looking for more than a quick wave of a decorator's wand. He was aiming for value. Solid rejuvenation, structural and aesthetic. He'd be living in the place, after all. He'd be holding on to it for the rest of his life.

He unfolded the plans for the renovation and placed them on the bar, smoothing the creases with his hand. He had a strict and meticulous budget he knew he'd be able to stick to—and a contingency in place if he didn't. He had seven toilets and he had to make a start on the renovations now, before he backed down and lost his nerve.

'Man,' he muttered. If it wasn't only ten o'clock in the morning he'd pull a cold one out of the fridge. He still wasn't sure how he'd handle the fall-out or the repercussions but he knew he had to make his move soon, before this stupid confidence issue took over his rationale. He wasn't usually bothered about what others thought of him but the truth was, he was no better a communicator than Charlotte or he would have told the townspeople about his plans, like she had. She hadn't been frightened of any flak—although she hadn't known she'd be getting it, which smoothed salve on his battle-damaged confidence. But if he wasn't careful how he handled things now, he and Red would be bickering over business too.

He'd bought the bar at below market value the same way Charlotte would have with the B&B—there was nothing in town to keep the market buoyed. There would be though, and he wondered if perhaps Red might be able to keep her little B&B going despite the likelihood of the hotel taking most of her business. He hadn't expected the B&B to sell before his hotel was up and running so hadn't been concerned about pushing anyone out of the market. Could they get along without being business rivals? Could they be friends, even? Maybe, if she was willing to back down as much as he was. He didn't want to hurt her business because that would hurt her, not just her plans.

Shuffling one large page over another, he studied the plans showing the pitch and ceiling heights of each of the seven rooms. He looked up from the documents as the door opened, and lost all thought of square metres and plumbing as an electrical current ran down his spine.

Red.

The light from the day outside shone around her, dappled a little because he hadn't opened the blinds on the front windows yet, hadn't realised he'd unlocked the doors, come to that, or he'd have been looking through his plans in the back room not the front bar.

She peered at him, but didn't come in, maybe waiting for him to speak, but his mouth had gone dry. She'd changed from that sassy little skirt she'd shimmied over her hips and down her slim legs last night, was back in her tans and whites.

'I came to say thanks for taking me home and sorry for your trouble.' She was using her prim voice. 'It won't happen again.'

Her hair was a little damp and looked as though she'd tugged a comb through it quickly after showering. Her skin was a bit pale but that was probably due to her disgruntled frame of mind at having to apologise to him, and nothing whatsoever to do with any vulnerability she *didn't* feel when around him. Although the veil of uncertainty in her eyes clutched at his heart.

'Did you hear me? I came in to apologise.'

He smiled at her. 'Come over here and apologise.'

She glanced at the street behind her, as though expecting someone to creep up on her. 'What?' she asked, looking back at him, brow creased.

It didn't fool him. She was trying her utmost to appear her usual flippant self but it wasn't working. Not today. 'I said come over here. I want to hear that apology again.' He gave her a serious frown. 'Do you have any idea how much trouble you could have got into? Could have got *me* into? Our reputations are at stake.'

She stepped forwards as though in a rush, then stopped as the door closed behind her with a clunk. 'I'm really very sorry.' She looked over her shoulder, maybe wondering if the door had locked behind her and she was stuck with him. Alone with him.

'It's okay,' he said. 'I was joking. Just want a closer look at your bloodshot eyes.'

Her resolve fired up, the clear whites of her eyes shining against the pupils. Ready to run or fight. Dan folded the plans and tucked them beneath the bar. When had he begun to read her so well? Or had he only recently started understanding what had always been in front of him?

'I'm still joking, Charlotte. Come on over here.' He beckoned her. She took a step and stopped again. 'Right up here.'

She walked to the bar, stopped in front of him and pulled in a breath. 'I suppose there's a pay off?'

'Yeah.'

'All right then.' She wiggled her fingers at him. 'I'm ready. Give.'

Cute, but was she really ready? Dan smiled as the adrenaline inside him rose at the expectation of what was to come—the heightened moment before a fight or a tackle, when the hairs on the back of his neck stood up and his blood pumped faster.

'Sock it to me,' she said. 'Do your worst.'

She expected a verbal exercise.

'I can take it,' she said. 'Don't hold back.'

'Okay, I won't.' He leaned forwards, took hold of her under her arms, pulled her over the bar and hit her mouth with his.

Her hands slapped on the counter to steady herself and suddenly the bar was too wide for him, too much of a barrier. She was braced on it, her waist against it, her feet off the ground but she made no attempt to move from his kiss. He pressed his mouth on hers, prising her lips apart. Holy Jesus, he was kissing Red. She tilted her head, giving him a better opportunity to taste her. Firecracker Charlotte had her tongue against his, soft and gentle, but probing nonetheless, and she wouldn't get an iota of an argument about it from him. He hadn't felt sparks like this in—not ever. Electric sparks in his fingers, on his lips, running down the back of his legs.

He broke from the kiss and let her down. She slid to her side of the bar, holding onto it, but she didn't lose his gaze. Lake-green stillness in her widened eyes. What would she do now? He straightened and put both hands to the counter. What would *he* do now?

She tugged at her shirt, fiddling with the buttons as though they'd come undone. Impossible. The bar had been in the way. If he hadn't had to keep her lifted with both hands, he might have unbuttoned one or two ... or all five.

'Well,' she said, unblinking, looking as though he'd sent a volley of flaming arrows her way. 'Some pay off.'

'What's that supposed to mean?'

'I'm not sure.'

Neither was he—of anything except the current still washing through him. He made his way around the bar.

'What are you doing?'

He didn't exactly know, but it was going to involve her mouth.

A car's engine revved outside. They both looked out of the half-shuttered windows of the doors as the car sped off from the petrol station.

'He's going too fast,' she said. 'Somebody ought to stop him.' She marched to the door, away from Dan. 'It's a main thoroughfare. Six cars an hour.'

Dan moved until he stood behind her. He studied the top of her head.

'It's a drive-carefully zone,' she said. 'There are signs everywhere.' She waved a hand at Main Street. 'Do you think he didn't see them?'

Her hair had feather-light streaks of paler auburn in it. He caught the smell of it, freshly washed, and he wanted to put his fingers through it. 'I think he noticed the signs,' he said quietly. 'He ignored them.'

She looked at him over her shoulder. 'Why would he ignore them?'

Dan shook his head. 'Don't know. Maybe he was being bullish about things.'

She turned to face him. 'It's reckless,' she said, her gaze a little bewildered-looking. 'People could get hurt.'

'Yeah.' He took hold of her arms.

'He's going too fast ...'

'Yeah. But he doesn't care.' He pulled her into his chest and lowered his mouth to hers.

Charlotte caught hold of the top of his arms as his mouth got closer. No way was he going to grab her and kiss her like he was in charge. Like *he'd* made the decision. If there was any more kissing to be done, she was in on it as an equal partner. She lifted her face for his kiss as his arms came around her. Their mouths touched, lips already parted. He pressed her to him tightly, tighter still. She wound her arms around his neck. His mouth was heaven. Strong coffee heaven. And his body …

A car horn beeped and they parted. A split second and they were out of each other's arms, breaths suspended.

He stared down at her but his focus was neither sheepish nor regretful. The shine in his eyes was one she'd seen before—the day outside the beauty parlour when she laughed and caught him smiling at her, as though he'd taken his first look.

'What did I say to you last night?' she asked. 'What did I do?'

'You said you had a memory like an elephant. Looks like you meant sieve.'

Anybody would forgive her for blushing—she'd been kissed unexpectedly. What woman wouldn't feel a little heated? 'I don't know where the kiss came from, but let's forget it.'

'I think it might have been heading our way for a while, don't you?'

She shook her head. 'I don't like you in that way.' Never had. Didn't want to start now. There was no time to start liking people … men—*Daniel*.

'So why did you kiss me back?'

Why had she? And why did she want to do it again? 'That was to put you off. I was about to lift my knee to your groin.'

His studious concentration broke as he smiled. 'Oh yeah? You think you had a chance?'

'I did three years of self-defence classes. I could have you on your back in two seconds flat.' More like one class a fortnight for six months, but she'd put her all into the expertise and exercise the classes offered.

He looked at her, challenging. 'Go on then. Get me on my back.'

She took a breath. 'You asked for it.' She took up her stance, feet apart, weight evenly distributed, elbows bent, hands spread, fingers eased but ready. 'Grab me.'

'Be my pleasure.' He lunged and caught her wrists, bending her arms at the elbow and bringing her captured hands up to her chest in a hammer grip.

He was fast, but this was the reality of being attacked and the calculated responses she'd learned came rushing back. She grabbed his right wrist with her left hand. She twisted his wrist, brought her bent arm up and under his, ready to put an elbow to his face—not that she would do that, but she had to make the move to show him she could hurt him.

Mistake. He pulled from her grip, spun her around to face the door and bear hugged her from behind, his arms firmly around her, pressing hers to her sides. Dammit. She'd gone lax for a second. Lost her ground and her advantage.

'Not bad,' he said, his face close to her ear. 'Next time remember not to lose your concentration.'

She sidestepped to his right, used her knee to smash the back of his and knocked him off balance—but not enough. He righted himself quickly, lifted her by the waist and turned her so fast her feet came off the floor in the spin. When she hit the ground again she was backed against him and he was bear hugging her again.

She twisted to look at him. His eyes were full of those dangerous lights. The ones that danced over her muscles and pummelled them like heavy rain on a rooftop. But she wasn't finished yet. 'That first move was a ploy,' she told him. 'I've got you exactly where I wanted to get you.'

He cocked one eyebrow. 'Really?'

'From this position, I could flip you over like toast and land you butter-side down.'

He chuckled, low and soft. 'Now you're getting sexy with me.'

'Don't move,' she told him as he breathed in, as though ready to make his next move. She tightened her quivering muscles as best she could. During those months of self-defence classes, not once had she encountered a situation where she wanted her pretend, proposed attacker to ... pounce her. With his whole body.

He lowered his head, his cheek brushing the side of hers as he moved his mouth to her ear. 'So what's *your* next move?' he asked, his tone a murmuring, mesmerising caress.

She gasped as the sensual drawl in his voice flitted through her. 'It's tactical. It might hurt and shock you.'

'Go for it.'

He fell for her ruse and released her from his hold. Charlotte turned, grabbed the thumb on his right hand, bent it back towards his forearm, and down towards the ground.

He let out a surprised laugh, edged with pain. She gave him a second to register what had happened to him, let go of his hand, caught him around the neck and kissed him.

This was showing him. Thought she was all ice and no fire, huh? Boy, was he getting a taste now.

His arms came around her again, but this time his move had a much greater impact on her. He was strong and fluid. Her body was taut, still geared up from the shock of the events of the last few minutes. His body was warm, and softened only the way a man with self-assured control could ever have. She felt his heartbeat. A strong rhythm, unlike hers, which was knocking a hole in her chest as though her ribcage was made of flimsy cardboard.

She wasn't sure if she'd released him from the kiss or if he'd released her, but either way, their mouths were no longer touching. She looked long and deep into his eyes until she saw the flecks of gold on mink and almost fell in.

He lifted his chin, indicating the doors behind her. 'I could lock them,' he said quietly. 'My room's thirty steps away.'

Thoughts of a dozen consequences skimmed fast and furious through her mind, battling with her yearning for what he proposed. It wasn't easy knocking friends back, and the friend she never expected to have was standing in front of her, offering something she'd gone without for—well, long enough for it to be termed a long time. It wasn't easy staying detached when her heart kept melting at things like the flocked wallpaper she was becoming fond of and a pink-flowering plant she'd watered and put into the shade early this morning. Not to mention home-brewed wines, and martinis mixed by the guy she didn't care for. The guy who was making her limbs tremble. The guy who was giving her serious thoughts about getting naked next to him. The guy whose abs were undoubtedly ripped. She blinked. It was always best to check before making such a statement. She glanced down to his abdomen, and further down, to his—

'Bet I can get you to make those noises you can't remember how to make.'

Thought he'd get somewhere with that smoky voice, did he? She reached out and pinched his waist.

He buckled slightly, a grin on his face. 'Hey, that's not fair.'

'You're ticklish. I told you my memory was fail proof.'

'Well if you'd like to step out to the back room with me, I'll give you something you'll remember through summer, autumn and possibly winter.'

She bit down the laugh rising inside her; knew by the light in his eyes he was being bold, not pushy. There was nothing cocky and boyish about him now. A man stood in front of her, ready to take her to bed and have sex with her.

His gaze narrowed on her and the mesmerising flecks threw suggestive thoughts her way. 'Want to play, Charlotte? Want to know where else I'm ticklish?'

Her heartbeat rocketed to full-thrust level.

'Ten minutes, that's all it'll take.'

'Is that all you've got?'

He reached over her shoulder and locked the swing doors. He pulled the blinds fully down on the windows. The little tassels on their thin chains rattled against the wood. He manoeuvred her until her back was up against the locked and shuttered doors. 'How long would you like it to take?'

All day and then some. Right through the night to the sunrise. Maybe until she saw the wildflowers bloom. 'Twenty minutes' worth or no deal.'

'Now you're bargaining with me?' He grinned his boyish grin but when he bent and nuzzled her earlobe, it was the thrill of a strong and terrific man making her shudder in pleasure. It tingled through her body, from her earlobe to her toes.

'All right,' she said, her mouth on the soft, glossy brown hair on his head. 'Five minutes would probably do it.'

'Now you're talking.' He put his mouth on hers and kissed her as if she was a fire he had to put out. He pulled her with him as he walked backwards, his tongue probing against hers.

Her body trembled like a firework about to shoot into the sky, and her blood heated to explosion level. She was flushed all over—beneath her clothing. Too many clothes. She wore too many clothes.

'You taste sweet, Charlotte.' His mouth did something monumentally tormenting to her earlobe.

'Don't talk,' she gasped. 'There's no time.' She nudged him with her hips while she grappled with her blouse. She tore it from the waistband of her skirt and searched for the buttons at the hem, fingers shaking with anticipation.

'Let me help you.' He undid the buttons on her blouse quickly, without ripping the material. He must have had some serious practice at this. She'd got lucky. The man had skills and she was about to taste them. All of them, hopefully. Her life had been a drought for so long …

He pushed the blouse from her shoulders so it dropped to the floor behind her.

They paused again.

They were in his bedroom, or his gym room. Charlotte didn't look around but the fragrance of a masculine space blanketed her senses. Worn leather and steel from much-used gym equipment, the tang of freshly laundered linen, melon and sandalwood aftershave, deluxe coffee berries ... and racy, stimulating desire.

She'd imagined him half naked on a tractor. She hadn't imagined herself half naked in his bedroom-cum-gym while he stood fully clothed in front of her, looking down at her breasts. Her about-to-be-exposed breasts. Her bra felt too tight but that was okay because any minute now that penetrating gaze of his would laser it off.

She drew in a breath as he pulled her close and took hold of the clasp on her bra. Her breasts were against the solid warmth of his chest but she needed skin. 'Your shirt,' she said as he undid her bra.

He slid the straps down her arms and dropped her bra to one side. 'Holy Jesus, look at you.' He bent and took a nipple in his mouth, his hands firm on her waist, holding her in place.

'Daniel ...'

'What was that about my shirt?' He straightened, and held her breasts, one in each of his large, steady hands. His palms were roughened with work, physical work, bench-pressing work, outdoor wood-chopping work, but the pads on his thumbs were gentle as they swept over her, back and forth.

'Take it off.'

He smiled.

'Take it off,' she said again. 'Please.' His chest expanded as he breathed deeply. A chest covered with too much shirt. She scrabbled for the buttons and managed to undo half of them.

'Steady, you're pushing me over.'

'I'm using my attack skills on you. Don't be frightened.'

He laughed and let her undo the rest of the buttons. She laughed with him, the shock of desire mingling with the humour they'd found. Who would have thought her first *close* friend would be Hotshot? She felt overwhelmingly friendly towards him, and looking below his waist, he obviously felt inclined to friendliness himself. His comfortable fit jeans didn't look that comfortable now.

Her knees buckled when he thrust his shirt from his shoulders and shrugged it off. The man was built like a champion. Strong neck, a pitch to his heavy-duty shoulders telling her he was used to tackles and scrums. She hadn't thought about his arms or what they'd look like but they were ball-throwing, hay-bale-lifting defined. She trailed her fingers over the solid curve of his shoulder, along his fine collarbone and down to his chest. She slid the palm of her hand over healthy pectoral muscles, fanned and taut. She let her hand and her gaze drift lower.

Everything below his glorious pectorals was in proportion. The bumps of his ribcage, the toughened muscles around his waist and … She inhaled the slightest of breaths. His abdominal muscles looked like they'd been placed with precision by the goddess of nature. She touched them with her fingertips. 'You've got abs,' she murmured.

'So have you.' His thumbs skimmed her midriff.

'Mine don't look like yours.'

'I'm kinda glad about that.' He lifted her chin with his fingers, caught her gaze and bent to kiss her.

She wound her arms around his neck, loving the touch of his skin against hers. He moved with her in his arms. 'Where are we going?'

'I need to get you to the bed.'

'No time.' What she needed him to do was get his jeans off.

'I want to do this right for you.' His hands swept down her spine, captured her bottom and pulled her into him. 'Let me get you on the bed.'

'We haven't got time.' She yanked at the waistband of his jeans, undoing the stud and searching for the zipper.

He groaned. 'Take it easy or it's going to be over before it's begun.'

'Stop talking. You're talking too much.'

'Yes, ma'am.' He pushed her hands away, took hold of the hem of her skirt and slid it up over her thighs and hips. Cool air rushed over her tingling skin. He hooked his thumbs into her pants and pulled them down the length of her legs. Her knees trembled as she stepped out of them. She was nude, apart from the skirt caught around her waist—and he was still half dressed.

She pointed to his jeans. 'Take them off.'

He held her hips in his hands, his gaze sliding from the tips of her breasts to the tops of her thighs. 'Man, would you look at you?' he said softly. He looked into her eyes. 'I'd like to take my time with you.'

If he didn't take his jeans off right now, she'd show him phase two of the hammer grip manoeuvre. 'The clock's running.'

He grinned. 'So it is. I forgot.' He picked her up. She laced her legs around his waist. 'Oh, that's good, Red.'

'I haven't actually done this in a while.'

'I can tell.'

'I'm out of touch.'

He thrust his pelvis at her hips until his ... Charlotte went a little dizzy.

'Remember what this is for?' he asked.

She nodded. And all this hardware was hers.

Dan didn't waste time. Time was precious because he didn't think he'd last much longer than it appeared Charlotte would.

Man, she was wrapped around him, all legs and arms. There wasn't time to hit the mattress, the woman wanted this done fast and he was happy to oblige.

He moved with her still in his arms, her legs wrapped around his hips and the heat from between her thighs resting against the heat in his jeans. He picked up a towel from a pile of freshly laundered linen, whipped it behind Charlotte and laid it across the dark green seat of his incline bench-press—didn't want her getting cold on the shiny vinyl. He popped her bottom down on the seat, straddled the lower section of the bench, keeping her legs around him. 'Don't go anywhere.' He reached out to the chest of drawers on his right. Charlotte's fingers scraped along his back. He stretched as far as he could without letting go of the woman waiting for him and managed to grab hold of the drawer handle. She ran her nails down his sides, sending lightning forks along his spine. He yanked the drawer so hard it came out of its housing and fell to the floor.

'What are you doing?' she asked, trying to pull him back.

He bent, grabbed what he wanted from the clutter on the floor. 'Just taking the appropriate precaution for the situation.' He had to let go of her in order to stand and get his jeans off first. He prised his shoes off and shoved his jeans and his boxers down and off his legs.

Her hands few to her mouth. 'Oh, bugger—I nearly forgot!'

Dan smiled at her. 'Don't worry, Red. I've got all your interests at heart. I'll deal with the safe side of things while you concentrate on having a very, very good time.'

Fully undressed apart from the necessary, Dan let Charlotte look at him for a moment. She parted her lips and took a ragged breath. 'Oh my God.' Her gaze went all dewy as she ran it over him.

He lifted her and settled her spine against the length of the slanted backrest. 'This too fast?' he asked, half disappointed things were happening so quickly he was missing out on foreplay, but mostly desperate to get inside her warmth.

'The clock,' she said, running sharp, sweet nips with her teeth along his jaw and down his neck. 'Don't forget the clock.'

'Tick tock.' Her pelvis against his, her upper body inclined at a 45-degree angle, Dan tilted her hips and slid inside her. Her head rolled back, wisps of red and auburn hair floating across her cheekbones. He leaned into her, holding the backrest with one hand, bracing himself, his other hand at the base of her spine, keeping her against him as the rhythm of sex pulsed between them. 'Holy hell, Charlotte.'

'Don't stop.'

'Not going to.' They were going to set a record.

'Daniel,' she said, clinging to him. 'I think I'm … I'm …'

'Don't apologise.'

'I wasn't going to,' she said, her voice downy and feather light. 'I'm just warning you.'

Dan didn't need a commentary to tell him she was at the ten-metre line.

'Just like that,' she said, voice tightened now. 'Don't stop that.'

She was under the posts and the crowd in Dan's head went wild.

Goal. Try. Touch-down. The impact of her body shuddering against his and the force he was experiencing with this exceptional woman in his arms left him in no doubt about what was coming his way.

She slackened, the breathy sounds from the back of her throat turning to vocalised sighs.

He tightened his hold of her. 'I think this means it's my turn.'

'Your turn,' she repeated, her eyelids fluttering, her mouth open and her sexy lips plumped from the pressure he'd been putting on them with his kisses.

He rocked into her, cradling her, keeping her against him, and ensuring neither of them fell off the bench. She had her hands on his head, fingers spreading through his hair and over his scalp. She was warm, tight, curvy, soft and womanly. A pale, slim-limbed firecracker sprawled naked on a piece of his home gym equipment, and he wasn't going to make it to the end of the next thought.

The powerful, sexual appeal of her surged in his groin. When it came it crashed over him like a wave and drowned him. For a few short seconds he was lost in a watery heaven and didn't want to find his way back to the coastline.

They were both breathing, hard—but the air was otherwise silent.

All too soon his body recovered. His heartbeat slowed. Then his mind took over.

What had they just done and what were they going to do now? She didn't speak. He paused for a few more seconds. What did he normally do after sex? What had he done with all the other women he'd been with? He couldn't remember and didn't want to drag out any reminders of other women while he had this passionate, beautiful one in his arms. Maybe he should kiss her. He wanted to. He'd kissed her dozens of times in the last minutes but the silence between them hummed in his head. What the hell should he do? Why couldn't he think straight? It wasn't the right situation to make a joke, no matter how small a joke—unless she made one first. He put his chin onto the top of head and held her against him. He'd wait and see what she did.

Charlotte's body sang and she was trapped in the rousing chorus. Did the man have any idea how gloriously he handled ... everything? She'd never had sex so fast in her life. No man had ever made her—not that fast. His jaw was on top of her head and his arms still around her. She lifted her chin a little and nuzzled it against his shoulder. His heartbeat slowed from the pounding beat she'd felt hammering against her as he took his turn. She relaxed into the satisfying knowledge she could make a big strong guy like Daniel get seriously hot and bothered. Fast. But what to do now?

She cleared the dreaminess of the moment from her mind, and swallowed the sweetened moisture in her mouth. 'Well.'

'Well?' he asked, leaning back and looking at her as though expecting her to answer some unspoken query.

She compressed her lips to halt the smile that wanted to flourish. He looked studious. Courteous. 'Um ...' Should she thank him? Kiss him on the cheek, move from him, pick up her clothes and get dressed in a nonchalant manner? One of them ought to say something. 'How long do you think it took?'

He relaxed his shoulders. 'I hazard a guess at three minutes.'

She half expected him to keep kissing her. To give her a cuddle or something but it looked like he didn't know what to do either. 'I'd best go then.'

He moved his shoulders as though to stop her and peered at her. 'Why?'

'I'm feeling vulnerable.'

He grinned. 'I think I am too.'

Such a relief, seeing his boyish smile appear. 'You?' She poked him in his chest. 'You're a well-developed, fit and muscly man. What have you got to be vulnerable about? I'm the naked visitor in your room.'

He ran his gaze down her throat, over her breasts and back to her eyes. 'Going by the clock, we've still got two minutes.'

Hadn't they already set a record? Or perhaps hot, speedy sex was his speciality—of course it was, she'd had a taste of his expertise—and maybe he didn't do soft-and-cuddly after sex.

'Reckon we could do anything in that time?' he asked.

Another round of pulsating, earth-shattering pleasure? Charlotte blinked. 'I only came in for a coffee.'

He smiled slowly and leisurely. He ran his hand over her brow, brushing her hair from her face, and lowered his until his mouth was almost touching hers. 'Let me get you a refill.'

Twelve

Charlotte's lips had been pummelled by his kisses. He might not want to do cuddly things after sex, but boy, the man knew what to do to a woman's mouth in the midst of the action. And all other womanly parts too. His soft touches said enough. She ought not to expect romance—not at this stage, if any stage, although she had a hankering for such frivolous additions. Probably due to surprise at what they'd done.

They hadn't made it to the bed the second time either, but there was something romantically risqué about doing it on pieces of his home gym equipment and he'd shown himself to be super fit with his repetitions and sets. He'd been caring, making sure she had her turn before he took his. And after, helping her dress. Handing her her underwear with a little bow, and fastening the buttons on her blouse.

As she walked out of his bedroom and into the bar, her responses to his masterful display of strength and energy sent the percussive rhythm of a rumba to her hips.

She turned to him as she got to the locked and shuttered swing doors. 'Do you think anyone saw me come in?' She shrugged and rolled her eyes. What a stupid question. Of course they had.

'Want to go out the back way?' he asked.

She chewed on her bottom lip. 'Ouch.'

He ran his thumb over her lips. 'Sorry. Are your lips sore?'

So much kissing. She shook her head. 'It's okay, they haven't been used for much more than—'

He compressed his lips, amusement shining in his eyes.

'Talking,' she said. 'Talking.'

He nodded. 'I knew you meant that.' He took hold of her hand. 'Go out the back way. Chances are anyone who saw you come in has forgotten about looking for you going out.'

He led her back through the bar, bypassing his bedroom and into a short corridor filled with silver kegs, bar paraphernalia and plastic glass-trays. He unlocked the back door, opened it and popped his head out. 'All clear. Saunter around the corner of the alley at the B&B end and call for Lucy—make it sound as though you've been out looking for her.'

Charlotte nodded, stepped to the door, and turned. 'Best if we don't mention this to anyone.'

'I won't be saying anything.'

'Your reputation will swing upwards, mine will grind to a halt.'

He smiled. 'Not by my count.'

She stared at him, a sudden, horrible thought of him telling tales across the bar coming vividly into her mind. Her concern must have shown on her face.

'I don't kiss and tell, Charlotte.'

Of course he didn't. She relaxed. 'Well, bye then.' Was this the point where she leaned up and kissed him? Or thanked him, or something?

He took hold of her arm. 'Was that a once-only episode or can we make a sequel?'

Oh, she'd prayed to the goddess who'd planted those abs on him that he'd make a suggestion about another round but hadn't wanted to appear pushy. She'd been more forward with him over the last hour than she'd been with any man in her life. 'Part two might be interesting.'

'Tonight? Your place?' He tipped his head, indicating the bar behind him. 'I send Lily home early on a Friday and I can get Josh to take care of things after that. I'll tell him I've got business to attend to.'

'Okay, but if you change your mind, that's fine.'

'Won't be happening.'

'Let me know though, would you? So I'm not waiting for you.'

'Knowing you'll be waiting will be hurrying me right along.'

His encouragement sent a thrill through her. 'So what time?' she asked.

'It'll be late. Can I get back to you?'

'How?'

He looked around as though searching for something he'd misplaced. 'Lucy. Send her down the alley about eight o'clock. It'll be dark by then. I'll slip a note in her collar and send her right back.'

'Wouldn't it be easier to text me?'

He lifted the corner of his mouth. 'Yeah, but that's boring.'

He wanted covert and exciting? Like snipers in the bush. Or in this case, sneaky lovers in the alley. 'Okay.'

Charlotte turned to the door, and on impulse, swung back to Daniel, reached up and kissed him quickly on his cheek. She didn't look into his eyes or wait for any response, just walked out into the late morning air, hoping she didn't look as dishevelled as she felt. She'd started a clandestine affair with Hotshot and couldn't tell anyone. There was no-one to announce it to, but she wanted to run up the hillside and bellow from the depths of her lungs: 'He's got serious hardware!'

Dan sat, propped his feet on the desk in his room, crossed them at the ankle and put his hands behind his head.

Now he came to consider it, he'd been wanting to do the deed with Red since he'd first seen her, and any number of wild fantasies about the next time were crowding his head. Most importantly, she'd liked what he'd done. Everything he'd done. Although next time, he'd make sure he got her on the bed. There were things they could only do if they were on the bed.

He'd liked what she'd done too. Fast, fiery little Red with enchanting curves and fascinating skills. He sighed, long and deep, and closed his eyes. Her words—*Oh I like that*; *Don't stop that*—were embedded in his memory as much as the imprint of her skin on his.

He opened his eyes and glanced around his room. He'd never be able to use the incline bench again without thinking about being straddled over Charlotte. He might dip the bench in gold and tuck it in a corner so he could stare at it in years to come and remember every delicious thing he and Red had done on it. Naked Red. Firecracker Red. Sexy—

He took his hands from behind his head and his feet off the desk. *In years to come*? Now there was a problem. How long was it going to last? Hopefully for some time, like a few months, but it wasn't dating. He doubted Charlotte would officially date him anyway, even if he wanted things to progress that way.

There seemed to be some unspoken understanding between them to keep things quiet, which was just as well. Along with the old-fashioned values in town came expectations of traditional courtship. Casual sex wasn't spoken of and neither would it be condoned. That sort of behaviour from Charlotte—not that it was anyone's concern what her decisions were about sleeping with Dan—might bring up new concerns from the townspeople, just as they were beginning to accept her. Those couples in or around town who shared a few fun moments between the sheets were usually on the road to marriage anyway but any diversion they found while on the relationship road to permanency, they kept private. Which is what Dan and Charlotte would be doing. Privacy that was, not permanency.

He checked his watch. Nine hours until eight o'clock. It would be more like ten hours before he could get over to her place. What was he going to do for ten hours?

He kicked back and put his hands behind his head again. He ought to stop calling her Red. 'Charlotte,' he said. There'd be times when they'd be soft and slow. Times where he watched her take more than one turn before he took his. Fast and feverish was great—surely no guy anywhere, ever, had complained about a hot quickie—but what Dan wanted with Red was a follow-up of slower, more ponderous sexual physical contact. He couldn't whisper little words of encouragement in her ear by calling her Red. 'Charlotte,' he said again, and thought up a number of words of encouragement he could use. 'That's another thing you've got to remember to do,' he told himself. Tell her good things about herself. Like how she felt when she was spooned into him and he was giving her a bear hug. He'd make sure he complimented her too. Not that he'd ever thought himself an inconsiderate lover. Mostly, he put his heart and soul into behaving like the perfect gentleman, before and after. And as much as he could during. With Charlotte, he had a feeling he'd be putting in more effort than ever before. She sort of made it easy for him to show that kind of gentlemanly display. What a beautiful woman. And for the moment—all his.

'Dan!'

Shit. Dan pushed off the chair and walked to his bedroom door. He'd forgotten Josh had a key to the front doors of the bar.

'Dan!'

'Coming.' He pulled his bedroom door open and faced Josh. 'What are you doing here this early?'

'Came into town to pick up more of Grace's pickles for the craft centre.'

'Right.' The craft centre Ethan and Sammy had started housed any number of things that showcased the skills in town. Home produce, quilting and sewing stuff, woodwork, like the rocking chairs Red had bought for her veranda. Some of Sammy's local landscape artwork. Even bricklayers and rope makers got a look in. 'So what are you doing in the bar?'

'You better get into the back alley quick.'

Dan's heartbeat skipped a deadly beat. Had something happened to Charlotte? 'Why?'

'What have you been doing?' Josh asked with a frown. 'Can't you hear it?'

'What?'

'The truck, Dan.' Josh raised his voice as though talking to someone who didn't speak English. 'There's a truck in the back alley dropping off seven shower units.'

'How about tomorrow morning? Ten o'clock?'

'Let me consult my social calendar.'

Julia laughed down the phone and Charlotte smiled into the mouthpiece. 'I'm not in the market for a new me, though,' she warned.

'Oh, come one,' Julia said in exasperation. 'Let's play.'

'And I'm not getting my hair cut.' She put her fingers through the ends of her hair. 'Maybe a wash and blow dry—and I think I need a treatment.'

'Great, I have this spectacular brand of products I've been dying to try out and if you think the ends of your hair are dry, you probably need a trim.'

Charlotte sighed. 'A quarter of an inch.'

'How are your nails? What about a French manicure?'

Charlotte wiggled her fingers. How long would polish last with all the renovations she planned? 'Maybe just a manicure.'

'With polish.'

Charlotte gave in. 'A light polish, pale pink or something.' Oh, bugger, there she went again—going for pink.

'Red.'

'Yes?' Charlotte answered.

Julia laughed. 'I meant red nail polish. What did you think I meant?'

'Oh, nothing.' Red was the name Daniel had given her. When had she started to think of it as a plausible, endearing nickname and not offensive? 'Red?' she asked, as the notion of what Julia was suggesting sank in. 'Bright red? Like my front door?'

'What other kind of red is there? I've got the perfect lipstick match too. This is going to be fun.'

Charlotte was tempted. The thought of refreshing herself appealed. A little time out. Nothing whatsoever to do with the fact that she had a man—or rather she'd had a man, about an hour ago—but a bit of pampering wouldn't go amiss for either reason.

'Do me a favour, would you, Charlotte? Wear something that isn't white or beige.'

That would be tricky. She had the rose-pink skirt but it was in the wash.

'Just because you're in the country doesn't mean you have to turn into Anne of Green Gables,' Julia continued. 'Although don't get me wrong, ivory suits you. In fact ivory is *you*. You need to make sure your wedding dress is ivory, not white.'

'I haven't got to your salon yet, and already you've married me off?'

Julia laughed. 'I could arrange something. Although there's only one available guy in town who would suit you.'

'No, thanks.' Charlotte had already *had* the only available man in town and as it turned out, he'd suited her fine. But not for marriage, so she needed to put Julia off the scent. 'I've got an indigo-blue dress.'

'Have you got shoes the same colour?'

'Yes, I do.'

'Great. Bring that gear tomorrow so I can check it out. Now I've got to go, need to call this guy I know in Canberra about being a donor.'

Julia hung up before Charlotte had time to form a polite enquiry about what kind of donor.

Charlotte paused when the doorbell pealed, a beige dress in her hand. It was only gone midday—that wouldn't be Daniel, would it? She dropped the dress on top of a pile of clothing on the bed, gathered the clothing in her arms, threw them into the wardrobe and kicked a stack of shoes she'd been trying on under the bed.

The doorbell pealed again. 'Coming!' she called, tucking the hem of her mint-green strappy top into the waistband of ivory-coloured shorts. She'd showered and blow-dried her hair, giving the shoulder-length ends a kick-up curl. One mad and fulfilling hour with Daniel, one five-minute telephone call with Julia and it felt like she'd been reborn as a girly-girl with froufrou on her mind. But she was not pampering herself to please Daniel. She was not. He'd seemed more than satisfied by what she'd offered earlier this morning but the Anne of Green Gables image had stuck in her head. Pampering would boost her morale and make her feel like a real woman again. She'd been putting all her energy into worrying about the renovations and how she was going to get the townspeople on her side. No wonder she hadn't been sleeping well—she hadn't given herself even a nanosecond to consider her mental health and wellbeing. Or her happiness. In her quest for completion of the B&B, she'd forgotten about her quest for happiness. Colours were happy and she hadn't much in the way of colourful clothes, so perhaps after Julia's beauty scrutiny tomorrow she'd drive into Cooma and shop. Life was suddenly fun. Two girlfriends in town—Sammy and Julia; a few neighbours who were warming up, and a powerful man capable of more than one hot shot a day.

The doorbell pealed a third time. 'Coming!' She raced down the hall and swung the front door open, throwing her hair over her shoulders with a bounce of her head and placing a surprised but pleasant smile on her face in case it was Daniel.

'We've got a problem.'

'Oh ...' Charlotte's eyes widened as she looked at the twins on her doorstep. 'Hello.'

'Can we come in?' the twin with the purple streak in her hair asked.

'We need to discuss something,' shell tattoo said.

With Charlotte? She stepped back and opened the front door wide. 'Come in. I'll make coffee. I've got some blueberry friands too, if you're hungry.'

As they walked down the hall in front of her, Charlotte studied their backs. They wore identical dresses apart from the colour. Purple's dress was ... purple, and Shell's dress was the colour of whipped cream. Both dresses were made of lightweight summery fabric, with capped sleeves; clinched and belted at the waist and full-skirted above the knee. The epitome of a couple of hangers-on in a 1950s Elvis movie.

'Mrs J said you were smart,' Purple said as she sat at the kitchen table.

'And we need some smart advice,' Shell said, sitting next to her sister.

'Well, let's hope I can help.' Charlotte filled the electric kettle with water, switched it on and gathered mugs, spoons and a jar of granulated coffee.

'Our dad isn't well at the moment and Mum's running the store.'

Charlotte stopped herself from questioning the girls on why they weren't helping their mum run the store. It was none of her business. 'Sorry about your dad. Does he have the flu or something?'

Purple shook her head as she took a friand and plopped it onto her plate. 'He's hoping for a weird experience.'

'Out-of-this-world weird,' Shell said, handing her sister one of the forks Charlotte put onto the table.

Charlotte made the coffees while the girls ate, and then put the mugs onto the table, sitting herself opposite her two unexpected visitors. 'So what can I help you with?'

'We've got to answer this letter from the guy's lawyer.'

'And we don't want to go to prison.'

'In case they split us up.'

'They're bound to split us up—just to make the punishment worse.'

'Punishment for what?' Charlotte asked, her imagination in overdrive.

'We were attacked.'

'In Canberra.'

'Walking home after a party.'

'Oh no.' Charlotte put her mug down. 'Were either of you hurt? What happened?'

'We were lucky. There were two of us.'

'And only one of him. So we attacked him right back.' Shell stabbed her friand with her fork.

'We didn't think we'd get into trouble for it,' Purple said, sipping coffee. 'But we did. That's why we came home for a while.'

'We're lying low, but his lawyer found us.'

'Wait.' Charlotte held her hand up. 'First—' She looked from one to the other. Apart from the different-coloured dresses, the only distinction between the sisters was the purple hair streak and the small shell tattoo. 'What are your names?'

'That's Jillian,' Purple said.

'And that's Jessica,' Shell said.

That made it *so* much easier. Charlotte needed a mental reference. Jillian Shell and Jessica Purple. 'Okay, back up a bit. You were both attacked and fought him off.'

'Yeah, but Knucklehead had a mate in his car who filmed it on his phone.'

'He must have nearly peed his pants when we turned on him,' Jessica Purple said.

'He would have screamed when Jessica did the Heimlich thing on him, if he'd had breath left to scream.'

'He was on his knees by that point.'

It sounded like Knucklehead hadn't figured on his targets fighting back, which gave Charlotte cause to feel proud of the girls, and of every woman who screamed out against such hideous crimes. If only her mother had been able to defend herself. 'Good for you. Both of you.'

'Anyway,' Jillian Shell said, putting her fork onto her now empty plate. 'Turns out Knucklehead has yet another friend who has a friend who knows this guy.'

'A lawyer,' Jessica added, picking up her plate and mug and taking them to the sink. 'A lawyer who wrote to us telling us that Knucklehead was pressing charges against us for GBH.' She paused at the sink. 'Can you beat that?' The look of outrage on her face was identical to that of her sister's.

'No,' Charlotte said, 'I can't beat that.' Forsters executives were bullies, but they hadn't tried any physical manoeuvres on her. Although they'd done their best to destroy her reputation after one of their sniffer-dog clerks discovered her history and made snide comments about her in one of his interviews with a journalist.

'Dad's supposed to be finding us a lawyer,' Jillian said as she joined her sister at the sink and put her mug and plate down. 'But now he's a bit overcome with his other problems.'

'So we thought we'd ask your opinion because we figure with you being smart, you've probably got a lawyer and maybe we could use him. Or her.'

'If he or she would take us on,' Jillian added. 'Because we haven't got much money.'

Nobody in town seemed to have an excess of money, except Charlotte. Possibly Sammy and Ethan. They ran a huge spread, about two hundred acres, although she imagined they ploughed their money back into their businesses and town interests. And Daniel—Charlotte sensed Daniel had money.

'Okay.' Charlotte crossed her arms and leaned forwards. 'I have a lawyer, but he's a property and real estate lawyer, so no good for you. But what we can do is ask him to refer us to the right legal aid. That will likely be a criminal lawyer.' Charlotte didn't know, but she'd find out. 'We can probably request a court-appointed lawyer, which means it'll be free.' If it got to court. It sounded more like a dispute that wouldn't even reach the courthouse steps, but Charlotte was prepared to search out the best possible avenue for the girls to follow. The attacker had been offended and his ego bruised because the girls had bested him. His friend in the car had filmed it, which was evidence of the attack. Served Knucklehead bloody well right. Thank God the twins hadn't been seriously hurt.

'Free would be good,' Jillian said.

If it wasn't for the coloured streak, the tattoo and the attitude they usually put across, both young women could be taken for lost and bewildered. They appeared quick-witted though, but had got tangled in something bigger than they or their parents could cope with. Mrs J had sent the twins Charlotte's way and Charlotte wasn't going to let anyone down.

'I'll help you,' she said, rising from her chair and feeling pride creep up her spine at being considered one of the pack: an unusual but smart woman around town.

'Thanks very much.'

'We really appreciate it.'

Charlotte walked them to the door.

'Dan's had his delivery then,' Jessica said, as she and her sister stepped outside.

Charlotte looked down the street as a truck backed out of the alley behind Kookaburra's.

'And he's unloaded them,' Jillian said. 'So he must be keeping them.'

'Unloaded what?' Charlotte asked.

'Seven pre-built shower units. They must be to go with his seven toilets.'

'He's building an apartment in the upstairs of the bar.'

'Yes, he told me,' Charlotte said. Wasn't it supposed to be a secret?

'Big space for a single-guy apartment, don't you think?' Jillian said.

It was. Charlotte had already thought as much but who was she to question what he wanted from the upstairs area of Kookaburra's?

'We think Dan's up to something.'

'Like what?' Charlotte asked.

Jillian shrugged. 'A hotel, probably.'

'It figures,' Jessica said, nodding in agreement with her twin. 'Seven toilets for seven bathrooms.'

'Seven bathrooms for seven hotel rooms,' Jillian answered.

Charlotte smiled. So that's what he was up to.

Couldn't pop over to offer you some of my spiciest recipes, could I? Promise to bring my biggest chilli.

Charlotte held her breath as she read the note she'd pulled from Lucy's collar. It was only three o'clock; he wasn't supposed to be here for another six hours. He wasn't supposed to tuck a note into Lucy's collar for another five hours. She couldn't help the inner glow of a smile at his more than obvious code. She was pretty sure chillies didn't get that big.

'Knock knock.'

Charlotte spun to the open laundry door.

Daniel put his hand on the doorframe and leaned inside. 'Hi,' he said. He ran his gaze down her body. 'You look good enough to eat.'

'You're early.'

He stepped inside. 'Did I disturb you?'

'No.' But the moth wings were back, fluttering in her belly as though she'd been starved for a week.

He took hold of the laundry door. 'Can I close it?' More code for 'Can I come in and can we have sex?'

'If you like.' Should she tell him she knew about his hotel plans?

He closed the door and locked it. 'I haven't stopped thinking about you.' He walked across the kitchen.

Bugger his hotel. That conversation could wait. Something far more tantalising than Daniel's secret plans had her rooted to the spot. He'd only been in the house one minute, possibly less, and she was over-thinking and organising the upcoming scenario in her mind. The bed linen was clean but had she made the bed? Would they make it to the bed? Had she put the jumble of clothing away? If he picked her up and she wrapped her legs around his hips, would he trip over the shoes still on the floor?

'I was having a bit of a tidy-up,' she said as he stopped in front of her.

He tucked a strand of her hair behind her ear. 'You smell amazing.'

'Lychee body wash.'

'Yeah?' His voice caressed her the way his smile did.

'Or it could be the orange-flower shampoo I use.'

He leaned towards her, put his mouth on the side of her head and inhaled. 'Could be.' His warm breath dived through her hair to her scalp. 'I like all your fruits.'

He smelled of coffee berries and melon wedges. Together, they could make a lusty fruit cocktail; an aphrodisiac delight. They could bottle it and sell it at the craft centre.

'You're thinking too much, Charlotte.'

'You caught me off-guard.' Her voice sounded hoarse, and how did he know a hundred thoughts were tumbling in her head?

'I'd like to catch you any which way.'

Her breathing heightened and her blood pumped faster. There was no way they'd make it to the bed.

'If you'll let me,' he murmured.

'You do seem to be having an effect on me.'

'Yeah?' He wasn't kissing her hair but the way he skimmed his mouth over her head felt like a bouquet of petal kisses.

'I got your note.' She lifted it, still in her hand. 'You've got a spicy recipe for me?'

'I'd like to see what sort of effect it has on you over the next hour.' He leaned away from her. 'How are you fixed for that?'

Where to start? The lemonade effervescence in her stomach or the crackle of buttered popcorn in her chest? 'Are you giving or are we swapping?'

'We can each have a turn.' A smile hovered on his mouth. 'I'd like to taste some of your sweet pastries.'

'And what do I get?'

'My spiciest dish. With hands-on instructions on the methods and procedures I like to use to make sure it's *just so*.'

Charlotte went lightheaded as an avalanche of thoughts about the techniques he'd use and how methodical he'd be nearly swept her sideways. She waved the note at him. 'Did you bring your chilli?'

His smile turned sinful and weakened her knees. 'Never go anywhere without it.' He brought his mouth to hers. The intensity of his kiss sent the moths whooping in her stomach and drew so much strength from her upper body that for a second she thought she might swoon. He wound his arms around her, cocooning her, and deepened the kiss.

Now, she begged him silently. *Pick me up and take me now.* Her arms trembled and the note fluttered in her hand.

He took the note from her, crumpled it, let it fall to the floor and lifted her off the ground.

Thirteen

'So what do you love about being a redhead?'

Charlotte met Julia's eyes in the chrome-framed salon mirror. 'The jokes.'

Julia laughed as she put another giant Velcro roller into Charlotte's washed and trimmed hair. Apparently the rollers were to give lift. Julia promised her the hairdo would fall and settle but Charlotte had doubts about that, given the seven barrel-sized rollers already in place.

'What did your friends call you as a kid?'

Charlotte fingered the lilac nylon hairdresser's gown draping her shoulders, wondering how she could answer without making too much of a deal of it. She hadn't had friends at first because her classmates had stayed clear. Probably at their parents' requests. She remembered being called weirdo a few times as she was taken from class for one of the numerous meetings with a counsellor or psychologist. But things had got better after that first year of torture.

'Is your mother a redhead? Or your father?'

'My mother. But she died when I was six.' Charlotte couldn't say anything about her father.

'I'm sorry, that's awful.' Julia paused. 'I lost my mum when I was fourteen.'

They were silent for a few moments. Charlotte pondered Julia's loss, and wondered if Julia was pondering the same. She glanced in the mirror to the back corner of the salon. Julia's folded stroller rested against the umbrella stand.

Julia picked up another Velcro roller and wound strands of Charlotte's fine hair over it.

'I like that it's rare,' Charlotte said. 'That I'm not part of a crowd.'

Julia smiled into the mirror. 'I knew you'd find a reason to start loving yourself.'

Charlotte tensed. 'What makes you think I don't?' She'd been in the beauty parlour for nearly three hours, getting pampered, tweaked and buffed. She and Julia had built a connection but Charlotte hadn't realised her new friend had been sussing her out.

Julia shrugged. 'Takes one to know one.' She put the comb she'd used to section Charlotte's hair into the tiered trolley by her side and pushed the trolley away. 'You're nearly done. Just got to dry your hair.'

Charlotte studied her reflection. She didn't often wear her long fringe swept back, so she took a good look at her face in the mirror. Since when had her pale skin taken on such a dewy glow? She looked like she'd been standing on a hilltop catching a sunlit breeze. Julia had been right about the deep blue dress she'd made Charlotte try on and parade around in. Lagoon blue against her vanilla skin. She wiggled her fingers, the nails manicured and bright red after all, despite a multitude of excuses for not wanting polish.

'Yeah,' Julia said, catching Charlotte unawares. 'You're a redhead and you're beautiful.'

Charlotte sucked on her bottom lip, trying to hold on to the smile wanting to form. Let it go, she told herself. She looked Julia in the eye and smiled. 'I am, aren't I?'

'It's a sin,' Julia said, walking across the room and picking up a garment bag on a wooden coat hanger, 'not showing off all that riveting glamour you've got. What are you planning to wear to Grandy's birthday party next Friday?' She unzipped the garment bag, pulled it off then held the hanger high.

'Not that,' Charlotte said, staring at the silvery gown Julia held up.

'Oh yes you are.' Julia shook the hanger. The sleeveless, floor-length dress shimmered, the sparkles on the bodice lighting the silvery cloth like fireflies around a moonlit stream. 'We'll all be dressing up and I'm not letting you go in one of your white and beige ensembles.'

'I couldn't wear that.' The pull of wanting to tore into her. What would Daniel say if he saw her in that dress? Would he speak or would his thoughts be readable from his expression?

'It's vintage,' Julia said. 'Stand up.'

Charlotte stood. 'Wow.' Julia held it against Charlotte's body and turned her to the mirror. 'Wow.'

'I bought it in Canberra. Haven't worn it though. Haven't got the bust for it. Haven't got the hips either, come to that. I'm a sexy twig, you've got sexy shape.'

'It's amazing.' Charlotte held the beaded bodice against her breasts with one hand, lifted the soft fabric of the floor-length skirt with her other hand, and ruffled the material. It rustled like soft tissue paper. 'This dress has anatomy.'

Julia tipped her head to one side, her gaze questioning and the kink of a knowing smile on her mouth. 'Anyone in town given you a double-take when you smile like that?'

'Like what?'

'Like the sun just lit your world.'

Charlotte laughed, pleasure reverberating in her chest and bumping against her heart. 'I could have an affair with this dress. Just me and it, forevermore.'

'I doubt you'd be alone for long,' Julia said. 'Who are you going to show the new you off to after you leave the salon?'

Daniel. Definitely Daniel.

'It's Saturday, you should have a date for tonight.'

'No date,' Charlotte said. 'But I'm having dinner tonight at Sammy and Ethan's place.'

'Daniel's going, isn't he?'

Charlotte nodded.

'I hope he's behaving himself.'

Not in the least. She could already feel his hands on her back, unhooking the beaded bodice of this exquisite gown. Slipping it off her shoulders. Staring down at her, looking deep into her eyes for a burning second before he let the dress fall to the floor.

'How are his mediating skills?' Julia asked.

'He's got a knack for expressing himself.' Charlotte didn't remove the blooming smile on her mouth. Julia would think she was still wrapped in pleasure by the dress. 'Are you sure everyone will dress up for the party?'

'To the nines. Wait until you see what Mrs J wants me to do with her hair.'

'But am I invited?'

'Why are you so troubled with yourself, Charlotte?'

Charlotte shrugged. 'I'm not. Not really.' Could she open up and tell her new friend, her bright, city-smart friend, about the burdens she carried through the night?

Julia grinned. 'Maybe next time.' She turned and headed for the corner of the salon. 'Of course you're invited. You'll have the guest of honour at your house. Grandy will want to walk you to the Town Hall.'

Charlotte's thrill and pleasure subsided a little. Daniel wouldn't be able to take her to the dance. They weren't in a real relationship, they were embroiled—for the moment—in covert sexual encounters.

Julia wheeled a cumbersome black leather seat-cum-hairdryer contraption forwards. The type of chair a person sank into, with a huge beehive-style hairdryer on top. A metal helmet that would come down on Charlotte's head and cover her brow, maybe her eyes. Fear shock-waved through Charlotte's system, stiffening her limbs, narrowing her arteries and bringing pain to her chest.

'Let's get that hair dried and out of rollers before someone walks in. Wouldn't want your mediator to catch you looking like you're wearing a plum tart on your head.' Julia plugged the lead into a wall socket. 'I know it looks old-fashioned, but believe me, it works beautifully. Dries your hair, sets the style and doesn't—'

'Sorry, Julia but I can't sit in that.'

'Why not?'

'I'm ...' *Afraid of being confined. Scared of the dark. Terrified of small spaces.* 'Claustrophobic ... I don't like being shut in.' Trapped with nowhere to go. Backed against a wall, gripping her mother's clothing in the wardrobe. Hiding while the terrifying noise of murder happened outside the flimsy plywood door. A gagging sound from her mother. A hard hiss of breath from ... him.

'Hey, are you okay?' Julia rushed forwards and caught the dress as it tumbled from Charlotte's hands.

'I'm so sorry.'

'It's all right. Sit down.' Julia hooked the dress over her arm and pulled the chair Charlotte had been sitting in earlier to the back of Charlotte's knees.

Charlotte couldn't sit. Her muscles had stiffened, her limbs locked. 'I can't be stuck. I can't be stuck in a small space. I can't be—'

'It's all right, Charlotte. Take it easy. Breathe.'

Charlotte took hold of Julia's hand and managed a smile. 'Got a little lightheaded. Must have been sitting down for too long.'

Julia frowned. 'Are you sure?'

Charlotte nodded, desperately trying to bring herself out of the panic attack. *Count. One. Two. Three … Breathe. Count. One. Two. Three …*

The door opened behind them, the bell tinkling in its brass housing.

'Hi,' Ethan said as he stepped inside. 'You girls busy?'

Julia glanced at Charlotte, concern in her eyes, and back to Ethan. 'A woman's work is never done,' she said with a smile. 'But we can take a break. What do you need?'

'Sammy wanted me to pick up some product you've got for her.'

Charlotte took the moment and settled the terror inside. She was here in order to clear the past and get a life. No, she'd never forget and neither was she supposed to. *Face the fear without reliving it. Deal with the negative emotions in the light of reason.*

'Excuse me, Ethan,' she said, her voice still wobbly as the panic subsided.

'You're looking a bit pale, Charlotte. Are you okay?'

Charlotte nodded. 'Yes, I'm fine. I just wondered if I could have a private word with you some time.' Sometime soon. 'Whenever you get a moment.'

'Of course you can.' Ethan seemed to lapse into an unsettled frame of mind. 'And I can guess what it's about.'

Charlotte stilled.

'I've told Sammy she's meddling in something that might be bigger than she is.' He grinned, and warmth flushed on his face, as it always did when he mentioned his wife. 'It's about Dan, isn't it?'

'Daniel?' She forced herself to think. Too many cumbersome thoughts were swimming in her head. Did he know about Daniel?

'It's all this matchmaking she's been doing,' Ethan continued. 'I imagine you find it embarrassing.'

She exhaled in some relief. If Ethan or anyone else guessed half of what was happening between her and Daniel, her embarrassment would be acute. But at least her panic attack had subsided. 'Actually, it's not about—'

'But here's the thing,' Ethan continued, his eyes riveting a hole into Charlotte's. 'Dan's a decent man.' He lifted his hand. 'I'm not pushing you into anything, Sammy's doing enough of that. But Dan's a friend. A good friend, and I can tell you that if anything did ...' He looked lost for a moment. '... Happen to happen between you,' he continued, 'I can vouch for him. And I wouldn't say that if I didn't mean it.'

Julia clapped her hands. 'Oh goodie! Things are really starting to heat up in this town.'

More than she knew. 'The only thing that's heating up is your sit-in hairdryer,' Charlotte said.

Julia unplugged it. 'And your cheeks,' she said with a smirk.

The doorbell dinged and all three looked around.

'Good morning.' A tall, thin man with a glowing smile entered La Crème Parfaite. 'I'm looking for Ethan Granger. Must be you,' he said to Ethan. He hooked a thumb behind him. 'Saw the ute outside with the vet's signage. I'm Ira Maxwell.'

'Isla?' Ethan said, stepping forwards.

'Ira.'

'Aren't you supposed to be a woman?' Julia asked.

Ira paused, looking across at Julia. 'Last time I looked, I was definitely a man.' It was surreptitious but Charlotte caught him giving Julia a quick once-over; head to toe and back to head.

Julia laughed. 'I'm sorry. Our mistake.'

Ira beamed at Julia. 'Not a problem.' He bounced on his heels, his smile an umbrella of warmth.

Ethan reached out and shook Ira Maxwell's hand. 'Good to have you here. You can follow me and I'll show you the surgery and the unit where you'll be staying.'

'Sounds good.' Ira turned to Julia. 'And where do you stay?'

Julia opened her mouth and blinked but didn't appear able to speak.

Ethan cleared his throat. 'This is Julia Morelly, and this is Charlotte Simmons. Charlotte runs the B&B.'

Ira stepped towards Charlotte and held his hand out. 'You'll have to forgive me if I don't recognise you next time we meet.'

'How do you do?' Charlotte shook his hand, liking him instantly and forgetting about the plum tart image she portrayed with all the rollers in her hair.

'And Julia Morelly,' Ira said, turning to Julia. 'You must be the crème part of le parfait.'

Julia still looked like a stunned gazelle.

Ira rubbed his hands together. 'I like this town already.' He dragged his gaze from Julia to Charlotte. 'Am I staying at your B&B?'

'No.'

Ira clicked his fingers. 'That's right—I've a unit of some sort, haven't I?' He turned to Ethan. 'I knew you had accommodation for me but I half expected it to be the local hotel.'

'The unit's comfortable but it's not a hotel or anything fancy,' Julia said.

'We don't have a hotel in town,' Charlotte said.

Ethan made a slight grunting noise. Julia laughed and looked over at Ethan. He queried her with a frown.

'Yeah,' Julia said. 'Caught wind of that a couple of weeks back.'

'Right,' Ethan said. 'This makes the playground of Swallow's Fall a little more interesting than usual.'

'Sure does,' Julia said.

They were talking about Daniel and his seven shower units. The twins had been right. Daniel was going to open up Kookaburra's as a hotel. It was a brilliant idea. Why hadn't he told her? She really should have asked him yesterday but they'd ... got distracted.

'We will have a B&B up and running soon though, won't we Charlotte?' Ethan asked.

Charlotte looked at Ira and smiled. A smile communicated nothing, except pleasantry. No further embellishment about the B&B and its prospective opening day necessary.

'I helped Ethan's wife, Sammy, decorate and furnish the unit,' Julia told Ira. 'And I dare you not to be comfortable in it.'

Ira turned his attention back to Julia and bowed his head. 'If you've had a hand in the furnishing, I'm sure I'll be more than comfortable.'

Julia lowered her chin and angled her gaze away, a little startled perhaps, but definitely charmed too, given her suddenly flushed cheeks.

'I'm sure you'll be comfortable and I'm hoping you'll stay,' Ethan said. 'No point beating about the bush, I'll give it to you straight: you're needed here. My wife is pregnant and due in three weeks so I'm wanting to stay close to home, as I'm sure you can imagine.'

Ira nodded.

'It's not only the general surgery practice and the surrounding farms you'll be handling, we also run a rescue and agistment centre on our property. We've got thirty horses who've been bequeathed to us or found in neglected circumstances.'

Charlotte noticed how Ethan always referred to the practice and the home they shared on Burra Burra Lane as 'theirs' not 'his'. Sammy and Ethan were a partnership, in love and in business. So different to herself and Daniel. She had no intention of staying in Swallow's Fall but hadn't told him. He had seven toilets and shower units for an apartment she knew he wasn't building.

'Just as well I'm a horse lover then,' Ira said. 'And a trained farrier.' He looked back at Julia. 'Don't judge a man's strength by the slightness of his frame,' he told her.

'I won't,' Julia said softly, eyes popped.

'Man, you look hot.' Dan came around the bar, a takeaway coffee in his hand, as ordered by Red via a note in Lucy's collar: *Could I have a takeaway coffee please? I need the caffeine hit if I'm going to be spending the evening looking at you over the Grangers' dinner table.*

He'd understood her real meaning: We need to get together and check stories before we go to Burra Burra Lane tonight.

Charlotte skimmed her hand over the thick waves of her hair in a self-conscious manner, as though she were unaccustomed to being sexy and fascinating.

'Julia,' she said, perhaps by way of explanation.

Dan took his time checking her out. One of the benefits of having an up-close-and-personal female friend. He could look at her for as long as he wanted, without apologising for his appraisal. Her pale skin looked like polished ivory against the deep blue of her dress. She wore tiny diamonds in her ears and a big silver locket was nestled at the swell of her breasts.

She'd done something sensational with her makeup. Eyeliner or eye shadow—or something—lined her top lids. The red lipstick on her full mouth just about gave him a heart attack.

'Sexy,' he said. He took her hand in his and looked at her fingers. 'Double sexy.' He brought her hand to his lips and kissed the bright red nails on her soft-skinned hand.

'I don't look too poshed up, do I?'

Dan ran his fingers along the neckline of her dress. 'No.' Stunning though. 'You look good, Red. I'd really like to mess you up.'

'There isn't time. We have to be at Sammy's by six. We take the southbound road out of town, and turn left at the fork on All Seasons Road, yes?'

He handed her the coffee and brought the thoughts in his head about going south on Red to a halt. 'I'll drive. I can run my hand up your skirt on the way.'

'They're expecting us to go separately. And they're expecting us to be antsy with each other, remember?'

He looked deep into her eyes. 'But we're not, are we?'

'No,' she said. 'We're not.' She put a hand to his chest as he lowered his face for a kiss. 'No kissing. You'll smudge my lipstick and although you haven't opened the blinds yet, the doors aren't locked.'

He groaned, deep and low in his chest.

'I think we can appear reasonably friendly towards each other though. Since you're my mediator.'

'Whatever you say.' Right this moment he wanted to negotiate her out of her dress. He looked down at her legs. They were bare and she wore high-heeled blue shoes. 'Are your toes red-tipped too?'

'Yes,' she said softly. 'I'm fully coordinated.'

Was she now? He looked at the skirt of her dress, hoping for x-ray vision. Red underwear? Somebody tell him no, or he'd bust a gut.

'Get your mind off my lingerie, Hotshot.'

Dan tipped his head and smiled at her. She was right. There wasn't time for hanky panky—unfortunately. Josh and Lily would arrive any minute and Dan would be opening the Bar & Grill in half an hour. They had to decide on a story that would put people off the scent of their secret relationship—and this was as good a time as any to take the opportunity of putting the story of what they were doing with each other right.

He'd had an uneasy rumbling of concern inside him since he'd snuck out of her house at six thirty this morning. He hadn't intended to hit on her that early, but after his run and seeing her back bedroom light on, he'd popped into the B&B. Taking a morning shower with Charlotte had invigorated him so much he hadn't felt the need for his usual weight-training session today.

'While we're sorting out our undercover stories,' he said, 'can I ask you something? I mean, I'm not worried about this either way, don't get me wrong.'

'You're worried about us having sex and where *whatever* it is we're doing might lead.'

Sharp and smart. 'I'm not worried, Charlotte. But I don't want you thinking I'm only coming around you for sex. I mean, what I mean is, I like you too. The *person* you.' He paused. 'And the woman you. All of you. I like all of you.' And he sounded like a tongue-tied teenager. 'Do you understand what I'm having trouble saying?'

She smiled. 'Yes.'

'And is it … okay with you?'

She took hold of his fingers. 'Yes. We're having a fun time.'

They certainly were. He brushed his thumb over her knuckles.

'Why don't we look upon our situation as time out?' she suggested. 'Me from the B&B renovations and you from building your—apartment.'

Was she taking about a timeframe? A few months? He hadn't thought it would go longer than that anyway but as he'd given some consideration to their situation this morning, his composure was rattled. After all, he couldn't speak for Charlotte and he didn't know what she wanted from this; she might have expected it to lead to the whole deal: dating, making it known around town, having people look at them as though they were a couple. And if Sammy got a hold of the secretive, scandalous news, he'd be in trouble—nesting trouble. That was probably the reason his composure had been rocked. He'd got it back now, thanks to his girl. Their relationship would be fun and bargain-free. The type he liked best.

He put a finger to her chin and tilted her face his way. He gave her mouth a ghost of a kiss, aware of the lipstick issue, and smiled at her. 'This is good, yeah? We're on the same wavelength.'

She nodded. 'Makes it easier all round, doesn't it?'

Man, he was about the luckiest guy alive. He winked at her. 'I'll drive out first, you arrive about ten minutes after me.'

'Okay, see you there.'

'Hey,' he called as she opened the swing door. She looked over her shoulder, impossibly beautiful. 'Take it easy at the junction of All Seasons Road and Burra Burra Lane. The road needs resurfacing. It's been wet through spring and all this sunshine we've been getting has made the bitumen slippery.'

She smiled. 'Thanks for the tip. See you there.'

Dan watched her walk out of his bar. Once they got through this dinner, he'd pop over to the B&B. They'd spend a few minutes discussing the events of the evening, they'd no doubt laugh at how sneaky they'd been in covering their tracks. She'd try to tickle him, he'd catch her in his arms, kiss the breath out of her and they'd get down to making each other sigh. Pleasure sank through his muscles and hit bone. Luckiest man alive.

Fourteen

'Looking a bit awkward there, Hotshot,' Charlotte said under her breath.

Daniel shifted on the dining room chair, his body rippling like the folds of a warm blanket, his arm curled around little sleeping Lochie. 'Be good, would you?' he whispered. 'We're guests, remember.'

'Just making an antsy observation.'

He shot her a look. The sleeping toddler in his arms was snuggled into a dark blue baby blanket, a toy koala clutched in his plump hand, sleepy and fragrant in the crook of Hotshot's long, muscled left arm. A cute picture and one Charlotte hadn't expected would make her like Daniel any more than she already did. How could she not like him? He'd charmed his way into her life and her bed. Well, they hadn't made it to the sheets yet, but Charlotte had hopes.

'How are you getting on?' Sammy asked as she came into the room with a stack of dinner plates in her hands.

'We're fine,' they said together.

'I meant Daniel with Lochie,' Sammy said, switching her focus to her two guests, like a judge evaluating leading witnesses in a courtroom.

'He's fine,' they said together. Daniel gave her a frown and Charlotte pressed her lips firmly closed. She smiled at Sammy as Sammy put the dinner plates onto the table.

Warmth and welcome enveloped the house, which was old in parts and still under various forms of renovation but scrubbed and glossed in love nonetheless. It almost breathed with the Grangers, as though it drank every move the family made. The affection in the air surrounded Charlotte immediately when she stepped through the door—fifteen minutes after Daniel. Sammy had painted a mural of wildflowers in the hallway so it was like stepping into a spring field. Maybe she could persuade Sammy to paint a mural in the hallway of the B&B. Once she'd found the time to steam the flocked peonies off.

'Alright, then,' Ethan said as he walked into the room carrying a large plate of roast leg of lamb. The aroma of rosemary and mint settled over them in a delicious cloud of expectation.

Charlotte glanced over the laid table. Six places. 'Are you expecting other guests?'

Sammy sniggered. 'Julia and our new veterinary assistant, Ira.'

'Ah.'

'Yes, ah,' Sammy responded with a smirk. 'One dinner, four lovebirds.'

'Okay, time out.' Ethan spread his hands. 'It's obvious that my wife has a fixation with matchmaking and I'm sorry to say it's unlikely she'll back down any time soon—so it's best if we all acknowledge it now because I don't want it to ruin our evening.'

'Puh,' Sammy said, but she was grinning.

'So you think Ira has a thing for Julia?' Charlotte asked.

'Absolutely.' Sammy sat and picked up a linen napkin. She nodded at the windows behind her. 'They're out in the kitchen garden.'

The bay windows in the dining room, which had apparently once been the living room, looked out onto the gardens at the side of the house and the lawn at the front. It was twilight now, so only shadows played outside but Charlotte could imagine Sammy in this room in the daytime, looking up from her sketch pad, glancing out the window and down the driveway to the people who drove up, tooting horns in welcome, dropping off the children who worked at Ethan's stables, or who came for art lessons with Sammy.

'Julia arrived unexpectedly,' Sammy said. 'And Ira turned up within three minutes of her arrival.'

'Three minutes?'

'More like two and a half, actually. Said he'd seen her turn into the driveway while he was closing the gates in the lower paddock and thought he'd wander on over to see if we needed a hand. I invited them both for dinner.'

Daniel leaned forwards and lifted the lid off a china dish. The wafting fragrance of roast vegetables made Charlotte's stomach rumble. 'I'm starving,' Daniel said, putting the lid back on the dish. 'Why can't we eat while your two lovebirds get cosy in the garden?'

'You're always hungry,' Sammy said, picking up her glass and sipping her wine.

'Yeah but I'm extra hungry today.' Daniel gave her a grin. 'Did an additional bout of exercise this morning.'

Charlotte picked up her wine glass and studied the merlot, willing the image of herself tumbling from the hot shower to Daniel's bare chest to disappear.

'Are you all set for Grandy's arrival on Monday?' Ethan asked her. 'If there's anything you need a hand with, just let me know and I'll set Dan onto it pronto.' Ethan smiled. 'Give you both a chance to get to know each other better.'

'Now who's being the matchmaker?' Charlotte asked. If they were all going to gang up on her and Daniel about getting it together, it might be best to let their banter roll on down the street and into every shop or house in town. Let them try to figure out if anything was going to happen between the newcomer and the mediator. It was unlikely they'd grasp the truth.

'So Grandy knows about my offer?' she asked Ethan.

'Yes, he does. In fact, he had a few things to say about you.'

'Oh, like what?'

Ethan shrugged. 'Not really sure what he was talking about, but he said something about having expected you.'

'He probably meant he expected someone to buy the B&B at some stage. He hated it being empty.'

Ethan looked from his wife to Charlotte. 'How are the renovation plans going?'

'Great.'

'What have you done so far?' Sammy asked.

'I'm in the middle of taking the flocked wallpaper off.' Had been 'in the middle' of that task for over three days.

'What else?'

Charlotte sipped her wine. What had she done? Nothing. Dear God, she'd done nothing yet. 'According to Mr Charm next to me, I need to get the banister fixed on the staircase.'

'Ask Josh. I'm sure he'd do that job for you.'

Charlotte nodded at Ethan and put her glass onto the table. 'I plan to take the old lino up and sand the floorboards.' If this conversation continued they'd realise she hadn't done any work yet. That would appear odd—and *was* odd; she hadn't done even the smallest of jobs. She'd been distracted by the attentions of the man she'd been bickering with and was now sleeping with.

No—correction—the man she was having sex with. They were unlikely to spend an entire night with each other.

'Josh—again,' Ethan said. 'He's your man for those carpentry jobs.'

'That would put money in his pocket too,' Daniel said.

'At this rate he'll have enough money to leave town by the time the B&B is up and running,' Sammy said. 'Not that I want to see him go.'

'He's planning to leave town?' Charlotte asked.

'That's been the only thing on his bucket list for the last few years,' Daniel told her, angling his left arm around Lochie and wiggling his fingers. Perhaps they'd gone to sleep, along with the toddler. 'He's had an argument or something with Gemma. They're not talking.'

Sammy poured more wine into Charlotte's glass then her own. 'That'll be something to do with his mum taking over Cuddly Bear. Gemma probably feels pushed out, especially if she has to leave town with her mum.'

'I didn't realise the toy shop was up for sale,' Charlotte said.

'Gemma's mum is getting divorced and moving to the city,' Daniel told her. 'Gemma doesn't want to go and her mum doesn't want anything to do with the shop, that's why it's hardly ever open for business.'

Charlotte had only been into Cuddly Bear's once—to get a better understanding of why the townspeople thought her yellow weatherboard would interfere with the lemon and royal-blue colours of the toy shop. 'It's a shame it hasn't been trading well.' Another loss for the town.

'Josh's mother, Pat, will get it up and running again,' Ethan said. 'I'm sure of it.'

'And Josh will be run off his long legs,' Sammy said. 'Keeping the craft centre going, working for his mum in the toy shop at the weekends and for Dan in the evenings.' She looked at Charlotte with an apologetic smile. 'I don't think he'll have much time for the jobs you want done at the B&B.'

'We'll all help, somehow,' Ethan said as he stood, picked up a carving set and sliced into the meat.

Daniel drummed the fingers of his free hand on the table. 'Shouldn't someone nip out and tell the lovebirds dinner's ready?'

Sammy held up her hand. 'We wait.'

'But it's going cold,' Daniel said.

'We wait,' Charlotte said.

Dan looked at Ethan. 'What am I missing?'

'Does it matter? We're not in charge, remember?'

Daniel indicated Lochie with a nod. 'This poor little guy doesn't know what he's got in front of him. Why don't you let me put him to bed, Sammy? I can tell him a story—one about how to handle women.'

Sammy tutted. 'As if you'd know. Anyway, we have to wait until he goes well and truly under, otherwise it'll take me an hour to get him back to sleep.'

Daniel sighed. 'How am I supposed to hold him and eat?'

'I'll cut your food up for you.'

'That's overwhelmingly generous of you, Charlotte,' Daniel said. 'Wanting to make me look vulnerable in front of everyone?'

'No problem.' Charlotte couldn't hold her grin. 'Let's call it a fringe benefit to add to your not inconsiderable mediation charms.'

'Well, Miss Simmons, I'm sure by the end of the evening I'll have thought of a way to repay you.'

Charlotte bet he would. She laughed, then stopped when she caught Sammy's analytical gaze. Ethan had paused too, studying her, the carving knife stilled mid-air.

'This mediating thing is doing wonders for you both,' Sammy said.

Fortunately the door opened and everyone's attention went instantly to Julia and Ira as they stepped inside.

'Sorry to keep you all waiting,' Julia said, looking like an enchanted cat.

Ira moved to the table, nodded at everyone and held his hand out to Daniel. 'Ira Maxwell.'

Daniel lifted his free hand and shook Ira's. 'Dan Bradford, I own Kookaburra's. Good to meet you, Ira. Come in for a beer one night. On the house.'

'Thank you, Dan.' Ira sat next to Julia and picked up his napkin.

'Can we eat now?' Daniel asked.

'How's your dog?' Ira asked Charlotte as Ethan put slices of lamb onto the plates and Sammy took the lids off the hot vegetable dishes. 'Lucy, is it?'

'She's fine. How do you know Lucy?'

'She popped into the surgery this afternoon. I checked her collar to see who she was.'

Lucy had run all the way to Burra Burra Lane? Lucy got out of the B&B more times than Houdini had got out of a straitjacket but she hadn't known the dog wandered this far.

'She often joins me on the hill when I'm out running,' Daniel said.

Charlotte took a laden dinner plate from Sammy. Despite the chatting around the table and the anticipation of a wonderful meal, a barrenness settled inside her. The dog wasn't hers to keep and the kind-heartedness around the table wasn't hers to bask in. The growth of the town wasn't hers to remark on. The man next to her would become a memory. The experience of a comfortable moment with them all would be short-lived, because in a month or so, she'd be gone.

Dan glanced at Red but she didn't catch his eye. Dinner had been excellent, both helpings. The second one easier to eat because Sammy had put Lochie to bed. He flexed his shoulder slightly.

The kid had been in the crook of his arm for so long, he kind of missed him.

He glanced around the table and listened to his friends talk. Laughter and gentle ribbing had flowed all evening. But not so much from Charlotte. He didn't think she'd gone quiet because she felt out of it, and he didn't think anyone around the table had noticed she'd withdrawn a little. Especially around the time the renovation plans for the B&B had come into the conversation for a second time.

He lifted his glass and gave her another look. The fun had left her. He sensed it easily enough and wasn't perturbed by his ability to read her any more.

'That was the best cheesecake I've eaten,' Charlotte said to Sammy. 'Did your mother teach you how to bake?'

They'd been talking about the McLaughlin River and how good Sammy was getting at casting a line and catching a brown trout. The unexpectedness of Charlotte's question made Sammy pause, and Ethan too, Dan noticed.

'No,' Sammy said. 'My mother didn't teach me to cook. She's a little difficult, but as the years go by, she's getting warmer. I taught myself, but I'm not up to your standards.'

'What about you, Ethan?' Charlotte asked. 'Do you cook? Did you mother teach you how to look after yourself in the kitchen?'

Ethan smiled. 'My mother was a fantastic cook but I didn't pick up all her skills in the kitchen, no matter how much she tried to teach me.'

'Was? Your mother died.'

'Yes,' Ethan said quietly. 'A long time ago.'

Charlotte turned to Sammy. 'What about your father?'

Sammy's widened eyes showed surprise at the fast-fired question. 'He died when I was three years old.'

Charlotte took her focus to Ethan. 'And yours?'

It wasn't a cold charge in the air but a wary one. It bristled like the brush of an echidna's quills as it crept beneath the footings of a tin house. Sammy went quiet. She had her smile in place but its effervescence didn't bubble in her eyes.

Dan glanced around the table. Ira and Julia had the look of wondrous new love on their faces. Charlotte's remark hadn't affected either of them.

Ethan picked up the napkin from his lap and held it in his hand on the table. 'I hope I don't appear rude by not answering your question, Charlotte, but I don't talk about my father. Not in public.'

Now Julia's interest perked up. She looked at Ethan, a query in her eye that had nothing, so far as Dan could tell—because it wasn't there long—to do with any knowledge she might have about Ethan's response. It was more like an understanding of a situation. Something long-lived. Something not spoken of. What had Charlotte done? What was he missing?

Julia picked up the bottle of merlot and topped up her wine glass. 'You know, you should ask Charlotte to cook up some of her fancy pastries for your restaurant, Dan.'

'Good idea,' Dan answered quickly, because he didn't like the feeling of discomfort around the table that Charlotte's enquiries had produced. 'Want to do that?' he asked her with a smile, looking at her and willing her, silently, to catch his gaze.

She turned to him slowly and the sensitivity in her eyes tied his heartstrings into a knot. 'Sure,' she said, her voice soft but toneless. 'Good idea.'

Whatever it was she'd done, she was shocked by the response, the atmosphere she'd created. She looked across at Ethan and smiled. A tender smile, a smile that asked forgiveness. 'I understand,' she said. 'Maybe we'll talk about it another time.'

She turned to Ira and asked him a question about his journey from Queensland as Ethan's brow furrowed. He was still for so long Dan almost knocked his beer over on purpose to break the executioner's look on his friend's face but Sammy moved first, scraping her chair back and bumping into Ethan's shoulder.

'I'll get coffees,' she said chirpily. The shoulder bump woke Ethan from whatever darkened thoughts had been in his head. He straightened in his chair, caught hold of Sammy's hand and kissed it. She patted his shoulder lightly.

A show of love and unity. Not unusual from either of them, but there was an unspoken thread of a story in this one. What had Charlotte done to Ethan by asking about his parents?

After late-night murmurs of thanks, kisses on cheeks for the women and handshakes for the guys, Ira set off down the drive towards the unit by the surgery and Julia got into her car, waving to Dan as he escorted Charlotte to her 4WD.

Charlotte unlocked the car, threw her handbag onto the passenger seat and stood quiet for a moment, her gaze following Julia's sports car. When the taillights rounded the bend from the driveway onto Burra Burra Lane, she turned to Dan.

'I'm a bit tired tonight.'

Code for not getting together. 'Yeah, me too,' Dan said as she got into the driver's seat. 'Drive safely.' He caught the door as she was closing it. 'I'll see you tomorrow.'

She paused, staring out of the windscreen, then sighed softly. 'It's hard to keep secrets in this town, isn't it?'

Dan bent to her. She'd said that once before. 'What is it?' he asked. 'What's scaring you?' She had locks on her doors and windows. 'What are you running from?'

She looked at him, her eyes wide and vulnerable. 'Nothing. I'm trying to get somewhere.'

'Do you want to tell me?' He should have insisted on driving them both tonight. That way he could have kept her at his side. Her fear was becoming his. 'It has to do with Ethan.' Pointless making it a question, everyone had felt the undercurrent around the table after her keen questioning.

She nodded, turned it into a shake of her head. 'I don't know.'

He nudged the door open wider and hunched down, on eye level with her. 'We've got a thing going on, Charlotte.' He indicated both of them. 'You and me. Don't you think I'd listen?'

'I won't bring you into anything.'

'I'm not asking you to, I'm saying—why won't you tell me what your problem is?'

She shook her head, decisively this time. 'I made a mistake tonight, I'm sorry about it but I don't want to talk about it.'

'I know about the bad dreams you have.'

'How do you know?'

'The night before we got together, when I took you home.' She sat as though trying to hold herself together. Fragile and lost. 'And you talked about a monster.'

No response, apart from her lips compressing. Dan stood and clenched his hands to fists so he wouldn't drag her out of the vehicle and pull her against him. 'I want you to talk to me. Really talk to me.' She was going to drive off alone and she didn't want to see him later. She'd be in the house on her own with some nightmare hovering in her mind, making her sleepless and restless while he sat in his back room in the bar, awake and listening—in case she changed her mind and knocked on his door. In case Lucy barked. In case she needed him.

She shook her head and stared ahead, hardly breathing.

Stubborn as all hell. Dan took hold of the door. 'Drive carefully. I'll be right behind you.'

She nodded, pulled the door closed, fired the engine, hit the headlights and drove down the driveway, leaving him with worry in his gut, tension in his shoulders and a heart full of something he hadn't sampled before. Helplessness.

Charlotte parked the 4WD in the carport behind the B&B, got out, beeped the lock and walked swiftly to the laundry door. She didn't look as Daniel drove his car down Main Street, halted when he reached her house, then turned into the alley at the back of the bar.

Her hands trembled as she took the keys from her bag. Lucy padded forwards from her bed and waited patiently as Charlotte struggled with the lock on the flyscreen. Stupid lock had jammed. Like her brain tonight.

Had Ethan known about Charlotte's mother and what happened to her? Had he known about Charlotte? If he had, and if he was her half-brother, he'd ignored her. He hadn't come forwards to claim her from the foster care the authorities placed her in.

Now she'd never know. She could no longer ask anything of anybody. She'd spoken out of turn and too soon. Couldn't swallow her words or take back her imprudent outburst. She wouldn't be in Swallow's Fall long enough for the impact of lost friendship to hurt, but she had a feeling the void would follow her for the rest of her life.

Whether she deserved the desolate feeling inside her or not, tonight, just tonight, she wanted to be wrapped in the comfort and safety of Daniel's arms. All night.

Through the dream and into the daylight.

Fifteen

Dan leaned his elbows on the bar and re-read the article from the British newspaper. This one had been written about a month before Charlotte had won over the big execs, and was giving him cause for real concern.

> Forsters have hinted a satisfactory conclusion is imminent. Their lawyers, McStone & Hulmes, say the information they have discovered on Miss Simmons was found, not by a deliberate act to seek the derogatory, but by chance.
>
> Although they have not put out any statement regarding the information, this reporter did discover the veiled—and to this reporter's mind, threatening—reasons why they are attempting to force Miss Simmons' hand in this manner.

Dan's unease heightened. They'd certainly thrown the works at Charlotte and he understood now that she hadn't won anything: she'd lost her home and a part of herself, and had been left with nothing but a healthy bank balance. A glamorous yacht without a mooring. Maybe that's why she was so tense all the time and hadn't let anyone know how wealthy she was. The reporter who'd written these articles appeared to be a journalist with a conscience, but Dan couldn't imagine what the big execs might have found on Charlotte and the article wasn't giving him any answers.

Miss Simmons' history should remain her own. It is neither a threat to Forsters nor any business ventures she is currently undertaking or intends to undertake. It is merely a reminder to society that we play hard, but not always by the rules.

Some might say this attempt to undermine Miss Simmons is the big boys' way of manipulating a situation by bullying but this is business and business is a confidence game. Regardless of Miss Simmons' personal and surely private past, this is a typical business-playground scenario—but one that might hold everlasting or at least long-term consequences for the small kid on the block.

The scenario was scaring the daylight out of his morning. More than losing her home and lifestyle, the article suggested she'd lost her childhood. This is where the monster came in and the nightmares. But what the hell did it have to do with Ethan? She'd been in shock when she'd first met Ethan on the walkway, and Dan had turned on her, thinking she was after his friend. Man, his blow must have been a tough one for her to take. He'd goaded her, pushed her. She'd dealt with it, hadn't backed down. A witty comment, a couple of self-defence moves and a bear hug later and she was in his arms. Making love and laughing. Sighing with him.

Dan's heart seemed to stop beating as the woman who'd given him such concern he'd hardly noticed night turning to day came through the doors of the bar, a smile on her face and a bounce in her step. 'Got your coffee machine up and running?' she asked, hand on the opened door.

Dan nodded, closed the lid on his laptop and slid it beneath the bar.

She breezed in, the door clunking closed behind her. 'Good. I could do with one. Got a lot to do today.'

Whatever had happened last night, she wasn't going to talk about it. Looked like she wasn't even willing to remember it. 'You had a good night's sleep?' he asked.

'Mmm. Didn't you?' She grinned. 'Or did you miss the sex?'

Pieces of information from the article he'd read filtered into his mind fast. Jesus. That was it: the bad thing in her past. Someone had hurt her. Is that why she'd taken self-defence classes? Alone and looking after herself, and doing a damned good job, after someone had ruined something in her life. Nobody—*nobody*—messed with his friends. Some guy, probably. He couldn't bear the thought she'd been abused. He'd had this woman in his arms and some guy … He didn't want to visualise it, couldn't see how any man could have—

He took a breath deep enough to push the wrath away and settle the shock to simmer level. If the man was still around, Dan resolved to find him. And if the man had put physical pressure on his girl, in any way, Dan would want to kill him. And might even do it.

When the blood came back to his head she was halfway across the bar, heading for the staircase at the far end, inside the family restaurant area.

'Where are you going?' he asked.

'Why don't you show me your apartment space and I'll tell you my new plans for the B&B.'

He'd renovated the staircase simply because it sat in full view of customers, but he'd put a locked gate across it so that kids and nosey punters couldn't wander up the stairs.

'New plans?' he asked, joining her and unlocking the gate with a key he kept hidden in a small wall cupboard.

'Yes.'

He led her up the carpeted stairs, hand on the polished wooden rail, their footsteps almost silent on the thick navy-blue carpet with plaid-patterned edges. 'When are you planning on opening up for business?' he asked.

'Haven't got that far in my plans.'

'Like I said, I might be bringing in a couple of guys soon who could be your first customers.'

'Who?'

'Work guys. Plumbers and electricians.' At the top of the stairs, he let her go before him. She made her way through the fallen partitions, weaving between plaster boards until she got to one of the windows.

Dan followed, and pulled her into his arms, moving them away from the window into a darker space beneath the rafters. It was good to have her next to him again. He'd missed her last night, no question and no argument, and he wasn't referring to sex. He'd missed Charlotte, the person. 'Can I say how good it is to be cuddling with you again? Thought I'd messed up last night.'

'Did you really think I fancied Ethan?'

Dan's hold on her loosened a little. Was she going to open up? 'You're a sharp shooter,' he said, with a grin. 'Where'd you learn that?'

She smiled and slipped from his arms. 'From Mrs J.' She laughed, spreading her arms and twirling around in the box-shaped area that would become bedroom number three. 'This is going to be a huge apartment once you've knocked the rest of the original bedroom walls down.'

'I like space.'

'Three hundred and fifty square metres' worth?'

A yearning to spill the truth rose in his chest and thickened his throat. He closed his eyes for a moment but all he saw was the B&B at the beginning of Main Street with a For Sale sign on the front lawn and a rush of customers coming in and out of Kookaburra's.

'By the way, the twins spoke to me about their predicament.'

Dan opened his eyes.

'I presume you know about it?' she asked.

'Yeah.' He nodded. He'd think about how to tell her what he was up to with the hotel once he'd given consideration to how she could keep her B&B running. Then he'd tell her the truth, followed quickly by a plan. So fast she wouldn't have a chance to look shocked and hurt and he wouldn't need to feel like Brutus. 'I think Ted's sorting out a lawyer for them.' He paused. 'Guess he might not have got around to that since he's been unwell.'

'I've got the names of two lawyers. I'll give them to you as well as to the twins. So you can keep an eye on things.' She frowned. 'What *is* wrong with Ted?'

Daniel shrugged. 'It's funny but it's not.' He paused for a second time. She was giving him the names of the lawyers for what reason? In case she forgot or something?

'Ted?' she asked, eyebrows rising.

Dan gave her the rundown on the space study and the aliens. 'It's relatively harmless, but we need to keep an eye on him,' he said, smiling broadly. 'It's good to see you smile like that, Charlotte.' She turned and sauntered to another window, leaving his arms aching with the want of holding her again.

'Has anyone considered it might be because Ted is bored?' she asked, drawing a box shape in the grime on the window. 'He runs the store and looks after the gavel but he must be bored stupid. He's got brains. Look at that letter he wrote me.' She added an inverted V-shape to the top of the box.

'I wrote the letter,' Dan reminded her.

'You typed it. Ted dictated it. The wording is all Ted.'

'True—but I put in more pleases and thank yous than he dictated.'

'There's quite a bit the people in town could do to help themselves, you know.'

'Oh?'

'I've been thinking …' She drew four squares and a rectangle inside the box with the V-shaped roof. A house. She scrubbed it out with the palm of her hand, turned to him and wiped her hands together, cleaning them of about eighty years' worth of dirt. 'I've got a lot of information on a number of the committee members now. Like Mrs J. How she lost her husband. Lily and her knuckling down together and making do. It must be hard on them. And Mrs Tam's all alone.'

'Yeah, but they're doing okay.'

'They could do better though. What this town needs is more tourists. They also need more recreation and community entertainments. The type of things that bind them but also allow them to grow in their own way. In their own time.'

'Well, we're certainly doing a lot of talking this morning.' He crossed the space but stopped before he reached her. Didn't want her walking away from him again if he tried to take her in his arms—that would be one rejection too many in a twelve-hour period. 'You been thinking all night, Red?' It was good to use the nickname again; it built a walkway over the gap between them, taking them back to yesterday, before the dinner party.

She shrugged. 'I'm just saying it needs to be their idea.'

'You should put it to them.'

'They wouldn't listen to me.' She raised her face to him. 'I was wondering if you'd like to take Lucy.'

'What?'

'She follows you everywhere.'

'She's yours, Charlotte. You found her. You rescued her, why would you want to give her away?'

'She's a community soul. I've seen her pop in and out of every shop in Main Street.'

'So keep her and just let her roam a bit.'

Charlotte shook her head. 'I've got a lot to do with the B&B and don't think I can give her the attention she needs. You take her.'

'No.' He moved towards her. This friendly little chat was scaring him and he had to get his hands on her.

'Oh, and one last thing,' she said, holding her hand out, palm up, to stop him. 'I've decided to keep the weatherboard pink.'

Dan stilled.

'You can tell the committee.'

'You're backing down?'

She shook her head. 'No, I see sense in it. Why spoil what they already have? They want it pink, they can have it pink.'

Dan sank his weight on his hip. 'What's happened?'

'I'm seeing sense.'

'Let me talk to them about the weatherboard. I'll bring them around to yellow. I'll even help you paint it.'

She smiled. 'Turn it to a mushroom colour, then hit them with honeyeater yellow.'

'It took me seven months to go from frog-green to navy. I reckon it'll take the same timeframe to go from pink to yellow.'

'That would keep us busy.'

She gave him her cheeky smile. The impish one he found impossible to resist. Yeah, he could take seven months with Red. He could probably take a lot longer.

'How are you getting on with the committee?' she asked. 'With your apartment plans?'

'I'm working on a way through.'

She turned to the window. 'Word around town is you took delivery of seven toilets and seven showers.'

'Yeah.' He put his arms around her, bear hugging her. 'It was an error in the order.' She didn't move from him. He kissed the side of her head. 'My handwriting, I suppose. They mistook a one for a seven.' God, it was good to hold her.

Charlotte wished she had the courage to turn and face him. To look into his eyes as he spoke so she could gauge how she really felt about him lying to her. She clamped her lips together to stop herself asking if he was planning to send six toilets and shower units back. As she was also lying to him by keeping quiet about why she was here and not telling him that she'd never intended to stay, there was nothing she could do about it.

'I need to ask you a favour, Daniel.'

'Anything.'

'Don't talk to Ethan about what happened last night. Please.'

He didn't move or speak for a few moments. She almost felt the pounding of his thoughts as he inhaled and exhaled slowly.

'Why not?'

'I made a mistake. One I can't fix or take back.' She had to let him know that much, but had no intention of following through with her questioning of Ethan now, and didn't want to put another lie onto her already full agenda. In the loneliest hours of the night, those just before dawn, she'd made her decision. Leave town. O'Donnell would remain in the rivers of her history; the fear of him would always be with her, bumping its way over the many boulders of her memories. But her past was hers and she didn't have any right to thrust it on others. 'Can you promise me you won't talk to Ethan and that you won't ask me any more questions about it?'

'That last favour is going to be hard.' He rocked her in his arms. 'You're hurting for some reason, and I don't like any friend to be hurt.' He brushed a finger over her cheek. 'Can't I help you out?'

She shook her head. 'Not with this.' She turned into his embrace and enjoyed the heat of his body as it filtered through her. 'You could help me with the staircase banister though. Or maybe the work guys you're going to hire could take on some extra work for me at the B&B.'

'Thought you were going to do a lot of the jobs yourself.'

'Changed my mind.' She showed him her bright-red nails. 'Might chip one.'

'So get Julia to do them again.'

'I think she'll busy with Ira for a while, don't you?'

'What's going on, Charlotte?'

How could she tell him? His plans would take business from the B&B, which worried her because the little house ought to be given a chance. Its history was important. *Why, it's practically heritage ranking, is our B&B*, Ted had said. The town was growing but progress would be suitably sedate. Daniel wouldn't fill his hotel with a rush of guests, not at first, and neither would the B&B, even without the hotel. A quiet town like Swallow's Fall didn't suddenly erupt onto the tourist scene, no matter how good Ted's photos were on the internet. It would take acceptance, patience and care from everyone to see the town prosper.

Daniel's plans would be readily accepted, she felt sure of it. They'd need some persuasion, but he'd encourage them gently, all the time caring for his town and everyone in it. He had the love of his townspeople. She wondered if he realised how big a deal that was.

'Will you help with the banister?' she asked.

'Of course I will. Whatever you want.'

He'd open the hotel all day. He'd serve breakfast, morning tea, lunch, afternoon tea and dinner. He'd be mad not to and there wasn't a fool's bone in his body. She leaned against him and let him put his arms around her. The B&B had one year in it, maximum, while he built the hotel rooms. She couldn't see a way it could keep going after that, let alone prosper. Which created one more concern she'd be taking with her when she left: guilt. She'd spoken to a realtor this morning and was waiting on his proposal for the sale coming to her over email. She'd sign the papers for a 'going concern' called the House at the Bottom of the Hill, pay for the advertising and sell the B&B under false pretences.

She put her arms around Daniel's waist and snuggled into the warmth of him.

'That's good,' he murmured. 'Have I got the real you back now?'

There wasn't a real Charlotte, just a lost and bereft homeless woman but how comforting it would be to hold the imprint of Daniel against her in her mind for those quiet, restless nights when the dream came after she left Swallow's Fall. Or for the moments when the void of loneliness couldn't be shaken and all she had was the memory of being with tall, muscular Hotshot, and how it felt being up against him. Being sheltered by the strength in his shoulders and delighted by the charming smile on his mouth.

'Are you alright?' he asked.

'Yes.' She tilted her face to his and ran her gaze over the planes of his face. She needed memories. Good memories, like the feel of his skin on hers, his heartbeat thumping along with hers, his body, so long and toughened with muscle, entwined with hers. The kisses from his mouth. The smiles. She'd remember his smiles forever. Each of them. The charming one she'd thought so smarmy. The boyish one she'd fallen for, and the smile of the man. The smile that sent dancing lights shivering over her body.

'Can we?' she whispered.

'Thought you'd never ask.'

He led her down the stairs, holding her hand. No need for speech. He knew what she was asking for and thankfully, he wanted it too.

He walked her into his bedroom, closed the door and turned the lock.

'What did I do?' Dan asked, propped on one elbow on his bed, looking at how Charlotte's hair spread like a display of red silk on his pillow. Yeah, they'd made it to the bed. Best place as far as he was concerned. He liked the length of her next to him.

'You want an explanation?'

No need for one. The images in his head were pleasing enough, but this time had been tender. 'Those little noises you made.' He moistened his mouth, smiled down at her. 'They weren't the usual ones, and I like them. Do you think you could do them again, next time?'

'Possibly.'

'You're teasing me.' He pulled the sheet up and over them, tucking it under her arms in case she felt chilled now the heat of their soft passion was over. 'Was it something I did differently?' he asked. 'To bring those sighs and cries out of you?'

'What was different?' she asked, gaze averted.

'Well … you weren't just sighing, you were holding onto me in a different way. You were like a purring kitten.' It sounded silly, but that's what it had been like for him.

'I was feeling softish, that's all.'

'It was romantic.'

She moved her head on the pillow to look at him, eyes widened.

'Yeah, I know,' he said. 'You didn't expect me to use the R word.' He hadn't expected to feel it in such a way let alone speak about it, but she'd done more than hold onto him, she'd sort of … given herself. He couldn't explain it, but halfway through he'd yielded to the newness and wonder and they'd connected. Not just physically.

She swallowed. 'I frightened you.'

'No.' He stroked her hair with his fingers. 'Nothing frightens me.' That wasn't quite true. In fact it was an outright lie, because she'd been frightening the skin off his bones all morning.

'Sometimes I like being charmed.' She grinned, although it looked forced. 'Let's not get carried away, Daniel. Just because you now know the different types of moans and sighs I make, it doesn't make us a couple or anything. We're not dating.'

He nodded, accepting the reality and relieved they were on the same wavelength. Presumably it was relief, he couldn't rightly place the sensation swimming through him. 'They weren't moans, they were tender little sounds. But you're right. We're too sneaky for dating.' So why was he pushing her to accept they'd had a romantic moment?

'We are sneaky, aren't we?'

He shifted her in his arms, turning her so her back was to his chest, her body spooned into his. 'I admit I threw a few jibes your way to begin with. But not now we're together. You don't think I'm still being a charm-boy hotshot, do you?'

'We're not together,' she reminded him. 'We have sex.'

He stared over her head, at the space he called his home. 'And that's enough for you?'

'Don't go thinking my softish spells mean anything. I'm a girl.'

'That explains very little to me.'

'Sometimes we naturally feel the need for a romantic moment.'

'But that's the thing, Charlotte, I had a romantic moment too. What was it I did?'

'Why? Do you want to repeat it?'

'Are you getting prickly with me, for asking?'

'Sorry.' She turned, rolling into his embrace and burying her face in his shoulder.

'Are you pissed off? I was just asking a question, didn't mean it to turn into an argument.'

'We're not a couple so we can't have an argument,' she said, her voice muffled.

'So what are we?' He tightened his embrace, almost fearful of her answer. He'd settled for seven months or longer; if she was going to end it sooner, he needed to know.

'We're friends,' she said. 'Who have sex. Regularly. And like it.'

He repeated her clipped response in his head. They were friends—that was good. They were having sex regularly—that was amazing. And they both liked it. And they'd shared a romantic moment. They were having a … nice time. She didn't want anything more, but it felt like he'd hurt her.

'I'd like to keep our nice time going for the seven months we discussed earlier. How would you feel about that?'

'Let's just wait and see, shall we?'

'Okay.' The timeframe wasn't flashing in neon lights above the bar, but if they were having such a nice time together, why end it? Why not wait until it fizzled out naturally? Perhaps she needed more romantic moments. He liked this gentle side of her, this womanly, wanting-a-cuddle side of her. He liked protecting her. He liked those soft sighs and cries and he wanted more of them. Wanted to give her what she wanted so he got what he wanted: more cries and sighs from sexy Red.

'It's just an instinctual need for cuddles. It's normal,' she added.

He kissed her head. Okay then. The cries were sexy, the sighs were romantic. And she was probably right. They ought not to push anything, just enjoy what they had.

He curled his arms around her tighter still. 'You know what, Red? I think we're getting good at this.'

'Yeah,' she murmured, but she didn't sound convinced.

Sixteen

'It's like the light bulb has blown in Ted's head,' Mrs Tam said, sipping the latte Dan had made her.

'More like the fuse,' Mrs J answered, a dainty espresso cup in her reddened farmer's hand.

Dan had trouble thinking of her as Clarissa, but hey, it kinda suited her. He nodded at Ruby pig, stuck on her lead and tied to the leg of Clarissa's bar stool. 'Would Ruby like an apple?'

'Thank you, Daniel, she would.'

Dan picked up the sliced apple he'd been about to eat before his unexpected visitors arrived, leaned over the bar and dropped the pieces on the floor for Ruby. Kookaburra's was a dog-friendly pub, so long as the dogs were on a lead and not in the family restaurant area, but the punters loved it when the pig visited. He might be able to make use of this in the future. He looked across to the alcove where he'd placed the monstrous twisted-metal Kookaburra sculpture he'd inherited from the previous owner. Maybe he could have an animal portrait section up there. Ruby, Lucy, one or two of Ethan's horses.

'So what's the news this bright Monday morning?' he asked the ladies. They'd never come in for coffee before and it was good to open the doors for them. Might get them used to the doors being open all day, every day.

'Grandy's due back this afternoon. Said he wants to take a look at Charlotte before he makes any decisions about staying at the B&B. Said to tell you if he doesn't like the look of things, he'll put a camp bed in your apartment.'

'Did he now?' Dan asked. News travelled fast—and far. How the hell did Grandy know about his apartment?

'Have you thought it through properly, Daniel?' Mrs Tam asked. 'It's ever such a big space. How many bedrooms are you planning?'

'Um … four. Plus a study. And a gym.'

'Enough for a family,' Mrs J said. 'Not thinking of selling up, are you?'

'Oh Daniel, please don't sell up.'

'I'm not selling.'

'Is business that bad for you too?'

'Mrs J, swear to God.' Dan slapped a hand on his chest. 'I'm not selling.'

'Good. So why an apartment that big?'

'I'm thinking of the future.' The little white ones were coming faster and easier, but he'd had some practice recently.

'Perhaps he's thinking of a family of his own,' Mrs Tam said, patting her bun.

Mrs J fixed her eyes on him. 'Got someone in mind?'

None of her business. And the best reason for him and Charlotte to stay under the radar. 'Not yet, but I promise you— once I decide to tie the knot, you two will be the first to know.' He didn't make promises he didn't keep and as he would never have the opportunity to call on these old dears to discuss his matrimonial affairs, the promise was sincere and secure. 'I'll even ask for your blessing.'

'I see Charlotte coming in for a lot of coffees.'

'Yeah, she's got an addiction. How's Ted?' Another skillset he'd polished—putting people off the trail of any gossip they thought they detected.

Mrs Tam shook her head. 'Worrying. He's scouring the space and alien web pages again.'

'It's the problem with the girls that's getting to him, not to mention how hard it is to make a fair living these days,' Mrs J said. 'But according to Grace he's not doing too badly and the twins are getting themselves organised. Getting a lawyer.'

'And they're helping Grace run the store while Ted takes a bit of time off. Jessica is handling the till and Jillian is doing a stocktake.'

Dan had a healthy suspicion the twins' sudden enthusiasm for work was due to Charlotte's assistance.

'Ted's bored,' he said. 'He needs something to get his teeth into. Something to fire him up and spark his enthusiasm for life again.'

Mrs Tam kinked an eyebrow. 'Not sure if Grace would want him fired up.'

'What Dan means is Ted needs to be kept occupied.' Mrs J peered at Dan. 'Isn't that right?'

Dan nodded. He hadn't seen Ted since he'd helped him write the letter to Charlotte and as far as he knew, Ted hadn't anything more than *Hay & Grain Weekly* to keep him distracted from either the problem with his daughters or his hoped-for involvement with aliens. Charlotte had said the townspeople needed hobbies and pastimes and Dan agreed with her, but a man like Ted needed more important distractions than the fortnightly visit from the mobile library.

'Ted's got some buddies at the shire, hasn't he?' he asked the ladies.

Mrs J nodded. 'He got chatty with a few of them when we were going through the rigmarole of getting approval for the renovation of the Town Hall. He used to play some online hangman game with them.'

'He's very good online,' Mrs Tam said. 'Surfboards the net everywhere.'

And Dan didn't want Ted wandering the internet ocean looking for Charlotte. He slapped his hands together.

'Tell you what, ladies. Why don't we do something to help Grace out? How about I offer up a suggestion to Ted that will keep his smart brain chugging like a steam roller?'

'Anything to keep him out of space,' said Mrs J.

'Like what?' Mrs Tam asked with a concerned look in her eyes.

'Leave it to me,' Dan said. 'I've got an idea.' There were varied means of support and goodwill in town. All Dan had to do was connect them, and Ted was the link.

'How do you do? It's so nice to meet you.' Charlotte stepped onto the veranda, hand out in welcome, although her fingers were shaking slightly. 'I've heard lots about you.'

'Have you now?' the old man asked, head tilted, his gaze steady.

It wasn't his towering height that surprised Charlotte most, it was the way he held himself. Relaxed, but the authority in his easy stance immediately told her she'd been wrong to think of Grandy as a cranky old man.

Grandy took the steps from the path to the veranda. He used a cane, but didn't appear too stiff. Old joints fluid, maybe a little too creaky for his liking. His mouth pursed as he trod the steps but if he was in pain, he hid it well.

'Charlotte Simmons.' He took her hand in his, his long fingers curling around Charlotte's hand, his papery skin cool and his grip firm. He looked into her eyes for a long time, gauging and searching.

'Well, well, well.' As though he understood his scrutiny created more awkwardness in her than she already felt, he looked up at the house and released her hand. 'Always did like this veranda. Looking forward to sitting on one of your rocking chairs. Weatherboard could do with a new coat of paint though.' He looked back at Charlotte and winked.

Of course he'd know about the sunflower yellow issue, people would have been tripping over themselves to tell him, but Charlotte had a feeling Grandy knew everything there was to know about anything, whether he'd been told or not. She lifted a hand, indicating Ethan and Junior Morelly as they hefted a Queen Anne–style winged-back armchair off Ethan's ute.

Contrary to her expectations of being shunned after her rude questions at dinner the other night, nobody had expressed doubt over their friendship with Charlotte. She hadn't expected the generosity of spirit and it only made her feel worse about what she'd come to town to do and more determined not to further her questioning of these genuinely kind people.

'Does the armchair mean you'll be staying?' she asked Grandy.

He nodded. 'Thank you kindly for the offer. Hope you don't mind but I like the feel of my own armchair. My old body has kind of moulded to it. Why don't you show me inside?' He looked at her, and Charlotte felt he might have seen right through her. 'Got a feeling we're going to get on just fine, little Charley.'

Charlotte opened the flyscreen door, her breath flickering in her chest as Grandy walked into the house. She looked over at young Mr Morelly and Ethan. They hadn't heard, were too far down the path. No wind today, no breeze to carry the conversation on the air, but Grandy's words unnerved her. Had Grandy just referred to her by the alias the authorities had given her, the six-year-old child who'd witnessed her mother's murder?

How in God's name did this old man know about Charley Red?

Dan looked into the stockpot of chilli as he stirred the thick, spicy sauce. Cooking gave him a breather, a chance to wind down and gather his thoughts as he chopped and browned and spiced the meat, vegetables and herbs. He and Lily liked the restaurant food to be fresh wherever possible, not frozen and re-heated for weeks on end.

'Dan,' Josh called from the bar.

'Yeah?' He turned.

'Ethan's out the back.'

'Okay.' Dan put the lid on his pot of chilli, turned the gas burner to low. He untied the chef's apron from around his waist, flung it onto a stack of plastic glass-trays then went to the back corridor. His thoughts were on the dinner party the other night, and his promise to Charlotte yesterday. He wouldn't bring the topic up with Ethan, not until he'd discovered once and for all what had happened to Charlotte and why it involved his best mate.

Ethan stood at the open door. 'All under control—Grandy's installed at the B&B.'

'Okay, that's good.' Man, he and Charlotte were going to have to be extra sneaky now. It was hard hiding anything from Grandy but Dan didn't want to be without Charlotte—and he needed to do something for her. Her sadness after they'd made love yesterday had pinned him to the wall. He looked down the northern end of the alley. *Made love?* Since when had sex with Red turned to making love? 'I've sussed out the gear we need for his farmhouse,' Dan said. 'Young Mr Morelly can get most of it from the stock they keep in Canberra. He's ordered the rest.'

'Should be here in a week or two then.'

'Yeah.'

Lucy appeared, winding her way down the alley with her young-dog gait. Dan checked the dog's collar. No note, which meant nothing to explain to Ethan, and also meant Charlotte hadn't sent her over. He wished she had, regardless of his having to explain sly, secret notes to Ethan.

The dog trotted up to Dan with a friendly bark and lashed at his boot with a playful paw.

'You've got a pal there,' Ethan said.

'Yeah.' Dan thought about what Charlotte had said to him. 'Charlotte asked me if I wanted to take her.'

'Why would she do that?'

'Not sure.'

'Everything okay?'

Dan grimaced through his embarrassment, but while he had the chance, he took it. 'I need to do something romantic.'

'Like what?'

Ethan hadn't asked for who. Was it obvious to those closest to him that he and Charlotte were together? Dan lifted a shoulder. 'I'm asking. What should I do?'

Ethan furrowed his brow. 'Depends what you've done wrong.'

'I haven't done anything wrong—I just want …' His mind was an empty cave, devoid of romance. He'd never been in a position to want to go overboard on the R stuff, but Charlotte needed the extra-special touch, and he wanted her to smile again.

'Flowers?' Ethan suggested.

'Nah, boring.' Flowers would only remind her of the pink-flowering wisteria he'd given her.

'I like flowers,' Ethan said.

'You like receiving them?'

'Don't be stupid. I like giving them to Sammy. She relaxes. Then she forgives me. Flowers. If you want out of the dog house.'

'I'm not in a dog house.'

'Dan, you think you haven't done anything wrong but I can pretty much guarantee Charlotte will have found something.'

Yeah, Ethan knew about the secretive relationship. Hopefully it was only those closest to him, the friends who'd keep quiet. 'You're getting the wrong end of the stick. We're not an item. We're not a couple. We're just … having a nice time.'

Ethan grinned. 'Flowers. If you think you're about to get a bucket of cold water poured over your "nice time".'

Charlotte flicked the cardboard lid into place on the boxed steamer and slid it into the cupboard, where it nestled tidily with the other tools.

How wrong of her to behave in an underhand manner towards the people of Swallow's Fall. How had she dared to try to sell the B&B as a growing concern? Shame on her.

She picked up the telephone from the hall table and dialled the realtor's in Canberra. After a few minutes' wait, she got through to the salesman in charge of selling the House at the Bottom of the Hill Bed & Breakfast.

'I need to make changes to the ad,' she told him. 'I'm no longer selling a business. I'm selling a house.' She nearly added 'a home' but stopped herself in time. No need for the realtor to know she'd gone soft on the lived-in tattiness of the house. On the pink-flowering wisteria. On the townspeople and their hopes and wants. Although someone, surely, would steam off the flocked peonies? 'How soon can you get the changes made?'

'Twenty-four hours. I suggest we keep the ad running until you've signed the new marketing proposal, in case someone's interested.'

She discussed the new terms, accepting the lower sale price—lower than she'd paid for the house due to it no longer being a business, and lower still in the hope it would sell sooner.

She ended the telephone conversation and rubbed a hand over the tired, tense muscles in her face. With the B&B sold as a house, not a business, Daniel could get on with his plans for Kookaburra's without creating unnecessary acrimony between himself and another accommodation business. No-one in town would be hurt. Thank God she'd seen sense in time. One guilt she wouldn't be taking with her when she left.

'Cup of tea time, Charley.'

Charlotte turned for the kitchen.

Charley. Charley Red. She bit down on her agitation and headed for the kitchen where Grandy waited. He was up earlier than the birds. Forget making his breakfast, he was the one who had toast and tea waiting by the time Charlotte dawdled from her bedroom at seven a.m. She'd never had such a perfect house guest. He made a damned good cup of tea too, insisting on tea leaves and teapot.

'Settling in nicely,' Grandy said, putting a cup and saucer in front of her with a steady hand.

'I'm glad.' Charlotte lifted the cup from the saucer. 'I would hate to think you didn't like it here.'

'Didn't mean me,' Grandy said, taking his seat and resting his cane against his long thigh. 'Meant you.'

'Oh?' Charlotte asked guardedly.

'You got friends in town.'

Charlotte pulled her mouth into a penitent smile. 'And a few enemies.' Pointless not admitting her foibles regarding her inept handling of the townspeople. 'Of my own making, I know that.'

Grandy chuckled. 'They'll come round. So what are your plans?'

'Oh, you know ... Fix the banister. Lift the lino and sand the floorboards. Some other stuff, just bits and pieces.'

'Didn't mean that either.'

Charlotte took a sip of her tea, cautioning herself against its heat but unable to think of what else to do with her hands. Being under Grandy's scrutiny was like being on the blind side of a two-way mirror. Questioning Grandy about whether he knew her history would have to wait until she'd sorted out in her own mind how he might know and where he was involved. If she didn't get that right, she'd only create more apprehension and unpleasantness for the people of Swallow's Fall.

'You haven't done what you came here to do,' he said. Charlotte knew he wasn't referring to her renovations. He shifted in his chair, took hold of his cane and rested his hands on top. 'Got a heap of questions in that head of yours, haven't you?'

Charlotte met Grandy's regard but couldn't speak. This was her opportunity—and she wasn't ready. She'd travelled seventeen thousand kilometres to find answers and the questions she'd decided not to ask were choked in her throat. She shook her head slightly and put her cup into the saucer.

He leaned across the table and patted her hand. 'Maybe the next time we talk will be the right moment. Let's discuss something else.'

Relief was a balm to her nerves.

'How long are you planning on staying?'

'Grandy …' Too soon, relief turned to nagging worry. This man knew things. He wasn't the type to give up, and Charlotte had to find the courage to ask him those questions.

'I hope you're behaving like a gentleman with Charlotte,' Julia said. Since she had electric hair clippers in her hand and was currently clipping the hair behind his ear, Dan didn't answer. Another one who knew about his 'nice time'. Not that he and Charlotte had shared anything more than a wave down Main Street since Grandy moved in. Three nights without her.

'She's my new friend, Dan, and I don't want her hurt.'

'What makes you automatically think I'm going to hurt her?' he asked, affronted.

'Just saying.'

'I have no intention of hurting her.' He glanced at Julia's reflection in the mirror. 'What about if she hurts me? Would you care about that?'

'Sure. But in this case, it's you who's likely to do the hurting. Keeping it all secretive, like you're scared to death people might make the assumption you're getting serious.'

'Maybe it's Charlotte who wants to keep it secret.'

Julia lowered her thin eyebrows and looked down her nose. 'Is that the reason for the little-boy-lost look?'

Dan shuffled on his seat and ran a finger beneath the neckline of the lilac cloak he'd been forced to wear. He was stuck so he might as well see where it led him. Ethan's advice hadn't been any use. Charlotte wouldn't want flowers. The pot plant hadn't been in any way romantic. 'We're both happy having a nice time, but I'd like to do something romantic and I don't know what.'

'Flowers.'

Dan sighed.

'Biggest bunch you can get—and I mean pricey.'

'No.'

Julia's eyebrows shot up, wrath brewing on her features.

Dan clocked the cutters in her hand. He didn't want a scalping. 'I don't mean no to spending the money—I don't care what I spend—but I'm looking for a gesture, not a bunch of roses.'

'Did I say roses? The language of flowers, Dan. Google it.'

Give a guy a break. 'So how's it going with Mr Assistant Vet?' he asked, changing the subject.

'Cool,' Julia said.

'You're looking dreamy-eyed. Is he the one?'

Julia glanced at him in the mirror. 'I've told him about my past and I've quit thinking about sperm donors. Truth is, I think I'd like to have Ira's babies.'

'Think? Isn't that something you should be sure of before you get all gooey with the guy? Why don't you just let things rumble on, see where it goes?'

'No time for that.'

'Why not?'

She put the clippers down and caught Dan's face between her hands, angling his gaze to the mirror. 'What do you see in my eyes?' she asked.

Dan studied her blue eyes and saw a gentleness, a kind of hazy glow. 'You're already in love,' he said quietly.

'Yeah.' She bent to kiss his cheek and looked into his eyes in the mirror, her hands willing him to observe his own brown-eyed gaze. 'And so are you, Dan.'

Facing the fourth day without his girl, Dan made his way down the back corridor of the bar wondering who was knocking with such persistence at eight o'clock on a Thursday morning.

He unlocked the door and swung it open. Daylight and Charlotte.

'Hi,' he said, sticking his hands in his jeans pockets as his insides turned warm and fuzzy. What better way to welcome the day than having a beautiful redhead smile at him? He nodded down at her Lycra shorts and sneakers. 'We going for that five-K run?'

She laughed, pulling at the knot of a pale-green sports wrap she was wearing over her white singlet. 'Not until I'm certain I'll beat you.'

Dan smiled at her. 'You forgot your hat.'

She reached behind her, pulling a folded baseball cap out of the back of her shorts and waved it under his nose. 'Got my mobile too.'

Dan's smile grew warmer as his girl's got happier. Of course he wasn't in love. Guys in love got serious about flowers and went bug-eyed every time the woman of their dreams walked into a room. Yeah, alright, he liked Charlotte a lot more than he was saying. He'd like to spend more time with her in an open and honest way but that didn't mean he was in love with her.

'I was looking for Lucy,' she said.

'Luce!' Dan called over his shoulder.

Charlotte tutted. 'I knew she'd be here.'

'She came running with me earlier.'

'She's more yours than mine,' Charlotte said as she bent and let the dog kiss her hand. 'You really ought to keep her.'

Dan bent to the dog. 'She's ours.' He caught Charlotte's fingers in his. 'You could have come in the front door. You didn't need to sneak down the back alley.'

'Habit,' she said, smiling at him.

'Hasn't been much of a habit recently.' They hadn't been together since Sunday. He squeezed her fingers gently. It would be good to walk down the street with her, holding her hand. Maybe draping an arm over those stubborn shoulders and pulling her into him as they sauntered down Main Street. He saw himself leading her across the road, a hand on her back as they nodded hellos to the shopkeepers. He saw himself leaning over Charlotte's shoulder to see her smile as he bearhugged her. Yeah. A natural progression to what they already had; no back alley sneakiness with Charlotte any more, he wanted to show her off. At his side.

'Lucy won't want another run if she's already been out with you.'

Dan straightened. 'Sorry. If I'd known you were going running I'd have made her stay in town.'

'It's alright. I don't mind.'

'Coming inside for a while?'

'Now?'

'We can exercise together.'

She grinned. 'You're trying to put me off my training. You're really scared I'm going to beat you, aren't you?'

She was playing for time, and maybe about to refuse. 'Come inside with me, Charlotte.' He wanted her in his arms, desperately.

He shooed Lucy, pulled Charlotte into him and held her with one arm as he closed and locked the back door. Lucy snuffled off to check out the empty bar.

Dan bent and kissed Charlotte, holding her steadfastly against him. Her mouth so tender beneath his, her body so pliant, that a craving to taste and hold onto her forever flew through him in waves of tenderness.

'Shall we go straight in?' he asked. 'Or do you want to have a chat first?'

She ran the tip of her tongue over her lips. 'You mean a chat before we …'

'Yeah.'

'What would we talk about?'

He shrugged in apology as he released her. 'I just don't want you to think I only want one thing from you.' She'd been away from him all week. He didn't care what they did first, so long as she was with him.

She gave him a sheepish smile and took hold of his hand. 'We've never chatted before.'

'There's a first time for everything, Red.' And he was beginning to understand exactly what that old cliché meant.

Charlotte took his hand and they walked in silence through the back corridor and into his bedroom. Inside, he pushed the door closed, locked it, and turned to her.

He pulled her into him and kissed her. She warned herself against getting too comfortable in his embrace. Theirs was a sexual pull. No need for passionate stuff to infiltrate the casualness of their affair, even though she'd felt passion with him recently.

She knew it didn't take much for either of them: the first touch; the release of sexual tension. The intake of breaths, bodies connecting, arms intertwining. They didn't have to lock eyes in some love-bitten simpering manner—a sexual urge flew through them and they each recognised it without needing to pretend otherwise.

'You're making those little noises,' he said. 'Those sighs.'

Making noises with him? Already? She hadn't realised. 'Sorry.'

'The breathy ones,' he said, butterfly kissing her throat. 'The ones I like best.'

Well, if he liked them, maybe it was okay to keep sighing them, because she didn't think she'd be able to hold them inside her.

'I want you on the bed, sweetheart.' He pushed her gently backwards until the back of her knees hit the mattress.

Charlotte allowed her body to sink to his bed. He'd called her sweetheart. What did that mean? And how did she feel about it?

He kicked his shoes off and undid the belt on his jeans, then the stud and the zip.

Charlotte drank in the sight of his abdominal muscles and then his chest as he pulled his white T-shirt up and over his head. A man made for loving. Body tanned, muscles defined. He discarded the trousers then bent to the dumbbell rack he used as a bedside table. He took what he needed from a box and slipped it on, his body already hardened and obliging.

Charlotte sighed at the glory of him as he lowered himself carefully on top of her, kissing her lips. 'I like this part.'

So did Charlotte.

'I love undressing you.' He pushed the cardigan off her shoulders. 'Seeing your flesh appear.' He threw the cardigan to the floor. 'I missed you.' Everything about him sent waves of familiarity over her; the scent of his body, the heat he threw off.

'Now this.' He lifted the hem of her singlet, his fingers caressing her midriff. His thumbs brushed over her breasts.

Charlotte raised her arms over her head and allowed him to pull the singlet off.

'Very nice underwear. But I'm going to remove it.'

Oh, God, yes please.

The warm smile in his eyes danced over her as he undid her bra, slid it from beneath her and sent it to the floor with a flick of his wrist. He undressed her, unhurried, taking his time to kiss each part of her body as her shorts, her pants and then her running shoes flew to the floor.

You couldn't get any closer to a person than this, she thought. They were breathing into each other, skin fusing where it touched, with a sensual current.

'Touch me, Charlotte. Put your hands on me.'

A wall of masculine strength, his perfect upper body raised from hers. She ran her hands from his shoulders to his tightened pectoral muscles and down to his waist. Then she gripped his arms, curling her fingers into biceps that didn't budge beneath the pressure.

'Alright?' he asked.

Charlotte nodded.

He took her hand in his, raised it to his mouth and kissed her palm. 'You're so soft. I love your skin.' He kissed her mouth, his lips open and warm. His clean-shaven cheekbones slid over hers and their noses clashed as they fought for satisfaction.

He ran his fingertips over her face then pressed his thumb against her mouth. Her lips parted under the slight pressure. His gaze moved over her features, down to her shoulders, to her breasts, her waist and to her hips.

Something about the way he was behaving, the way he was treating her, sent ripples of astonishment through her.

'I thought you wanted to talk,' she whispered.

'We are talking.'

Charlotte tried to regain some balance, wanting time to speed up so that she reached the spine-tingling moment of release, while at the same time, fascinated by the rising anticipation he created in her.

'I like this part of you.' He took her face in his hands and kissed her forehead. 'And this part.' Her cheek, then her mouth. She tilted her chin so he could reach her throat. His hands moved down her body and cupped her hips, moving to between her thighs. 'And especially here.'

Oh, my God! She rose to his touch and arched as his fingers brushed her.

'Am I getting this right?'

She nodded, unable to speak.

'You're raising my temperature, Charlotte.'

His? Hers was off the scale. 'My heart's thumping …'

'I feel it.'

'Yours isn't.'

'It will, I promise you.' He smiled at her. 'This isn't going to be over soon. I'm going to take my time with you.'

Wow. This was some chat.

Up until now their love-making had been a game. Filled with sexual fervour, yes, but a still a friendship game. They'd had fun, had laughed and teased during and after. This felt consummate.

'Stay with me. I've only just got started.'

She'd do her best.

He slid his body down hers, slowly and deliberately feasting, and up again, covering her. She knew how every part of her body felt beneath his lips.

'Now my heart's thumping,' he said, looking into her eyes.

'I feel it.'

Where was the jocular dialogue they used to get themselves into sex and out of it? Those words smoothed the way for each, until they got dressed, kissed briefly and said goodbye. Without them she didn't know what to do next because she felt so much passion; it outweighed lust about twenty to one. What *was* this?

'Are you ready?'

She'd been ready for what seemed like hours. She tugged him to her, willing him to do it.

He took her slow and steady. Cradling her yet sculpting himself against her. Her skin burned and her mind went into a frenzy as delirious shockwaves engulfed her. Full-bodied sensations from slow, deliciously tantalising sex sank into her muscles and her bones. He smelled so Goddamned wonderful. If desire had an aroma, Daniel wore it and the fragrance enveloped the air, wrapping them both. Their limbs were tangled and warmed from their energy. Her legs were around his hips, pulling him in further. His arm anchored her body, hand at the base of her tingling spine, holding her and leading her.

'Daniel ...'

'I know.'

He knew how to wind her up and keep her there. How and when to let her down. Oh, please let that be soon.

He curled his fingers in her hair, fastening her to him as he moved her towards the moment. Their eyes held. She wanted him physically and emotionally and in a split second she recognised the same want in him. 'Now we're running,' he said, his voice low and his words devoted only to her. 'Run with me, Charlotte.'

To hell with running, Charlotte's blood galloped through her veins.

Pressed together, holding onto each other, moving in unison Charlotte felt, for the first time in her life, the joy when two people shared the moment. Coming together heightened the feelings and the release. It tightened the bond between two bodies willingly joined in mind-blowing physical exertion, leaving her overwhelmed, dazzled and breathless.

She stared at the ceiling and the little bubbles of flaked paint around the lighting fixture as her breathing relaxed. Daniel lay over her, his head buried next to hers in the pillow. No movement from either of them yet—they were all sighed out—but this time, there were no soft jibes at each other either.

Eventually, he lifted from her. He laced her fingers with his and kissed her.

'Daniel, we ... I mean, we, you know—at the same time.'

'Yeah, and that's normally something people have to work on.' He kissed the tip of her nose. 'The timing thing.'

'Yeah,' she agreed with a nod. 'We must have pushed a button, or something.' It had never happened to her before and she hadn't expected such powerful sensations.

'The passion button,' he said, a Hotshot smile so wide on his handsome face, she knew that he was filled with the same infinite gratification at what they'd achieved as she was.

Wow. So this was the aftermath of extreme pleasure. It left her feeling emotionally shattered.

Dan shrugged into his T-shirt as Charlotte stepped into her running shorts. He snuck a glance at her. He usually hid his interest in how she got dressed. Didn't want to embarrass her. She seemed to prefer it that way, although any number of times he'd wanted to hug the breath out of her and thank her for making him feel so ... whole. On this occasion he was almost ready to get down on his knees and ask her to move in with him.

'We've got the party Friday night,' he said.

'I know. Julia's booked solid all day.' Her mouth curled in a smile. 'I think Mrs J wants fancy treatments—probably to impress Ray the farmer. I only just managed to get a late appointment so I can posh myself up.'

'I was wondering, Charlotte ...' He watched her slide the tight singlet over her head and shoulders. 'If perhaps you'd like to come with me. As my date.'

She looked across the room at him. Her mouth opened. Her fingers held the hem of the singlet. 'You're asking me on a date?'

Given the long pause, Dan didn't feel he had to repeat himself. He nodded.

'Wow,' she said softly, eyes widening at him.

'*Wow* good or *wow* bad?'

She went back to the singlet, pulling it down over her bare midriff. 'Actually, Daniel …'

Dan's heartbeat skipped. *Actually, Daniel* … Here it came. A negative. 'Yeah?' he asked, his throat thickened.

'I was thinking perhaps we ought to back off for a bit.'

'Really?' *Why*? The unspoken word burned in his mouth.

She lifted her face, hands resting at her sides. 'It's a little tricky now that I have Grandy at the house.'

He shrugged and slid his hands into his jeans' pockets. 'It's not sneaky if we come clean.'

She shook her head. 'Not a good idea.'

'Why not?'

She sat on his bed, picked up her sneakers and slid her foot into one. 'Let's wait until I've got the committee on my side, shall we?'

'So that's not a definite no?'

She let out a bewildered-sounding laugh, then slipped her other sneaker over her red-painted toenails and onto her foot. 'Please don't push it. Please.' She looked up suddenly.

Dan smiled. 'Have you gone shy on me, Red?'

She returned his smile, warmth on her cheeks. 'A bit.'

'Sorry. Forget I asked.' He moved to the end of the bed and picked up her sports cardigan. 'Come here, then. Let me do the gentlemanly thing and help you with your coat.'

She stood and turned her back to him, sliding her arms into the sleeves of the cardigan he held out. Dan unclenched his fingers from the soft material and slid his hands down her arms. Maybe he'd try again later, when she'd had time to think about his offer. Hell, when *he'd* had time to think about it. He'd extended a romantic offer her way and she'd refused.

'Hey,' he said as she ran her fingers through her hair, neatening it from the tumble his hands had left it in. 'Got a few ideas about the tourist thing you were talking about.'

'Oh?' Interest sparked in her features.

'Yeah.' He pushed his hands into his pockets again. 'I was thinking we might see what we can come up with at the party. You know ... chat to a few people about what they'd like in town and what they wouldn't.'

'I've got a few ideas too.'

'Great.' He headed for the bedroom door, unlocked it and held it open. 'Let me get you a coffee, see if we can hatch some plans for this quaint old town of ours.'

'Good idea. I'll switch the machine on while you put your shoes on.' She looked over her shoulder. 'I don't fancy a run now.' She walked into the corridor. 'I probably look like I've been for one anyway.'

Dan stuck his feet into his sneakers and laced them. So she didn't want to be with him while Grandy was living at the B&B. It would take up to two weeks to get the gear to fix Grandy's farmhouse. Dan wasn't sure he could take another two days without Charlotte, let alone two weeks. And he wasn't talking about being in bed with her. He meant *with* her. Next to her, laughing with her, touching her. Just ... *with* her.

He followed her into the empty bar. 'Okay.' He pulled the portafilter from the coffee machine as Charlotte settled onto a bar stool. 'One flat white coming up.' *And don't draw a heart in the froth.* But he wanted to draw two hearts, intertwined. Man, what was happening here?

He packed the ground beans into the filter. Maybe she'd said no to a date because of everything that was going on with her. Everything Dan didn't understand. He had to know what had happened to her and the only way he could do that was to drag the internet one more time. And how would that make him feel? Like a damned traitor.

Seventeen

Charlotte turned to Grandy at the open door of the Town Hall, her arm tucked in his.

'Ready?' he asked.

'You look so handsome, Grandy.'

He pulled at the knot of his green tie. 'I look like a stuffed turkey about to be carved.'

Charlotte laughed and squeezed his arm. 'Thank you for escorting me here. I'm a bit nervous.'

'No need. You got friends here now, you know that. And just wait until Dan sees you in that dress.' He winked.

The warmth of the summer evening cloaked Charlotte's bare shoulders and arms. The skirt of her vintage dress swirled around her legs and the diamantes on the bodice shone in the moonlight. Music from the jukebox Daniel had provided for the evening bubbled on the air, joining the chatter and laughter to dance down Main Street.

'You know about Dan and me.'

'Don't worry, Charlotte. Not about anything. Not tonight.'

'Sounds good.' She had need of some freedom. A need to smile and chat and feel reasonably whole, even if only for a few hours. She stepped inside, the town's patriarch and guest of honour at her side.

Someone turned the music down and Slim Dusty's voice faded beneath the cheering and clapping.

'Nonsensical,' Grandy murmured.

Charlotte laughed. 'Enjoy it. This is all about you.' She stepped back and applauded along with everyone else as Grandy gave a bow.

People came forwards and shook his hand. The men slapped him on his shoulder and the women kissed his cheek. Charlotte retreated further. She smiled and nodded at those who spoke to her and felt a flush from the welcome but she longed to turn and greedily search the room for Daniel.

She glanced around the hall. Red, white and blue bunting lined the walls. The glitter-ball spun from the highest rafter. She brought her attention down and found Daniel. He stood over by the food-laden committee table, hands at his sides, staring at her. She held her breath, then nodded hello.

He moved towards her, his pace steady, eyes not leaving hers. He didn't break the connection even when he stopped right in front of her.

'Thought you'd never get here,' he said at last.

'I was asked to make an entrance with the birthday boy.'

'Lucky birthday boy.'

'Looking good.' She smiled and nodded at his jacket. He looked so tempting she wanted to take a bite. Tan leather deck shoes, cream chinos, white shirt, and a chocolate-coloured jacket. No tie but he didn't need one to look striking, clean-cut and altogether handsome. A twelve out of ten rating kind of handsome.

He tilted his head and gave her a smile she couldn't read. 'You're not being fair, you know that, don't you?'

She moistened her lips, tasting her cherry-red lipstick. 'Oh?'

'Bad Charlotte,' he said quietly. 'Very bad.'

'Why? What have I done?'

He leaned closer. 'You look beautiful beyond belief and I can't do more than kiss you on the cheek.' He kissed her cheek, his mouth lingering on her skin a fraction longer than normal. 'Man, I'm not going to be able to take my eyes off you all night. That dress was built for you, Red. Dance with me so I can touch you.'

She laughed and stepped back from his hot words, his hot breath. 'Maybe later.'

'Don't tease a man who's enchanted.'

He lowered his voice as people walked by them, heading for the catering table, dragging chairs into circles and getting themselves sorted for the evening. 'I'm gonna make you dance with me at some point.'

'Later. We've got work to do tonight, remember?'

'My mind went blank the moment you stepped into the room.'

She snuck a hand out and pinched his waist, beneath his jacket. He stepped back, hands raised. 'Just warning you. Keep your eyes peeled and your senses humming because this bartender is going to catch you in a bear hug at some point.'

He backed away, grinning, then turned and headed for the area next to the committee table, and for Ted, who had been given pride of place on an old velveteen sofa Charlotte remembered seeing at the town meeting two weeks ago. Poor Ted, but at least he was here, and he'd been given a throne to sit on.

'Hey, Charlotte.'

Charlotte turned to the twins. 'Hi.'

'The oldies know how to put on a decent party,' Jillian said, nodding at Kookaburra's jukebox, which was now thumping out an array of 1980s music.

'Except there's hardly any men our age to dance with.'

Charlotte glanced over the girls' shoulders and spotted their dashing hero, Josh, talking to Mrs J.

'Ask Daniel,' Charlotte said. 'He's dying to dance.'

'Great. We'll catch him later,' Jessica said. 'Anyway, just wanted to let you know we got ourselves out of that mess.'

'Yeah,' Jillian chimed in. 'We're not getting prosecuted.'

'In fact we're not even going to court. Nothing. Whole thing is over and that lawyer you sent our way put us in touch with the cops, who've apparently given Knucklehead a real dressing down.'

'We got the chance to prosecute *him*, but decided not to since Dad's not well and Mum is under the hammer at the store.'

'Well, at least the police know what happened, you're both out of trouble and Knucklehead dare not make another mistake, because the police will be watching out for him.'

Jillian kissed Charlotte's cheek. 'Thanks very much for everything.'

'I really didn't do much.'

Jessica kissed the other cheek. 'Yeah, you did. Thanks.'

'No problem at all.' Charlotte stood alone as the twins left, heading for Josh, she noted with a smile.

'Those two will turn out just fine.'

Charlotte greeted Mrs Tam with another smile. She would enjoy this evening, and there was the promise of being bearhugged in a dance with Daniel later, but for now, there was work to be done. 'Mrs Tam, I've had an idea and I'd like to run it by you.'

Dan pulled up a chair next to Ted's velvet sofa. 'Glad to see you here, Ted. How're you doing?'

Ted snuffled. 'Not feeling too good.'

'I reckon you're bored, mate.'

'Too right, Dan. Too right.'

'Well, if you think you might be up for it—I was wondering if you'd help me out with something that's bothering me.'

'Oh?' The rise of one of Ted's eyebrows wasn't entirely enthusiastic, but at least Dan had got his attention.

'You've noticed yourself that we've been getting a lot more tourists coming through town these last couple of years.'

'I have.'

'And I've been trying to think up a way we can utilise this.' Ted didn't speak so Dan ploughed on. 'You know—turn a profit here and there.'

'For all of us?'

'Absolutely. I'd like some advice on how you think we can develop Swallow's Fall into a viable destination.'

'You're talking about a tourist manifesto.' Ted frowned, but the slight glee in his eyes told Dan his interest had puffed up along with his pride.

'Am I?' Dan asked. 'Not sure I'd know how to go about that. Sounds like it would involve quite a bit of work.'

'Oh, it would.'

'Sounds like something we'd have to involve not only the committee and the townspeople in, but also the shire.' Dan slapped his hands on his thighs. 'Not my field, I'm afraid. Damn it. And I thought I'd got it all figured. Hang on—haven't you got buddies up at the shire?'

Ted nodded, mouth pursed.

'If the committee like your idea of the tourist manifesto, do you think you'd see your way clear to do all the high-level work for us?'

'There's more involved than chatting with the bigwigs, Dan.'

Dan nodded. 'Think it might be too big an endeavour to take on?'

'I'm not saying that.' Ted shuffled on the sofa. 'It can be done, with the right management.'

'Well, if you don't mind my saying so, I think you're the man for the job.'

'No doubt about that,' Ted agreed, not looking in any way modest. 'What worries me is the money side of things.'

Dan had that covered, but he gave Ted a chance to think things through.

'We'd need to get the Town Hall finished.' Ted counted off on his fingers. 'We'd need someone to organise a tourist walk around the historical areas on Main Street. We'd need to get a little museum up and running somewhere, perhaps at the Town Hall. And we'd need to re-do the website. We need a sponsor.'

'How about me?'

'You? How?'

'Kookaburra's could sponsor your tourist manifesto.'

Ted mulled this over, pushing his tongue into his cheek. 'What would we owe you for doing that?'

'Nothing. It'd be a business expense.'

'Well. I could likely spread the idea around. Would you be willing to assist?'

'Anything you'd like me to do, Ted. In fact, Charlotte's talking to Mrs Tam and Mrs J about how they could help—if they want to.'

'Oh, they'll want to. Mrs Johnson would be the ideal person to do the history walk.'

'Great idea.'

'Mrs Tam could keep an eye on the museum since the petrol station is right next door to the Town Hall.'

Dan grinned. 'You've got it all sussed.'

'Shame the craft centre isn't in town.'

'Yeah, but you've come up with some smacking good ideas. I'm impressed.'

'Thank you.' Ted crossed his feet at the ankles and laced his fingers over his comfortable stomach. 'Wouldn't be worth much to the committee if I didn't have a finger or two in the networking pies up at the shire.' He looked out on the dancing crowds. 'You know, Dan—this idea could help everyone in town.'

'Get us all moving a bit.'

'We're normally quite a cruisey bunch, but if I speak the right words to the right people, I can bring them around.'

Dan stood and held his hand out. 'We're lucky to have you, Ted.'

Ted shook Dan's hand. 'Give me a day or two to get something down on paper and we'll have a meeting.'

'Hey.'

Charlotte smiled up at Daniel, happy to have him close after two hours of communication with Swallow's Fall's elite about the tourist manifesto they had cooked up between them yesterday at the bar. 'How's it going?' she asked.

'Good. Ted's on board. Now it's dance time.'

'Not yet—I haven't told you my news.'

'Don't want to talk, I want to dance.'

'I just danced three times.'

'Not with me.'

'Hold your horses, Hotshot. Let a girl get her breath back, would you?'

Charlotte expected his smirk but instead he frowned down at her. 'Okay,' he said, 'this is getting kind of strange, so I'm going to ask you something outright.'

'Sounds official.'

'Have I been treating you badly?'

Surprise stilled her. 'In what way?'

'Have I been giving you the impression I'm only with you for sex?'

The way he angled his face as he waited for her answer did nothing to lessen her wariness about discussing their … association. He'd asked her the same thing yesterday. She hadn't answered then, either.

'Hey, you two.'

Daniel took his attention off Charlotte and smiled at Sammy. 'Hi, Gorgeous. Want to dance?'

'No thanks. My bulk and I are taking it easy.'

'Feeling okay?' Charlotte asked.

Sammy beamed her answer. 'Just the tough last two weeks. So—why aren't you two dancing?'

'She won't have me.'

Sammy poked Daniel in the ribs. 'Are you trying hard enough?'

'We're talking about our community mission,' Charlotte interrupted, changing the subject.

'Charlotte's got Mrs Tam raving about her idea of a Sell, Swap, Trade noticeboard at the petrol station.'

'And Clarissa's keen to be in charge of the historic walks each day,' Charlotte chipped in. 'She's going to bring Ruby along.'

'Any ideas about the craft centre?' Sammy asked. 'It's not doing good business, and I'm thinking of closing it down and creating a child-care centre instead.'

'Leave it to us,' Dan said. 'We'll work on the idea.'

Sammy clapped her hands. 'You're quite a team. Now go dance, will you? Give the town something to gossip about. I'm going to sit down.'

Suddenly they were alone. 'That's a great idea of Sammy's,' Charlotte said.

'Yeah. It's something that's needed. Looks like there's a lot of changes about to take shape and actually, I'm thinking of … kind of branching out a bit with Kookaburra's too.'

'What a good idea.'

'I'd need quite a few staff members, though, if I expand the business.'

'There are heaps of smart people around town. I don't think you'd have a problem staffing your … pub.'

Daniel turned to her. He caught her hand. 'Charlotte, about us. Some people already know about—about the nice time we're enjoying.' He squeezed her hand. 'The thing is—are we enjoying it?'

He was bringing up issues as though they had a proper relationship, not a liaison.

'Of course we're enjoying it,' she said in a lowered voice. 'I mean, you're always gentlemanly. I always feel respected and liked.'

'I do like you. Very much.'

'I like you too, Daniel.'

'So if we value each other so much, what's going on here?'

She shook her head but still couldn't meet his gaze. 'I don't know.'

He drew a deep breath and turned his attention to the room. 'Okay. I'm really feeling the strain now.'

'Behaving?' Grandy asked.

'Doing my best not to.' Dan slipped into the seat next to Grandy. 'And you? Hope you're being a perfect house guest.'

'Doing my bit. Thanks for offering to put in the old-age equipment at my place. Real good of you.'

Dan laughed. 'I'm gonna hide that twenty-foot ladder too.'

Grandy shucked that off with a smile. 'How's your apartment?'

'Jesus.' Dan shook his head. 'You know I'm not building an apartment, don't you?'

'Reckon you'd be wasting the space. Reckon you could use that space for something more viable.'

'Like a hotel.' Dan wasn't going to hide anything from Grandy. Didn't even feel the need.

'So when are you going to tell folk?'

Dan sucked in air. 'Got a few things to sort out first, but soon.'

'Heard about some of the conversations you and Charlotte have been having with people. Good ideas coming out of you both.'

'I'm glad you approve.'

'I do.' Grandy paused, then took a breath that sounded arduous. 'Best be quick though. Property seems to be moving.'

'Whose property?'

Grandy turned his gaze to Dan. 'The B&B. Didn't Charlotte tell you? She's put it up for sale.'

Charlotte looked around the room. Night had settled inside as well as outside. The balmy evening air drifted through the opened windows. The bunting fluttered in magical waves and the glitter ball sprinkled starlight over the floor and the walls. Bubbles of light skipped over the heads of the quietened townspeople as the soft, jazzy blues playing on the jukebox turned as sultry as the evening.

She caught Daniel's eye. He left his place by the top committee table—plates and platters now almost empty, lonely sandwiches and party pies sitting among the crumbs—and headed for her.

Dancing couples paid no attention to him as he wove his way through, lost in their own dreams and the satisfaction of a successful evening.

'This is it. We're going to dance now. I'm not taking any more refusals.'

The night was nearly over; her moments of freedom about to come to an end. 'Yes please.' She stepped into his opened arms.

'You're beautiful. Have I told you?'

'About five times.' And the thrill of each would sit with her forever.

'Had a good evening?'

'Yes.' Wonderful.

'So can you do me a favour?' His hand firmed at her back. 'Pretend you're with me. Really with me,' he whispered, his mouth close to her ear.

She gave in and drew the moment deep inside her as Daniel danced her around the room. To be remembered forever.

He stopped them by one of the opened windows but he didn't take his arms from around her.

'Charlotte,' he whispered, his scrutiny soft but committed. 'I want more of you.'

Music floated over her in curls of emotion. The gentle rhythm of the singer's voice spoke of dreams and wishes and pennies from heaven. But not her heaven. 'I can't.'

'Don't say that.'

She pulled from him. 'We can't be seen together.'

'I don't want us to be a secret any longer.'

'I'm not staying, Daniel.'

The light in his eyes dimmed. 'What do you mean?'

'I have to go. I need to walk Grandy home.'

'Charlotte, don't leave like this.'

She'd dressed for him this evening, not for herself. Her pride in her appearance had always been for her own sense of self but tonight, as she'd slipped into the dress, she'd been thinking only of how Daniel would see her. And now he was asking for more—but she wouldn't be around for more. She couldn't let this go any further. Her few hours of respite were over.

'This wasn't supposed to happen, Daniel.'

'What?' he asked, taking hold of her hands.

Charlotte bit into her bottom lip.

'What?' he asked again.

Love. She wasn't supposed to fall in love.

Eighteen

Dan wandered the lonely path home, his jacket slung over his shoulder. She had a list of excuses as long as the street for not going public with him. She had to leave. Had to protect her reputation. Had to walk her guest home.

Bullshit.

She hadn't meant she had to leave the party without him, she'd meant she was leaving town. She'd put the B&B up for sale, for Christ's sake. She wanted him to take Lucy. She'd been sorting out the lives of the townspeople. Why do that if she intended to leave? Did she want to make redress for something?

He unlocked the back door of Kookaburra's and headed for his bedroom, pulling a cold beer out of the corridor refrigerator as he passed. Burning some midnight oil might ease his frustration. He flung his jacket on the study table in his bedroom, sat, and fired up his laptop. He checked the real estate pages first.

There it was. Too damned easy to find.

For Sale: Charming bed and breakfast business, tucked away in small town in the Snowy Mountains. Rare opportunity

> to leave the bustle of the city behind and head into the heart of the High Country to run your own business. Quaint town, unique atmosphere, tourist attractions abound in the vicinity of Swallow's Fall. The house offers the owner a comfortable home. Two ensuite bedrooms offer guests peace and tranquillity. For more information ...

'Jesus.' He took a swig of his beer and deliberated leaving it be. Letting his need for a relationship with Charlotte go. Letting her leave.

Look at your mother. His father's words came to him and sent him back, once again, into his childhood.

'Yeah, Dad. I hear you.'

Look at Red, Dan had been saying to himself all night. *Look at Charlotte. Look at my girl.* He'd watched her dance with others, chat with others, laugh with others. He'd followed her every move around the dance floor of the Town Hall, studying her from every angle. The way that sexy dress swayed between her legs. The way her cherry-red mouth curved into a smile on her pale face. A goddamn beautiful face. And he couldn't deny it any longer.

He was bug-eyed in love with her. Eyes burning just looking at her, heartstrings pulling when he touched her. Completely in love.

He put his beer down. If he was going to win her, he'd have to venture into her history so he understood how to handle all the messy situations without hurting her, or himself. Nah, stuff hurting himself—he was hurting now, and if she left he'd be hurting for a lot longer than a few hours in a sleepless night.

He opened the electronic folder on the desktop where he'd stored the information he'd found to date. Words bounced from the screen to his mind. *Lost ... Thriving home and small business ... Forsters ... Manipulating a situation by bullying ... Miss Simmons' past ... Australian-born ...*

Only one avenue he hadn't searched yet: Charlotte's childhood in Australia. He opened up a new tab and typed into the search engine: *Charlotte Simmons, news reports, Australia*—and the year—twenty-three years ago.

One million, three hundred and eighty thousand results in 0.44 seconds.

'Jesus.' The night sprawled ahead of him.

He found what he'd been looking for at four a.m.

His chest tightened as he read the article from the online archives. The words swam in his vision. He scrunched his eyes tightly closed, released the pressure and read it again.

Woman murdered. Child, 6, hides in wardrobe at scene

A 6-year-old has been taken into custody after being discovered in the wardrobe of her mother's bedroom, where it is believed she hid while her mother was killed. The victim, a 32-year-old British-born Australian resident and single mother, was strangled to death. The gruesome discovery was made by a neighbour in the early hours of the morning.

It is unsure if this was a planned attack or a domestic dispute gone terribly wrong. Fingerprints of a suspect have been found at the scene, both in the bedroom where the tragedy took place, and in other areas of the small house in Campbelltown, in Sydney's southwest.

It is believed the suspect is known to police and wanted for vicious attacks on two other women eleven and eighteen months ago. To date, the suspect has not been found. Police are advising it's likely he has fled interstate. Police have interviewed residents of a town in the Snowy Mountains where the suspect is believed to have lived and the investigation continues.

Meanwhile, the child, who has become known as Charley Red, is in foster care while she awaits the arrival of her maternal grandmother, who is travelling from England.

Dan's breath wouldn't come. His heart pounded but his lungs had collapsed at 'Charley Red, is in foster care ...' *Charlotte. Sweetheart. God almighty.*

The black and white photograph alongside the news report showed reporters jostling against two women in suits, their arms around a child wrapped in a blanket large enough to trip her up, but not pulled high enough over the child's head to cover a tumble of sepia-coloured long hair. Titian hair; so different in hue, it stood out even in black and white.

He typed in a new search: *Swallow's Fall, suspect, police, murder.*

Alleged murderer Thomas O'Donnell found dead south of Canberra

O'Donnell, 56, a drifter described by police as violent with malicious intent had served two jail sentences for attacks on women in the Northern Territory. He was also wanted for questioning in relation to the murder of Campbelltown single mother, Lillian Simmons, three years ago. At the time of the murder, police were unable to locate O'Donnell whose fingerprints were found in the flat where Ms Simmons lived with her only child, and believed he had fled interstate.

O'Donnell's last registered address was Burra Burra Lane, Swallow's Fall, where he lived before abandoning his family. It is believed police will return to the rural town in the Snowy Mountains to once again question residents and possibly close the murder case.

Ms Simmons' child was in foster care after the killing and was then taken to Britain by her maternal grandmother, Olivia Simmons.

Dan pushed his study chair back from the desk. Six years old. Man, how could any kid go through such torment and get out of it the other side?

'Twenty-five minutes, Lucy.' Charlotte jogged on the spot at the top of the hillside, Lucy darting around her legs. 'Getting faster.' They'd taken the back route up the hill this morning, although the dog had been up to the top twice, pelting back to Charlotte as though encouraging her to keep going. But there was no satisfaction in Charlotte's endeavours. She looked down at the town below and came to a standstill, her heartbeat still racing.

Swallow's Fall, a dot on the map with one street and less than a dozen establishments. But it didn't look lost in the folds of the countryside, it looked settled.

'Oh, God,' she said quietly. 'Look at it.' Love hung in the air on the hillside and inside Charlotte's heart.

The flamingo pink of the B&B stood out against the darker hues of royal blue, stately grey and lemony-yellow of the town's businesses. Even from this distance, the little house at the northern end of Main Street looked special.

The townspeople weren't hanging on to traditions because they were frightened of growth or scared of change. They didn't see themselves as disadvantaged—they saw themselves as lucky. A strong community, one Charlotte found deeply heroic. And one to which she didn't belong.

Pointless hiding the truth from herself any longer, out here on the bluff of the hillside, surrounded by nothing but summer. Last night she'd fallen. In Daniel's arms, beneath the bunting and the glitter-ball in the funny old Town Hall, with sultry jazz playing on a jukebox. She'd fallen desperately in love with him.

'Bad timing, Red,' she murmured. 'Real bad timing.'

I want more of you, Charlotte.

She squashed the hope his words had given her. More of her? To offer a person any kind of love, she had to first find her own balance, and doubts tipped the scale.

'I have to love myself first,' she told Lucy. 'And I can't do that here.' Lucy jumped up, paws on Charlotte's thigh. One day,

Charlotte would be as lucky as Daniel. She'd find her home, but it couldn't be here, and it wouldn't be with Daniel—the first man she'd ever been in love with. She'd lied to everyone and was still lying, no matter how much good she may have done by being part of the tourist manifesto. She'd be leaving the townspeople an empty, unrenovated pink house with a big For Sale sign out the front.

She made her way over the ridge towards the town. The dog galloped ahead, skirting the trees and sniffing around the boulders.

The grass squished beneath the rubber of Charlotte's sneakers, the morning dew still fresh. The sun would dry it soon. She looked up at the sky and wondered how it would feel to have snow dampening her shoulders and chilling the tip of her nose as she walked this hillside. How would the snow gum in her garden look, laden with white?

She paused and studied the ground. The tips of new growth dotted the grass, many of the plants already in bud.

Her heart tumbled to her stomach. 'Oh great. That's just great.' Surely they weren't supposed to appear before January? She wasn't supposed to be here long enough to see them. Now she'd have to tip-toe down the hill to make sure she didn't squash Daniel's wildflowers.

'Sold?' Charlotte stumbled in the hallway, her knees almost buckling. 'Sold?' she asked again, steadying herself by bracing against the hall table and gripping the telephone tighter.

'Quite something, isn't it?' the realtor said. 'Apparently just the type of property this company is looking for. They'll be doing it up.'

'As a house?' Charlotte asked.

'I must say, Miss Simmons, I was thinking along the terms of a fast sale taking six months, not six hours.' He chuckled, his delight obvious.

'Will they use it as a house—as a home?' Charlotte asked again.

'No idea.'

'What is this company? Where are they located? What do they do?'

'Sentinel Renovations is the company name. Registered address is Victoria. This is a cash sale, Miss Simmons. A cash sale.' The realtor laughed, no doubt counting his commission.

'So what happens now?'

'I'll email the documents, you sign and return to me by both email and in hard copy.'

Charlotte hardly heard him. *Sold.*

'I'm working double-duty for you, Miss Simmons. The buyer wants a quick settlement and as the cash is on the table, so to speak, I can get this done fast.'

Done. Gone. Was this was she wanted for the town? Would they care who bought the house when she left? Would Charlotte care?

Yes, she would—but what was the point in stopping the sale from going through? There'd be no business for her, Kookaburra's would take that over. She didn't need money to live on, but she needed to use her brain and her hands. And how could she stay in Swallow's Fall under the cover of lies and deceit? How would she bear it when her relationship with Daniel ended? What would she do if he found someone else? If he married and had children with some other woman? The image of little Lochie cradled in the crook of his arm came to life in her mind. A blast of love spread through her chest at the thought of Daniel being a daddy to any child she might have. But from this point on, she'd need an iron grip on such thoughts, because at this moment, there was no way on God's earth she could envisage herself loving any other man enough to have children with him. Not when the essence of Daniel filtered over her and through her, soaking her heart with a desperate kind of love.

'Alright,' she told the realtor. 'Please email the papers and I'll sign.'

Charlotte disconnected the call and turned to the sunlight at her front door. Pushing open the flyscreen, the temperate air flowed over her. She inhaled the scent of eucalypt, the newly mown grass of her front lawn, and let the breeze heading down Main Street waft over her. But it was no longer her front lawn and the gentle wind didn't blow away the cobwebs of regret around her heart.

'That's your lawn cut for a fortnight,' Grandy said as he trod the steps from path to veranda.

'You didn't have to get someone to cut the grass, Grandy.'

'Got to do something for my keep, and anyway, Josh needs the extra money.' He lowered himself with grace into one of the rocking chairs by the front door.

Charlotte smiled. 'I like your waistcoat. It's very … yellow.'

'Ain't it just? Got Julia to nip into Cooma. She got it from one of the second-hand stores. I call it sunflower yellow.'

Charlotte sank into the chair next to Grandy's and rocked, nursing her hurts. 'What are you doing, Grandy?'

'Just letting folk see a bright yellow waistcoat on a craggy old man.'

'Against a peeling pink weatherboard.'

'Terrible colour,' Grandy muttered. 'You paint it yellow, Charlotte. And while you're at it, open up your heart to what surrounds you.'

'What do you mean?'

'Sometimes we don't see what's right in front of us because we're too busy chasing the dream to colour our hearts with the shades of love already there.'

Charlotte studied her guest. His rugged features, the sparking light in his watery blue eyes and the way he held himself. Old, yes. Decrepit? No. This strong man had lived fully, had given his energies to those around him, whether family or neighbours. This man didn't need to look for friendships, he could hold his own without them and that was the characteristic that made him so compelling. His safe, almost stately personality brought people to his side and made them listen to his quiet instruction. People wanted to hear his wise words. And Charlotte wanted to hear how she could colour her heart.

'Got a few things that need doing, Charlotte, and I need your help.'

'At your farm?'

'No. I won't be going back to the farmhouse.'

'Why not?'

Grandy leaned over the arm of his rocking chair and took hold of Charlotte's hand. 'There's a folder in the desk drawer in the back bedroom.' He pulled a small key out of a fob-watch pocket on his waistcoat. 'Give this to Ethan and Junior. Tell them everything they need to know about the legal stuff is in that folder.'

Charlotte took the key. 'What legal stuff? Are you going to sell your farm?'

'I'll be leaving it, that's for sure.' He smiled at her, his tanned face creased and consideration sparkling in his eyes. ''Bout time too. I need to be somewhere else. Just like you do.'

Was he saying he thought she needed to leave town too? There were lessons in his eyes and Charlotte wanted to be taught. She suspected he'd been born a teacher and over time, with many experiences, he'd become a professor. One that stood in front of the blackboard of life and chalked up notable recommendations for all to read, if the lesson was necessary. She'd kept the child she'd been at a wary distance since the terrible event in her past, but she had a suspicion Grandy saw the little girl still hiding inside her.

He nodded at the key in Charlotte's hand. 'Got three boys. Didn't know that, did you?'

Charlotte breathed deeply and brought her attention back to what he was telling her. He had his son, Junior, here in town and a son in Victoria—a farmer, Mrs Tam had said. She hadn't heard of another son.

'My boys won't fight when they find out. It's my girls I'm worried about. They won't take kindly to the news.'

'What news?' Charlotte asked.

'Totally independent from me, my girls. Have been for years. I got this hope they still have brains enough to recognise that what happened, happened and what is, is.' Grandy looked over at Charlotte and patted her hand. 'Go talk to Ethan, Charley Red. That's why you're here, ain't it?'

A chill crept over Charlotte's shoulders and down her spine. 'You know why I'm here.'

'Been expecting you for years, but I guess you had your life to live in England first.'

'How do you know?' *What* did he know?

'O'Donnell,' he said, his tone roughened with disgust.

Dan pulled into the driveway at Ethan and Sammy's homestead, taking the curve faster than he should. He'd been up all night, thinking, rearranging the puzzles in his head, getting nowhere. If he wanted to keep Charlotte in town, he was out of time for second-guessing. He needed answers.

Charlotte was in Swallow's Fall to search for O'Donnell, she had to be. O'Donnell had lived here at some point. Dan had never heard of the man, but there was only one house on Burra Burra Lane and Ethan had been born in that house, had grown up in that house, and now lived it in with his family.

Gravel spat and crunched as he brought the car to a skidding halt outside the house. He slammed the car door, jumped the steps, made his way along the veranda to thump on the open front door. He pushed it wide and walked through. 'Ethan!'

'You've kicked up gravel in my driveway,' Ethan said, coming out of the kitchen, a tea towel in his hands as though he'd been washing the breakfast dishes. 'What's up?'

'Hi,' Sammy said as she stepped out of the dining room. 'What are you doing here so early? Is everything okay?'

Dan looked from one to the other and hoped to God he wasn't going to be poking sticks in old wounds by mentioning Charlotte's history. He nodded a sort of apology before speaking to Ethan. 'I need to talk to you about Charlotte. About you ... and about some guy called O'Donnell. He used to live here, in your house.'

Ethan stilled quickly, his stance the same except for the response in his eyes—stony, cold. 'You don't mention that name in my house.'

'Our house,' Sammy said, stepping beside Ethan and taking hold of his elbow. She looked at Dan. 'We don't mention that man's name in our house.'

'I'm sorry, guys, I really am.' They'd gone as still as they had that night Charlotte had asked Ethan about his parents. They were hurting, but Dan had to keep going. 'I need answers. It involves Charlotte.'

'How?' Ethan asked.

'O'Donnell killed her mother.'

Sammy gasped, her hand flying to her mouth.

'She was just a kid,' Dan said. 'Six years old. She hid in the wardrobe while he murdered her mother.'

'Holy shit.'

Dan blinked. Yeah, he'd heard Ethan swear, but the intensity in his tone rocked the rafters.

'What?' Dan demanded.

'I need to speak to Grandy, and you need to talk to Charlotte.'

'Why?'

'Not my place to say.' Ethan turned, walked down the hallway and into the kitchen. 'Sammy,' he called.

Sammy looked at Dan, helplessness and worry in her demeanour. 'I need to be with Ethan. You should talk to Charlotte.'

'He's long gone,' Grandy said. 'He can't hurt you any more than you let him. And I'm hoping you're going to let go of all that fear and beat him.'

'He killed my mother,' Charlotte whispered. 'He might have killed me too …'

'But he didn't.'

'Is Ethan my brother?'

'No.' Grandy looked at her, his eyes creased at the corners. 'O'Donnell wasn't Ethan's father.' He squeezed her hand. 'He wasn't your father either.'

Charlotte crumpled, pulled her hand from the old man's as a racking sob escaped her chest. She pressed her hands to her face, holding on, remembering everything through her tears. *Face it without reliving it. Thank God. Thank you, God.* The bastard wasn't her father.

'How did you find us?' Grandy asked.

Charlotte swallowed the unsavoury moisture in her mouth and looked at him. He'd given her answers to questions she hadn't asked and he wasn't finished. She breathed deeply, needing to find the moment again. 'I discovered newspaper clippings after my gran died,' she told him, a catch in her voice. 'The official paperwork was there too—all the correspondence between the police in Sydney and my gran. The police said they'd spoken to an Ethan Granger, O'Donnell's son, who was training to be a vet at university and they'd informed him of his murder. They mentioned Swallow's Fall too. It was easy to find Ethan after that. I just looked him up on the internet and found his veterinary business.'

Grandy nodded. 'You tell Ethan why you're here. Tell him soon.'

Charlotte shook her head. 'If he's not related to me, why upset everyone by bringing up old news?' It would hurt Ethan—and Sammy. 'It isn't their problem, now I know he wasn't my father and that Ethan didn't know about me.'

'I knew about you. Came to visit you in the foster home.'

Someone had cared enough to visit her. Grandy had cared. The knowledge overwhelmed her. Comforted her, even. 'How do you know so much?'

'Your mother came here.'

'To Swallow's Fall?'

Grandy nodded. 'You were about five years old.'

Charlotte had been here before? It was incomprehensible.

'She'd come looking for Thomas. She'd been with him for a couple of months and he'd disappeared on her, taking a few hundred of her dollars with him.'

Charlotte gasped. 'She wanted him back?'

'She had courage, your mother. She came here hoping to get her money back, but mainly to put wrongs to right as much as she was able. She'd recently suspected he was married. She wanted to know the truth, and to apologise for the wrongs she'd done to his wife and any children.'

Charlotte gasped. 'He might have been here.'

Grandy lowered his jaw. 'Thank God he wasn't. I warned her to stay clear of him.'

'But he found her.'

No need for an answer.

'The only other person who knows something—but not everything,' Grandy continued, '—is Mrs J. She was with me when your mother arrived. We both spoke to her and she seemed so emotionally exhausted by the journey that we suggested she stay in town the night. You both stayed here, in the B&B.'

'Good God.' Charlotte gripped the arm of her chair, holding herself still as her heart beat wildly in her chest.

'There's a longer story, Charley.' Grandy grabbed his cane from its resting place on his thigh and gripped it, his fingers tight around the curl of the handle. 'Ethan can tell you more, and he will, but the short tale is—I'm Ethan's father.'

It took a few seconds for this second astonishing piece of information to settle in Charlotte's mind.

'Nobody knows except Ethan and Sammy. My kids don't know—yet. I kept it from prying eyes and flapping ears around town all these years too. But things are about to change.'

'You're going to tell your children now?'

'I have to.'

'Because of me?' Discomfort travelled through her. 'You don't have to tell anyone. I'll leave and they'll forget about me … and about O'Donnell.' She spoke the man's name on a hushed breath, as though his ghost might turn up any second and scare her to death.

'Some stuff has to be told,' Grandy said, contemplating the wooden floor of the veranda. 'Somebody killed him, Charlotte. Knocked him out cold, then gave one last punch, I reckon. Someone ended his life and before they did it, maybe that someone had a word with him. Put him straight.'

Some man had killed O'Donnell and by doing so, had undoubtedly given life to others. 'He was a monster.'

'A violent man,' Grandy agreed. 'He'd have killed again. Just wish that *someone* had got to him before he killed your mother. You didn't deserve what happened to you.'

'I always harboured fear it was my fault—because I didn't do anything. I should have screamed, should have got out of the cupboard and run for help.'

'Sweet Jesus, Charlotte, you were six years old, love.'

'I know, but it lives with me.' As a little girl she'd thought fear was normal. That darkness meant loneliness, hurt and shame for being so unable to help.

'It lived with the child, the emerging teenager and the young adult you were. Now you have to handle it.'

'I'll try.' If she didn't, she'd never be true to herself. 'Do you know who my father was?'

Grandy shook his head. 'Sorry, but I don't. I know it wasn't O'Donnell because for two years before you were born, he was causing trouble up in Darwin. Did a spell inside. The cops told me that. They came down here too, looking for answers after his murder. They didn't know he wasn't Ethan's father and I didn't tell them.'

Relief helped pour salve on her fatherless state—O'Donnell wasn't her father and that's what mattered to her most. Perhaps her mother had loved someone who'd left her. Or had simply found herself pregnant and alone.

'And I don't care where anybody's morals lie on the killing issue,' Grandy said. 'O'Donnell did damage to many people, to people I cared about. Far as I'm concerned, he met the right end.'

Charlotte nodded. A man like O'Donnell would have always found a grizzly end. The discovery of his killer would never have concerned her, unless it was to offer thanks. She reached out and put her hand onto Grandy's, gripping the long, stiffened fingers, and couldn't stop the next thought in her head: Did Grandy kill O'Donnell?

'Don't let him beat you, Charley Red.'

'I think I can walk away now.' She'd put the knowledge of what Grandy *might* have done for her, for her mother and for the other people he was referring to—Ethan, probably—to the back of her mind. O'Donnell had deserved his death.

'Do something for your mother, would you?'

Better memories bounced on the cobwebs of fear around Charlotte's heart. As though her mother were above her, around her, within her. 'I miss her.'

'Live for her. Live your life for her—she'll want that.'

'I sometimes wonder if she's watching me. If she's here with me.'

'Oh, she'll be at your side, love, when you need her. But she can't live your life for you. That's up to you.'

'I'll try.' No more than a whisper, this second promise.

'I'm asking a lot of you,' Grandy said. 'But that's because I think you've got it in you. You got brains, but you haven't figured out yet what it is you've got in front of your eyes.' He held his hand out, palm up. 'It's in your hands.'

'A life?'

Grandy nodded.

Away from here. The emotional cobweb would need unpicking but she'd have time to heal and the stitches could be woven once more. She'd lost so much in her life. First her mother, then her gran, then her home and business, and now the person she'd thought she was. It would be hard, looking for her real self all by herself, but she'd do it.

'Charlotte, would you do me another favour?'

Charlotte's mouth had gone dry. She couldn't speak.

'Be a friend to Julia, would you?' Grandy asked. 'Looks like she's found herself a decent man at last, but I think she'll need a good friend too. With you, and Sammy, she won't feel so lost when she realises she's settled in town for good. It's what she wants, but she's been feral for so long, it might come as a bit of a shock to her that she's finally got something she wants. She'll need a friend to tell her she's doing the right thing and not to be scared.'

Charlotte swallowed the lump that had formed in her throat. Tears prickled her eyelids. 'She'll have you,' she said. 'You tell her.'

He shook his head, ever so slightly. 'Won't be here to do that.'

Charlotte gripped his hand. 'Grandy, you're scaring me.'

Nineteen

Charlotte chewed on the tip of her pencil, telephone pressed to her ear as she waited to be put through to the realtor in Canberra. Since her conversation with Grandy, her stomach had been knotted, as though she'd swallowed the chain of horrendous events and they'd settled in her gut and rusted there.

What a mess she'd made of everything. Falling in love with Daniel was a heart-aching discovery, but she could deal with it, on her own and in her own time—no matter how long it took. Falling in love with Swallow's Fall gave her a much greater complexity to handle, and one that needed to be addressed now.

She tapped the pencil in a furious motion on the hall table. Before the astounding conversation with Grandy, she'd signed the sale agreement and emailed it back. A cash sale meant a settlement date could be set as soon as all the documentation had been dealt with. The purchaser didn't want an inspection, didn't even want a cooling-off period. No need for all parties to meet up, the actual settlement would take five minutes in somebody's office in Canberra. Take the cheque and hand the keys over. Wham—done deal.

She had to get in touch with this company now, today, in the next five minutes, and explain why she was not going through with the sale. To do less would leave her with one more guilt. She had enough shame on her shoulders not to right this wrong.

'Right then, Miss Simmons,' the realtor said. 'You're in charge.'

The realtor thought her mad and perhaps she was, but the heart of the town was at stake. She pulled her shoulders back and breathed deeply. There was only one thing she could do to make reparation for all the things she'd done wrong: take the house off the market and bequeath it to the town. Her parting gesture.

If Sammy was going to close the art and craft shop and turn it into a child-care centre, there'd be nowhere to show off the local skills of the townspeople—of which there were plenty. So they could have her pink house. Daniel, Ethan and Josh could refurbish it, knock down dividing walls and create a gallery. Whoever ran it could live in the upstairs rooms.

'If you could give me the address and telephone number of the director of the company, I could call myself.'

'Well ...'

Charlotte heard the sounds of papers rustling.

'Ah, here it is. Got at pen? Let me see ...'

Come on! How hard could it be? Why hadn't he just opened up his computer, hit a key and *found* the bloody information? Charlotte waited, pen poised.

'The owner of Sentinel Renovations is Daniel Bradford.'

Shock punched its way from her brain to every part of her body, then surprise turned just as quickly to hurt, swamping all the memories of lying with Daniel. Of kissing Daniel's mouth. Of laughing with him. Play-fighting, tickling, talking and falling in love with him.

Daniel had bought her house. Behind her back. How could he do this? *Why* would he do this?

This day—what had this day done to her? Had she deserved this torture, she asked herself, and the heavens, and anyone who was able to hear her innermost thoughts—had she deserved this struggle? She was only trying to find herself. She'd been given her answers but her quest had turned to heartbreak.

She replaced the telephone without speaking another word to the realtor and couldn't find the energy to worry about her rudeness.

Thunder rumbled outside.

She turned to the hallway and ran a tear-stained gaze over the staircase, the flocked peonies on the wallpaper, the tatty hall carpet. All Daniel's now. Daniel's house. Daniel's problem.

He could have it. She'd go through with the sale. It was all his. He could take it. And she would leave.

Dan left his car parked outside Kookaburra's and headed for the B&B, an intensity inside him so strong his heart ached.

He quickened his pace, rain pelting over his head and shoulders, drenching him.

'Hey, Dan, where you going looking so charged up?'

Dan glanced over his shoulder and threw a wave to the Tillman twins, who were standing outside their father's store, huddled under one purple umbrella. Dan focussed on the expanse of lawn outside the house at the bottom of the hill, the shingle pathway to the veranda, and the cherry-red front door. Same shade as Charlotte's fingernails. Same red as her lipstick from last night. Same colour as his heart: bright red and bleeding.

'Charlotte!'

The door flew open and there she stood, behind the flyscreen. 'What have you done?' she demanded, her features a blend of disbelief and wrath.

Dan stepped back.

'You bought my house.' She held herself straight and tall, her slender shoulders angled slightly, matching the challenging tilt of her chin. 'You bought my house,' she repeated.

Jesus, how had she learned that so quickly? And here they were, bickering again. 'You put it up for sale,' he said, hopelessness about how to untangle the knot of deception swirling inside him. 'Were you going to tell me?'

She yanked the flyscreen open, stepped onto the veranda and poked him in the chest. He tried to take hold of her hand but it was gone from his body as fast as it had struck him.

'How did you find out it was for sale?'

He'd known he'd have to tell her, but her fury stalled his thoughts. 'Small town, Red.' He gave her a smile.

'Don't call me Red.' Thunder cracked above them. 'Who else knows?'

Dan took a breath. 'Nobody.'

'You went behind my back.'

'You put it up for sale behind *my* back. Were you going to tell me?'

'No.' The rain pounded the tin roof of the house and the metal awning, almost drowning out her softly spoken response. But Dan could lip-read the one syllable, and he could read her thoroughly. She was off-kilter, unsure of what was happening but he could make it better for her.

'Come on, Charlotte. Let's take a second, shall we?' He'd been breathless all night at the thought of her leaving. Hearing her admit she was going released the apprehension in his chest. He stepped forwards and held his hand out. 'Come here, would you? I want to hold you.'

She didn't step back but neither did she move to him. 'Why did you buy my house?'

'You didn't want it.'

'How did you know I didn't want it?'

'I know.' He swallowed. 'About you … why you're here. The little girl. Your mother.'

She gasped, her skin paling. 'You spoke to Ethan?'

'He wouldn't tell me anything. He said I had to talk to you.'

'You promised me you wouldn't speak to Ethan. You promised me!'

'Charlotte, sweetheart, I've got a real big thing about you—you must have guessed that last night. Of course I wanted to know more about you and I want to know the whole story.'

'And how did you find the scent of this story?'

Dan paused and considered his answer. He ran a hand over his wet head, then wiped it on his jeans. There'd been enough deceit between them. 'I researched you. On the internet.'

'Oh, God.' She covered her face with her hands, her shoulders sinking, as though she wanted to hide from the world.

It didn't look like she was crying, she was breathing deeply, maybe trying to get herself together. She dropped her hands and looked him in the eye. 'Does everyone know?' Her eyes were veiled with uncertainty, or maybe total despair.

Christ—this wasn't the way things were supposed to go. 'No—I don't think so, but some of them recognise you …'

Stubbornness appeared in the way she straightened her shoulders. 'You went behind my back.'

'I'm sorry, sweetheart, but you didn't want the house.' She couldn't deny that, surely?

'And you do?'

Dan shook his head. 'I bought it so I could—'

'So you wouldn't have to fight for business when you turn Kookaburra's into a full-blown hotel.'

How long had she known? What was this making him look like? A total idiot. Dan looked over his shoulder. Half-a-dozen people stood in the street. Unfortunately, the important half-dozen. The Tillmans, Mrs Tam, Mrs J—the ones he'd lied to. 'Can we take this inside?'

'It's not your house yet.'

'I have serious plans, Charlotte. The hotel would give people work. It would bring in revenue for the town, not just me.'

'I could do it, you know. I could make this B&B work.'

'I know that. I want to help.'

'Even with your hotel up and running, I could make it work.'

'So make it work. Let's make it work together.'

'Together? You just bought my house!'

'You sold it!'

Dan spun around in frustration and found half the shopkeepers on Main Street staring at the B&B. He turned back to his girl and moved closer to her. 'I want to be with you, Charlotte.' Lightning struck high in the sky. 'Up front, honest and square. I want everyone to know you're my girl.'

'Honest?' she asked, her expression tight with incredulity. 'So why did you lie?'

That wasn't fair. They'd both lied. From the start. 'Why did *you*?'

'Getting a bit heated out here, ain't it?' Grandy said as he pushed through the flyscreen.

Dan faced Grandy. 'I can explain,' he said. This wasn't about Dan, it was about Charlotte. It wasn't about arguing, it was about wanting to make her feel secure. Wanting to be with her. Forever. 'Can we take her inside?' he asked Grandy.

'She's had a difficult time, Dan.'

'I'm trying to help her.' Her distress sucked the guts out of him. 'Charlotte, come here now.' He held his arms out to her but she backed from him.

'I'm afraid I might have punched a hole in her world this morning by giving her the answers,' Grandy said.

'Answers to what?' Dan asked, then turned to Charlotte. 'I want to know why you're here. It's got something to do with O'Donnell and with Ethan. I know that much.'

'No,' she said. 'You're wrong. And I was wrong. It has nothing to do with Ethan. Thomas O'Donnell killed my mother. I thought Ethan was his son, and my brother. I thought O'Donnell was my father but he wasn't—he wasn't Ethan's father either.'

'Afraid I'm going to have to interrupt here,' Grandy said, his voice thick, like he'd swallowed gravel.

Dan's attention spun to the old man. One look at the pale, stricken features and he leaped forwards to take hold of Grandy. 'Charlotte—quick.' She was already at his side, holding Grandy's arm and bracing his tall body against her own slight one.

The old man stumbled backwards. 'Need to see Junior.'

Dan put his arms around Grandy. 'Get the phone,' he told Charlotte.

She dashed inside, picked up the telephone, thumbed through a little book on the hall table and dialled.

'Call … Ethan,' Grandy said, the words punctured with a grunt.

'We're calling the air ambulance.'

Grandy looked into Dan's eyes. 'Happening a bit sooner … than I thought.'

'I've got you.'

'Just as well. Don't think I can stand.'

Grandy collapsed into Dan's arms, the jolt of a sudden pain etched on his face. Dan lay him on the floor, checked that Grandy's airway was clear and then put him into the recovery position as Charlotte's troubled voice punctured the air.

'This is Charlotte Simmons, Lot 183, Swallow's Fall. We need the air ambulance. A resident is having a heart attack.'

Twenty

Why did a hospital hold such a clinical hush within its walls? As though antiseptic and systematic care from experienced strangers could settle the stress and frantic worry of those who stood by, watching and breathing. Loving. Hoping.

The air ambulance had transported Grandy and Charlotte to the hospital in Cooma. Daniel had waited at the B&B, getting hold of Ethan, Julia and eventually Junior.

Ethan had driven to Cooma with Sammy. Junior arrived three hours ago, having been in Canberra for the night, overseeing something at the Morelly storehouse. While they worked on Grandy, Charlotte had left the hospital waiting room and wandered the corridors between the cafeteria and the gift shop, giving Junior and Ethan time to talk. What they'd spoken of, Charlotte didn't know, but it appeared the truth about Ethan's parentage had been told because when Charlotte returned to the waiting room, Sammy, looking strained, had stuck to Ethan's side and Junior had looked stunned.

When Junior Morelly gave them the news mere seconds ago the light seemed to seep from the brightly lit, sterile waiting room. Charlotte closed her eyes as the darkness descended in her mind and behind her eyelids.

'They'll let us see him now,' Junior said.

There were only the three of them now. Sammy had gone into labour forty minutes ago and had been taken by a nurse to the maternity wing where she was being monitored. Ethan had accompanied her, but had come back to the coronary care unit when Charlotte went in search of him to let him know the doctor wished to speak to Junior, and that Junior wanted Ethan with him.

'You must go in too, Charlotte.' Charlotte forced her eyes open and glanced at the two men standing in the space, looking like lost warriors. She shook her head at Ethan. 'I've caused everyone too much pain already, if I hadn't …'

'This is not your fault.' Ethan took her arm. 'It's not your fault.'

'It's alright, Charlotte,' Junior Morelly said. 'My father took the time to talk to you … to tell you so much. And he knew his time was close. Please come in.'

Charlotte hesitated but walked towards Junior when he held a hand out for her, wanting very much to say her goodbyes to the man who had been not only her unexpected guest, but her saviour.

'He wouldn't have got here without you,' Junior said as he took her hand and led her into the care unit where Grandy lay. 'And Ethan and I wouldn't have been given the chance to speak to him, if it wasn't for you.'

This was the first time his family had been allowed to see him since Grandy had suffered a second heart attack, and Charlotte felt like an outsider. She looked up at Ethan, who stood apart, waiting. 'Are you coming in?'

Ethan glanced at Junior for acceptance. Junior nodded. 'Of course he is.'

They moved into the unit, Charlotte trying to ignore the busyness around them as nurses and doctors tended those still living.

'They said he rallied,' Junior told Ethan as they walked into the curtained-off area. 'Enough to tell them he didn't want any more help.'

Charlotte shuddered.

Junior stood on one side of his father's bed and indicated that Ethan should move to the other side. Charlotte closed the curtain behind her to give the space some privacy.

Death had been soft, she thought as she looked at Grandy's features. There was a hint of serenity on his face and no horrid contraptions in his mouth or throat. There'd been no time. He'd gone. Never to come back.

'He told me he saw my mother,' Junior said.

'He loved her,' Ethan said softly.

Junior took hold of his father's hand. 'Looks like he loved yours too.' He glanced up at Ethan.

'For one night,' Ethan said. 'He told me it was only the once.'

Junior nodded. 'He was the best man I ever knew. Didn't think he had secrets, but I was probably too close to him to notice.'

'He didn't mean any of this to hurt any of you.'

'Of course he didn't.' Junior seemed to recover from his pain, and cleared his throat. 'I'm sure going to miss him. But there's only you and me here now, Ethan. So let's get this done for him.' He bent and softly kissed his father's forehead. 'Thank you for everything. Say hi to Mum, would you?'

Hot, sharp tears prickled Charlotte's eyes as she said her own, silent farewell to Grandy.

Ethan gave Junior a long look, mouth drawn. 'If you don't mind, I'd like to say something to him I've never been given the chance to say before.'

Junior nodded. 'Now's the time.'

Ethan lifted Grandy's hand and held it in both of his. He looked down at his father. 'I love you, Dad,' he said quietly.

Charlotte swallowed the lump of emotion rising in her throat.

Junior looked up at Ethan. 'I've said that to him many times.' His mouth moved as though he were chewing the words before he spoke them. 'But I reckon hearing you say it for the first time was the best time I've heard it said.'

Ethan put his father's hand back on the bed. 'I'm so sorry, Mr Morelly.'

Junior gripped his father's hand tighter. 'We don't apologise, Ethan. We're brothers.' He looked across Grandy's body into Ethan's eyes. 'And my name is Edmond.'

Ethan inhaled a ragged breath, and Charlotte slipped out of the curtained room.

She walked the length of the empty and silent corridor for the umpteenth time and turned as the doors creaked open at the other end. Daniel walked through and paused.

Charlotte gazed at him. He'd come. He must have driven. The joy of seeing him was almost too much in the light of everything that had happened and all they'd shared before now. They'd bickered and quarrelled. They'd lied to each other. They'd argued in the rain a few hours ago but still, he was the only comfort she wanted.

He walked towards her, his arms out and Charlotte ran to him. He crushed her into an embrace and rocked her.

She breathed in the living aroma of him. 'Grandy died,' she said, face against his shoulder.

'I know.'

'Edie was born.'

He stroked the back of her head. 'I know.'

'And I'm not talking to you.'

He laughed, gently and softly. 'So what are you doing buried my arms?'

'Taking a bit of comfort.' She'd been alone for two hours. Ethan was with Sammy and his new baby, and Junior had left to visit his sisters on the outskirts of the city. 'I wanted a hug from someone and you're the only person available.'

He held her tighter.

She should leave the security of his arms before the strong, steady impression of him melted the last of the emotional strength she had left. 'I've done everything wrong,' she whispered.

'So have I.'

They shouldn't be having this conversation. Not here, in the hospital where she'd said goodbye to one life and welcomed another. But the remonstrative words tumbled out anyway. 'You shouldn't have bought my house.'

'I'm giving it back to you.'

'I don't want it.'

He tightened his hold of her. 'We have to talk, Charlotte, but not here. I came to get you.'

'You didn't have to. I was going to hire a car.'

'Capable as ever,' he said, a smile in his voice.

How wrong could he be? His soft tease brought with it the many thoughts of the struggles she still faced. Her house, and what to do about it. She wasn't even sure which of them owned the house. Did signatures cement the sale? Or would she have to wait until Daniel's money hit her bank account? How long would it take her to pack? Would she even get to see baby Edie again? And Lucy—would Daniel take the dog?

Too many sensitive issues to think about in the hallway of a hospital. She gathered her thoughts tight and focussed on the now. 'Did you come with anyone else?' she asked, pushing away from him, sniffing back the tears and wiping her eyes with her fingertips. 'Julia?'

'No, Julia's in town looking after little Lochie and helping out with ...'

Charlotte looked up when he paused. 'What's happened?'

'I came to get you because for a moment I forgot how capable you were.' He smiled. 'I didn't even think about you hiring a car. But we have to get back to Swallow's Fall now.'

'Can't we wait until we see Edie and Sammy?'

His smile faded as he shook his head. 'I've got more bad news.'

Charlotte's heartbeat thumped in her chest. 'Is it the house? Is it Lucy?'

Daniel looked into her eyes, compassion and focus in his gaze. 'Ted's gone missing.'

One a.m. The emotional whirlwind she'd been through in the last hours had left Charlotte unexpectedly calm. Maybe it was the night sky laid above her like an iron-black mantle, or the cool, still air she walked through. She smelled more rain in the clouds that appeared like shadows in the sky. Maybe ghosts crossing the wilderness of life into the tomorrow of somewhere heavenly. Charlotte hoped so. Heavenly sounded perfect this late at night.

Her limbs ached. Her heart beat steadily but it ached too. Her mind raced and her stomach rumbled. She hadn't eaten properly in almost twenty-four hours. But that had been her only foolishness since Daniel had dropped her off at Mrs J's house four hours ago.

She heaved the backpack more firmly onto her shoulder as she and Mrs J trod the wet, slippery land. The bag was packed with a spare torch and batteries; water; a minimal first-aid kit—the only one she'd had at home—some biscuits they'd been nibbling on as they walked the High Country in the darkness; a flask of coffee; a coil of nylon rope; a space blanket and a tin box full of matches and dry kindling.

'Are we heading in the right direction?' she asked Mrs J, who wore a padded body-warmer, tweed trousers and Wellington boots. Charlotte has slowed her pace over the last hour of trudging through fields and up and down hillsides. Mrs J hadn't spoken for twenty minutes, her breathing hard in her chest, telling Charlotte she was tired, and probably couldn't walk through the rest of the night searching for Ted.

'We're on the back end of Ray Smyth's farm,' Mrs J said. 'We'll descend from here onto the heritage trail.'

'Where will the others be?'

Mrs J stopped walking. 'Most likely Dan and Josh are skirting the other side of Ray's place. I reckon the volunteer rescue folk will be fanned out around the hillside by the town.'

'Here.' Charlotte slid the backpack off her shoulder and put it onto a grassy mound. 'Sit down for a while. Let's take a rest.' She led Mrs J to a seat-sized boulder and made her sit, then got the flask of coffee and two plastic cups out of the bag, and sat on the boulder next to Mrs J.

Mrs J sipped the lukewarm but still refreshing coffee as Charlotte wrapped her numbed hands around her own plastic cup. Summer or not, the night was cooler than she'd expected. Perhaps it was the air that floated around them in the silence and the unknown outcome of their endeavours that chilled her the most.

'Will we find him?' Charlotte asked.

'Like as not.'

'Has he been gone this long before?' He'd been gone fourteen hours now.

Mrs J shook her head. 'Only went missing once before. Four hours he was gone, although he thought he'd been away for weeks. Daniel found him at the bottom of the field behind the stock feeders'.

'Poor Grace.'

'She does her best.'

'You all do.' Charlotte had been more impressed by the gathering of people in the town when Daniel had driven her down Main Street around nine p.m. than with anything she'd ever witnessed. Every nook, shadowy corner and crevice around town had been searched. Every shopkeeper had opened up, switched on the lights in their shops and pulled blinds, lighting the street. Ted hadn't been found. A two-kilometre radius had been combed, the townspeople calling out, shedding the beams from torches onto the verges and into every bush. Charlotte and Daniel searched Grandy's farmhouse—skirting the perimeter of the gardens and driveway, and eventually breaking into the house to search that too. Daniel did it as carefully as possible, wrapping an old sack around his hand to smash a pane of glass on the farmhouse back door.

Charlotte hadn't worried about being in Grandy's house. His spirit wasn't there; it was someplace better. But she'd felt the emptiness as they left, Daniel covering the smashed pane of glass with the hessian sack, and locking up behind them. Who would love the farmhouse next?

'Just hope Ted regains consciousness,' Mrs Johnson said, bringing Charlotte back to the night and the endeavours ahead of them.

'You think he's had an accident?'

'Possibly. But I mean mentally back, not physically. If he's hurt, I hope he found himself somewhere safe to shelter from the thunderstorm.'

Charlotte peered at the grass, thinking about Ted and his woes. 'Many normal people say they've been taken by ... by extra-terrestrials.' Saying the word out loud felt silly, but she was determined not to make light of Ted's issues.

Mrs J looked across. 'You saying you believe Ted?'

'I believe he believes it.'

Mrs J nodded. 'I think we both know it's a kind of post-traumatic stress.'

'The twins?'

'Things haven't been so good at the stock feeders' either. Fewer people coming in wanting goods. Less money to spend around town.' Mrs J nodded at Charlotte's backpack. 'Hadn't you better call Dan? Let him know where we are?'

Daniel didn't know Charlotte had persuaded Mrs J to take her with her. Daniel didn't know Charlotte was out on the hillside—and Charlotte knew he wouldn't like it. 'He'll be busy. I'll call him later.'

Mrs J frowned. 'Doesn't know you're with me, does he?'

Charlotte was pretty sure a wisp of a smile slid across Clarissa's face. 'I'm not talking to him.'

'So how come you were with him in town earlier, hooked to his side as you both looked for Ted?'

Charlotte shifted on the boulder and settled more comfortably. 'He coerced me into staying with him.' She'd run into Daniel's arms at the hospital, and he'd been tender, but silence had settled between them on the drive back to Swallow's Fall.

'Man of force, our Daniel,' Mrs J said with a hint of teasing in her tone. 'What a thug, making you tag along with him—especially as you're not talking to him.'

Charlotte grimaced. 'He said he didn't trust me not to go wandering off on my own.' He was right, of course, but she wasn't going to give him the benefit of knowing that just yet. He'd sent her to stay with Mrs Johnson and Lily up at their house and she'd gone, ostensibly willingly. But there was no way Charlotte was going to be held back from helping the search for Ted.

'There's a lot can be said without words, Charlotte.'

Charlotte didn't want to continue this conversation. The secrets and lies uncovered in the last twenty-four hours had been mostly her fault—apart from Daniel going behind her back and buying her house, which was surely underhand. She didn't know, and didn't have time to think about it now. He'd said he wanted to talk later. Charlotte was done talking. She needed to get out of town and give herself time to recuperate and ponder the many events of the last five weeks. Events that had turned her from a self-assured woman into a saddened, lonely person hoping the quest had an end. Once Ted had been found, she'd pack all her belongings into her 4WD and leave Daniel to deal with his house and the townspeople. Although if she ever found out they'd allowed him to paint the weatherboard yellow, she might march straight back into town and show him phase three of the hammer grip manoeuvre.

Mrs J threw the contents of her plastic cup on to the grass at her feet. 'Best get on.'

'Why don't you wait here, Mrs Johnson?' Charlotte asked as Clarissa struggled to stand. 'I'll keep going.' She stood up and helped Mrs J to her feet.

'You don't know where you're heading.'

'I'm unlikely to get lost if I hit the heritage trail soon, and I've got Lucy with me.'

At the sound of her name, Lucy padded up to Charlotte, cocked her head and waited.

'I'll rest a bit then make my way down the hill,' Mrs J said.

'You don't have a mobile phone?' Charlotte asked as she repacked the backpack.

'Can't afford one. Wouldn't need one anyway, I'm only a twenty-minute walk into town.'

'You're a two-hour hike from town now. Here.' Charlotte pulled her mobile phone out of the backpack and handed it over. 'I'll leave you the coffee too, but I'll take the water in case I find Ted.'

'Don't know how to use a mobile.'

Charlotte unlocked the phone so anyone could use it, and showed Mrs J the screen. 'If someone calls,' although Charlotte had no idea who would—unlikely to be the realtor at this time of the night, 'you press Answer. If you want to call someone, press Call and punch in their number.'

'All right. I got that. I might give Lily a quick call. I'll pay you for the cost, mind.'

Charlotte couldn't help the laughter that tumbled through her lips at Mrs J's politeness. 'We won't worry about that now.' She lifted the torch from the darkened grass.

'Take it easy on the downwards slope, watch your footing. It's slippery.'

'I will.' Charlotte patted Mrs J's shoulder, and in a moment of sudden appreciation, bent and gave her shoulders a quick hug.

'You should hit the heritage trail in about an hour,' Mrs J called as Charlotte tramped away, keeping the white tip of Lucy's bobbing tail in view. A full moon tonight. Maybe Grandy had sent it to guide her.

'She's *what*?' Dan stared Josh in the eye, blinking against the sweat running down his forehead. Five hours he'd been out looking for Ted. Not a lengthy time. He suspected the rest of the night and the day was ahead of him, but given the trauma of everything that had happened, his body was holding up but his mind told him he was whacked and needed a break.

'What's the problem?' Josh asked.

'I told her to stay with Mrs J. That's where I left her.'

'You didn't really expect Mrs J to stay at home, did you?'

'I expected Charlotte to follow my instructions.'

Josh stepped back. The duskiness of night and the boulder crops and tussocks around them would have put him into shadows if it hadn't been for the full moon and the torches each held. 'Settle down,' Josh said. 'What's got into you?'

Dan breathed deeply. His girl was out in the night without him, that's what had got into him. He pulled his mobile phone out of his back pocket and called Charlotte's number.

'Come on. Answer.'

After what felt like an eternity of ringing in his ear, a voice spoke.

'Hello?'

'Mrs J? It's Dan. Are you alright?'

'Fine, Daniel. How are you?'

'Is Charlotte with you?'

'She was.'

Was? 'So where is she now?'

'Probably just hit the heritage trail behind Ray's place.'

'You mean she's on her own?'

'I got a bit tired, so I'm taking a rest. She left me her telephone so I could talk to Lily.'

'You didn't think to call *me*?'

'You're busy, aren't you?'

Dan sucked in air. 'Mrs J, are you alright?'

'Of course. I'll make my way down to town in another ten minutes or so.'

'I'll send Josh for you. Where are you?'

'For goodness' sake, Daniel, I know this hill like the veins on the back of my hand. If you feel you've got some spare time to perform your heroics perhaps you and Josh could head off to the heritage trail, because I've got a feeling Charlotte is going to find Ted. And I've got another feeling that Ted is hurt and Charlotte is going to need help.'

'This is the reason you should have called me,' Dan said sternly.

'I was about to, and don't use that pinched tone with me, young man. I couldn't find your number on this damned stupid mobile telephone. I've been—'

'Alright.' Dan raised his hand in placation, his mind focussed on two things: Mrs J needed help whether she wanted it or not, and Charlotte was out there, alone. 'Alright,' he said again. 'I apologise. Does Charlotte have Lucy with her?'

'Honest to goodness, Daniel, it's time you gave that woman some credit. Not only has she got the dog with her, she's got a backpack full of the necessaries. God give me strength to handle men who think they have the—'

Dan cut her off again. 'Where are you, Mrs J?'

'Is that Clarissa?'

Dan turned to Ray Smyth, the farmer whose property Charlotte was currently wandering alone. He nodded.

'Give the phone to me.' Ray took the mobile off Dan. 'Clarissa? Now listen up. Where are you? Okay, got it. Stay put—do you hear me? If you take one step from that point I'll personally kill you.' Ray nodded into the night as he listened to whatever Mrs J was saying. 'That's good. I'll tell Dan. And I'll be with you in one hour. One hour, Clarissa, and mark my words, if you're not within two foot of that rock formation in that field, you'll be answering to me.' He punched the End Call button, looked up at Dan and grinned. 'Gutsy women. They'll be the death of us.'

'Where's Charlotte?'

Ray didn't mince words or time. 'I'll get Clarissa, you and Josh head to the heritage trail at the point where Slowdown Creek meets Pebble Hill. I reckon that's where your Charlotte is. And if I'm right, that area will have been swamped in the rain we've just had. There could be a landslip.'

'Got it.' Dan took the mobile phone from Ray and stuffed it into his back pocket. 'Josh,' he called. 'Get over here.' He looked back at Ray. 'Thanks.'

Ray grinned.

Despite his unease and the worry churning inside him, Dan grinned back. Guys in love got more than bug-eyed about their women. Guys in love got protective. Charlotte wasn't his friend at the moment, let alone his girlfriend, but he was damned well going to chase her until she was or she told him to get lost. Which he would be, without her.

He turned as a loudmouthed guy barked his displeasure to the rescue team. '... and I've got a day's work to do tomorrow,' he said. 'I've spent the whole night looking for this nutcase. I'm off.'

The loudmouth from the bar last week. Dan glanced around, and sure enough, his team mates were ten paces behind him, nodding agreement and packing up their kit.

'Hey,' Dan called as he walked towards the group.

The mouthy guy paused and looked Dan's way. 'What's your problem?'

'You.' Dan smashed his fist into the guy's face, punching him hard enough to knock him down without breaking his jaw, although it was likely he'd split the talkative mouth and maybe knocked one or two teeth out. He damned well hoped so, because if the guy got up with another complaint, Dan had a healthy desire to knock him down again.

'Vhat ... Vhat vas at for?' the guy asked, then spat on the ground.

Dan grabbed him by the wrist and yanked him to his feet. 'That's just a meet and greet, mate. Next time I hear you badmouth anybody, you stay on the ground.' Dan clenched his teeth, attempting to hold on to his anger. 'And if I see you or any of your buddies in my bar, you get thrown out. In fact, if you're seen within a five-kilometre radius of town I reckon you'll have more than my fist to deal with. We look after our own. And you're not one of us. Now get going. You're not needed.'

Dan turned and headed for the makeshift tent the rescue team had erected hours earlier. A five-minute breather would help settle his fears and clear his mind. He wouldn't be any use to Ted or Charlotte if he lost his focus now.

He looked up as a shadow crossed in front of him. Josh, headed towards the temporary tea and tucker table Mrs Tam had set up.

'What's got into him?' Josh asked, jutting a thumb towards where Dan had walked and obviously thinking Dan couldn't hear him.

'He's in love,' Mrs Tam said.

Dan stepped back into the shadows. Did everyone know? And how long had they known? And why had it taken Dan so long to figure it out?

'He's what?' Josh asked. 'With who?'

'Charlotte.'

Josh paused for a long time. 'When did that happen?'

Mrs Tam tutted. 'Where have you been, Josh?'

Twenty-One

'Oh, bugger.' Charlotte aimed the torch at Lucy, who barked and twirled as though she were doing some sort of rescue dance. If the dog had found Ted, it didn't look good. Not for Ted or Charlotte.

Charlotte told herself to be calm. The eerie night and the damp air sucked heat from her flesh after the trek down the hill and along the heritage trail in the dark. She picked her way to the edge of the uneven granite pathway and shone the light on the rubble in front of her. Thousands of pebbles the size of chicken eggs and rocks like watermelons covered the rest of the naturally hewn trail, halting her journey.

Lucy yapped again and Charlotte lifted the torch. Beneath the excited barking, another cry punctured the otherwise quiet night.

'Ted!' Charlotte called.

Again, a muffled, woebegone human voice.

'Ted! It's Charlotte. I'm coming.'

Charlotte moved carefully, inching her way over the rubble. She stopped and shone the torch upwards. Earth, grassy tufts and rocks littered the steep incline of the hill that should be sheltering the trail. The rain had been hard but she wouldn't have expected the vibrations to create such a slip. Angling the torch up further, she saw the large, craggy shadows of a tree root. A big snow gum, like the one in her garden. It had obviously once crowned the top of the hill but had fallen on its side, uprooted during the rain, and now looked like a shipwreck on a mudslide. A creek ran down the side of the landslip, bark and branches bobbing in the fast-running water.

'Hello.' Ted's voice.

Charlotte focussed on her pathway. 'I'm here. I can hear you.' But she couldn't see him. 'Where are you, Ted? Keep talking so I can find you.'

'I'm down a blasted hole.'

A smile of pure relief touched Charlotte's lips. If Ted was annoyed it meant he wasn't too badly harmed.

Lucy barked, only a few metres away. Charlotte moved to the dog, shoved her backpack off her shoulder and stretched herself out on the wet, dirty, stony ground. She peered into a narrow hole, shining the torch.

'It's pretty dark down here,' Ted said.

Charlotte rotated the light and found Ted. He was on his back, about a metre-and-a-half down. The roof of his cave sat so low it only allowed Charlotte sight of his feet, legs, hips and waist. She couldn't see his face.

'I've twisted my ankle or something,' he said. 'Can't move an inch without feeling a bit of pain.'

'I'm so sorry, Ted. Please stay still.' Charlotte sat the base of the torch on the ground and pulled the bottled water out of the backpack. 'I've got water, Ted. I'm going to reach down and see if I can pass it to you. Will you be able to turn or lean forwards and take it from me?'

He grumbled indistinctly. 'No,' he said at last.

Damn. 'Okay, don't worry. I'll think of something else.'

She flashed the torchlight over the mound that enclosed Ted. It looked like a natural cave. A huge, flat, rectangular boulder served as a roof and from the moss in its cracks, it had been there for decades. She didn't have her phone and it was too late to regret that.

Scrabbling in the backpack, she found pen and notepaper. She wrote a hasty note, describing where she was as best she could. Any of the townspeople would know this area. They'd find her and Ted.

'Lucy, come here, girl.' She folded the note into a concertina and tucked it into Lucy's collar, twisting it under and over and lacing the end securely in the silver buckle, the way she had any number of times. For additional emphasis, she unwrapped one of the bandages in her first-aid kit and tied that to Lucy's collar too, making a big white bow. The note wouldn't be immediately visible, but they'd see the bandage and wonder why the dog was wearing it. She took the dog's warm face in her hands and kissed the top of her wet nose. 'Go find Daniel, Lucy. Where's Daniel?'

Lucy perked up, her lithe body taut, expression alert.

'Go find Daniel.' Charlotte had used the words over and over, every time she sent a note to Daniel. Lucy only had to make a minute's journey from the house to Kookaburra's, but she'd never failed. The dog loved working. And Lucy wandered these hills every day on her own. She'd know the way back to town— or to wherever Daniel was.

Lucy bounded into the night, the rubble and muddy earth hardly bothering her nimble legs, and a few seconds later she was gone.

Charlotte peeled her jacket off, then her long-sleeved jersey. It took only moments to find a broken tree branch tall and sturdy enough to shove into a softened-earth part of the track. She braced the branch and secured it by piling rocks and rubble around the base, then took off her white sports singlet. The cool air nipped and brushed at her naked torso. She re-dressed in the jersey and the jacket, and then secured her singlet to the top of the branch, tying the shoulder straps to the top and making a flag. *Please find us soon*, she prayed silently. It would be an hour or two, maybe a lot longer. What she planned next would be hard. Hardest thing she'd ever done or was likely ever to do again. She had no option.

On her stomach once more, she threw the fastened backpack into the cave, making sure it skimmed the wall and slid down to land by Ted's right leg. His left leg was bent as though he'd found the most comfortable position for his injured ankle. She reached down and put the torch onto a ledge in the cave, jutting out like a shelf. She waited, her hand on the torch to ensure it wouldn't fall from its resting place, then she squeezed through the narrow aperture.

'Ted,' she said. 'I'm coming in with you.'

By Dan's reckoning he and Josh were about an hour and a half from the area where Mrs J said Charlotte was headed. They'd left Ray to find Mrs J and skirted around the hill behind Top Field farm, running most of the way, relying on their torches to spot potholes in the sloping fields. They'd slowed the last half-hour as they hit the heritage trail from the northern end and were taking it at a fast stride.

Small landslips and fallen rocks told Dan what to expect about the state of the trail further south. The rain had been heavy and the closer they got to the denser middle section of the trail, the more he realised the danger Ted could have got himself into. Charlotte was working that section, and whether she'd found Ted or not, she'd be having a tough time.

Give the woman some credit, Mrs J had said. Dan would be happy to, as soon as he found her. She wasn't used to the area like he was. She wasn't as physically strong as Dan, and who knew what she was in the middle of if she'd found Ted.

'I'm holding up a sec, Dan,' Josh said behind him.

'What's wrong?'

'Bootlace.'

Dan stopped as Josh hunched down to attend to his unlaced boot. 'Take the chance for a drink, too,' he said. 'And eat a chocolate bar.' He turned to the trail again and looked through the misty darkness as he grabbed his own water bottle from his backpack and took a slug.

Why was Charlotte so special to him and why hadn't he understood before now? God only knew what he was to her, but to him she was light on water. Without her light, he wouldn't see the ripples on the surface or know how deep the water was. Wouldn't know where the shore was. If she left, the images of her might disappear, leaving him only an essence to hold on to, coming to him at the oddest moments in his day. Opening the doors of the bar. Pulling a pint. Running the hillside, trying not to squash the newly sprouted wildflowers.

He bent and plucked a flower off a wild geranium tumbling along the verge. A weed, although his mother had kept pots of the plants outside the front door of his childhood home. It meant gentility and esteem. He knew, because Charlotte wasn't the only thing he'd Googled. Yeah, he thought, as he pocketed the flower. What he hadn't researched were his own reasons for loving Charlotte.

'Okay, let's go,' Josh said.

Dan concentrated on the way forwards as they got back into their pace quickly, but his thoughts were still on Charlotte.

Look after Red, Mum. Look after my girl until I get to her. Charlotte encompassed the gentleness he'd been missing since he'd lost his parents. So maybe it was his mother's turn to tap his resolute shoulder. Maybe he could make Charlotte understand the connection they shared through flowers after all. Along with his own damned foolishness, because the geranium also meant stupidity.

Would Charlotte ever know how sentimental he'd turned? Half of him hoped so, and the other half preferred to retain his masculine and sceptical outlook. It felt like words were being spoken from the heavens, or the afterlife—or whatever the hell went on that wasn't of this earth. Or maybe Dan was just going crazy, not knowing where his girl was. Not knowing if she was in trouble.

Charlotte had never wanted to know how it might feel to be incarcerated in a submarine, but she was getting a taste of it now. There was hardly room to do much more than shuffle herself into a slightly different position in order to ease the pain of the rocky floor jabbing into her hips and back. Which was more than Ted was able to do, with his heavier weight and throbbing ankle.

Charlotte had slipped the silver first-aid blanket over Ted's torso. At least his arms and body would be warmed.

'I've been doing a lot of thinking while I've been lying here,' Ted said. 'About my space research.'

'Just lie still.'

'I am still. Can't move in this place. Especially with you in it too.'

Charlotte turned her laugh into a cough. 'Well, I'm not leaving you, so you'll have to put up with me.' She unscrewed one of the water bottles and offered some to Ted, holding the plastic bottle to his mouth. 'Just a sip.' She didn't have much first-aid knowledge and regretted not having done a course or something. She'd bet all the townspeople knew first aid. They'd have to, living so remotely from clinics or doctors.

'How did you get down here?' Charlotte asked, hoping the conversation would eat into the time it took for the rescue people to find them.

'Don't know. Woke up and here I was. Think I might have slipped, although I don't know how I managed to get in head first. I remember a heavy crashing noise.'

'That must have been the tree uprooting above us, on top of the hill.'

'It's the rain. Makes some parts of Top Field farm more like a creek of shingles.' Ted paused. 'Miss Simmons—'

'It's Charlotte, Ted. Call me Charlotte.'

'I've been re-evaluating my priorities. My wants and needs.' He cleared his throat. 'I've been concentrating on my space studies too much as a way of ignoring what's really happening. I've been deceiving myself. It's all down to environmental factors, you see, and times have been a touch hard.'

Charlotte patted his hand. 'Don't worry about that now.' He'd been down here for hours in this cramped quarter and must have had nothing to think about except his troubles.

'It's time I came back to earth and gave my attention to the women in my family. And it's not that I'm discounting the possibility of life outside our universe, but I no longer have a desire to be taken by anything considered alien. I don't think it'd be pleasant.'

'I wouldn't want you to be taken. What would the town do without you? Or the ladies in your family who love you?'

'That's a kind observation, Miss Simmons.'

'We're stuck in a cave together, Ted, I think it's okay to use first names.' She grinned at him.

'Doesn't seem right. I haven't been the friendliest or most hospitable, have I?'

Charlotte patted his large hand. 'I don't blame you. I charged in like a shot from a pistol with all my ideas.'

'Oh, that you did. Stirred us up alright.'

'Will you accept my apology?'

'If you'll accept mine first,' he said with staunch politeness.

Charlotte squeezed his hand.

'Best turn the torch off, Miss Simmons. We need to conserve the batteries in case they don't find us.'

'They'll find us.' Charlotte aimed the torch at the opening and flicked the light on and off rapidly. The night sky lit up in pockets of white light. Then she switched the torch off and took a gulp of the darkness. 'And they'll find us before daybreak,' she told Ted.

He quietened, his breathing slowing as he rested. Charlotte blinked up at the opening above her and into the night, full of stars outside. What was this strange sensation rushing within her? A meeting of fear and peace? An amity with the dark? She was enclosed in an extremely confined space—trapped, because she wouldn't leave Ted, and she wasn't scared.

'There. Look.' Dan pointed into the dark. 'There,' he said again as a flash of white caught his eye.

'It's Lucy,' Josh said.

'Yeah.' Lucy's white-tipped tail bobbed as she raced towards them from the southern end of the trail. 'Luce!'

The dog barked as she bounded for them.

'Good girl, good girl, Luce.' Dan bent and undid the bow on her collar. 'Shine your torch for me, Josh.' Dan got rid of the bandage and flung it to the ground. He inhaled deeply. There it was. A note.

He unwound it from the collar and opened it, his fingers tingling at the tips.

Have found Ted. We're in a cave—a landslip. Please call Daniel Bradford if you find this dog.

Dan's heart swelled. She'd asked for him.

Can't give position or grid ref as haven't got a map but we're southern end of heritage trail. Granite hillside. Big snow gum at top has uprooted and fallen. So sorry for any inconvenience but please get in touch with Daniel.

'Jesus, sweetheart.' So damned polite—at a time when she must have been scared, no matter how intelligent and brave her written words were.

Dog's name is Lucy. She might lead you back to us. 2.45 a.m., Charlotte Simmons, Swallow's Fall resident.

Dan scrunched the note, shoved it into his pocket and picked up his torch from the ground. 'She's found Ted,' he told Josh. 'We're close. They're by the snow gum on the granite hillside.'

Josh turned to the trail. 'We might make it in fifteen minutes.'

'Let's go.' Dan took hold of Lucy's head and tickled her under her chin, the way he always did when he wanted her to take a note to Charlotte. 'Where's Charlotte, Luce?'

Lucy didn't wait to be asked a second time, she yapped and headed back the way she'd come.

'Ted—listen … It's Lucy.'

Charlotte grabbed the torch, aimed it at the opening and into the early morning sky, switching it on and off rapidly.

Lucy's barking got louder and closer.

'Charlotte!'

Daniel. Relief rushed through her at the sound of his strong voice. He'd come. He'd found them.

'We're here!' Charlotte called, surprised to find her throat gravelly. She coughed, swallowed a couple of times to get more moisture in her mouth and called out again.

'Jesus Christ.'

Charlotte flung the torchlight upwards. 'Oh, Daniel. Thank God.' So used to seeing the sunlight at his back as he stood in her doorway, Charlotte's breath hitched at the sight of his head and shoulders above her, haloed in torchlight.

'Okay, sweetheart, angle the light away. You're blinding me.'

'Sorry.' She swung the beam downwards.

'Are you hurt?' he asked.

'No. But Ted's twisted his ankle. It doesn't look broken but I'm not expert enough to tell. I gave him painkillers about two hours ago.'

'It still hurts like billy-o,' Ted said. 'But it's not broken.'

'Alright, Ted. We'll get you out.'

Daniel moved from the opening. Charlotte heard Josh's voice, answering something Daniel asked him. She breathed deeply, excitement mounting at the thought of being pulled out of here. Two big strong men had come to their rescue because of one beautiful, smart little dog.

'You need to get Miss Simmons out first,' Ted called up.

Daniel's face appeared at the opening again. He swung his torch into the cave, swinging the light around. The torch gave off enough light for Charlotte to see a frown, and his thinned mouth.

'What we need to do, Ted,' Daniel said, 'is get you turned. Charlotte—move so that you've got your back to me.'

Charlotte curled her legs up to her body and turned on her side, using her hands and feet for momentum. She bumped her head on the rock of the roof with every movement, but eventually she had her back to the opening where there was room to sit up straight.

'You know what I want you to do?' Daniel asked, but Charlotte had already leaned forwards to Ted.

'I need you to lift yourself up, Ted,' she said, taking hold of his arms. 'There's enough room for you to swivel around on your side. I'll help by holding your left leg, but it'll hurt.'

'Could take my boot off,' Ted said, 'and bind my ankle.'

'No,' Charlotte told him. 'We don't know what damage you've done; it's best to keep your boot on.'

Charlotte didn't know how many minutes it took but enough wetted dust and sandy particles kicked up with each hampered move Ted made to have her choking and coughing. His groans of obvious agony shuddered through her but she kept his left foot and calf lifted in her hands as he moved. When space became a premium, she had to let go of Ted's leg while he turned himself further. She gritted her teeth and tried not to think of the pain he was enduring. No complaints from him though. Not one.

'Okay, sweetheart,' Daniel said when at last Ted was turned enough to have his back and shoulders in front of Charlotte.

Charlotte looked up. She wished he'd stop calling her sweetheart. She wasn't his sweetheart. And she'd told him she wasn't talking to him. After they'd got Ted out, she wouldn't be talking to him any more than she'd been talking to him before. No matter how glorious it was to see him.

'That's you out, Charlotte. Put your arms up and I'll pull you up.'

She lifted her arms above her head and jolted when Daniel took hold of her wrists. She used her hips and legs to kick herself up and winced as her bottom scraped sharp rock. She bit her bottom lip. If Ted could do what he'd done without moaning about it, so could she.

'I've got you, Charlotte.'

She'd feel more comfortable if he called her Red.

He had his hands under her arms now. He lifted her easily, and she was out and on her feet, fighting the urge to throw her arms around his neck and thank him. To kiss him over and over and tell him how amazingly wonderful and strong he was. But she couldn't do that because she wasn't talking to him.

'What the hell were you doing down there?' he asked.

'He was hurt. He needed water and painkillers and the blanket. I couldn't leave him.'

'Sit down,' he told her, and turned for Ted.

There was enough room for Dan and Josh to put one arm each through the aperture and haul Ted out. He did groan this time as his bad foot trailed on the floor of the cave.

When they got him out, they laid him on the ground. Daniel took his jacket off and used it as a makeshift pillow for Ted's head as Josh got water out of his backpack. They washed the dust off Ted's face, and then gave him sips of the water and another two painkillers. He murmured his thanks and lay back.

'I called the rescue guys after I found Lucy,' Daniel told Ted. 'They're on their way. They'll have a stretcher. We'll carry you to the end of the track and then you'll be driven into town in the back of the rescue ute.'

Ted lifted his hand and gestured behind him at where Charlotte sat. 'She was marvellous. Just marvellous.'

Daniel nodded. 'You take it easy. Not long and you'll be home enjoying one of Grace's fattening lamb casseroles and a pint of my finest ale.'

'Sounds just the ticket.'

Dan glanced up at Charlotte, stood and walked over to her.

She scrambled to her feet. 'He'll be alright, won't he?' she asked as a means of stalling whatever it was he was about to do or say.

He nodded, then put his arms out and pulled her into his body, cupping the back of her head, holding her face against his shoulder.

'Jesus, Charlotte,' he said, his voice low and rushed. 'You feel wonderful.'

'I'm stressed and tired.'

'I know you must be emotional and all that, but you feel terrific.'

'Could you let me go, Daniel?' Not only was he squashing her bones in his hug, he'd forgotten that she wasn't talking to him. Had he also forgotten about buying her house from under her feet? He wasn't getting hold of the key to the front door until she'd had a shower and a damned good cry beneath the hot water.

'I'm so proud of you, Charlotte.'

He was? Bugger. That almost melted her resolve. 'Don't forget I'm not talking to you.'

'Looks like we're even on that bet,' he said, ignoring her warning and running his hands down her back until they landed on her bottom. 'Tight,' he said. 'I figure you could run five K easily now. Probably more.' He grinned at her, looking boyish and relieved and too bloody gorgeous for her torn emotions.

'Get your hands off my bum,' she said, struggling to loosen herself from his hold. 'And I have no intention of running all the way back to town.'

He squashed her even more, his arms like a vice. 'I'd carry you if I had to.'

'No need. I'm fine.'

'You scared the life out of me.'

'You can let me go now.'

'Got so worried, I hit a bloke.'

'What? Daniel—let me go.'

'He deserved it, mind you.'

'Daniel!'

He let her go. 'What is it? Where are you hurt?'

Charlotte pushed him in the chest. 'I'm not hurt. You were squishing me too hard.'

He stepped back, mouth open in some sort of bewilderment. 'I'm trying to take your mind off your experience.' He pointed at the cave. 'I know what it must have felt like for you after your ... after what you went through as a kid. I've never been more proud of anyone in my life.'

Charlotte halted the words of remonstration on the tip of her tongue. She hadn't been frightened in the cave. Not a jot. It wasn't Daniel's fault he thought she might have been scared. He knew about the little girl hiding in the darkened wardrobe, but he didn't know the whole story. He didn't know how she'd fought all her grown-up years to hide her fear. And how could she explain to him what she'd felt, or how her terrors had faded in the dark of a cave, lying next to Ted and tending him?

These were the emotional issues she'd be taking with her when she left. And she was leaving. She'd made up her mind because there was no choice. She was leaving Daniel and taking her love for him with her. Never to be revealed to anyone.

'I'm not talking to you,' she said.

'I don't care. I was worried.'

He would have been. They'd all been worried. Charlotte had been worried, why else would she have tramped into the night to help? Daniel's kind of worry had tethered her to Mrs J's house, not because he didn't believe she had enough gumption to do something on her own but because he wanted to show her his manly, protective side. The side she couldn't face. What was the point when she was leaving?

'Maybe we'll talk later.' She turned and walked over to Ted and Josh.

'You're damned right we'll talk later,' Daniel called after her.

Bugger. Now she'd pissed him off again.

Charlotte hadn't been in Kookaburra's when it was open for business, and she'd bet Daniel a ninety-K run he'd never had so many people in his bar in the entire six years he'd been in town.

Neither was it normally open for business now, at 5.30 a.m, but Daniel's coffee machine was thrumming and throwing off enough steam to drive the Flying Scotsman as Josh made coffee for anyone who wanted it. Lily moved back and forth from the kitchen with fried egg and bacon sandwiches as though her life depended on making sure the townspeople were fed and fattened.

Charlotte sipped her flat white, the taste welcome in her mouth and the caffeine hitting her veins in a much needed blast. How much love from a reserved, resilient community not big enough to be defined as a town could one outsider take? She hadn't accepted a fried egg sandwich because it reminded her too painfully of Grandy. She wouldn't be able to swallow any food anyway—her stomach was twisted in knots of anxiety.

Everyone was in the bar, even townspeople she'd hardly seen, and those who lived further out. Ira and Julia offered a loving picture as they stood together, little Lochie asleep in Ira's arms. Charlotte didn't think Grandy had much to be concerned about if he was looking down at his granddaughter.

Tiredness, sadness and bewilderment filled Charlotte's consciousness. The chatter around her was all about Grandy, baby Edie, Ethan, Ted—and Charlotte.

'Absolutely splendid effort,' Ted said to Ray Smyth and Mrs J—and everyone else in the bar. His twisted ankle hadn't affected his vocal cords. 'Top notch, if you ask me. She didn't bat an eyelid—just popped on down beside me.' He'd been placed in an old wheelchair Mrs Tam had retrieved from the Town Hall. Ira had tended Ted's injuries, delighting everyone with his knowledge of first aid and Ted's leg was now propped up by a plank of wood and duct tape from Morelly's. 'Although there was hardly any room for her,' Ted added.

'Might be time to go on that diet I've been harping on about for the last year,' Grace told him, her hand on his shoulder as she sat on the arm of his wheelchair. Ted simply patted her hand.

'What a night.' His voice lowered. 'We'll never forget this night. Not any of us.'

Charlotte huddled into a wing-back armchair and decided she didn't want to dwell on the events the town would never forget, since she'd had a hand in all of them.

'Best get on with it then,' Mrs J said loudly, bringing everyone in the room to silence. 'Firstly, we'd like to thank Charlotte for everything she did tonight.'

People murmured their responses but Charlotte didn't want any thanks for what she'd done for Ted. Anyone would have done the same.

'We've lost Grandy,' Mrs J continued, sorrow diminishing her usually crisp tone. 'But it looks like we've found family, and Grandy would want us to acknowledge that, and not our loss of him.'

Bobbing heads and quiet calls of 'hear, hear' swept around the room. Charlotte wondered how they'd celebrate Grandy's life. They were bound to have an additional ceremony after the funeral, maybe a remembrance service at the Town Hall.

'We've got little Edie to welcome home in a couple of days,' Mrs J said, and then paused in what Charlotte decided was a dramatic manner. 'And we've got two brothers who have only just found each other. So let's get this out in the open now before rumours spread.'

Charlotte hissed in a breath and gripped her coffee cup.

'Here's the story,' Mrs J said, 'and I'm going to make it succinct. Grandy had an association with Ethan's mother and that's none of our business.' She challenged her audience with a stare but no-one spoke. 'What *is* our business is our duty of care to everyone in this town, so what I'm saying is, we let Junior and Ethan sort out their new family ties in their own way, and we don't interfere.'

'Are they talking?' someone asked. 'Or arguing?'

Mrs J stabbed the man with a glare. 'They're brothers and they're supporting each other the way their father would expect them to.' She took her pointed gaze off the man and directed her attention back to the other townspeople.

Charlotte snuck a look at Ted, surprised he hadn't piped up. He was still frowning but he didn't look tortured or annoyed, he looked keenly perceptive, his focus entirely on Mrs J as though she was the captain to his commander, which, Charlotte supposed Mrs J was.

'We all thought Ethan's father was Thomas O'Donnell,' Mrs J said, 'and we all know what he was like and what he did. He caused trouble and pain for the Granger family—and for many of us in town—with his drinking and his disgraceful physical abuse of Ethan's mother, and of Ethan himself. But that's in the past and the Grangers have helped us move towards the future. We don't forget that.'

Appreciation and wholehearted acceptance sang around the bar.

'We've also got old news to discuss.'

Charlotte bit into her bottom lip.

'Mrs J.' Daniel stepped from the bar and walked through the gathering. 'How about we do this later?'

'Later won't fix rumours, Daniel. I want this out in the open and understood.'

Oh, bugger. Charlotte's skin flushed in mortification.

Mrs J leaned up to Daniel and spoke quietly in his ear. Daniel nodded, mouth pursed but obviously agreeing with whatever she'd told him. He stepped back and glanced over at Charlotte. Concern creased his brow but he dipped his chin to her, as though telling her it would be okay.

Charlotte stared into her coffee cup, willing herself somewhere else. His frustration at her for not talking to him wasn't helping her to understand what he might be trying to say.

She glanced up. Daniel ran a hand over his now bowed head, his other hand on his hip, looking as though he loathed what Mrs J was about to say as much as Charlotte would. But he didn't speak up or try to stop Mrs J from going on.

'So.' Mrs J put her hands into the pockets of her body-warmer. 'Turns out we have more than blood ties to deal with today.'

Here it comes, Charlotte thought.

'Turns out that Charlotte Simmons was also a victim of O'Donnell's abuse.'

Charlotte squeezed her eyes closed.

'The man killed her mother when she was a child.'

'You saying she's the kid who hid in the wardrobe?' someone asked.

'I remember that,' said another. 'We had the police down here asking questions.'

Charlotte didn't need to open her eyes to know that all eyeballs in the room had rotated her way.

'And we're not going to discuss the particulars,' Daniel said, his voice loud enough to stop the chatter.

'So why did she come to Swallow's Fall?' someone asked.

'Did she know about Ethan and Grandy?'

For the first time ever, Charlotte didn't hear disparagement in the voices, but a genuine interest.

'I said we're not discussing the particulars.' Daniel's voice had firmed as though he was talking through gritted teeth. Charlotte didn't know, she still had her eyes closed. Every muscle in her body was tense.

'Yes, we are discussing particulars, Daniel,' Mrs J said. 'From what I've gathered after talking on the telephone to both Ethan and Junior, and from the conversation I had with Charlotte while we were looking for Ted …'

Charlotte opened her eyes. She hadn't discussed her history with Mrs J.

'It's common knowledge O'Donnell murdered a woman who had a small child,' Mrs J continued. 'We all know that because we lived through the nightmare of O'Donnell and had to answer to the police all those years back when they were looking for him. It was a relief when he was killed.'

More murmurs, but otherwise, Mrs J had a rapt audience.

'Charlotte bought the B&B and arrived in town without having a clue what she was heading into.'

Charlotte sucked her breath in and held it.

'The poor girl discovered she was in the town her mother's murderer had lived in. Imagine the terror of that. A coincidence, certainly, but one that was fortuitous for us. The B&B will be up and running again soon, and as we've all signed consent for the tourist manifesto, the B&B will prove a worthy addition to our town. So thanks are due, again, to Charlotte.'

Oh no. Charlotte struggled with her conscience as Mrs J poured fabrication onto fabrication. The B&B would never be up and running.

'I'm buying the paint.'

Charlotte stared at Ted.

'For the B&B,' he said. 'Yellow paint.'

God bless him, but he was too late.

'But Dan bought the house, didn't he?' a woman asked. 'Wasn't that what they were arguing about before Grandy had his heart attack?'

'That's between me and Charlotte,' Dan said. 'We've got some things to discuss.'

'Like what?'

'Like none of your business,' Daniel said.

'I'm still buying the paint,' Ted chimed in, and slapped the arm of his wheelchair. 'Whatever colour.'

'There'll be no changes to anything until Charlotte says there can be.' Daniel stepped forwards. 'And there's something else you all need to know, since we're stemming a flow of rumours.' He pulled his shoulders back and heaved in a breath. 'I've got plans underway to turn Kookaburra's into a proper hotel.'

The entire room stilled.

Charlotte looked straight ahead of her. The blinds were open on Kookaburra's big windows and the dawn glowed through the glass in tones of hazy lemon-yellow. She didn't want to be a witness to Daniel's explanations of how or what he intended. Didn't want to know what he'd be using the B&B for either.

She put her cup of coffee onto a table beside her armchair and slowly stood.

Nobody noticed as she walked carefully along the perimeter of the restaurant area, snuck behind the bar and made her way down the back corridor. She opened the door, stepped out into what might be her last day in Swallow's Fall and walked along the alley to the B&B. She had no idea what she would do next. Except head for the shower.

Twenty-Two

Dan waited for the squall. He'd seen Charlotte slip out the back and wanted to run after her, but he had to deal with this first.

Silence still. Perhaps they hadn't understood him.

'I mean a proper hotel,' he said. 'Open all day. Seven ensuite bedrooms. Paying guests.'

'We know that,' Ted said.

Dan swung to him. 'You know?'

'We're cautious, not daft.'

'I didn't know,' someone piped up.

'Well, you know now,' Mrs J said.

'I mean a real hotel,' Dan said, swinging his arm at the doors and indicating the street. 'Tourists tramping around the town seven days a week.'

'Can I have a job?' a young voice asked.

Dan looked across at Gemma Munroe, standing next to Lily.

'Of course you can,' Dan told Gemma.

'Can I change my working hours to daytime instead of evening?' Lily asked.

'Anything you want, Lily.'

'I've always wanted to work behind a bar,' an older resident said, thumbs hooked into his braces. 'Wouldn't mind a part-time position, since we're all putting our hands up for one.'

'I'll teach you how to pull a schooner,' Josh said, smiling. 'Then you can have my job.'

Dan stepped forwards, hope building inside him. 'There'll be plenty of work around.'

'Have you got your all-day trading licence?' a man asked.

Dan nodded.

'Couldn't purchase a whisky from you, could I?'

'It's only six o'clock in the morning,' a woman said.

'And it's been a hell of a long night.'

Dan grinned. 'Josh, open up. There's a tot for anyone who wants one. On the house.'

As people moved around the bar and once more began tucking into the breakfasts Lily and Gemma had made, Dan took a steadying breath. He could slip out now, he wouldn't be seen.

'Saw her leave,' Mrs J said, suddenly at Dan's side. 'Not pleasant for her, having her past discussed like that but as I said to you, Daniel, it was best to get the story out in the open.'

Dan nodded. 'I agree, and thanks for softening it, but I should have stood next to her and held her hand or something.'

'Doubt she'd have let you. She's not speaking to you.'

Dan winced. 'She says she's leaving.'

'What do you expect her to do, now you've bought her house? And why did you buy it?'

'I have every respect for you, Mrs J, but you know damned well why.'

'Haven't got a first clue. And don't swear.'

'I want to marry her and live with her in the house. I love her.'

Mrs J cocked an eyebrow. 'Oh?'

Dan straightened. He had everything in place to get his girl, but there was one promise he had to keep first.

'Mrs Tam,' he called, 'could you come here for a minute please?'

Mrs Tam padded across Kookaburra's with a glass of sherry in her hand. 'What's going on now?'

'Daniel's going to marry Charlotte.'

'Lovely.' Mrs Tam smiled. 'And?' she asked Dan.

Dan cleared his throat. 'I promised you both I'd ask so here goes. Do I have your blessing to ask Charlotte to marry me?'

'Do you need it?' Mrs J said.

'No.'

'Well, thank the good Lord for that. If you'd said yes I'd have pronounced you soft in that masculine head of yours. What are you waiting for?'

'Go get her,' Mrs Tam said.

Dan headed for the doors.

'What's happening?' he heard Ted ask.

'Dan's going for Charlotte.'

'Now? Grace! Quick. Take the brake of this infernal chair. Dan's going for Miss Simmons.'

Jesus, there was nothing private around here but Dan didn't care. He pushed through the doors and strode down the walkway, people falling out of Kookaburra's behind him. He jumped the steps to the road, swung open his car door to grab what he'd been stealing from people's gardens and picking from the hillside and the verges all night.

He turned to Lucy, who'd trotted out after him. 'You shouldn't be at my side,' he told the dog. 'You should be with Charlotte.'

Lucy tilted her face and looked at him with a forlorn expression.

'Yeah,' Dan said. 'I know, Luce. You want to be with both of us, don't you? Well, here goes. But I'm going to need your help. Take this.' He handed Lucy her parcel. She took it in her mouth. Her eyes glazed as she tasted it. 'Don't bite through it,' Dan warned.

He bent and stuck the note he'd written earlier into the dog's collar. 'Okay, Luce. Thanks for your help here.' He turned for the B&B. 'I'm gonna need it.'

Chatter and clatter followed him as the townspeople got themselves into some sort of order. Dan didn't look back. The cherry-red door was in sight—the rest of his life behind it.

'How are we going to get the wheelchair down the steps?' someone asked.

'Get me out of it,' Ted yelled. 'There's important town business going on and I need to be at the front.'

'He's going to ask her to marry him,' someone said in an exasperated tone. 'What decisions are *you* going to make?'

'How dare you!' Ted's voice boomed behind Dan. 'There'll be a memorial, a christening and a wedding going on in town and where do you think we'll be holding the services? In our Town Hall, that's where. And who's in charge of the Town Hall regulations? Me, that's who.'

Dan kept walking. He knew there'd be memorial and christening services but he had no idea if a wedding would be taking place.

Metal and wood crashed and rumbled behind him. Shit. It had to be the wheelchair.

He turned to the walkway hoping Ted wasn't in it. Ted stood at the top of the steps supported by Grace and one of the twins, his bound left leg thrust forwards. The other twin jumped down the steps and righted the wheelchair. 'Come on, Dad,' she called. 'Get your bum in the chair. This is important town business.'

Dan couldn't hold onto his smile. He loved this town. But he loved Charlotte more, and if he had to move out of town and follow her to the Starfoot Lower-forest place in England, he'd be doing that. Even if it meant he never came back here. He couldn't be whole without her.

Once he saw the townspeople rally, helping Ted to hobble down the steps and once more allowing him to take charge, Dan squared his jaw and turned for the house at the bottom of the hill. He hoped like crazy the words inside his head made their way from his brain to his vocal cords without getting mangled by his tongue.

Charlotte paced the hallway, back and forth, her mind in a spin.

She'd had her shower, hot and stinging on her dusty skin, but she hadn't cried. Not a single tear. Why? Because her resolve had backfired. Perhaps she'd faced more than her fears in the dark of the enclosed cave. It looked like she'd found a new type of courage.

So, she asked herself silently once more as she paced, should she stay? Stick it out and accept whatever the consequences would be? Yes, she had the courage for that.

She halted. Maybe she didn't have the courage for that—not if rejection was the outcome. She flung her hands in the air. *Make a decision, woman.*

Her time in Swallow's Fall had shown her so much about other people. She'd been taken out of the misery of being Charlotte Simmons, holding herself aloof in case the world noticed how lonely she was, and had been transformed into Charlotte, grown woman, still lost but hoping.

Maybe she could talk to Ted and Grace. To Mrs Tam and Clarissa. She'd ask their advice on where they thought she stood— and what chance they felt she might have at winning Daniel back.

No. What was she thinking? She couldn't spread the news of her love for Kookaburra's owner. It wouldn't be fair on Daniel. He might not be in love with her. She had a healthy suspicion he might love her, a bit—the lower-scale bit where affection for a person turned into love for a person—but his type of love might not hit the higher-ranks, whereas Charlotte's love hit the sky in a roaring display of fireworks she wanted lighting the night forever.

She groaned, buried her face in her hands. Make a bloody decision!

'Knock knock.'

She dropped her hands, lifted her face and blinked.

'I know you're not talking to me but I've got something to say and I need an answer.'

Charlotte inhaled and settled herself. Since what she wanted most in the world was standing right in front of her, she'd better find that courage or she'd miss her chance. She moved to the doorway and opened the flyscreen.

'Actually, I am talking to you now.'

'I'm a bit out of my depth,' Daniel continued as though he hadn't heard her. 'So I'd appreciate it if you gave me a moment to get my words right. And as you can see, I've got a following.'

Charlotte peered over Daniel's shoulder. Blood drained from her head when she saw the entire town gathering at the end of her lawn. Damn it—Daniel's lawn.

'I want to move in,' Daniel said.

'You want to move in right now?' she asked in a barely there voice.

'If you'll let me.'

'What's going on?'

'Sorry about the audience, but you know what they're like.'

'Are you all here to kick me out?' Oh dear God, surely not? She hadn't started packing. All the utility surfaces needed a wipe down. There was five weeks' worth of dust motes in the kitchen, and a lifetime of regret in her heart. Neither of which could be swept away at a moment's notice.

'Actually, Charlotte, it's more a case of me being kicked out if I don't get this right.'

'Get what right?'

'You and me.'

'There's a you and me?'

'What did she say?' someone called from behind Daniel.

He turned to the crowd. 'I haven't got to that part yet.'

'What are you waiting for?'

'Privacy!' Dan turned to Charlotte. 'Can I please come inside?'

Charlotte stepped back from the flyscreen and he entered the house. She had a split second to notice the wonderful sunrise shadowing his handsome face and his tall, beautiful body in rays of morning glory before he spoke.

'I brought Lucy with me.'

Lucy looked up at Charlotte, her eyes wide and her mouth full of a posy.

Dan retrieved it from Lucy's mouth, wiped the stems and handed it to Charlotte.

A small posy of flowers. Some looked wild, or as though they'd been picked from gardens. 'They're beautiful.' This had to be the moment she hadn't expected so why wasn't she feeling elated and brave? Why wasn't her head listening to her heart? Because she couldn't quite believe that this might the moment she found all the right colours of love around her.

Daniel pointed at the flowers. 'The geranium means stupidity. Entirely on my part. The freesia next to it asks if you'll trust me. The viscaria asks if you'll dance with me, because ...' He paused, the tan on his face fading a little as he looked Charlotte in the eye, then looked down at Lucy.

He nudged the dog with his foot and she trotted to Charlotte.

'Open it,' Dan said, pointing at the note tucked in Lucy's collar. 'It says everything I want you to know.'

How many notes from Daniel had she read? Dozens; each full of coded meaning or jocular fun. She hardly dared read this one.

'Please open it,' Daniel said again.

Charlotte unfolded it, her fingers shaking, and was instantly blinded by tears.

The primrose means I can't live without you.

She looked up at Daniel from beneath her damp lashes.

He shrugged a shoulder, head cocked to one side. 'I Googled it—the meaning of the flowers. I wanted it to be right. It's my gesture, Charlotte.'

'I love you.'

Daniel stalled, his eyes widening. 'I love you too.'

'You do?' He did? Top-of-the-scale love? 'How much?'

'Enough to tie you down and keep you prisoner in town until you understand how much.'

'Oh, Daniel.'

He crossed to her and grabbed her, wrapping his arms around her and nuzzling his face in her hair. 'I love you, Charlotte. Will you marry me and give me and Lucy a place at your side for the rest of our lives?'

'In this house?'

'Our house. Say yes.'

The house at the centre of her universe.

'Do one thing for me,' she said.

'I want to do a hundred and one things for you.'

'Don't forget to think of me as Red sometimes.'

He leaned back, still holding her. 'That scares the hell out of me. What do you mean, sometimes?'

'Is there a flower for stubbornness?'

He shook his head. 'Don't know, but I'll look it up and plant a garden full of them. I was stubborn as all hell. Right from the beginning. I fancied you and refused to acknowledge it. I liked arguing with you and making you prickly because I loved the sparkling light in your eyes.'

Oh, how wonderful. He loved her prickly nature.

'When I look at you, I see laughter and love, Charlotte. I love you the way I love the wildflowers in spring. I would no more squash the flowers in your heart than I would tread over those wildflowers on our hillside. They're one to me.'

Charlotte had stopped breathing long before he'd finished speaking. She'd probably forget the majority of his words, but she'd remember the look on his face and the intent of his tone forever. And the flowers.

'Please don't leave me alone with memories of how you look,' he said, 'because eventually they'd fade and I'll be left with nothing but a soft picture of you and that's not enough. I want you. With me, beside me.' He paused. 'Can you forgive my stubbornness?'

'I didn't mean you,' she said. 'I meant me. I was stubborn and proud, with you and the townspeople. I'll regret that for the rest of my life.'

He released her and spread his hands. 'What's to regret? You've done nothing wrong—you've opened us up. You brought us light, Charlotte.'

'Red,' she whispered. 'You can call me Red.'

'I just want to call you mine.'

Charlotte looked over his shoulder and out the flyscreen door. 'I have to be sure of something.' She moved around him.

He followed and put his hand on the flyscreen to stop her from opening it. 'I'm not letting you go.'

She looked into his eyes and saw love; felt loved. Recognised she was part of something wonderful, which meant being whole. She pulled a freesia stem from the posy and handed it to him. 'Trust me.'

He let go of the flyscreen and as Charlotte stepped onto the veranda, she remembered the little girl she'd been—the one *before* the event. That little girl had returned to the woman and the woman wanted a future. The house had no owner yet. It stood empty, incomplete. But this house would never be unoccupied again, if Charlotte had her way.

She heard Daniel step outside behind her as she faced the citizens of Swallow's Fall. And perhaps one member in heaven, who might have guided her mother and her gran to this place too, to witness Charlotte's moment of truth.

'Daniel has asked me to marry him,' she told the gathering.

No response.

'The problem with this is …' She faltered, then pushed aside the dread of rejection. 'The problem is, I want to, desperately. I love him. But I'm not sure if you want me to.'

Charlotte couldn't tell what the silence meant but she guessed every person looking at her was holding their breath. 'I love him,' she said again, her voice firmer. 'I love this house. I love your town.' From the shuffling, she could be sure they'd heard that last bit. 'I'd like to be a part of you all.' Her voice was steadier, much more the Charlotte she wanted to be.

'So—this is my proposal. I want to marry Daniel and live with him in Swallow's Fall. I want to be part of your community. We would live in this house.' She indicated the flaking paint with her hand. 'We'd call it the House at the Bottom of the Hill but it would be our home, not a business.' She nodded down Main Street. 'We'd work together at Kookaburra's, running it as a hotel and making sure everyone who came to stay was treated with welcome and with courtesy. But we'd ensure they respected your town. We wouldn't put up with any nonsense.' She looked over her shoulder. 'Would we, Daniel?'

She waited for him to speak. His features had softened, his lips parted, his eyes on her, full of wonder. Eventually, he shook his head and closed his mouth.

She swallowed, then licked her lips. They probably wanted more assurances from her about her feelings or about how this marriage might affect their town. After all, she'd been pretty strong-willed during the first weeks of her stay and that characteristic was likely to remain.

'Daniel would run the bar and restaurant as he does now,' she said, hoping Daniel didn't mind her making these decisions for them, let alone voicing them as they came to her. 'I'd do the morning and afternoon teas. We'd need more staff though; if anyone wanted to work for us we'd be so happy to have you on board because we'd want our business to have a special tone of friendliness about it for all of us. You, our visitors, our hotel guests, everyone.' She glanced behind her again. 'Would that be alright?' she asked Daniel in a quiet, personal tone.

He nodded, a whisper of a smile of his face.

Charlotte turned back to the people of Swallow's Fall. 'I've been searching for a place to live, a place to love and to breathe in and … to just be. And I think I've found it.'

She glanced at Ted. He sat tall and proud in his wheelchair. He had the gavel in his hand. He twirled it gently, lowered his chin and frowned at Charlotte.

Charlotte gave him a nod of understanding. A warmth trickled through her. Ted was awarding her the gavel, telling her he was happy for her—probably only in this instance, but what an important instance—to be doing his job.

'I want to stay,' she told everyone. 'But we have to do this properly.' She raised her chin, lengthened her spine. 'Those for,' she said, voice loud and resolute. 'Raise your hands.'

Lots of hands shot up but Charlotte couldn't count or see properly for the tears filling her eyes. She blinked them away but more formed as fast as the first ran down her cheeks.

Daniel's footsteps sounded behind her on the veranda floorboards. The scent of him surrounded her and his presence pierced the bubble of nerves in her heart. Coffee berries and love. A cocktail of joy.

'And those against?' she asked the crowd, her voice cracking. If even one hand went up she would not have achieved her goal.

Nobody moved. She waited, scanning the group. Waiting for one perturbed, argumentative townsperson to raise their hand and tell her she wasn't wanted.

'There's no need for another call, sweetheart.'

Charlotte stepped back and leaned against the length of Daniel. Not for support but to feel the love of him, the strength of him, the warmth of him and the happiness he gave her. Happiness she wanted to cast down Main Street with outstretched arms and share with the people in her life.

She had a life. She'd found it all by herself. She'd messed up and she'd made mistakes but so had everyone else and the gathering in front of her and Daniel were smiling at them.

'I found it,' she said softly to Daniel. 'I've got a life.'

'Yeah.' Daniel curled his arms around her and pulled her against him. He tilted her face to his with his fingertips and kissed her. 'Looks like you're home, Red.'

Acknowledgements

Firstly, my praise and heartfelt thanks to Kate Cuthbert, Escape Publishing, and also to the wonderful team at Harlequin Australia.

A writer writes with an almost hunter-gatherer instinct, foraging for words and chasing the tale. When she finishes the draft, she sends it to special and trustworthy people for opinions and feedback long before the story goes to her publisher. Without the keen, often humorous and always superb feedback from author friends Lily Malone and Juanita Kees, this story might not have reached the publisher at all.

Thanks again to Romance Writers of Australia and all the wonderful people I now call writing friends. Special thanks to my readers—without you, I'd be writing for myself which wouldn't be quite as much fun.

Never last, merely the finest—to my home team. John and Liz, you're the best. The very best.

talk about it

Let's talk about books.

Join the conversation:

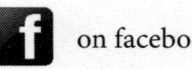

on facebook.com/harlequinaustralia

on Twitter @harlequinaus

www.harlequinbooks.com.au

If you love reading and want to know about our authors and titles, then let's talk about it.

Keep an eye out for more of your favourite
HARLEQUIN authors in print and eBook!

harlequinbooks.com.au

HARLEQUIN